The Body in the Smokehouse

Guida M. Jackson

Library of Congress Control Number: 2009908329
ISBN: Hardcover   978-1-4415-6458-0
               Softcover   978-1-4415-6457-3

Portions from this novel have been published elsewhere. The author wishes to acknowledge The Center for Texas Studies, University of North Texas Press, which published "Liminal Space" and "The Hired Girl" in its literary journal, *New Texas*, edited by James Ward Lee.

This book was printed in the United States of America.

To order additional copies of this book, contact:
Xlibris Corporation
1-888-795-4274
www.Xlibris.com
Orders@Xlibris.com
52109

In loving memory of Vivian and Mildred who never knew each other but possessed in common the valor to keep going against great odds

PART I

The Body in the Smokehouse

1

The October daylight, which had flared out in one swift flash across the plain, showed reluctance to recede in the late afternoon. The light held on through every possible combination of hues as if it could not leave until the awful thing was uncovered. Otherwise, she might not have seen it, because she'd had no premonition.

The Victorian house of her grandfather was spooky enough on the best of days. It remained for her a liminal space, where she was caught between two worlds: the past and the present. It was a threshold place, like the Wailing Wall, that was so freighted with meaning or layered with human experience that just by wandering close to it she fell prey to a collective clout capable of altering her perceptions.

At certain times she experienced the past as accordioned so immanently against the present, merging with it, really, that the ability to focus on the present vanished. So it was when she returned to the big house rising stark up on the hill just outside of town. Anywhere else the configuration would've been considered a rise. In the Texas Panhandle, it qualified as a hill.

She saw no use standing there pounding on the door and letting the wind whip her to smithereens. Already she was infected by the remorse of the place, impregnated by its desolation. If Snider was conscious, he had spotted her through the bushes overgrowing the window and had decided to ignore her. Besides, he didn't have to see her to know she was about. Even at his most inebriated, they had maintained that uncanny bond, much closer than most first cousins, more like that between identical twins.

On second thought, considering the hour, he was probably already rotting for the afternoon, his pattern except for brief periods of grace which seldom coincided with times when she needed him.

She bent against the wind and went around to the side windows to peer into the dining room. There was no evidence of dishes or clutter: not a promising sign, considering Snider's perpetual slovenliness. She ought to go on home. Instead, she went down the side steps, dodging a flailing piece of loose millwork, hoping her persistence was irritating the tar out of him. She went around to the back yard, which was even bleaker since he let the chickens die, and hollered through the open kitchen window. Between the yellowed curtains belling out against the screen she could see that even the kitchen was tidy. Too tidy. The place almost had the look of a woman's touch. But that couldn't be. He used to threaten to find himself a wife, but she'd told him, "I'm aghast at the thought of you breeding."

She knocked half-heartedly on the back screen. There was no use trying to rouse him: even if he'd had only a few drinks he'd have about as much snap as a radish by now. She turned to go, but a sudden slackening of the wind brought one of those stark shifts in perception. The yard, overlaid by a momentary haze of suspended dust, became a liminal, transmitting space, a tender evocation of childhood.

It hadn't always been such an awful place. They had once scampered around this chicken yard with no notion other than that it was the finest place in creation to be. She could still close her eyes anyplace on earth on a soft morning and hear the meadowlark calling from the prairie out in front of the house.

Grandfather had called them heathens because their extraordinary brightness allowed for their easy unspoken communication with each other. He accused her of directing Snider's activities without a word passing between them. Out of earshot, Adrian took pride in the designation, telling Snider, "At least heathens aren't hampered by the belief that somebody else is going to make their blood sacrifices for them." They used to make blood sacrifices routinely, pricking their fingers and performing solemn rites which were mostly of her devising. The ritual was particularly comforting to Snider, who was forever looking for a savior.

She had worn herself out hammering, standing out in the blowing sand, battering away much as she had beaten against his young and helpless spirit in years past, alternating periods of high and intimate camaraderie with sudden spates of cruelty which surprised her as much as they wounded him. Finally, long ago, to have any life of her own that he could not enter just by willing it, she had shucked him off like a dirty sock, even though she had not succeeded in establishing other relationships any more than had he.

Still, from point of practicality, they remained related, sharing no familial traits—she was pale and slim, he, ruddy and bulky—other than a puckish satyr peak of the eyebrows and a casual proclivity to lust. Always much more than cousins, because they could not help dipping into each other's minds, they were the last of the clan, joint executors of the estate. At times she suspected that in addition, she was the only client he had left. And small wonder, as inaccessible as he had made himself.

The sound of the banging door had been there all along. It only just now brought prickles to her spine. She looked across the chicken yard and saw that the hasp was not fastened on the smokehouse door, which thudded heavily in the resurging wind. Only last week she'd tried to phone Snider to ask him to check the smokehouse, rationalizing that she wasn't inventing excuses to check up on him, that she was genuinely curious to know if Granddaddy had left any smoked meat when he died. If so, it ought to be removed before it attracted coyotes.

She'd been informed by recording that his phone had been disconnected—again. It happened periodically when he forgot to pay his bill. He was like that. His whole life had been dimpled with acts of self-undermining, as if he deliberately and manfully determined to play out the part his detractors had assigned him years before.

She crossed the chicken yard and made for the smokehouse, scuffing up dirt into her shoes, grumbling at the trouble he invariably caused her. By the fierceness of her defense, she used to spare him the persecution of childhood peers who were tempted to taunt him because of his weight—reserving his torment jealously for herself. Nothing had changed in these years. She and Snider could not seem to come together in an orderly exchange, even on the subject of mutual business. They seemed to crash into one another, be thrown back, and bounce into each other again, on rare occasion meting out sexual favors in the process, becoming more inventive as his girth expanded. They ground against one another whenever they met, sharpening their fighting skills, honing themselves in their interminable grating relationship.

And soon they would be graying and growing dull of tooth and still be no less the squabbling intimates they'd always been, still oddly dependent upon one another, still free as with no one else to macerate one another unmercifully and to complete each other's thoughts despite her best attempts to prevent it. And she had dragged his degenerating reputation behind her like a gunnysack of decaying bones through her live-long days.

Despite that it had been flapping in the wind, the old door scraped on the ground when she tried to pull it open: evidence of how the shed had settled. One part of her weighed the effort to gain entrance against curiosity. It was as if she were caught in a darkened vestibule between the old and the new. The door on the past closes; the door to the future is still unopened. In either direction can be heard faint whispers. Intuition warned her that a certain period of endurance in this limbo was necessary before crossing the threshold.

The opaque air inside the smokehouse was dungeon cold and only marginally thinner than the dust-laden wind outside. The only window was blackened with smoke so that light no longer sifted through. She wondered why Grandfather had put a window in the smoke house in the first place.

So she had no warning.

She stood just inside the doorway until her eyes became accustomed to the dark, aware of the sour air and a suspended feeling like a trapeze artist who has let go of one pair of hands but hasn't yet caught another. She took a step backward, but she caught a glint in the center of the floor and knew it to be his Masonic ring, the one that had belonged to Grandfather. She went over and picked it up from a large dark spot on the concrete floor. It was as weighty as a weapon.

Now the shadows began to take form: she could make out the old salt box used for curing hams sitting against the right wall, the fireplace in front of her and a large iron pot to the left of it. The shadow overhead was a carcass, hung from the beam to be smoked. Usually it would be a deer carcass, but this one was too large. Probably a spindly cow—

She stopped breathing, not looking up, but seeing it all the same. In the crepuscular light it might almost be a gutted corpse with a large cavern where its entrails ought to be, hanging from a rope tied under its forelegs, its almost human features smoked black beyond recognition. The presence of the head upon the carcass jarred her like a thunderbolt.

She stumbled backward and held onto the door jamb, blinking against a light-headedness this side of unconsciousness, knowing she must be hallucinating. It had something to do with liminal space that had altered her perception. In a moment she would step back inside and look again, but now she was blinking in the concave aura of a blood-red sundown outside the smokehouse. She must not be well. If she could just get into the house so that she could sit down—and ask Snider what in God's name that was, hanging there. But in a second she knew, from the way the hair stood on the back of her skull, that she did not have to ask. But it couldn't be Snider. Else she would have remembered doing it herself.

She had a long-standing acquaintance with his anatomy, including its nether regions. The shriveled legs and genitals, so blackened and insignificant, couldn't be Snider's, couldn't even be human. Or was it conceivable that once the fluids drained, once the folds of fat melted to a crust by long and gentle smoking—why hadn't she looked, forced herself to look at the features? No. No need. The sight was permanently etched on the back of her brain. This place, that specter, would cast its miasmal pall on the rest of her days.

She sat on the ground and shook and waited for sanity to return, hearing, finally, the faint screams of night creatures. It could not be Snider. She had heard no call from him. Please God no. He would never leave her.

On her hands and knees, she dragged across the chicken yard over to the back door and cried to him weakly. Then she put her head down on the back step and shook and pleaded, with all the stubbornness that she could call up, that he would come out and find her.

2

One year earlier

As soon as Snider opened his eyes, he knew.

No matter how far into the night he drank, testing how close he could come to the edge without going over permanently, he could never sleep past six in the morning because of the hawking from the adjoining bedroom, when Grandfather began clearing the phlegm.

This day the silence woke him.

For a while, caught between two worlds, he lay staring at the ceiling, figuring it wouldn't be true until he looked. But it must be true. Briefly, Snider wondered if he himself, in a blind drunk, had staggered in during the night and put a pillow over the old man's face. But no, even when he was pickled, he'd have better sense. Grandfather's Social Security check was all that stood between Snider and trouble. With that source gone, something new had to turn up quickly. When the estate was settled and Adrian discovered—but that mustn't happen.

Again he rehearsed what he'd been going over for years when Grandfather would at last quit circling the drain. Now, by degrees, all that was fluid or spongy or labile had gradually precipitated, leaving the finite and solid, the hard and fixed: a state of which the old man would soundly approve.

Still, Snider felt light, as if he might float off the mattress. Except for the years when he was off in college, he had lived under Grandfather's absolute authority since he was five.

He had maintained a fascination with the goddess of crossroads, Hecate, who occupied his musings during evening bouts with the bottle. What would his life have been like if at that crossroad after high school graduation, he hadn't gone into law as Grandfather wished, if he had simply majored in history at Podunk College? Would Grandfather have cut him off, refused to pay for his education? Could he have mustered the stamina to make it on his own? Had he ever had a consuming passion for a vocation that would have required such sacrifice?

Or what would have happened if, after law school, he hadn't returned to Attebury, had escaped dependency on Grandfather's money and, yes, his intolerable lust for Adrian, and had gone to Seattle or LA? He might have found an entry-level position with a semi-prestigious firm and eventually worked himself into a partnership; might even have found a woman and married her—but no, that thought was insupportable. That would have involved another crossroad: there might have been children. On the other hand, an heir would have overjoyed Grandfather.

It always got back to the old man. Those under his roof had succumbed to the unspoken dictum that everyone must be as he wanted them to be or feel the sting of rejection. Perfection reigned, and those who fell short kept the fact a deep secret.

Grandmother had once explained, "It's nothing personal. Your grandfather's just not able to acknowledge the existence of anyone different from himself." Which wasn't wholly so: He certainly had acknowledged Adrian. And also Grandmother . . . or so Snider supposed.

But maybe that's why Grandmother had died so young: she needed love, not edicts.

After these many years, he closed his eyes against the still-welling ache, remembering happier times: the hours alone with her in the kitchen, or in the big bedroom where she sewed. He would sit on a stool beside her, listening to the measured tick of the marble clock on the desk, while her needle made careful punctures in the cloth. The natural rhythms of his body fell in step with her slow stitches. It was the same pace as the beat of the prairie out in front of the house, where he spent his solitude hunting Indian blankets and horned toads after school.

He might have dozed for a while, untroubled by thoughts of crossroads not followed, lulled instead by fleeting currents of serenity evoked by childhood memories. But his eyes popped open when he remembered the looming hassle if he didn't act quickly. By law, a person who dies in his own bed must undergo an autopsy unless death is certified by an attending physician. He must contact Doc Strickland immediately.

Or maybe he wasn't dead. He might've only suffered a stroke and couldn't call out.

It required great effort for Snider to hoist himself from bed. He scuffed to the connecting door, opening it enough to see the inert shape, the colorless gnarled claws resting atop the hobnail spread. He had no intention peering at close range into the face of death. He could see enough to confirm that Grandfather was truly gone. He would phone Doc to high-tail it over.

Then, a sudden movement: he watched in morbid fascination as the onyx ring inset with diamonds slid down on the bony finger as if by magic and came to rest against the next arthritic joint. Snider took it as a sign. Grandfather would want his only grandson to have that ring, not his granddaughter. But there was no use throwing the subject open to debate.

He could almost hear Adrian's protest: "It's a keepsake; his most prized possession. You'll only lose it, or pawn it. Whereas, if *I* take it . . . ."

He was at another crossroad. It might be possible, now that the old man—his alter-conscience—was gone, to put one over on Adrian. She needn't know Grandfather hadn't given it to him days ago. He stepped inside, averting his eyes from the chalky face, and forced the ring past the enlarged, stiffening knuckle. It wouldn't fit his third finger, so he slipped it onto his pinky. Then, feeling pleased, he stumped to the hall to phone the doctor.

Out of long habit, he went to the screened back porch, picked up the sack of chicken feed and rattled a portion into the waiting bucket. It was not yet light, so he flipped on the halogen spot before he carried the bucket into the yard and dumped it over the wire fence into the pen. Even as the feed hit the ground, he heard Grandfather's voice in his head: *Did you remember to feed the chickens?* Dammit, the old fool was still dictating his every move.

Later, after he'd had breakfast and the doctor had left, someone came to carry away the remains. Snider watched out the oval glass in the front door until the hearse drove off, hearing the quiet tick of the little marble clock and then its dignified chimes announcing the hour: nine o'clock. Six hours until three. He seldom took a drink before three.

Might as well call Adrian and get it over with.

She sounded brittle, using her take-charge tone. Had he made any arrangements yet? Called the church? Notified the lodge? Grandfather would want a full Masonic funeral, with lodge members officiating. They'd have a reception following the burial; she supposed the best place was the house. What shape was it in? Did he still have Madam coming in twice a week?

He had long since let Madam go, figuring she was one more unnecessary expense. They used only two bedrooms, a bath and the kitchen. A housekeeper wasn't worth it, just to wash a few dishes and change a few sheets. He had engaged Miz Puckett to do the laundry for much less money, and he could do up the dishes himself, whenever they ran out. In theory, at least.

Now he said to Adrian, "I'll get somebody in to straighten up. Won't need much."

She sounded dubious, but she had more urgent things on her mind. "Call the minister and fix a time for the funeral. Then we ought to meet with the mortician, pick out a casket."

The thought of the expense of a casket brought a surge of panic.

"I'll ask if he can see us around three this afternoon," she went on.

"Three might not be good for me. If I don't make it, you go ahead without me."

She paused then said, "Fine!" He could tell it escaped through clenched teeth. "But I'm coming to see what the house looks like before the whole town comes traipsing through."

After she hung up, he glared at the phone briefly before his wits gathered and knocked him in the head. He looked up banker Vogel's number and wrote it on the wallpaper. Hell, he could write anywhere he wanted now. He dialed and told Neva to put him through to Vogel in a hurry.

Ignoring Ernest's wary greeting, Snider got to the point. "The old man's dead."

Before the banker could get in condolences, Snider said, "He left everything to Adrian and me—except this house. He'd already deeded it to me for taking care of him all these years."

Ernest sounded bored. "I trust you'll discover there're no funds to meet your obligations."

"Quit the sarcasm," Snider said. "I've decided to sell Adrian my half of his ranch. That ought to generate whatever you think I need to pay."

Banker Vogel was silent for a moment. Then he said, "She'll need money to make such a purchase. Where'll that come from?"

"My God, think like a banker for once! She can put up her half of the land as collateral and borrow what she needs from the bank! She won't ever have to see any money."

Again, silence before Ernest chuckled. "You're right, of course. I'll get on it at once . . . or have you discussed this with her yet? You know how unpredictable—"

"I'll handle her," Snider said, well knowing what he was in for.

Vogel laughed again. "I'll just bet you will." Everyone knew how Snider managed Adrian. Everyone except Adrian, who thought it was the other way around.

Snider bundled up Grandfather's bed sheets, hunted down the keys to Grandfather's Chrysler, and drove off toward the Puckett place. A plan was forming in his mind. Miz Puckett had three offspring: Mozelle, the one with half a brain who worked as a maid-of-all-work for Adrian; Mozelle's twin brother Sael, the doofus who did odd-jobs oddly; and the youngest and dullest, Elsie, who must be fourteen by now. Big enough to hire out, cheap. Snider figured Miz Puckett would come along to help her get started. He'd get two for the price of one.

And if Elsie worked out, he'd keep her on. There was something to be said for having a kid dumb as a stump to run his errands, deliver messages, maybe a little something more.

Someone with the curiosity of a speed bump who would never think to ask questions.

3

Since Grandfather had been a Mason in good standing for seventy of his ninety-four years, he was accorded a full Masonic funeral, conducted with contrived magnanimity on the minister's part at ten o'clock Saturday morning at Holy Trinity Episcopal Church. The local chapter provided six pall bearers wearing little white aprons. Another apron draped the coffin.

As the only family members, Snider and Adrian sat in a cloistered section behind the choir where their grief would be sheltered from Masons and congregants alike.

Following the minister's ridiculously effusive eulogy for a man who was essentially a despot, the mourners trouped up to the bleak, wind-swept Citizens' Cemetery, where the Masons did the burial honors. The elder reader, reciting his part from memory in a high nasal sing-song, was required to remove his hat and gaze heavenward at each reference to "the Lord," a gesture that convulsed Snider and Adrian—he could feel her go rigid with the attempt not to crack up.

At the end the Masons sprinkled dirt on the coffin and recited a passage which seemed to promise everlasting life to Oliver Alton Greene. The idea of Grandfather hovering forever nearby, plaguing them in death as he had in life, was enough to jerk Snider from momentary sentimental fantasies about Good Times with Grandfather. He leaned forward as the mortuary attendants stepped forward to begin cranking Grandfather into the hole.

He allowed himself a moment of empathy for the obdurate corpse, finally free of the soul that had infected and dissatisfied it for so long. By reason of its lust for power, its fancies and pride, it had moved Grandfather to destructive action repeatedly. Where do wars come from? They are occasioned by the lust for power that has to be acquired by force to satisfy the hubris of the spirit. If ever one takes a moment for contemplation, the soul breaks in to inflict turmoil and confusion not only on the thinker, but ultimately on those weaker, those subjected to him.

As the first spadeful rattled onto the coffin lid and the assembly surged forward to offer condolences, Adrian whispered to him, "Are you sure everything's ready at the house?"

He waved her off. "Place is swarming with Altar Guild biddies. Just shut up about it."

Nevertheless, he could feel her agitation, as with each embrace, each handshake, she backed another step closer to the limo.

Finally, Snider had had enough. The wind had picked up, swirling sand from the grave into his eyes. He raised his voice so as to be heard over the subdued din and called, "Everybody come on over to the house." Then he grabbed Adrian by the elbow and hustled her into the limo.

Once they reached the house, they found, to Adrian's obvious relief, the women of Holy Trinity in firm command, herding the mourners toward an overloaded dining table. Miz Puckett and Madam were washing dishes and Elsie was scouring pots.

After Snider and Adrian had entertained guests, including banker Vogel, for a good half-hour, he filched an empty glass and slipped across the hall to Grandfather's room for a quick libation. It was past eleven: in view of the circumstances, civilized stimulant was overdue.

But soon the guests drifted away, and there were sounds of the last bustling Holy Trinitarians driving off. The Pucketts must be tidying up; too frequently sounds of clattering cutlery or crashing china echoed up the hallway from the kitchen.

Snider sat at Grandfather's desk with a glass of Scotch when Adrian came in and turned the lock behind her. In his warmly inebriated state, she looked fetching in black silk. Nowhere near thirty-seven. But the last person he needed when he was trying to quench his thirst.

"Fancy finding you here." Her voice ground with sarcasm. She plopped onto Grandfather's bed, kicked off her shoes and eyed the drink. Which meant she wouldn't mind having it herself.

He shifted over to sit beside her, handing her his Dewars. "This is the only glass I have." Thinking, *Damn you to hell.*

She took a large gulp, made a face and gave it back. She unclenched her palm, revealing a wadded tissue which she dabbed at her eyes.

"Oh Jesus," he said. *Not this.* He thought she smelled like lilac. *Dammit. Not now.*

But she surprised him by saying, "Here's an idea. Grandfather probably left us everything jointly. So what about if I buy your half of the ranch? Then we'll be done with each other."

He snorted. "I doubt there'll be enough cash for you to buy me out."

"I'll get a loan. Ernest Vogel just suggested it, in fact." *Good old Ernest.* As far as she was concerned, the matter was settled. *Greedy bitch.* Let her think it was her idea.

The clock ticked noisily. She looked around, studying everything. Looking for valuables, maybe. Or thinking that it was the end of an era.

She gave him the customary command with her eyes. *Crappola.* He sighed in resignation, downed the rest of the Scotch, let the glass drop to the floor because it was too much work to bend over, and lunged for her. He could feel the tears wet on her cheek as he brushed his mouth against it in their old practiced way. Never a kiss. No form of affection, for there was none between them. There was never time for undressing, no foreplay for this rite of transition, perfected after each trauma, fair or foul, in their lives.

He pushed her onto her back, grabbed her legs, still dangling over the edge, and pulled her forward, stripping off her undergarments without help. He clutched a leg under each arm and entered into the union with little difficulty. They had come to this position out of necessity after his girth made more traditional arrangements impossible.

Neither spoke, having reached their shared suspended, otherworld realm as he ground away, attempting to quell inner civil war, to recapture beyond this frenzy the natural, slow rhythm of life, to quiet, through this manic activity and its inevitable recapitulation, the soul. He saw in the act the possibility of *tertium non datur,* the third not known, the transcendent function described by Hegel: thesis and antithesis wrestling interminably until a synthesis emerges. This tension of opposites must yield a numinous state of some sort. It was a goal they had never reached up until now, but there was always hope that this would be the time.

He knew precisely when she would climax, and he could usually hold out until then. Experience had taught him that it was better to pace himself than to endure her wrath. He paid a tremendous toll in sheer physical torment; often imagined that this was how he would die: panting, straining, heart pumping, not in tangent with his thrusts, but racing ahead, galloping, sending blood pounding against his sweating temples until water poured down his face and he gasped in a sort of gray blindness.

Quickly they were both spent and she pulled away. The littoral zone ebbed as well, without appearance of the phoenix, the third transcendent thing. He clutched the mattress and gulped free air. Seldom was he allowed to fall beside her for a brief respite, but today he had no time, anyway. The clock had already chimed twelve. With one shaking hand, he swiped water from his eyes, while with the other, he clung to the bed to keep from passing out. Gradually his wheezes subsided and he knew he had survived one more ordeal.

"I got an appointment," he said, rising with difficulty and rearranging himself. He retrieved her things from the floor and pitched them to her. "Lock up when you leave. Oh—you might pay the Pucketts a little something for their trouble."

As he unlocked the door, he couldn't resist a glance backward. She still lay half-off the bed, staring up with vacant eyes, the white rise of her belly almost as firm as it had been twenty years ago. Her body's secrets had been his special domain these many years, but there had been a finality about today. The old man was gone, and with him the forbidden frisson. Grandfather, with his unbending list of taboos, had been their *raison d'etre*. He wondered if Adrian sensed it, then knew that she did. She probably thought it first.

But no: The prospect of a life without this, their shared madness, brought intolerable grief. Even though it bored him now, the vacuum would be unthinkable. He shook off the idea at once.

Anyway, there was that elusive third thing.

Still, a niggling voice prodded, might not that numinous thing be nothing more than escape from bondage? If so, freedom would entail a gradual loosening of bonds. The wild horse of his libido that dragged him in its wake, pummeling him against the stones of exigencies not faced, was too rapacious to be tamed except by degrees. He was still too weak to cut the fetters.

He pulled Grandfather's watch from his pocket and fastened it around his wrist. So. Adrian hadn't noticed the ring; wouldn't notice the watch when he wore it from now on. She had no clue that he had deceived her. A heartening development. Perhaps he was at least rid of her meddling in his mind. Maybe he had come to another crossroad and had made a sharp left.

This might be easier than he thought.

4

From the day the traveling roller rink showed up, Snider had managed to remain sober long enough to hang around the tent for hours each afternoon. If anyone had asked he'd have been hard pressed to explain his presence. It had been ten years since he'd seen his own feet, much less put on a pair of roller skates.

But no one would ask. Nobody ever asked him anything. They thought they knew everything there was to know about Snider Greene. They had looked him over long ago, when he was the pudgy and disconsolate pariah child of the Greene household, forever cowering in the shadow of his darling cousin, weak with yearning for her smallest notice. They had judged him to be a putz, had condemned him to bumbling ineptness, to remaining in his assigned place well behind the middle of the pack.

They did not know, could not guess the dreams coloring his evenings alone up in the old house. They misjudged his creative genius. Someday he would surprise them, as he had surprised more than a few when he went off to law school. But the town had belittled his grasp of the law, had stayed away in droves when he came home and hung out his shingle.

No, they would take no note of him sitting in his car, watching. Most of the town would be there, parked around the rink's perimeter. It was an annual event, the arrival of the rink. According to old-timers, except for the time of the Seven-Year Drought of the 50s, it always hit Attebury when the blush was on the maize, while school was out for cotton-picking and youngsters had money in their pockets. It had been three years since the last decent stand of dry-land cotton anywhere up past the Cap Rock, three years of shoveling out fence posts buried in drifts of sand almost as bad as back in the old Dust Bowl days of the 30s—three years since the skating rink had come through town. There had been general rejoicing over the good crop this year, because school dismissed the last two weeks in October for cotton-picking. And as if it had received word on the breeze, the flatbed bearing the rink materialized on the prairie late one afternoon through the ominous red haze shimmering to the west.

The rink consisted of a large portable wooden floor which was flung out on the vacant lot at the near end of Main. It was covered with a canvas top with the sides left open, so townspeople could park around the edges of an evening and watch the action. You could skate all afternoon and night for five dollars, including renting the skates.

It had mystified Snider, this fascination with the rink. "What gets into people?" he'd groused to Adrian three years ago, back when he'd had no intention of showing up himself.

"You know why they go," she'd said. "They go to watch the Man."

All traveling shows had a Man: a star to attract the crowd. With the rink, the Man was Calvin Huddle, a sinewy, ginger-haired boy of no more than twenty, whose sensual gyrations on skates sucked females onto the floor in droves. There was a controlled volatility about the way he ignored them, gazing over their heads as if caught up in the Vision Glorious of when he would be Discovered and whisked to Hollywood to star in a string of hits.

A body would have to be hard up to take to traveling with a tent show, Snider figured. He had watched them unload, studied them bracing against the stubborn wind while they set up the tent on the weed-covered lot across from the video rental store.

Anybody who'd work that hard could use some extra money. Besides, as soon as they'd wrung the place dry, they'd be moving on, and Snider had need of someone who'd be long gone.

After he left Adrian in a post-coital fog, he hurried down to the seedy motel where the rink people had rooms. Snider suffered from the heat even in a cool spell, so he parked the Chrysler nearby in the meager shade of a luxuriant trumpet vine wrapped around the telephone pole. There he waited, dozing, but alert as a crab, until Calvin emerged and headed for the café. Then he gave his horn a tap.

"Boy," he called in his best barrister tone. If there was one lagniappe for his obesity, it was his rich, resonant voice. Whisky and cigarettes had added to its timbre. "Can you spare a sec?"

Calvin eyed him warily and ambled closer, as if drawn by some aura of greed. He peered through the passenger window, keeping his distance, stunning Snider with his beauty at close range. He flung back a ginger forelock and said, "Yeah?"

Snider stuck out a limp card that read, "Snider T. Greene, Attorney At Law." Calvin squinted at it but didn't reach inside to take it. It was just as well. Snider had no intention of allowing his name to be found in Calvin's possession.

"I don't need a lawyer. So bug off, fat man."

Snider allowed himself a hearty chuckle, which he surmised they both knew was deprecating. "Get in son. We have business to discuss."

"No way! I haven't had breakfast." But Calvin had hesitated before he answered.

Snider tapped impatiently on the steering wheel, saw Calvin hungrily eye his watch, the Masonic ring. The Man looked over his shoulder to make certain that nobody else was about, shrugged, opened the door and got in. Snider grinned; he hadn't misjudged his quarry.

With an exertion that left him puffing, Snider wheeled the Chrysler in a full circle and headed for the city limits through his own swirl of dust. Calvin hadn't closed his window; in fact, he sat with his arm gripping the outside of the car as if he might bolt if they slowed down.

"Where we going?" Calvin shouted above the engine's roar.

"Just out of earshot. Oughtn't be anybody at the cemetery this time of day." Snider took off onto a dirt road which angled to the right, barely missing several scraps of humanity who were camped on the highway's shoulder. He felt an uneasy superiority over the migrant workers and almost in afterthought, he stuck up a thumb in universal greeting.

They bumped along the caliche road, assessing each other. Calvin shifted slightly, and Snider could feel him eyeing the greenish elbows on his old black coat, the gravy stains on his tie, the gold watch fob he had found the day before among Grandfather's things.

"You a Mason?" Calvin hollered. "Ain't that a Masonic ring?"

Snider's head jerked imperceptively in appreciation of the boy's keen powers of observation. "I am a Mason," he lied, "but the ring was my late grandfather's. He was a thirty-third degree man. That's what the diamonds mean."

"He give you the watch, too? Or is it a knock-off?"

Snider allowed a smile. Then a thought struck. "I wouldn't try to lift them, if I were you."

Calvin laughed, and Snider knew they understood one another.

They jounced into the cemetery entrance, drove well beyond where grave diggers were still covering Grandfather's remains, and came to a stop beside a fair-sized mesquite tree which clung stubbornly amid granite headstones and rocky ground. Snider turned off the motor and waited for the dust to settle. It was restfully quiet. A bob-white tweedled, and he thought it was unusual that a bob-white should be singing at high noon in October. The wind twanged through the bare branches and rustled the dry spear grass lining the caliche drive. Snider considered getting out, measured the effort, decided against it.

"What else he give you? This old bomb?"

"How's that?" Snider felt a certain panic, felt Calvin gaining the upper hand, felt Calvin trying to fit him into a mold, the same mold the whole town tried to put him in.

"Your granddad. What else he give you? Any money?"

He came within an inch of pointing to the big house clearly visible on the hill across the gully. But it wouldn't be wise to tell the Man too much about himself. He grinned broadly and reached into his shirt pocket, intent on dispelling this ambience of suspicion. "Let me remind you that I'm a practicing attorney beholden to no one, especially relatives . . . . Smoke?"

Calvin shook his head and patted a packet of Beechnut protruding from his shirt-front. "Not before breakfast. So get to it, fat man. I'm not noted for my patience on an empty stomach."

Snider returned the cigarettes to his pocket. "Suit yourself. Shows I wasn't mistaken about you. I took you for a man who could use some cash."

Calvin's tongue moistened his lips. He was looking straight ahead, but Snider could see his Adam's apple working. It was only a matter of time.

Finally Calvin snorted in indifference. "I don't do anything illegal."

"Bless me, neither do I! I require somebody to fill another man's shoes for about thirty minutes. Can you show me where that's illegal?" Snider threw back his head and feigned a deprecating snort that ended in a spasm of rattly coughing.

This performance did not divert Calvin. He tossed the ginger-colored shock in a self-conscious gesture which Snider guessed he had practiced before a mirror. "That bad, huh? Well, if you can't even tell me what it is, it'll cost you plenty, old man."

A sudden whirlwind sent a cloud of grit through the open window. Snider sputtered and turned on the ignition to roll it shut, glad for the diversion. But Calvin was not to be put off.

"Well, grandpaw? What is this shoe-filling job? And how much money we talking about?"

Snider hesitated; knew immediately that it was a mistake. He should have spoken with authority at once. "For this trivial little job, which requires absolute discretion, I could go as high as . . . fifty dollars. Cash."

Calvin snorted. "You brought me out here for that? Must be mighty little shoes."

"I assure you, it's a matter of small consequence. More of a favor I'm doing for my client." He paused as if in thought then said, "All right. I feel sorry for you, son, scratching for a living in a tent, so I'll make it seventy-five. More'n you make in a week at the rink, I bet."

Calvin glared. "I mean it, shyster. Take me back to town and get yourself another sucker. 'Fill another man's shoes.' My ass! Probably robbin' a bank."

Snider ignored that and grinned. "Smart boy! Unless I miss my guess, you don't care what it is, so long as the price is right. But I can see I'm up against a hard-dealer. I like that in a man. Tell you what: because I need to settle this for my client, I'll give you one hundred smackeroos."

Calvin put one foot on the ground. "Okay, big spender, that's it. If it's too big to talk about outside a cemetery, it's worth more than one bill. I'm walking back to town."

Snider watched him stalk off down the drive, stumbling over loose pebbles and cursing loudly. It was part of the game; he wasn't worried. He reached for a cigarette and punched in the car lighter, which popped back stone cold. *Damn piece of junk. Soon's this deal goes through, I'm going to drive this bucket of bolts off a cliff in Palo Duro Canyon.*

Calvin had disappeared onto the main road. He'd give him a minute more. If he knew Calvin, now that he was out of sight, he had slowed his stride. Snider started the car.

Sure enough, as soon as Calvin heard the engine behind him, he picked up his pace, swinging his long arms vigorously. Snider smirked. The deal was as good as done.

When he was alongside, Snider slowed, opened the window and hollered. "Okay, kid. Final offer. One-fifty, take it or leave it." It was fifty less than he'd figured to pay all along.

Calvin shot him the finger and moved along at a jaunty gait. Snider swore again, letting the Chrysler idle along beside him. Sweat was pouring down Snider's cheeks. Calvin was getting to be a pain. And it could be ruinous to let him walk off now.

"Two, then, dammit!" he shouted. The Chrysler sputtered, backfired and died. Snider let out an oath and ground on the ignition. Nothing.

Exasperated, feeling the gods conspiring against him just like always, he popped the hood and heaved himself onto his feet.

Calvin was now moving off at a canter as Snider leaned into the car's innards. Sweat streaked off his body, and hot tears were close to the surface. His face felt flushed. He straightened, raking water from his forehead. Doc Strickland had warned him about exertion. All the while Calvin was getting father away.

He hadn't handled it well, not like in the old days. He was out of practice. Even when he had a chance, it wasn't going to work, because he was out of practice.

Just as Calvin reached the paved road, Snider caved. He had to have Calvin now. It would be too dangerous to let him get away. He called, "Hey!" Calvin turned. *Damn little bastard.*

Snider took a deep breath. "Two-fifty," he yelled, mourning his loss as deeply as any he'd ever felt. He had so little. He hoped his heart could stand the strain of being easily out-euchred.

"Two-fifty, cash?" Calvin sprinted back up the road, arriving barely winded and grinning like a sick calf. Snider was nearly prostrate with grief at the way things were going.

His dry tongue clacked. "Fifty now and two hundred when the job's finished."

"Make it a hundred now."

"Impossible. I don't have that much on me. I've only got—fifty." It was almost the truth.

Calvin extended his hand and Snider saw the unlined palm of a child, in spite of the grime and calluses. It wasn't fair that money should come so easily to the young while he'd had to scratch all his days. He hated the sense of deprivation that comes with putting up a false front.

When this deal was finished, he didn't intend ever to feel that way again. It was too bad nobody would ever know. Back in town, they thought he was a fool. But a fool who succeeds is called a big shot.

5

Because the house lent itself to a liminal state, long after Snider left, Adrian lay on Grandfather's bed, where her mother had been conceived, and Snider's father before that. Now she and Snider had added their stamp, but there would be no new generation scampering about, hiding in the closet between musty flannels that smelled like Ben-Gay.

They were all gone. She was the owner of the ranch. Now let Tom James ignore her. He was *her* foreman now.

It was the beginning of a new era. She refused to believe life had passed her by. Snider wasn't the reason she had remained in this town. No, besides Daddy's lingering cirrhosis, and after that, her helpless mother, there was Grandfather, who had depended on her as he never could on Snider. But she hadn't remained *because* of them. Or Tom (Mobeetie) James.

The tryst with Snider had not released her tension. An encounter with Ernest, the second in a week, added to her agitation. It took no finely-honed skills to figure he was sniffing around.

Her discomfort had become a vague urgency that bore into her like the Texas sun, penetrating the shallows to erode her concentration. It pressed in so she could almost smell it, suffocating as dust tumbling from the Colorado plateaus, sifting into every crevice. The urgency was there when she woke, hovering outside her periphery, a pendant cloud. It was incessant, like the moan of a wind that won't let up with the night. It confronted her in the dull faces of migrant workers shuffling west on the highway, young men bent old by the dust, their gaunt-eyed women, bellies swelled by knobs of despair, trailing children lank as scraps of siding ripped away by the wind. But she looked aside, intimidated by their doggedness, ignoring some warning. *What was it?*

The urgency was her grim and secret anguish. She seemed to have lived with it forever, knowing it like a mouse that lives somewhere in the walls. But lately it had taken a bold step into the light. She fled from it, barely kept ahead of it, felt it nipping at the hem of her consciousness, but she ground her teeth and stomped the accelerator harder. That she was functioning in a state of directed turmoil, she knew, but she couldn't recall when it began, or if it began, really. Maybe she was born with this need to do something, be something, have something. Maybe it just grew, like a tumor that begins from a tiny speck, no more than a dark spot at first.

She was always caught in a false frenzy of festival in October, answering chill mornings with a sharp pain of counterfeit joy, banking the smoldering disconsolation which would flame up with winter's gray onset. She would ignore the inevitable a long time, increasing the velocity of her dance, willing it to last. She knew about the sharp sweet sorrow of autumn, but this "spell" was more than her usual druid dance. It was a specter demanding to be acknowledged, like a ghost that keeps popping out of the closet.

Once she had lived in this house for two years, and although she wasn't Grandfather's target, she was occasionally wounded by the glancing blows which he inflicted in an unending barrage upon Snider's spirit. She shared with her cousin the certainty that they could not help their impish behavior, that the punishment was designed to make them better than they ever could be. So they maintained constraint in his presence and glib abandon out of his sight. She, being more adaptable, was better equipped for their deceptive dualism than Snider, who daily broke his traces and suffered the inevitable consequences. Perhaps it was much harder on him once the hill became her home, when she was almost nine.

The move had come several weeks after The Terrible Night, two years after she'd prayed Baby Sister into being. Children are like that: able to make up companions with such fervor that the imaginary ones eventually begin to believe in their own existence and come to life. She used to think it was a deliberate thing she did: Adrian wanted Baby Sister to re-live her own life, which she suspected even then was doomed, in spite of her innate sense of privilege: being of the right sort of family and something of a beauty, and polished with singing and dancing lessons, designed to make her more desirable for someone rich like Ernest.

But she had hoarded her talents, giving only a portion, coveting the rest in her strive for survival. Still, she performed adequately—because she played to no one but Daddy. Because while she did, he was hers.

Out back, the old windmill groaned, socked by a sudden gust, and she started, as if she hadn't heard it a hundred times before. This time the sound reached into her gut and wrenched something loose. It was the timing of the sound . . . .

It wasn't Baby Sister's arrival that made Daddy drink. There were always nights when he wouldn't come in, and Mother would lie on her bed and let the dusk seep in and take over, leaving Adrian as a small girl to wander the murky house in despair, or crouch on the corner of Mother's bed and wait for her to stop sniffling and fix something to eat. At that age she had already established standards which Mother's conduct violated as badly as Daddy's. Then, when Daddy came home, Mother would use her. *Ask him where he's been*, she'd say. *Go in there and tell him you were worried to death.* Thus awarding her the authority she already felt.

Once Mother said, *Tell him you know about the*—she whispered the word—*liquor.*

Adrian gave token obedience to confronting Daddy, resenting it mightily—except that she balked at mentioning the liquor. Then he would have had to invent an excuse, shaming them both, leaving them *both* tarnished beyond retrieval.

She grew up knowing Daddy's drinking was a secret even within the family. *Don't tell your grandfather*, Mother warned often. Adrian sensed he hadn't approved of his daughter Vee's choice in husbands. Will Craddock wasn't from the best family, and in Attebury, no one overcomes that. By the time Daddy died, everyone must have known, but even Grandfather was too polite to mention it, especially since an unexpected insurance policy made her and Mother comfortable. But then, she was never meant to be poor.

Ever since, when Adrian entered the bank, they always trundled out Ernest Vogel himself. She knew what they said behind her back, because it was shameful that while most of the country didn't have two shares of IBM to rub together, Adrian Craddock just kept getting richer. On her visit to the bank the day before, Ernest had strutted out of his office, picking up his feet with a toe drop like a rooster freshly preened. In his twenties, when he'd courted Helga with Teutonic intensity, he'd been rail lean and speckled as a Dominicker chicken. Adrian had never liked him then, not because of his looks. It was the whole package: how he held himself apart, as if he were better than the locals. Since then, he'd fleshed out so his collar threatened to strangle him, and the sun had done its work merging the freckles into one beefy mass. He moussed his reddish hair cockscomb-stiff, adding to the illusion that he was poised to crow. Since Helga had died, he'd begun to add some dash with flashy ties that didn't suit his tunic-and-epaulets personality—for he appeared to live by some buried military myth.

He gave her fingers a moist press. "Adrian. Just the girl I wanted to see." She grimaced and withdrew her hand—and the urgency swamped her. *Girl, indeed.* Mother's admonition that a woman becomes invisible at middle age caught her by the throat.

So the problem must be *time*, slithering away before she could do anything with it, squandered by the thoughtless young fool she'd been. She'd staved off its headlong rush by constant activity, but one thing was certain: she'd never succumb to a downhill slide toward invisibility, poverty. She'd be rich, be *Somebody*, by God! She wouldn't be like those migrants, accepting whatever came. She would fight, like always, at least, ever since Baby Sister arrived.

She could hardly remember Baby Sister now. After her birth, Adrian, feeling the weight of her responsibility and determined Baby Sister would have a perfect life, prayed fiercely to Jesus that they would be a proper family. But Jesus, once he'd delivered Baby Sister, ignored her. She was left to handle things herself.

Now, she got up from Grandfather's bed, unwilling to entertain a flood of memories. Maybe Miz Puckett and Madam had finished cleaning up after the Altar Guild women and were waiting for someone to pay them. It was like Snider to duck out and leave her to settle up. Probably he had fabricated his important errand so as to dump this responsibility onto her. She put on the rest of her clothes, patted down her hair, and hurried to the back of the house.

Madam had already left, returning to the sod half-dugout she'd lived in forever on the far side of Grandfather's property. The two other women—if skinny, wan Elsie could be called a woman—waited stolidly by the kitchen sink, being too servile to sit at the table. With scarcely a glance in their direction Adrian apologized for the delay and paid them twice what Snider would have doled out. A spot of color appeared on Miz Puckett's cheeks at the sum, but she poked it into her worn pocketbook without a word. Adrian saw them out the screen door, still distracted by the childhood scene she held at bay. When Miz Puckett called back about delivering Snider's laundry, she waved vaguely without responding, lost in thoughts of that night that changed the course of things, when Daddy was near dawn in coming home.

Adrian had lain frozen next to Baby Sister when Mother's voice had suddenly scissored out with the only curse word ever uttered in their home.

"Get the hell out of here!" Adrian waited for Jesus to strike her dead. Then Mother shrieked, "Adrian, come quick! He's got a *gun!*" Her burdened heart went wild, and she leaped up and flew along the hall, knowing the end had finally come unless by some heroic act she could do what Jesus chose not to do; knowing panic and relief that one way or another she would be freed from the pain that knotted her insides for years.

Still, she had felt foolish: the nine-year-old adult, quaking between them. Daddy, bleary-eyed, swaying a little, held a silver revolver she had never seen before and said, "I was only going to tell her if she wants to shoot me, go ahead." *Yes, he must've been that miserable.*

At the time, Adrian had felt cheated, as if somebody had crumpled her insides into a wad. At once, she was convinced that Mother was using her again, drawing her into the drama. She turned without speaking and stalked back to bed, heart still hammering, hating them both. It didn't occur to her until later that the child she had been had received no comfort, no assurance, following that awful moment. No one ventured to her bedside; there were no hugs, no whispered words of love to dispel the trauma. Nothing was ever said of it again. Odd that it had not occurred to her sooner—although the scene had played hundreds of times—that she might reasonably have expected some solace for having been put through such an ordeal by these very proper people. She recalled thinking at the time, as she stretched out stiffly beside her sleeping sister, *This could ruin my life if I let it, but I won't let it.* And she never told a soul about it in all these years, not even Snider. She did not ever plan to let it go until it blessed her.

Now, she looked around Grandmother's kitchen and wondered if she would ever see it again. If Grandfather had signed the house over to Snider, there was no reason to come here anymore. The thought was like an anvil tied around her neck. She sank into a chair to think.

Only yesterday at the bank Ernest had greeted her with a courtliness that wearied her. She caught the glint of his manicure and acknowledged that his hands looked better than hers. His smile hung heavy between them, but she, consumed with a dull hopelessness, wished for the security of her own home where there was no need for pretense. Outwardly, she put on a chary aloofness, her first line of defense.

He quickly removed his glasses. So vain, refusing to admit he wasn't the man he used to be. His close-set Germanic eyes flitted to the photo on his desk of his late wife. He nudged it with his elbow and said, "I've learned never to beat around with you. I'd like to—come over."

God, he is so tiresome. She answered, "So what do you want, a written invitation?"

The moment had been mangled, to her surprise, because she thought of Ernest as an insensitive automaton. He polished the glasses furiously with a monogrammed handkerchief. "You know what I'm getting at. Is this so startling? Don't tell me it never crossed your mind. Helga and I were very devoted, but a man gets lonely."

Since childhood she had come to expect things to happen. She'd lived in a perpetual state of both anticipation and apprehension, knowing they would be either very good or very bad, because she knew her life was not to be ordinary. Sometimes when it seemed ordinary, she would assure herself, *This is temporary; this is not the way it's going to be.* Grandfather used to say that beauty commands the extraordinary performance, and she'd proved the truth of that. She was never surprised when anything astounding occurred.

But sometimes, she had to make them happen, like after the Terrible Night.

The night was actually so named because of its aftermath. Following it, she sensed a subtle shift. Her parents turned on her, allies at last against the only witness to their degradation. She was unprepared, puzzled, mangled by their niggling gouges. Baby Sister became their child, while Adrian became the step-child. To her shock, even beloved Daddy criticized her. Soon her tears, hidden at night beneath the covers, became so common and cheap, they no longer meant anything. And still there was no one to tell; it was her duty to protect them, for no one must know they weren't a proper family. Besides, how could she admit even to Grandmother the intolerable: Daddy's cold despite. She had lost him. She had to escape or die of anguish. Her picture of the perfect family had been desecrated, and she felt responsible.

So, communicating scathing censure, she had coolly asked if she might go live on the hill for a while. Mother had studied her sharply for some sign as to whether she intended to tell Grandfather about the *liquor* or the *gun*. But she must have recognized the pride and known their secret was safe. Mother protested half-heartedly, but Adrian could see there were no bones under her words. She saw Mother's relief that she was removing herself from their sight: with her condemning eye, accusing them of failure, convicting Mother for turning Daddy against her.

Anyway, there was Snider, so elusive now but omnipresent back then, a refugee like her, perpetually underfoot like a mud-mat, slavishly adoring and beholden out of proportion for any crumb of attention. Old sloppy, faithful Snider, abandoned by his druggie parents and looked down-upon by the relatives because of it. That was when it had begun: taking physical comfort in each other the only way they knew how. Adrian had thought more kindly of him after that, yet it was his presence that drove her to higher ground, to the notion that with her talents, she would never be accessible to him except physically, an assessment with which he instantly agreed.

Nor was she now available to Ernest, whose words at the bank the previous day hadn't stunned her, even though for a moment she'd been unable to think of an answer. Lonely? Ernest was hardly alone in that McMansion. What about Bobby and his wife? That army of servants? Anyway, even if there were no one, he might imagine himself capable of loneliness, but she knew with an instinct that Ernest had never coveted or cherished anything but more wealth.

Across her mind flashed a picture of what she could become if she let it happen: she would be rich, yes, but eventually her whole life might be shot full of gray, and she would become no more than a spare willow, listless skin going slack over her long bones, shoals forming around her eyes, a small-town frump exchanging inanities across the bridge table at the country club. No. She wasn't part of that world. Now she had the ranch. She was a rancher.

Besides, she had many good years left. She had good bones; she would hold her shape better than her spherical and resigned counterparts. Too, she had brains. All of which would go to save her until—*what*?

But that was yesterday. Now, the windmill out back creaked again, like old joints. She got up from the kitchen chair and headed for the front of the house, turning only once to look down the long hall. Maybe Grandfather *had* deeded the house to Snider, although she suspected it was another of Snider's sleight-of-hands. Not that it mattered. She'd never live in this place anyway.

She turned the key to the front door and headed down the walk toward her car, congratulating herself that at least her grief hadn't gotten out of hand when they had finally put the old man into the ground. She had long practice in bearing up.

Coincidence. Did she believe it? That only an hour ago, on this momentous day of release, Ernest would make his case so pointedly? She hadn't been surprised to see him at the funeral. As Grandfather's banker, he would naturally make an appearance, would draw her aside and explain that a copy of the death certificate would be required when she and Snider wished to open his lock box. Would voice his willingness to assist them personally in transferring the assets. Would suggest the efficacy of her buying out Snider's share of the ranch.

But when he intimately touched her shoulder and whispered, "Join me for dinner next Friday," it hadn't been a question. She wasn't prepared. Her reaction had been slow.

She had glanced up quickly to assess his intent: too large smile, pudgy cheeks falling away to jowl, angry shaven neck folded over the stiff collar. She felt violated by his cloying cologne.

He had gone on talking, but she had trouble registering his words. "We're both well off, hard-working, self-disciplined—" But there was a difference between self-discipline and being driven. She was tired. And weak. With the suspicion that maybe Ernest was the best she could do, the relentless urgency sprang up again and grabbed her by the throat. Something like fate was probably at work. She felt an oppressive inevitability about the whole thing. Besides, his cologne filled even the corners of the room. There was no air left even in the crevices of the old damask drapes; cologne had sucked it up. She felt a strangling sensation and knew she had to get away. That was when she had escaped to Grandfather's bedroom to be with Snider.

So it had come to this: She was reduced to a portly Prussian Hun. But he was already rich. What did he want of her? Surely not more money. Respectability, maybe, to surmount the town's welling resentment of his wealth and his non-Anglo Saxon forebears. Perhaps he needed a hostess to entertain his important guests, or a traveling companion, or someone to oversee the household staff, or a glorified nanny to keep the *puer aeternus* Bobby in line. Possibly he merely wanted someone to look after him in his dotage.

But she had other options now. She'd soon be Tom James' boss. The cowhands called him Mobeetie, after the XIT town where he was born. That's what she would call him from now on. He was still young and virile, no more than ten years older than she—the thought brought her up short. She couldn't bring herself to think about intimacy with another man. Sex to her and Snider had been about survival: two outcasts against the world taking comfort in each other. Sex had nothing to do with love or even pleasure.

On the drive home, a fresh ache for Snider gripped her. Where was that sonofabitch when she needed him?

6

Immured by his own excesses, Snider had forgotten about Elsie when the noise roused him the next morning. It was barely eight o'clock. At first he thought the pounding was in his head. When it became apparent that someone was at the door, he pulled himself off the bed and stumped out to open it in nothing but the shirt he'd neglected to remove before he passed out.

Elsie Puckett, downcast eyes focused on the porch floor, scratched an infected chigger bite on her leg, and made a stiff bob. Then Snider remembered why she'd come. He congratulated himself on his genius. Virtue cannot know its own virtue, but genius knows its own genius.

Now that she was here, he wondered how to go about communicating. He decided to yell. He led her into the long front hall, stirring up in his wake lint balls that had accumulated in the brief hours since the Alter Guild ladies departed. He pointed into the fusty front room, where rotting canvas supporting the yellowed wall paper had pulled away from the ceiling.

"Give this room a right smart going-over," he hollered. "I got important company coming this afternoon. Seems to me like there's a carpet sweeper in the broom closet."

Elsie bobbed again and headed for the kitchen but stopped at the door and turned a puzzled face to him. He looked past her, seeing the sink again piled with dishes, cabinet and floor stained with goo. He had no recollection of having been in the kitchen since the funeral.

"All right," he bellowed. "Start in there, then. Just be sure the front room's clean by two-thirty. A fine lady's coming, so do a good job, hear?"

One thing she seemed to know was dishwashing. By some miracle, she brought the kitchen to a semblance of order in a mere half day. He made no mention of lunch but motioned her toward the living room, which didn't seem bad in comparison. Maybe he was overpaying her.

At two o'clock he called her across the hall into Grandfather's former bedroom, now his paper-strewn study. He sat at the desk, holding Grandfather's key ring with the raised Masonic emblem. Looking her over while she squirmed and tugged at her dress, he sighed at the momentousness of his burden. "Get back yonder and wash that wad of dirt off your neck. Look in the medicine cabinet and find a comb. Spruce yourself up some. I've got an errand for you to run." All that yelling left him breathless, but at least she seemed to understand.

She scurried out, and he heard the whine of the bathroom plumbing. After the little marble clock had ticked away ten minutes, she appeared looking only passably better, head hung low, small hands wringing, the white line where the washing began ending in a drop of dirty water still clinging to her elbow. She gave him a quick beseeching gaze, anxious to please, so he nodded his approval and handed her the key ring.

"You think you can hang onto this? Don't you lose it, you hear me? You lose it and I'll tan your hide so you can't sit down for a week." The small face blanched in fear and he felt satisfied.

"Take it down to the skating rink and give it to a guy name of Calvin." As her forehead furrowed and her eyes searched for an escape, he gave her a scrap of paper with Calvin's name.

"If you do a good job taking the man this key ring, I've got this ticket you can use at the rink. You can skate until it's time to go home to your momma."

Elsie took the ticket and the scrap of paper and the key ring, never looking directly at him. But a secret light came into her eyes as she closed her hand over the ticket. She started for the door when something occurred to him. He called once more, louder than before.

"Girl. Go get you a biscuit. And some of those leftover cracklin's in the oven."

She raised her head, and he could see a certain fragile comeliness in her wistful, pinched face. Her eyes were hazel, the color of ripe maize: large, frightened eyes that darted to the side as if she expected a momentary attack.

No use the scrawny wretch starving. He decided to let her eat at noontime from now on.

7

Elsie did as she was told gladly, for she was famished. The biscuits were hard and the cracklin's rancid, but she had learned to excuse. She went off down the walk nibbling tiny bites from her biscuit to make it last longer, and clutching to her chest the cracklin's, the paper, the key ring and the precious ticket. It was a passel to keep up with, more than she'd ever had. She made a decision and tossed the cracklin's into the bar ditch as soon as she was out of sight of the house. Such wealth. She felt proud beyond belief as she kicked up little eddies of caliche dust and marched down the road which ran directly from the hill to Main Street.

From a long way off she could squint and see the tent. When the music wafted up on the wind, her heart beat faster. She had not dared to come near the rink before, for fear that some of her tormentors might hurl insults at her. Besides, she'd never had the price of admission before, and Mister Snider Greene did say she was to use the ticket at the rink.

As she reached the curb her steps slowed. Timidity flooded her with fear. The crumpled paper and the ticket had grown damp in her fist. What if she couldn't find the Man?

But he rose from a bench where he must have been watching, and glided over to the entrance, smiling down. "Snider Greene send you?"

Not raising her head, she nodded and held up the scrap of paper for him to see, feeling a pounding in her ears. Scarcely hearing a taunt from the rink: "Hey! It's dumb ole Elsie!"

She peered past his knees at the rink floor, squeezing the last of the biscuit in her fist and dropping it to the ground behind her back, dismissing her hunger as unworthy on this grand occasion. Again, a voice from a skater: "Hey, estupido!" And laughter.

"He give you anything for me?" the Man said as if he hadn't heard.

She had almost forgotten. She felt her cheeks grow hot. Still not looking up, she held out the fancy key ring. He took it and pocketed it then said the most amazing thing.

"You want to skate, girl?"

She swallowed as two jeering skaters flitting by. "I ain't sure how," she whispered.

He caught her arm, so slender that his hand wrapped around it, and led her up onto the floor of the rink. "I'll teach you. Let's fit you in some skates."

She took a deep breath. This wouldn't be so bad.

At times in her life, she had a recurring nightmare in which she tumbled helplessly through space, unable even to scream. She felt the same stark terror when she tried to stand on the slippery skates and found that she had no power to prevent them from sliding out from under her. But Calvin Huddle caught her firmly before she met the floor. Gratefully she clung to him and allowed him to drag her, slithering like a rag doll, around the rink.

Gradually she lost a measure of her fright. Calvin's strong hands warmed her sides, and sometimes his hand wandered up near her chest or down onto her backside, giving her a quivering breathless tingle, though she scarcely had time to think about it. Her fleeting world kept whizzing before her eyes, the same counter and loud speaker, same hecklers coming around again and again, the music growing dimmer, then louder above the rumble of skates. She shrieked and whooped, cackling with ecstasy, never knowing such freedom before.

A yellow Hummer cruised by and headed up the hill. Like everyone else, Calvin paused to look, pulling Elsie to a stop as well, to see the face of the driver.

But Elsie could only wait impatiently for Calvin to begin again. She had been caught in a wild rapture, whirling in the arms of the Man. She could not believe her good fortune and knew in that moment that Momma had spoken the truth when she'd held her close and promised, "There'll be other Christmases when he won't have so many poor children's stockings to fill."

Elsie knew now beyond a doubt that Heaven's streets were paved in gold, that the things she'd seen on TV were real. She pretended it would never end, that she would go on like this until she dropped, and she would then die willingly, knowing no further happiness was due her.

At length, before she had a chance to protest, Calvin swept her across the floor to the bench. "I believe you've had all the skating I can handle for one time, Missy. Come on, take off them skates and I'll walk you over to the drug store for a Dr. Pepper."

She gasped. Maybe she'd heard wrong. It was so outlandish, what he said, that it almost spoiled the afternoon. Of course she couldn't go. Even thinking about such a high adventure sent spasms of fear rocketing against her ribcage. She ducked her head and thought fast.

"I got to get home, help Momma," she mumbled, as she spun around off the bench and dashed for the street, carrying her shoes.

"Wait!" He raced after her, catching her arm, as if he had a right. Like a startled cat, she widened her eyes as his grip tightened. "Come back after supper. Your ticket's good all day."

She hesitated, turned frantic glances in the direction of home, still straining against his grasp but less violently now. "I . . . might."

He released his hold. "Good. You come on back. I'll be waiting."

Elsie drifted the five blocks home, charged with an electric vitality, throbbing with new energy. Now that she was safe from her tormentors at the rink, she dismissed them, chose to remember only the adventure itself. The leaves underfoot looked like bright pennies scattered along her path. They were the small, sparse leaves of the Chinese elm, a hardy survivor of the unforgiving drought. They were her trees, the only ones she knew outside of the geography book. She wondered at their skeletal beauty, longed to stop someone and share her joy, ached to tell the whole thing, to hide behind the lilac bushes by the swing set at recess and whisper the Whole Thing to the other girls, who in her imagination wouldn't snicker but would listen with wide eyes. She had not expected such joy, had never expected much, learning very early that too much hope brings pain. She kept her hopes always at a minimum.

But memories were another thing. Memories could never disappoint. Some might hurt, if she let them, so she never did. She danced by the hurtful ones, grinding them down with her heel like soft caliche pebbles. The good ones she took out often and sang little songs about when she was alone. Sometimes, when she was telling them to the tree trunks, she made them even better.

Daddy was half-lying against the porch railing, as usual. "Where in creation you been and it almost dark?" He slurred his words the way he did along about this time of day, but she knew what he was saying, knew it by heart.

"Working for Snider Greene," she said, feeling guilty for not mentioning the rink.

"Yeah? How much he pay you?"

Momma met her at the screen door. She glared at his back, the way she often did when he couldn't see. "He's paying by the week. And it's not any you'll be seeing of it, neither. We got bills to pay."

She opened the screen and ushered Elsie inside, studying her face with what Elsie took for dread. "Elsie! What's happened, girl? What happened at Snider Greene's, for crying out loud?"

Elsie did not know how to hide anything from Momma. "He give me a ticket and said I could go skating!" She was gasping with the delight of telling.

Momma frowned and appeared to consider something. She pressed a straying hairpin into her bun of hair and said, "You probably got it wrong. Well, get on in yonder and set the table. Mozelle and Sael'll be coming in soon starving to death. Don't say nothing about this, hear?"

Elsie nodded, disappointed not to be able to share her secret. She turned to go, then she came back and stood by the old daveno, picking at the loose mohair. "The Man at the rink said my ticket is good all day."

Momma pressed her lips together. "Your daddy would never allow it, if you're asking to go back after dark."

Elsie closed her eyes, wincing, resigned, and shuffled out of the room. Then she heard her momma call softly, "Elsie."

She came back to the doorway, waiting for some new assault, some new assignment.

Momma hesitated, as if she were studying hard. "Maybe your daddy'll drop off early tonight. I just wouldn't say nothing about it if I was you."

Elsie wasn't sure she understood, but she read the warm look in Momma's face and her spirit soared. Maybe she was going to get to skate again. Maybe the Man would slide his hand on her waist and hold her hand and glide around the rink with her, like this afternoon. Then she put the hope quickly away before it consumed her. It would be almost as good to lie on her pallet and remember the afternoon over and over—better, maybe. Nobody could take that away.

But at about half-past seven Momma went out on the porch and poked a foot at the old man. He didn't move. Elsie, watching from inside the screen door, knew he wouldn't.

Momma motioned to Elsie to come. "Your pa's done dropped off. Go on up yonder to the rink if you've a mind. Only don't be past nine getting home, hear? Listen for the court house clock, hear?"

Charged with wild elation, dumbfounded by her turn of fortunes, Elsie raced, skipped, danced in circles the five blocks back to the rink. While she was still two blocks away, she could see its string of lights, hear the music and the rumble of skates. Then she remembered the people, and her steps faltered. She stopped and picked at the bark of a spindly tree, trying to decide.

Yet something drew her on, even though her pace became slower and slower the closer she came. She kept thinking of the ticket, already paid, and of the Man. Then, as she timidly approached the tent, she heard him call.

"Hey girl. Over here."

He circled the floor and spun to a stop at the entrance, holding out his hand to her. He pulled her up the steps and led her over to the bench, where her skates were waiting for her.

Three boys swept by. One yelled, "Hey look. Old flea-brain is back!"

Elsie shrank down, knowing it was her due, chastising herself for being there. She was afraid to look at the Man. Maybe he didn't hear; he kept on buckling her skates, as if nothing had happened. The boys circled the floor and came around again. She watched their progress, knowing a dark welling dread as they neared.

"He-y-ey, estupido!"

Sometimes if they caught her at nighttime, they hurt her, took things from her. How had she forgotten? It was a mistake to come. She wasn't safe after dark. Terrified, she slipped off the bench, kicking the skate free as she stumbled out of the tent, great hot tears blurring her sight.

"Girl!" Calvin, taken by surprise, tried to follow. "Wait till I get my skates off!"

Behind him, she heard another voice, deeper. "Calvin. Back to work. Keep 'em moving."

Elsie didn't turn around but ran quickly home, sobbing the whole way.

Much later, when Momma had tucked her into her pallet in the bed-sitting room without asking too many questions, and had poured the drunken old man into his bed nearby, someone knocked on the front door. Nobody except Miss Adrian ever knocked on the front door. Sael and Mozelle, crouched close to the small TV, didn't stir. So Momma waded past them and opened the door just a crack. Elsie hardly opened her eyes.

But Mozelle perked up. "Hey, it's the Man from the rink."

Elsie sat up quickly, trying to see, but Momma's back blocked her view, and her voice had an edge to it: "What do you want here?"

Sael leaped up to tower behind his mother, and Mozelle crowded close beside him. It seemed to Elsie as if Calvin Huddle swallowed and stammered as he answered.

"This here key belongs to Snider Greene. Would you ask your girl to take it back in the morning?"

Momma took the key ring and shut the door without another word. Sael fastened his gotch-eyes on his mother questioningly, then returned to his post in front of the television. Momma leaned against the door and studied the key ring, as if she were trying to puzzle out something.

8

Elsie knocked for a long time before Snider Green flung open the door and swayed there looking as if he didn't recognize her. He clutched a metal box under his arm. Papers stuck out of it, as if he had just grabbed it up. Seconds went by, and she ducked her head and waited.

Finally he said, "Oh yeah. All right, dammit, get on in here and make me some coffee, if you think you know how."

She always did as she was told. As she stepped inside, he said, "Hey girl. Did Calvin Huddle send me something?"

Elsie thought hard, searching the dead red eyes for a clue of what he was talking about. Then she grinned and opened her fist to reveal the key ring. He groaned as he took it from her. He shook his head and clucked his tongue, filling the hallway with his putrid breath, muttering something about, "I just hope I've got the right man."

She shuffled to the kitchen, dismissing what seemed to be his displeasure, just as she had dismissed yesterday's hurt, as she always dismissed the unbearable. She let her thoughts tread the air like dragonfly's wings, darting out of reach of the dismal chores ahead of her. Finally, she pursed her lips, trying to remember how to make coffee, a chore which consumed most of the morning, what with pouring it out and trying again.

But it didn't seem to matter to Snider, who apparently had forgotten about coffee, anyway. So she filled the time with small mechanical chores the way Momma would: wiping counters, sweeping, straightening. Dreaming about skating with the Man.

At two o'clock Snider called her into his study and handed her the same key. His voice was gruff: "You're going to have to run another errand. Take this down to Calvin Huddle at the skating rink."

She felt her cheeks grow warm. "I done that yesterday."

He raised his voice. "Well, it's got to be done again, ding-bat! Here." He handed her a five-dollar bill. "You can go skating. And get you some cracklin's and biscuit to eat on the way."

She folded the bill around the key ring and put them in the pocket of her skirt.

"Girl. Don't show up for work until ten o'clock tomorrow, hear? Ten o'clock. Got that? You can listen to the courthouse clock. When it strikes ten times, then you can knock on my door. Not a minute earlier."

She thought about this hard so she would be sure to remember, then nodded and scurried out. Since the cracklin's were rancid yesterday and the biscuit hard, she wanted to skip them. But she always did as she was told, so she got them and hurried out of the house.

She scuffed off down the hill, humming the way Momma did and sniffing from time to time under her arms. Last couple of years she'd noticed a new smell about herself. Her nose liked the odor. She was proud of her scent, which got better toward the end of the week. Even her dress smelled that way under the sleeves when she took it off at night.

It happened that as she neared the bottom of the hill, holding her arm up and savoring the way she smelled, Miss Adrian Craddock pulled her big car alongside and gave her horn a toot.

"Get in, Elsie," Miss Craddock said. "I'll take you home."

A proud feeling stole over her as she climbed into the fancy front seat. "Ain't going home. Going to the roller place."

Miss Craddock smiled, but her eyes looked sad. She said, "Would you like to go skating? I'll give you money to—"

"Oh, I'm going. Mister Snider Greene done give me money to use for it." She patted the precious lump in her pocket and leaned back to watch the skating tent grow closer.

Miss Adrian kept murmuring, but she didn't seem to expect Elsie to answer. "What in thunder? He never gave away anything in his life."

The rink was almost deserted. No sign of the boys, who were probably still in school. Elsie had almost forgotten about them until now.

Calvin, who leaned against the counter, beamed as she got out of Miss Craddock's car, as if he was glad to see her. But his smile darkened as she groped in her pocket and brought out the key ring. He took it and tossed the shock of ginger hair. Then he said, "You come to skate?"

She held out the money, swelling with pride, and followed him to the bench for her skates.

Even though she didn't skate any better than the day before, he held her effortlessly, and she enjoyed her frequent slips and slithers for the opportunity to feel him grab places on her body to keep her from falling. Sometimes he gave her an extra pat, too.

He steered her around for a long time. Then, as the crowd began to assemble, she glanced around and stiffened. The boys were coming. Panic rose in her throat. Suddenly she broke away and skidded to the bench.

"Got to go," she called back.

He didn't argue, but followed her and helped her remove the skates. His breath smelled like Juicy Fruit gum. Then he caught one ankle and held it while she struggled to free it. "Girl, before you go, I want you to think about something. Think about it real good, and don't say no until you think about it, hear? Will you walk across the street and have a co-cola with me? Just a co-cola, nothing else. No funny business or nothing. Coke sure would taste good, huh?"

Oh my. She tried to pull away, but he had a firm hold of her ankle. She heard the voices of the boys and knew she had to escape. "All right," she said, growing frantic, looking around toward the exit.

It was the first time ever that anyone had treated Elsie to a drink at the drugstore. She didn't know what to order and feared she would fall off the high stool. The cocky guy behind the counter tapped his foot, waiting, but she, being consumed with gripping the edge of the counter so as not to fall, could think of nothing to say. But Calvin chuckled and ordered two cherry Cokes. She watched with rapt attention as the guy squirted and fizzed and slid the drinks toward them. Her lips closed over the straw and she sucked. It was syrupy.

She bent low over the straw, a scraggle of hair falling across her cheek and obscuring the Man so she felt safe to enjoy herself. She took tiny sips, making it last as long as possible. When she was down to the ice, she sucked it long, liking the clucking sound. But finally she knew the pleasure was over. With reluctance, she pushed the glass from her. "Gotta go."

He was right behind her. She looked up, startled to find him at her side to hold open the door. Then she remembered her manners and said, "Much obliged."

He caught her hand. "I'll walk you home."

She started to protest, but she remembered the boys. So she nestled her hand in his and thought that in a way, this was just like the cherry Coke.

They walked along silently, for there was no talk unless Calvin initiated it, and he was very quiet. In front of the Craddock place, he pulled her up short and turned her face up to his.

"Will you meet me later, girl?"

She was puzzled, trying to understand whether he was commanding or asking for an answer. Dusk was rolling in, and the wind whipped up a few dust whorls from the unpaved cross-street ahead, where she lived. It was growing dark, and she couldn't read his eyes. She didn't know what to say. Then she remembered the cruel boys. "No. Can't come back."

He held her arms so that she couldn't leave. "I don't mean at the rink. I mean after it closes. Will you meet me then?" Again, the smell of his breath, blowing close to her face.

She felt deeply perplexed. "What for?"

His hands moved to her cheeks. He put his lips on hers, forcing them apart with his hard tongue. It was her first kiss.

She wrenched away, stammering, blinking, not looking at him. "Got to go. Got to go." And she fled and ran home as fast as she could.

But as she reached the front stoop, she heard him calling. "Girl, wait up! I forgot."

He caught up with her at the step, took her hand and closed it around the key. "Take this back to Snider Greene. Tell him the deal is off. Can you remember that? The deal is off."

She felt a warm surge as his hand lingered. Then the old man in the porch shadows stirred.

"Who'n hell's out there?"

She pulled away, giving Calvin a shove as she scampered up the step and inside the screen. She heard Calvin saunter away, whistling.

"Answer me, dammit! Who's out yonder? Sael!"

Her brother pushed her aside, his enormous frame filling the doorway. "You call me?"

"Go see who's prowling around out yonder in the dark."

Sael banged open the screen door and took off. She hoped Calvin could run fast. Even after Sael returned to sit at the kitchen table, she kept thinking about it, wondering what happened.

She came very near to going back to the rink, just to see. She was gripped by a seething unrest that caused her to press her knees together. She propelled herself through the kitchen chores on the strength of this agitation, and when Momma sent her to bed, she slipped thankfully between the covers, knowing, hoping that she wouldn't sleep. She swirled in a swivet of romance, better than anything on television.

When Mozelle slid in beside her, Elsie tuned out her blather in disgust: nothing must interrupt this ecstasy. She was in her own nether world of rapture.

And while she was there, it seemed that she was forgetting something. Something Calvin had said to tell Snider. But it had gone clean out of her head.

9

By midnight the cold snap had lent a definite texture to the air, especially inside the Pucketts' drafty house. The moonlight spilled cold against Elsie's cheek through the rattly window pane. She burrowed deeper into the covers and squeezed her thighs together, trying to relieve the strange uneasiness.

The Kiss, relived for the hundredth time, got longer and better as the hours wore on. She was a glamorous star like Brittney Spears, in a shimmering costume, and her hair was a mass of yellow curls clear up to the roots. Her mouth, glistening and full, left the soda straw often to close against the eager lips of the Man, over and over again the whole blessed night.

By daylight her fervor had whipped to such a pitch that she panted for breath. The far cry of snow geese drew her to the window next to her pallet. She leaned over, pressing her forehead against the cold glass so that she could see the wedge they drove into the chill sky. There was pain in the sight, and a wan longing in their call.

She dressed and went into the kitchen where the others slouched about, squabbling among themselves, paying her no mind. She picked at her oatmeal without tasting it, biding her time until Momma said she could go. Then, with a surge of energy, she started out for Snider Greene's with the magic key ring in her jacket pocket.

"He's gonna send me to the place, gonna send me to the place," she said, making a cadence of it. She marched down the street near where Miss Adrian lived, then, fearful of calling attention to herself, began to make her way through alleys and vacant lots, careful not to disturb the inertia of the town, until she got over to Main and past the now-deserted skating rink.

There, she turned south toward Snider Greene's, but halfway up the hill, she remembered: seemed like Mr. Greene said something about not showing up until the courthouse clock struck ten times. Disappointment welled up and dragged at her. A gentle gaff sent the tail of a nearby windmill into a tinny squawk that set her own heartstrings vibrating. She turned aside.

Instinct drew her to the dove-colored prairie, and she headed east down a gully and up the other side until she hit the quiet cemetery road, thicketed on either side by wintering mesquite.

Here and there the land fell away over a lime-white bluff, tufted on top with grey sage and tumbleweed. She sucked in the cold air, feeling faint and heady by what she saw as the dazzling beauty of the craggy landscape. From atop the low mesa, she had a clear view of the surrounding rises, dips and rabbit-brush plains. She looked back toward the hill where the old Victorian house lorded, but found it bleak and lifeless, like a corpse.

She hunkered down by the side of the road out of the wind and snapped off the stem of a goathead. What to do? The courthouse clock struck eight times, the sound carrying plainly on the cold wind. She could tell, by the light coming through a strange opaque haze, that it was a long time until ten o'clock, and even longer than that until Snider Greene would send her on another errand with the key ring. She took it from her pocket and let the medallion swing in the wind.

Then she got to her feet and looked back across the field of swaying buffalo grass toward the houses below. She knew what she would like to do. She would like to go see Calvin now. She would like to take him the key ring, even though she didn't get to skate.

She wallowed the thought around, turning it every which way, and her spirit felt like the sun breaking through the dust. At times it was hard to plan what to do, but this time it was easy.

Might ought to just go ahead and take the Man the key ring right now, before she went to work, since she had all this time. Key to Calvin, key to Calvin. She gave a little cackle at her cleverness and scampered down the cemetery road, kicking up sandy flurries about her feet.

The wind sang along the overhead wires, and two winter sparrows chattered as they were driven off their perch by the sudden gust. Elsie's heart thumped in happiness. The rink would be empty, that much she knew. But she knew where to go, knew where to go. Key to Calvin, key to Calvin. It didn't matter that clods bruised the bottoms of her feet through her thin shoes, and the cold wind made her lungs swell almost to bursting as she ran against it.

She hit the main highway still running as fast as she could manage, for the rough caliche had torn the toe of one sole loose, and it dragged against the ground if she didn't pick up her foot high enough. With the sole flapping with each step, she took off down the highway toward the only motel, where Calvin must be, doing a skip, hop, skip, hop, almost like the way she had seen the girls do at school. It was hard to keep it straight: when to hop and when to skip. She gave up and trotted the rest of the way to the Budget Nights Inn.

She crossed the stunted Bermuda grass lawn and walked along the hard-packed dirt close to the side of the place, peeking under the blinds into each room. From somewhere a rooster crowed. Most of the rooms were empty. But one was not. She sucked in her breath as she recognized Calvin's plaid shirt thrown over a chair. Timidity could not chain her now. She broke free of it, driven by a new overpowering urge: a wild desire that made her dance.

She tried the door. It wasn't locked, being so warped that it wouldn't even shut all the way. It scraped open stiffly when she leaned her shoulder into it, and propelled by a fierce urge, she charged across the threshold, giving the door a backward kick.

A dazed Calvin leaned up on one elbow, blinked and blew the ginger hair out of his eyes as she plopped down onto the bed. He smelled of dried sweat, man sweat, like Daddy or Sael. Some alarm stabbed deep in her memory, but she pushed it aside. She had almost forgotten about the pain until now, but she didn't study why it was brought to mind. She twined her arms around Calvin's neck and pressed close to the covers, finding his mouth hungrily, keeping his arms pinned under the bedclothes. She was certain that he was kissing her back.

Wriggling an arm loose, he grabbed her and bore her closer, and she knew his craving was like her strange one. When he pulled away, holding her off so he could look at her with his green glinting eyes, she resisted. She didn't want to stop, and she was afraid he would tell her to go.

"Boy hydie, you just never know what a new day'll bring," he said with a grin.

She let her hands explore his chest—she had just noticed it was bare—marveling at the few reddish hairs on his thin shoulders. She sucked in his smell while she thought what to say.

"I brought the key." She produced it and held it up to him, wondering as she did how much of him was bare. She shuddered in spite of herself, remembering her loathing for the ugly slack body of her daddy forcing himself on her ever since she could remember, and the large hairy body of her brother, misusing hers. The Man wasn't anything like either of them. He was like, like Justin Timberlake.

He was eying the key ring, taking his time about fingering it. "Seems like I recollect telling you to tell Snider Greene the deal is off, didn't I?"

Distress came in waves. She had a sick feeling in her stomach. She hadn't connected the message for Snider Greene with the key, did not know it would mean he wouldn't send her with it again. She hung her head, feeling her cheeks grow hot, and scratched at the covers.

"I forgot," she said in a tiny voice.

An alarm clock jangled somewhere past the thin wall. The plumbing soon clanked and wheezed, and somebody switched on a radio to a tune by "Asleep at the Wheel."

Calvin seemed to come to a decision. He tossed the key onto the floor and put his finger to her lips. "That there's my boss waking up," he whispered. "We got to make this fast."

He pulled her under the covers and groped beneath her cotton dress, touching her. At first she was too surprised to react. Then she knew he must be angry. He was punishing her, and yet he was trying to kiss her at the same time. She wanted to resign herself to the way things were, but buried memories pushed between them. Despite that she was still aroused from a night's love-making in her fantasy, she struggled to shove him away. She let out a small pleading moan.

He clamped his hand hard over her mouth, and she tasted blood. The music stopped and the boss rapped on the wall and called, "You up in there?"

Calvin's eyes were brittle green, watchful. He put his mouth against her ear and hissed, "Will you shut your yap? Now you got to get out of here before you get caught and we both get throwed out."

With a whimper, she did as she was told. She crept out of bed and scurried to the door, anxious not to displease him any more. The sprung door stuck again. She tugged frantically, knowing that he must be getting angrier.

He came over and closed his hand over hers on the knob. "You got to lift up on it like this," he said in a quiet voice.

He seemed in a hurry. He had no clothes, though. She turned her face away and waited for him to free her. But just as she slipped through the narrow crack he made for her, he caught her arm and pinched her on the chest where it stuck out. She thought she saw him grin again.

"You're not real bright, are you? But you ain't half bad looking. That was a real nice surprise. Now *git!*" He shut the door and left her squinting in the morning smaze.

It was still a long time until she was due at Snider Greene's, she could tell. She had no place to go. Afire with a new misery, a restless unspent longing, she trudged back toward Main Street, wringing her hands. But he liked her; that was something. It was even comforting that he knew about her now, about not being very bright, just as the needling about her leg hair by each year's crop of ever younger classmates was somehow comforting. But Momma said that after this year, maybe she could quit going to school and quit being in the same grade every year.

The October wind bit into her bare legs. She gave a violent shiver as the gale sucked at her thin clothing. Looking around for shelter, she saw she was in an alley about halfway between the Church of Christ, on the block behind Main, and the picture show, up on Main. The church's doors might be open at this time of day, because the cleaning man often left them unlocked. Still, it was no contest. She made for the partial shelter of the alcove of the Pastime Theater, where she could look at pictures of Scenes of the Current Attraction.

She usually tried to imagine what the pictures were about, but today her mind wouldn't work, wouldn't settle down. She didn't feel good anymore. She stood in the back corner of the alcove and faced the wall and pressed her fingers between her thighs, trying to get shed of this feeling that wouldn't go away, even though she knew Momma would hit her if she knew.

After a bit, she felt better, and when the clock finally struck ten times, she turned to go. A darker layer of rust-colored air hovered off to the northwest. The wind picked up the road dust and hurled it against her as she left the haven of the picture show and started up Main Street toward Snider Greene's.

Her throat was dry, and so was her nose. She stuck her finger up her nose, trying to do it the way Brittney would. Or J-Lo, who had very slippery lips and thin curved eyebrows. Elsie thought about her own thick eyebrows. She pinched a wad of hairs between her finger and thumb and tried to pull them out. Now it was late. She would have to run.

The old windmill out back of Snider's house was groaning as it was buffeted about. Somewhere a loose door flapped. With reluctant steps, she clumped onto the front porch and pounded on the screen, chattering with a chill that had seeped into her bones.

Snider was a long time in answering and when he finally opened the door, he wove unsteadily, glaring as if he had no notion who she was. She began to think he had forgotten. Or maybe she had made another mistake.

"I come at ten, like you said."

He seemed to recall at last. Raking a bloated hand over his mouth, he stepped aside. "Oh yeah. Get on in, then." He shuffled off toward his room, muttering so softly that she could hardly understand him. "Go in yonder and put the key ring on the cabinet, so you don't lose it."

Dread filled her belly. Maybe he would be peeved at what she had done. She tried to think of how to tell him. Finally she murmured, "I given it back."

He wheeled and studied her hard. She couldn't tell if he was mad or not. She squirmed, ducked her head, scratched a piece of dried oatmeal off her dress. Her stringy hair—not anything like Brittney's—fell across her cheeks, protecting her eyes from him. Seemed like Calvin had told her to tell him something last night, and again this morning when she first got to the motel. Now Snider Greene was so mad at what she did that she couldn't think what Calvin said.

"You don't have it? You mean he didn't give it back to you?"

She didn't know how to answer, didn't know how to tell him Calvin gave it back last night. She didn't have the words to explain about this morning, but she had to try. "He give it to me, but I taken it back to him."

"You what?" Snider was almost in her face, trying to see into her eyes. "When?"

She bent her head lower. "While I was waiting to come here this morning."

He didn't say anything for a while, so she added, "I thought it might save time . . ."

"Dammit, nobody's paying you to think, missy! You're just supposed to do what you're told." He turned and stumped off. "Well, later on this afternoon you can go down and check on it, make certain he was able to use it."

Her spirits sailed to the sky at the prospect of going to the rink once more, and she lunged into her work to make the time come sooner. On every side the weather stripping twanged in the gathering wind, a lonely crying sound. But unlike other times when things cried out to her, this time she was certain the sound did not augur disaster.

10

Elsie skipped out of Snider Greene's on that last errand with the money in one hand and some white bread in the other. She scampered toward town, trying to hum with the zinging telephone wires east of the road. To the west, the dark billows boiled, an ominous curtain between Attebury and the sun, with the already discernable smell about it of Colorado topsoil. But it wasn't the time of year for a killer storm, which always came when the little birds flew back after winter. Still, the wind was whipping up a frenzy among the scraggly trees, twanging under the corrugated roof of a building near the midpoint, rattling every loose board along the way. They were bleak sounds that often pressed on her, burrowing deep to touch a kernel of melancholy.

But today the desolation could not accomplish eroding her spirit, because she refused to heed it. She was tuned to a higher music from morning: "That was a real nice surprise."

Halfway down, she felt an overwhelming urge to turn and look back at the big house. Snider Greene was standing on the porch, watching. She waved gaily, but he didn't wave back. From all the way up on the hill came the mournful keening of the windmill.

Snider went into the house. She bit into the soft bread and swallowed it without chewing.

The sun, no longer high overhead, was a cerise ball in an opaque sky; she looked at it without squinting. Seemed like the day was going to end early—maybe before she had a chance to skate with Calvin. She took one more bite, threw down the rest and took off like a jackrabbit.

Calvin was waiting just for her, she was sure of it. As the tent hove into view, she saw his face light up hungrily, and he signaled while she was still a long way off. "I'm going to skate, going to skate," she shrieked into the wind, shucking off a tumbleweed trying to bar her way.

He glided over to the steps taking her hand wadded with the money Snider had given her.

"Where you been?" His voice was husky, urgent. "I'd just about give up on you."

She couldn't think of anything to say, just beamed in contentment and swung her arms to the rhythm of the Beatles singing "Help!" barely audible above the roar of the wind. Again she tried to give him the money, but he looked around toward the counter where his boss stood.

"Do we have to skate? If you'd of showed up sooner, we could of snuck off to the motel."

But Elsie was edging eagerly over to the benches, anxious for the adventure to begin again. She sat on the nearest bench and stuck out her foot, waiting. The speakers scracked out another old tune: "Wipeout." The gusts kicked up a flurry of grit, making her choke and claw her eyes, but she knew the skaters would come, because they were used to privation, used to the sand.

Suddenly the air was stifling with particles as the day went an eerie orange-black. The tent flapped wildly. Vicious wind tore at them, stinging like thousands of prickly needles, blistering, choking, burning the throat, making it impossible to keep their eyes open. Calvin held a handkerchief over his face with one hand, grabbing her arm with the other.

"Looks like we going to be blowed out—what's your name?" His voice was muffled through the cloth, although he was shouting above the creaking guide lines of the tent.

"Elsie." Her thin voice was ripped away by the gale. Maybe he didn't hear. She clenched her fists and tried to think what to do. She wished they could just go on and skate.

"'At's right. Why can't I remember that? Come on, Elsie, let's you and me kite off to the bushes. Looks like this might be a right good time to disappear."

But she heard Calvin's boss bellow as they clattered toward the steps. "Calvin! Better tie the top down before it gets too dark, else this storm's liable to whip it clean off."

Calvin cursed. "Fat bastard!" His eyes pored over her from behind the handkerchief for several seconds, then he said, "Screw it!" Pulling her roughly by the arm, he jerked her off the steps and half dragged her around behind the tent into a waist-high stand of dried-out Johnson grass. There he pushed her down and fell upon her.

Elsie cried out as the brittle stalks stabbed her dry skin, but the gale's howl had reached such a crescendo that her cries were carried away even from her own ears. She felt the panic of bewilderment, as if she had fallen asleep and missed part of the action. Even though the banked fire of her passion flamed up when he pulled her into the grass, even though she would readily have responded, eager to feed his ardor, he gave her no chance. With one thrust he seemed to cut her in two. A searing pain tore her flesh, bringing back childhood nightmares of Daddy and Sael.

Not counting the times, before she was eight, when they both had regularly assaulted her, Elsie had been raped before, and instinct guided her to go limp, lose consciousness if possible, to minimize the injury. But she could not uncoil. She writhed to escape, thus inflicting worse punishment on herself. She knew, but she couldn't help it. She jerked her head up and clamped her teeth solidly upon him, gouging her nails into the soft tissue of his ears in the bargain.

Calvin tore away, screaming in rage and pain, but his flesh remained within the tenacious clamp of Elsie's teeth. Her mouth filled with blood. She had, God forgive, bitten off his nose.

Still bellowing, Calvin Huddle clutched his spurting face, all the while flailing her with his skate, battering her maniacally, stomping her until his own blood seemed to blind him.

But Elsie felt no more than the first two of the mangling blows, although she could see they were still coming. She screamed, not in hope of being heard, but in unbidden agonal rattles.

Finally, still bawling, Calvin staggered off toward the street. Elsie, lifeless Elsie, wasn't sure she was alive, wasn't sure whether the wind subsided or she was losing consciousness. Wasn't sure whether the music summoned the skaters or whether that was heavenly music.

Did not get to tell her lover goodbye.

Calvin didn't collapse for several minutes, not before it occurred to him that Snider Greene owed him money, and if he died Snider wouldn't ever have to pay.

11

When the dust storm hit, Adrian had hoped Ernest would cancel their dinner date, but he was on her doorstep on the dot, braving the grit. She presumed they would go to the country club. Instead, he drove her out to his estate, so-called.

He described his choice logically. "You've never been outside the public rooms of the place, and I thought after dinner you'd like the grand tour."

Ah. Job orientation.

Along with everyone else in town, Adrian had attended the Open House that Helga had thrown when they moved into the monstrosity. By the time it was completed—a process that took over three years—it had become the scandal of the state. It was purported to contain sixty-three rooms and cost from forty to eighty million dollars. Snider, who sometimes had inside information, had confided that, including furnishings and grounds, the price was double that.

In the beginning of construction, Ernest had often boasted about its size, while Helga regaled the Garden Club and Altar Guild with accounts of European jaunts for antiques. But as time wore on, and the edifice rose out on the prairie like Disneyland, people began to mutter about excess. Such things might be common elsewhere, but Panhandle folks had better sense.

Thus, the big party when the estate and its sumptuous gardens were finished was an obvious attempt to gain the town's approval. Helga also announced plans to host musical soirees in the salon and a cotillion each spring for the local debs, but soon after the first party, her cancer had been discovered. Their first fling had been their last.

Helga's death did not blunt the town's animosity toward Ernest's monument to greed, and tonight, as the iron gates swung open onto the tree-lined drive to the house, Adrian wondered if he was trying to buy their good will by winning her. Certainly Snider would think so. A brief stab of guilt pricked her as she wondered why she hadn't mentioned this date to Snider.

Snider had been so secretive of late, as if she cared. She wrapped a scarf around her head as the Bentley pulled into the porte-cochere.

There was no sign of staff, but there must be banks of servants lurking. Ernest led her through a side entrance to a smaller dining room, where Helga's old maid, Precious, served them unaided: Ernest, wearing an Italian silk suit, sat at the head of the enormous table; Adrian, woefully underdressed in a tan sheath, sat to his right.

Apparently Bobby and his big German wife were out for the evening. Ernest didn't say, and Adrian didn't ask. But now that she thought about it, a live-in son and daughter-in-law weren't assets to someone on the prowl for a new wife.

Without the usual distractions of a public dining room, every clink of silver against china echoed, even above the howling wind outside. Precious' feet shuffling from sideboard to table provided the only other relief from the silence. When she left with the soup bowls, Ernest's mastication of veal was clearly audible. When he swallowed his wine, she could track the liquid all the way down.

As for Adrian, she had difficulty making even the tiniest bite go past her throat, but she made the effort for Precious' sake. Precious' idea of French cooking was actually quite good, if only there weren't that "grand tour" looming ahead.

For desert, Precious reverted to type and served a sturdy slab of apple-pecan pie—and won Adrian's heart. She could almost bear living in this place if Precious kept this up. If only she didn't have to look at Ernest.

Throughout the meal, he had made no attempt at small talk. He sat to her left, bolting his pie, washing it down with gulps of coffee, like a pig slurping in the trough. A peasant's forelock escaped the carefully styled hair, spoiling the princely bearing he had apparently been going for.

They had scarcely exchanged more than a dozen words since he called for her an hour before. Had it been only an hour? It seemed like five.

She nibbled around the edges of the magnificent culinary triumph, wishing she could box it and take it home. Finally, when she could stand his snorts no longer, she made a delicate show of daubing her mouth and folding her napkin and said, "Precious seems to have vanished. Mind if I step into the kitchen to compliment her?"

The suggestion took him by surprise. The Andy Rooney eyebrows raised then lowered over a scowl. "If you want."

She left him to finish his pie and stepped through the swinging door into the butler's pantry, Precious' staging area. She proceeded on into the huge kitchen, where the maid-of-all-work, loading an oversized dishwasher, looked up in astonishment.

Now that she was here, timidity washed over her. She smiled. "I wanted you to know how much I enjoyed your cooking. Especially the pie."

The woman's large round face opened into a wide-mouthed grin. "Yes ma'am." She seemed not to know what to say, either.

Adrian's gaze swept around the restaurant-sized kitchen, which was easily well-equipped enough to prepare a banquet for a hundred guests, toward the double French doors off to the right, obviously leading to yet another eating area, now dark. A glassed-in morning room behind it still glowed faintly with light. On impulse, she said, "I hope I didn't disturb the younger Mister Vogel and his wife. Are they eating in there?"

"Oh, Bobby and Inge? No ma'am. They don't ever eat down here. They take they meals in they own part of the house." She indicated a door in the wall opening to a dumb waiter. At the end of the kitchen, a door led into another hall, where she could see a flight of back stairs, probably one of many flights.

No wonder Ernest needed a wife. Now she could readily believe him about being lonely.

Having no other excuse to remain in the kitchen, Adrian returned to the dining room, where Ernest waited to show her the rest of the house.

As the gale whistled outside, they wound their way through the house. She lost track of the rooms downstairs, which she had seen before. On one side of the large circular foyer with its baronial curving double staircase, several sets of double doors admitted to a music salon, a library, perhaps more. On the other, identical doors led to a drawing room with solarium and a larger dining room. At the back of the hall was an elevator flanked by two marble powder rooms.

Ernest whisked her through another reception hall, beyond which she could glimpse a billiard room, and the music salon, which boasted, besides two grand pianos, a harpsichord, a harp, and a state-or-the-art sound system. It was just as well that she wasn't given time to linger. The sooner she raced through the place, the sooner she could go home.

As he ushered her onto the elevator he said, "There's a ballroom on the third floor, and a movie theater with Surround Sound and plush seats. I built dressing rooms and a green room. Helga planned to have some play productions. I put a dance exercise room up there—Helga had ideas about staging a ballet—although of course, there's a full gym in the basement with a racquetball court, and exercise rooms in each of the master suites."

They got off on the second floor, where Ernest and Helga's separate suites occupied most of the front of the house. Adrian barely stuck a toe into Helga's suite and thought that the King of Saudi Arabia couldn't have any more gold leaf than this. It was ghastly.

Several bedroom suites led off of the u-shaped hall, but Ernest merely motioned toward the wing to the right and said, "Bobby and Inge have their own suites there. I seldom see them."

"But surely you see them sometimes, when they use the elevator," she said.

He shook his head. "They use the back elevator."

After a tour of the third floor, Adrian, impressed despite her best efforts not to be, said, "You seem to have forgotten nothing except an indoor swimming pool."

His porcine face brightened. "You didn't see that the last time you were here?"

Like a gleeful child, he scurried her into the elevator and swept her back to the ground floor. On the other side of the stairway, a passage led to a side entrance. To the left, near the outside door, was an opening to the glassed-in morning room which she'd glimpsed from the kitchen. But when Ernest switched on the lights, she saw much more than a morning room. It was, in fact, the near end of another solarium, and a glassed-in garden room, complete with swimming pool which ran a quarter of the back of the house. He'd brought the tropics to the Panhandle.

She walked around the deck to peer out the back wall of windows at the tennis courts beyond, where wind tore viciously at the nets. "You have *four* tennis courts?"

"Would you like to play?" He sounded so anxious to please.

She managed a laugh. "Have you forgotten there's a dust storm raging? In fact, I was just about to suggest that you'd better take me home before I crater. I'm very tired. Must've been that great meal," she added lamely.

In a matter of seconds he was escorting her into the Bentley.

His effort at conversation as he drove her home consisted of, "Now you see how I live . . . ."

"It's very nice," she said, a bit too primly.

"You can see how I rattle around."

She cleared her throat, which threatened to close off. "You might consider moving."

It was the wrong thing to say. He was as touchy as Helga about criticism of his excesses. He brought the Bentley to a screech at her house and scuttled her through a blinding wind up the walk. At her door he clicked his heels and said gruffly, "Thanks for your company."

"And thank *you* for—" But she was wasting her breath. He was already halfway to his car. Well, she'd blown that one. Or maybe it was just the storm that he was escaping.

She closed the door and sighed. There was no way on God's earth that she could stand—

Ernest's car had scarcely roared away before she heard the sound of heavy steps on the porch. As soon as the insistent hammering began, she knew it couldn't be Ernest. She was not frightened at the obvious urgency of the knock. She never considered stopping for a precautionary peek out the window. She flung open the door, then caught her breath as the great heaving hulk of a man confronted her. At the same moment, a blast of dust hit her in the face.

It was the idiot Puckett boy, Sael, his gotch eyes tumid with fright. Saliva dribbled from between the gaps in his teeth, rolling past his thin lips onto the unshaven chin. He was literally foaming at the mouth. She felt her vulnerability as always when he was about. She made it a point to keep a safe distance from him when he came to mow the lawn or do odd jobs, especially if they involved the use of a hoe, a hammer or a shovel.

As she had done many times on every sort of occasion with Sael, she drew herself up and assumed an austere authority intended to intimidate him, hanging onto the door as much for support as to keep it from slamming against the wall. "What on earth is it? And for goodness sake, wipe your mouth."

The boy panted and slathered, his way when he was over-stimulated. It took a while for her instructions to sink in. She frowned at his chin until he finally ran a sleeve over it. It was only then that she could look into his eyes, but their maniacal glint did nothing to assure her. She gripped the doorknob and held her ground.

He waved his huge ungovernable arms in the direction of the Puckett shack, somewhere out there in the dark turbulence.

"Momma says come over quick. Poor Elsie's done been mashed flat!"

12

Two garage musicians happened upon the girl in the weeds—probably sharing a roach, Adrian figured when they told her about it later. Not wanting to bloody their van, they formed a gory single-file procession, one grasping her under the meatless arms, the other riding her legs against his hip. With the wind and sand to their backs they plodded the five blocks to Pucketts' with her limp body dribbling a trail of its vital fluids.

They plunked her upon the Pucketts' futon and backed out the door, unnerved by Mozelle's wails and the old man's drunken front porch ukase that someone would pay for this outrage. Miz Puckett stood by, bearing her distress in rigid calm after she had summoned Sael from the kitchen to go for Miss Adrian.

Adrian met the musicians heading back to town as she ran down the walk, following Sael, who identified them as Elsie's rescuers. One described their gruesome find, then told her, "No need to hurry. She's probably already dead."

But Elsie was not dead. Adrian passed the night on her knees beside what was left of the child, bathing her wounds, forcing small drops of liquid between the grey lips, chafing the flaccid wrists. Listening to the wind whining to get in, rattling the panes. Tasting the grit in her dry mouth, smelling it. Ordering Mozelle and Miz Puckett to boil more rags. Praying to a God she had long since renounced, cursing that devil of a rinkman who most surely had ravaged her. Feeling the weight of her thirty-seven years in her joints as, toward dawn, she labored to rise.

The sandstorm's original fury had been quickly spent, but even as Adrian tottered home for breakfast, the dust was only beginning to settle. It was difficult to get her breath.

Sarah, who was coming out for her morning paper as Adrian passed, stopped her and said, "Have you heard anything about The Man at the skating rink? Somebody said he got hurt bad."

But Elsie was much too small to hurt anyone very badly. Maybe Adrian was wrong about who injured her. She asked her neighbor to keep her informed and hurried on inside.

Too worn out to eat, she first fell asleep sitting in a kitchen chair while waiting for the coffee to make, then she roused long enough to creep off and throw herself across her crochet bedspread, where she slept for hours and woke with the pattern embedded in her cheek.

The telephone roused her; it was Sarah with an update. "Thelma down at the hatchery said the rink man lost his nose, but he wouldn't say how. Doesn't that beat all? She took him someplace to get help but I didn't ask where."

As she hung up, Adrian glanced at the clock with alarm. She hadn't meant to sleep so long. If only Miz Puckett weren't so proud, they could have called a doctor. Maybe Elsie had died, or wouldn't they have come for her to redress the oozing wounds? A bitterness consumed her. Damnit, Elsie shouldn't have to die before she'd had somebody to love.

Still, Elsie had a family. She belonged to someone, whereas now with Grandfather gone, Adrian had—well, she wouldn't think about it. She went in and drew a bath and lowered herself stiffly into the soothing warmth, where she stayed only as long as she dared. Then she devoured the first meal she'd had in almost twenty-four hours: an empanada, only half warmed.

Her physical self revived, she hurried to relieve Miz Puckett's vigil at Elsie's side, reminding herself that the girl had the resiliency of youth in her favor.

But as she opened her front door, she was astonished to find Ernest Vogel standing at attention, spit-and-polished in a knobby striped sport coat purchased out of town somewhere. Great-Grandfather's ornery prize rooster Hitler came to mind. For Ernest, though, the suit was a dashing departure and Adrian was not displeased.

"Why, Ernest, you look—" She stopped before she said something mawkish. Still, at the very moment when she was feeling unloved, his presence was like a sign from the universe. She stood aside, allowing him to strut past, painfully aware of her baggy sweats, hair hurriedly tamed, not a smidgeon of color on her fatigue-drained cheeks. Her hand went to her throat in automatic attempt to hide the place where her skin was going slack: a constant indictment.

He brandished a folder. "I've completed arrangements to transfer Ernest's part of the ranch to you, pending your signature on the loan papers."

Oh, so that was what this was about. Just business. "I could have come to the bank to sign them later," she said, following him back to the den, addressing his broad back. "The truth is, I wasn't expecting company. I was on my way over to help Miz Puckett—"

He turned, and his square-faced glower silenced her. "Adrian, why do you insist on mixing with town trash? Have you no respect for your station?"

She pulled the neck of her shirt, ootching farther down. If only she had a spot of blush.

"Am I invited to sit down?" He sat without waiting for an answer and brushed the toe of his loafers—loafers, for crying out loud! "Or must I rise until you decide to light somewhere?"

She wiped her hands down her sides. Her disadvantage was just too great. "Please wait. I—have to get out of these work clothes."

It took longer than she planned; still, the results weren't bad. She shucked off the sneakers and sweats, replacing them with flats, slacks and a lavender cowl-necked sweater whose folds mercifully masked the abominable gullet. The hue somehow caught the same shade in the delicate skin around her eyes, making them appear striking and deep violet. Fussing with her hair proved unrewarding. She slathered her face recklessly with makeup, pinched her cheeks, then decided a little lip liner wouldn't be obvious. A spritz of cologne and she was finally ready.

Ernest was glowering and drumming on the couch arm when she returned. She wondered at her own fear. He labored to his feet, obviously ill-at-ease in his sporty finery.

"How about tea?"

"Don't you have anything stronger?"

She pretended to be shocked. "At this hour?" She glanced toward the window and realized the sun was low in the sky. Where had the day gone?

But apparently Ernest hadn't noticed the hour, either. He sighed and sat down. "You're right. A man needs a woman to remind him of these things." It sounded like an act to Adrian. Then he added, "God, how I miss Helga sometimes."

She hurried off to make tea, muttering, "Helga. Always Helga."

It no longer seemed peculiar that Ernest should try to win her. She marveled at how quickly she had adapted to the idea. All it took was the thought of dying without ever having been loved. Clearly, the man needed taking in hand, and of a sudden, the task didn't seem so unpalatable. The stimulation of being courted was the payoff. And wait until Snider found out!

To keep him occupied while she scrounged around looking for something to serve, she called, "Thanks for the tour last night. Your place is impressive."

There was a pause. "Can you picture yourself living there?"

She swallowed and turned her attention to the menu. If only she had some evidence of at least a smattering of uxorial skill. Not that she had definitely decided to give a flip: the game was first to win and then decide.

"I wonder. If, as you say, you rattle around, why did you build such a huge mansion?"

His laugh was more of a disdainful snort. "Because, Adrian, I could!"

"But you own so many houses. All those hovels across the tracks. Seems like you could've spread the wealth around," she said as she finished a fruitless search of the freezer for Sara Lee. What was it Grandmother used to do when she heard Grandfather coming home? She'd be sitting there on the piano bench with the children gathered around, but when the car rumbled up the hill, she'd leap up and direct Adrian to put on the water to boil and throw in an onion, while she made cinnamon toast. The two would scurry around while Snider looked on enjoying the joke, and by the time Grandfather came in, the kitchen was full of steam and the pervading odors of onion and cinnamon, and Grandmother was peeling potatoes with a vengeance. For all Grandfather ever knew she'd been in the kitchen all afternoon.

Ernest hadn't answered. Maybe he hadn't heard. She slipped several slices of cinnamon toast under the broiler and went to find a decent cutwork napkin to put on her best silver tray.

She tried again. "I didn't know bankers were all *that* rich."

"The decade of the nineties was a time of unprecedented wealth."

Not for the Pucketts, she almost said. *They never even got closer to the table.* But there was no place to break in. He was elaborating on Reagan deregulation, and she quit listening.

For all her preparation, Ernest was unimpressed. She should have been warned by the ugly flush that had swamped his features. As she entered with the tray, he was muttering, "There are some women who wouldn't be averse to the attentions of a man with money."

She sat opposite him and carried off as well as she could manage, offering the county's richest man a measly piece of cinnamon toast. Still, her Sophie Newcomb training stood her in good stead: "I hope you'll join me in a bite of toast. Much more heart-healthy than a heavy pastry, don't you think?"

Ernest waved it aside. He frowned into the cup. "Is this tea?"

She tried not to bristle. "Is something wrong?"

"Looks like piss."

Time for more bluff. "This is a rare blend from the East Indies. It's much stronger than it looks." She jumped up and took his cup. "But I can get you ordinary—"

"Never mind," he said, sighing. "I'm out of the mood." He looked at his gaudy diamond-studded Rolex. "All I came for was a signature." He handed the folder to her and hoisted himself from the squashy cushions with effort. She'd never noticed before how chintzy they looked.

Dutifully she took his pen and affixed her signature where he indicated, then smiled. "But we've hardly—uh—" She tried to summon some semblance of long-forgotten feminine wile.

"I know," he said. "You've been on the run ever since I got here. Giving me the third degree from behind a swinging door."

She let out an exasperated sniff. "If I'd been warned you were coming—"

"*Warned?*" He puffed up like a bull, clicked his heels and wheeled for the foyer. "Someday, Adrian, you'll learn to curb your tongue. Don't bother to see me out."

She followed, floundering. "Ernest, I didn't mean . . . ."

But he was gone in a huff, crashing the door behind him. She watched through the side glass as he stomped away, a martinet with pride held high. She chuckled, weak with relief. Now that she was sole owner of the ranch, maybe Mobeetie James would give Ernest competition.

With a pang of guilt, she realized she must relieve Miz Puckett, who'd probably stood vigil over poor Elsie the live-long day. Not bothering to change into the sweatshirt, she slipped on a jacket and hurried along against late afternoon gusts toward the darkened shanty.

It was a pitiful hovel. You could set the whole place down into Ernest's entry hall and have room left over. The country had just created more wealth than any other economy in the history of the world, and people like the Pucketts had been written completely out of the script.

She stood on the crumbling porch in a wind that would skin a jack rabbit, but no one answered her knock. Her teeth clacked from the cold. She hammered again, less assured, wondering if even now Elsie was lying stiff and grey over at the funeral home.

Heavy footsteps finally neared. Someone peered at her through the small glass. She considered with sudden trembling that the unpredictable Sael might be playing games with her. Finally the door lurched open a mere crack.

She steadied herself, but her quaver betrayed her. "Miz Puckett? I've come to help with Elsie." Knowing full well that it was not Miz Puckett, and probably not Mozelle, either.

The door did not swing open as she expected. With mounting alarm, she assumed the imperiousness of a headmistress. "Well? Aren't you going to invite me in?"

"Naw." It was the choleric old man. "The heat is getting out. Besides, ain't nobody here."

She pushed against the door to prevent him from closing it. "But Elsie? Good lord, she isn't—she didn't—"

"Elsie Mae ain't here. Ain't nobody here but me, I tell you."

"But where are they?"

"Gone. Wal-Mart, maybe. How should I know? They left soon after Elsie did."

The drunken fool was making no sense. Poor, battered Elsie "left?" That was not possible.

"Where did Elsie go?"

"Who the hell knows? Snider Green just come and taken her away, that's all."

Adrian felt as if she'd been slapped. There was no need to answer, as the old man had already closed the door. She hurried back home in a blind fury.

Just wait till she got hold of him! Snider Green was going to get such an ear-scorching that he would never forget it. He did this deliberately, dragged the poor girl away behind Adrian's back just to get Adrian's goat. She loathed that man for once again pushing her buttons. He knew exactly how to drive her to distraction.

What had happened since Grandfather died? Snider had changed. Time was when he wouldn't make a move without consulting her. Furthermore, she used to be able to fathom his thoughts long before he said a word. This time, he had deliberately driven past her house without so much as stopping, had marched into Pucketts' place, scooped up that sick child, and carted her off—for medical help, she presumed. What else was she to think but that he did it to irritate her?

Why else on God's earth would he intervene in Elsie's behalf? He never did anything remotely like that unless it was for a legal fee.

That was ludicrous. Miz Puckett had no money. If she could pay, she'd call a doctor.

Maybe the girl had been running an errand for Snider in town when it happened, and maybe he, fearing a lawsuit, had decided to look benevolent. But if so, how did he even learn that she was hurt? Had Miz Puckett sent Sael up the hill to tell him?

"The least he could've done was phone me," she muttered savagely as she fumbled for her front door key. "He ought to at least keep in touch."

Without turning on any lights, she stomped through the house into her bedroom and promptly struck her shin against a chair. The pain was all out of proportion to the injury. She grabbed her leg and cried out as she hopped to the bed. Tears sprang to her eyes, and she knew, from their volume, that this was about more than just a lick on the shin.

With this admission, she fell back onto her pillow, wracked by sobs.

One by one, beginning with when Baby Sister was born, she had lost them all: Mother—long before she actually died—Grandmother, Baby Sister, for whom, out of jealous spite, Adrian had eventually quit praying, Daddy, felled by the protracted sickness that knotted her insides for years, and now Grandfather. Snider was the last, and he was turning his back on her. Without Snider, there would be no one left to show. What? That she would endure?

No, Snider mustn't desert her. Not young Snider, so defenseless against the whole family: claiming their pity from those small pleading eyes all but lost in the fat cheeks, wincingly awkward among the so-clever relatives. Not Snider, who could infuriate Grandfather just by being in the room. Dear Lord, not Snider, against whom and without knowing why, she often turncoat took up the cudgel of deprecation and whipped him, almost reveling in his look of startled dismay.

She had led him around by the nose from the day she moved up on the hill—no, long before that. He'd been such a needy child that it was natural that he should turn to her, and she, unable to vent her jealous rage against the baby who had stolen Mother's love, had focused that rage on Snider. She saw it plainly now. And although he returned her jibes tit for tat, she suspected he was often surprised and maimed by her viciousness. She knew it even then, but she could never seem to help herself.

They had not been friends for so many years that she had lost count. Even as children they had ground against one another with no small degree of relish. Like small lion cubs, they sharpened their fighting skills on each other. Who hones us better than our grating relationships?

They had no other confidants. Their pattern of comradeship interspersed with enmity exploded once they reached puberty, as soon as their early and anxious self-conscious experimentation had expended itself—being conducted for the most part out behind the chicken house or in the old smoke house and occasionally, when they felt brazen enough, under the covers in his bedroom with the aid of Grandfather's flashlight—until she realized that he intended to possess her with more than mere lust, that he had made her the center of his life.

But when had he become the center of hers?

13

Calvin Huddle, holding the place where his nose ought to be and screaming to high heaven, had staggered across the street toward Attebury Feed and Hatchery before he collapsed in the doorway, spurting blood to mix with the rime of dirt building rapidly across the threshold.

The proprietress, a giantess named Glenda Miller, stopped culling cockerels and dragged his inert frame out of the blow. She stemmed the spurting wound with an empty feed sack, gave him a poke with her toe and said crossly, "I can't have this mess around my newborn chicks. You're going to have to get on back across the street."

Calvin tried to lift himself to his knees but fell back with a howl. Glenda stood over him for a while and finally said, "Well, I might give you a lift out to Madam's. If she can't fix you nobody can. Go on out and get in the truck. But don't bleed all over everything."

She returned to her culling table, while Calvin, in semi-shock and thus spared the full brunt of his suffering, half-crawled through the dust storm out to the curb, pressing the prickly cloth hard against the pain.

In a while the good woman left her chicks, climbed into the pickup beside him, and took him out Main, up the hill past Snider's place and down into the gully behind. There she pulled on the brake, nudged him and pointed through the gritty windshield.

"See that little half-dugout yonder? Woman by the name of Madam might could ease you."

With that, she reached past him, opened the door and booted him out beside the caliche road, which had narrowed to a single pair of ruts.

He rolled over twice before coming to a stop. He might have caught himself if he had been able to use his hands, but he couldn't let go of his nose, couldn't bear the thought of the agony any movement would cause. He lay in the stunted grass and heard the truck pull away.

His eyes stung and watered, not so much from the dust as from the large quantity of his own blood which had spewed at the time of the injury. Try as he might, he couldn't hold his eyes open longer than a second before some unbidden reflex clamped them shut again. Still, in time he was able to make out the hut in front of him, could see the lamp burning in the window. It was maybe an hour until sunset, but the dust-darkened sky created the illusion of night.

Still gripping the cloth to his nose, he crept on elbows and knees up to the house of the Madam, who, he supposed, had heard the truck and stood watching his approach from her front stoop. He saw her long skirts at eye level as he bellied closer, and he sensed her rejection even before he saw the bat she held.

"Halt right there. Don't come closer." The guttural voice, descending upon him from a face he couldn't see, was thick with accent and animus-edged.

"I need help," he mumbled.

"You won't find it here. I have one room—no place for a man." She bent and pulled his hands away from the bloody mess, displaying extraordinary strength even for a robust woman. He squinted and saw surprise register on her warty face.

"Well, I can stop the bleeding, at least. You might heal."

She disappeared into the house and returned in a moment. Calvin strained to lift his face up to her. He thought he would faint when she touched the laceration. She pressed a piece of some substance against his nose and secured it with a fresh cloth, tying it at the back of his head.

"I collect these from the ranch across the fence. I use them for burning, but they are useful for healing wounds. And for growing tomatoes."

"What is it?"

"Cow dung. Perhaps they will take you in at the bunkhouse, if you make it that far. Follow the road. You can crawl under the barbed wire. But hurry. It grows dark in another hour." Quickly she retreated and shut the door. He could hear a scraping sound, as if she were moving something heavy against it.

His head lay as she had dropped it, cocked sideways, so that he could have watched the dusky sky if he could've kept his eyes open. He could hear no sound other than the wind sweeping across the gully. He rolled over and allowed hot tears to spring into the already burning eyes. He lay huddled in a heap and bawled like a newborn.

How long he was there he wasn't sure, but it was long enough to attract the attention of an approaching horse, which whinnied so insistently that its rider veered over to investigate.

"What'n hell's this? So this is where you ended up."

Apparently news had traveled, despite the storm.

The man hoisted Calvin's limp body across the saddle of his bay stallion much as if it were a sack of feed. He mounted behind the saddle and trotted toward a fence about a quarter of a mile away. Each jounce sent incredible pain shooting through Calvin's face.

With a practiced hand, the rider opened the gate without dismounting and shut it once they were through. Then he took off at an excruciating gallop toward the distant bunkhouse.

When they had reached it, some of the other ranch hands lifted Calvin off and laid him out on the ground while the first man, called Nasty, went to fetch the boss. Calvin, hanging onto consciousness, had long since elected to surrender without question to whatever ministrations anyone would offer. It was of comfort to matter to somebody, even remotely.

"Who's this sucker?" came a crisp authoritative voice.

"This here's the Man from the skating rink. Pert near dead, looks like. He come upon Elsie Puckett's teeth, I hear," Nasty said.

The foreman pulled the crude dressing aside and shone a flashlight into Calvin's face. Calvin heard several of the men gasp, heard one run off a few feet and wretch on the ground. "Sonofabitch," someone said.

"Take him up to the main house," the foreman said. "Might be we could do for this one what we done for that heifer that got her teats tore off in the bailer."

When they lifted him, he lost consciousness and did not regain it until someone forced his head up, pried his lips apart and poured a quantity of whisky down his throat. Then he lapsed again into a dead sleep.

By what magic the boss brought about his survival, Calvin Huddle never knew, for the next hours were filled with hallucinatory dreams from which he woke innumerable times, always to find the lean dark-eyed man whom they called Mobeetie sitting nearby.

When Calvin came to a day or so later, he could tell by the relief on their faces that he was going to make it. Already the pain had become bearable. He was even able to take a few sips of the juice from slumgullion stew.

"I'm much obliged," he said to Mobeetie, letting his head drop onto the pillow. "I don't know how, but I think you saved my life."

"Any time," the foreman said. "You relieved the monotony. Besides, we don't take kindly to folks dying on us."

Calvin closed his eyes, vaguely worried by the foreman's folksy manner. All during his coma, Calvin had the feeling that he may have rambled on about his recent business arrangement with Snider Greene.

And during his rambles, every time he opened his eyes, Mobeetie had never left his side.

14

Before breakfast, Adrian phoned Snider to find out what he was up to. If he had taken Elsie to a local doctor, she would have been home by nightfall the day before. He must have driven her to the city, possibly to be hospitalized. Maybe he suspected it was The Man who had beaten her, and he was trying to prevent him from finding her to finish the job.

Uncharacteristic as that would be . . . unless there was something in it for him.

Snider didn't answer, although he must have noted her number on Caller ID. It was much too early for him to be out. She had to be content with leaving a voice mail, asking him to buy her a bottle of fine sherry, some Chardonnay and Merlot, and a fifth of Johnny Walker Black when he went up to the county line. That would send him hopping. About the only thing she could count on him for these days was to keep her supplied with booze.

He would come now, she was sure of it. He would drag himself out of bed and drive to Groom, and he would buy her something dry and expensive. Nothing pleased Snider more than to replenish her liquor cabinet. Any excuse to make a trip to the package store where, so long as he was there, he'd stock up for himself.

When he came, she wouldn't grill him about Elsie; wouldn't even mention her. After all, what was Elsie to her? The girl was even less important to Snider, who didn't like anybody very much. If Adrian mentioned her, he'd think she was jealous. As if she cared a rat's ass what Snider did or with whom. He wouldn't be interested in Elsie in *that* way, in any case. Even stretching it, she couldn't be sixteen yet, and he was almost forty. Elsie was mentally lacking, to boot.

Finally she sat down to her coffee and morning paper. As she anticipated, Elsie's beating and The Man's injury went unnoted by the local press.

Apparently, if your name was Puckett or Huddle, you weren't newsworthy. Adrian gave the paper a healthy snap and turned the page. "I'd give a nickel to know what happened to that bastard," she said to no one.

Her gaze lit on a half-page ad from a Mercedes dealership in the city. "Trade Up Today! Must Make Room for New Arrivals."

Until her dinner at Ernest's mansion, Adrian had been satisfied with her five-year-old Camry. But since acquiring the ranch, she had begun to view her surroundings with new eyes. The place was shabby. Her clothes were out of style. It was as if all these years she'd been dressing for nobody but Snider, as if he'd ever notice what she wore or what she drove or where she lived. Maybe she should make some effort to spruce up, even if nothing ever came of her relationship with Ernest. Maybe she owed it to her ranch staff now.

After their encounter last night, it would be an uphill slog if anything ever did come of it.

She put down the paper and glared out the window. Even if Snider had been standing over the telephone when she called, he wouldn't leave for the liquor store immediately. It might be hours before she heard anything from him. Probably mid-afternoon, at least. She would sit here and grind her teeth all day unless—

The decision was made. She went to her desk and rummaged around for the car title. Mustn't think too long about this or she might change her mind. As soon as she found it, she grabbed up her keys and left. On the way she would phone the dealer to be sure that she could take immediate possession of a new car today.

When she rounded the corner of the house, Sael Puckett took her off guard, as he invariably seemed to do. She wondered whether he did it on purpose. She took pains to hide the start he gave her, but he grinned and rolled his gotch eyes as if he took pleasure in unnerving her. She'd never put up with him if Miz Puckett didn't depend on his income and if his strength weren't needed for odd jobs. She straightened, assuming command. "Rake out the rest of the leaves from the beds, roll up the garden hoses and put them away for the winter. When I get back, I'll have some things for you to carry to the attic."

She started for the garage then knew she couldn't wait any longer to ask. "What's this I hear about Snider Greene taking Elsie away?"

He had already headed toward the shed for the rake, but he trotted loosely over to her, never the slightest bit intimidated, no matter how hard she tried. "Yes ma'am. I done carried her to his car myself. She looked about dead to me." He showed no trace of emotion, the broad grin still spread over his untroubled face.

"You mean she was still unconscious?"

He looked puzzled, grappling with the large word.

"Never mind," she said. "When you finish your chores, stack the lawn chairs and clean up the litter in the alley." He wouldn't remember half of that, she knew. Once she was out of sight, he'd probably flop on the chaise and stare at the sky until he heard her car in the drive.

Without too much forethought, she took a detour up the hill to Snider's place. She got out and knocked, but he didn't answer. She moved to the window of his room and peered inside at the lump of covers. Just as she suspected. Probably sleeping off a drunk. She returned to her car in disgust. She had plenty of time to get to the city and back before he came to.

On the drive north toward Amarillo, she pictured Snider's puzzlement if he should arrive to deliver her liquor before she returned. He'd probably sit in front of her house for a while in Grandfather's old Chrysler, drumming his fingers on the steering wheel. Wishing for a drink. Oh, she'd keep him guessing, the same way he was doing with her. Wondering why she was buying Scotch, for one thing.

You're not the only one with secrets, she thought.

It was the end of October, and furrows had begun to freeze hard at nightfall. She could see evidence, the farther north she drove, that they hadn't thawed under the cold morning sun. Farm workers worked with a frenzy in the flat fields, doubtless anxious to finish before what promised to be the setting in of an early winter.

Soon it would be Halloween, and the weekend after that, regardless of the weather, the Attebury Coyotes and Claude Buffaloes would meet for the homecoming game, and at the half-time some radiant shivering sixteen-year-old in a strapless ball gown would be crowned homecoming queen. But not Elsie. The world was not full of options for a girl like Elsie.

What had he done with her? And why?

The questions so distracted her that she lost all interest in the project at hand. She drove into the Mercedes dealership and bought the first car on the floor, knowing that even so, and even though she would pay cash, it would be hours before the salesman would be through determining the trade-in value of her Camry so that she could get back home with her new car. Now she couldn't think what possessed her to leave town when she knew Snider was bound to come soon.

She tossed a deposit check across the desk to the startled salesman. "I've just remembered an important appointment. No need to prep the new car. I need it right now. Call me when you've decided what you'll offer me for my old car." Then she made a brisk exit and drove rapidly toward home, thinking that was no way to get a good deal on a car.

Some other day, when she wasn't in such a hurry, she'd shop for some new clothes, maybe when she came to settle up accounts with the car dealer. A new car did make her feel more like shopping, but not today. At present, she couldn't get her mind off Snider.

"That boy is up to something," Grandmother used to say, "else he wouldn't be such a loner." It was true that Snider kept to himself. He considered himself the perpetual underdog. But whatever his mischief, Adrian had never known him to do anything criminal. Shady, yes. Criminal, no. He was too clever for that.

One thing Snider knew was the law. He knew what a man could do and stay on the right side of it. Hardly anybody appreciated the art of that.

Grandfather had. He had advised young Snider, "An attorney writes his own ticket. You could do worse."

But Adrian had only snickered when he told her and said, "You look more like a Holy Roller preacher to me." Why had she perpetually tried to hurt him?

But he'd given it right back. "You are the gnat in my clabber," he used to say. "The splinter under my toenail. The tick in my groin. Somebody needs to take a switch to you."

But nobody did. She was much too pretty. Grandfather used to chuckle about her contrariness, like Teddy Roosevelt saying he could either govern the nation and or control Alice, but not both.

When Snider finished high school, Grandfather had said, "You've not been much count so far, but I made a pact with the Lord that if he prospered me, I'd see my children properly educated. The Lord would hold my feet to the fire if I didn't extend that to my grandchildren."

Adrian figured the real reason Snider went to law school was that there weren't many women there. Women invariably intimidated him. She'd seen to that.

As she sped toward Attebury, she picked up her cell phone and punched in his number. Not that she expected him to answer, but—

Snider came on the line immediately. "Yeah? What is it now?"

"Did you get my liquor?" she said.

"What liquor?"

"You didn't listen to your voice mail? You mean I'm rushing back home for nothing?"

"Home from where?"

"Amarillo. I've been car shopping."

"Then go by way of Groom and get it yourself."

"It's too late. I'm almost—" But he had hung up. *Hung up on her.* Furious, she jabbed in his number once more. When he answered, she said, "Don't you *ever* do that again!"

She could hear him swallow; knew she had interrupted his drinking. "What the hell do you want, Adrian? I'm busy."

"What did you do with Elsie?" She blurted it out before she could stop herself.

He chuckled and took another slug of something. "So that's what this is about."

Blood rushed to her head, and for a second she swerved across the center line. "I'm very concerned about the child." She emphasized the last word, in case he was under any delusions.

By now he was laughing between raspy coughs. "Don't forget who you're talking to. You don't care shit about anybody but yourself." And he hung up again.

Adrian felt betrayed. She probably sounded sharper than she meant to. Like a waspish old woman. It was a stance she'd come to assume with him ages ago. But her tone usually got results. At least, it used to.

From girlhood on, she leaned into the storms of discouragement, the subtle dissuasions of Grandfather and the rest, with a dogged stubbornness, leaving vulnerable Snider as the only one to take the old man's advice about keeping your head down to prevent Fate from noticing you.

Despite Snider's terrible health habits, he seemed to thrive without practicing the various forms of manipulation by which women have managed to survive through the ages. Yes, manipulations. Here she was, like every other one since the cave woman, playing games, baiting a trap. Only this time, it was for a man she didn't even want: Ernest Vogel.

It was just that she felt the thrill of being in the game again, of being part of the chase, not being counted out yet. She'd felt the zest of the tides rise once more in her veins.

Possibly she had carried it to extreme. She certainly hadn't meant to snap at Snider on the cell phone just now.

When she arrived home, it was almost a relief to find Sael sitting on the back steps. She pointed to a box of summer picnic things on the patio and directed him to carry them up to the garret storage room. Then she handed him a sealed envelope containing his pay, with the usual admonishment to take it home to his mother. "And here's a dollar to spend."

No sooner had Sael gone than Snider appeared at her front door, as if he had been lurking around a side street waiting for her to show. The man couldn't ever stand without wobbling anymore. He loomed there, florid of face and reeking of sour mash and tobacco, with a box of bottles in his arms. Had he just returned from Groom? She doubted it. He *had* heard her message, the old toad. She took it from him, swallowed her revulsion and astonished herself by asking him in. He surprised her by accepting.

Suddenly ill-at-ease, she seated him in the front room on her damask couch. She took a straight-back needlepoint chair in the far corner which she hardly ever let anybody sit on. Snider hadn't washed in a very long time, she could tell. For her, he could at least have bathed.

He gazed around at Mother's hand-painted knick-knacks as if he'd never seen them before. It made her nervous for him even to look. He wiped his mouth with the back of his hand. "I don't suppose you'd have—"

"No," she snapped, fashed that he would ask. "I'm saving the liquor for a special guest."

He could at least exhibit a shred of curiosity, but he didn't. Still he sat. Waiting for his money, she supposed. Well, he'd wait a little longer, until she had some answers.

"You never told me what you did with Elsie."

"She's being well cared for."

"Where?"

"The fewer people who know that, the better. Think I want you poking around, bringing half the town behind you, to have a look? Think those Pucketts could keep quiet if they knew? Especially that idiot Sael. Nobody finds out until that low-life Huddle leaves town."

"So why don't you bring charges against him in her name? Get him locked up."

His glance darted to the windows, and he fidgeted with his watch. There was something about the watch, but—she hadn't time to think about it; she knew his avoidances well. He was stone-walling. He said, "Sooner or later he'd get out and come looking for her."

"Then sue him."

He lifted his corpulent shoulders. "What would be the point? Huddle has no money, and neither does his boss. Anyway, he might counter-sue. He's the one who lost a nose." As a signal that the subject was closed, with some effort, he rose up on one hip, extracted the liquor bill from his back pocket and tossed it to her. "No extra charge for the house call."

The sum was more than she'd anticipated. She went to find her checkbook, quickly wrote out the amount and handed it to him. "You'll have to wait until I get to the bank to cover this," she said. "I wrote a rather large check in Amarillo today." She paused for effect before she added, "I bought a new car. A Mercedes. Paid *cash*."

He frowned and sucked an imaginary bit of tobacco from his canine tooth: a sure signal that he was about to find fault as he always did. "Who're you trying to impress? Don't you ever worry about spreading yourself thin?" He said it as if he cared, but she knew better.

She laughed, feeling tough and superior. "You've got to spend it to make it." It was her pattern to gouge him, remind him that she had it to spend, whereas he . . . .

He kept frowning. "Hope you don't forget there's now a big note on that ranch."

"If the Milo crop is good again, and if we have a fair-sized herd of calves, I'll be in fine shape. If not, if we have another year of drought, well, I can always cash in some elevator shares." *Or die and leave you to solve it, you fat bastard.*

She couldn't even tantalize him with promises of her demise. He just didn't care anymore.

Snider's unruly eyebrows lifted languidly. "You still have those shares?"

She wondered what he was up to. "Of course." He knew she still had them. Ernest had bought them for her ages ago, when he was made her trustee. If she had sold them, Snider would have had to co-sign—reason enough not to touch them.

He hoisted himself to his feet. She knew he wouldn't stay unless she offered him a drink, but she kept silent. Almost sick with dread, nevertheless, she showed him out, then watched from behind the curtains as he drove away without a backward glance.

She was losing him. And she didn't even know why.

15

Adrian should return the courtesy and have Ernest to dinner, but the task seemed too daunting. Yes, she thought of it as a chore. She fretted for several days about what to serve, if and when she summoned the nerve. She would opt for plain, down-home fare, which she suspected he preferred anyway.

And still she put off calling him.

Cotton picking was finished by the first week in November, youngsters were sent back to class, and the skating rink moved on—minus Calvin Huddle, who hadn't been seen since the day of the sandstorm.

"Maybe he's one of the Chosen and we're all Left-Behinds," Sarah speculated to Adrian.

In analyzing the phenomenon of the rise of "Rapture" mentality, the editor of the *Attebury Advocate* noted the feeling that people no longer had control over their lives. Things were getting too big, out of hand, in the lagging economy which would only get worse, what with business going to India and China; in the vicious whims of the weather that had turned against farmer and cattleman; in world conditions at the mercy of the maniacal machinations of terrorists.

"Hysteria is always just below the surface," he wrote. Adrian wondered why that comment lingered with her so vividly.

Soon after the rink left town, she heard that Elsie had returned home, still bruised and walking stiffly. Adrian figured the worst wounds were marked on the poor child's spirit, a new layer of misery on top of old. Still no explanation from Snider, but now Adrian doubted she would ever know the whole story. It might be that Madam had been caring for her.

Time was when she could read Snider's every thought, when he simply opened his mind to hers. Now a curtain had dropped between them, and he drifted farther away. Her isolation made the prospect of Ernest's company more comforting, if not welcomed. If she did decide to invite him over, Adrian hoped her neighbor Sarah wouldn't see; she didn't feel up to explanations. She hardly knew the reason herself, except that she judged her gloom and anguish to be unworthy, that she must shake herself out of it, for the world, gripped in grim self-destruction, would consider her "plight" laughable, no plight at all.

Finally, she telephoned Ernest and invited him to dinner. He accepted with grace, as if their last awkward meeting had never happened. The day before the big event, she went over to the salon and had her hair done. The stylist fashioned a ridiculous rasher of curls over one eye.

The hairdo went unnoticed by Ernest, although he did comment that she looked very nice. Otherwise, the evening didn't start well. As soon as he was seated on the sofa, she offered him Scotch only to find that he preferred bourbon. "I don't have bourbon," she said crossly.

"Then I'll take a beer," he said, obviously equally miffed.

"No beer, either. *My* mother always taught me to accept what's offered and be happy to get it." With that, she stalked to the kitchen, leaving him to twiddle his thumbs with no drink.

Her admonishment didn't faze him when it came to dinner wines, despite the fact that Snider had chosen very good ones. Ernest didn't care for her selections, saying he always drank Piesporter. He was being impossible. How could anyone live with such a prig?

To the Great Man, she served an entrée of chicken-fried steak and for dessert Miz Puckett's chocolate meringue pie, standing by in a sort of hand-wringing anxiety while he sampled it and—possibly—gave a grunt of approval. Up until dessert, their mealtime conversation had consisted solely of his comments about the food and her questions offering him more. But his mood became more agreeable as the pie disappeared.

Finally, her curiosity got the best of her. She put down her glass and said bluntly, "Whatever possessed you to build such a huge house? And don't say it was because of Helga. She always seemed to be slightly ashamed of all that ostentation."

She was surprised she hadn't offended him, but he appeared to be anxious to explain.

He said, "It's simple. Ever since I can remember, the crowd in Austin has treated this part of the state like a step-child. Their laws benefited Dallas or Houston, but never the Panhandle.

"Finally, when Boone Pickens began flying his execs to thousand-dollar-a-plate fund-raisers, lawmakers took notice of the Panhandle. But only because of Mesa Petroleum."

Adrian said, "So I guess that came to an end when Boone picked up his marbles and moved Mesa to Dallas." She recalled that after a flap with Amarillo leaders about who would control how his donations were spent, Boone and Bea had left in a huff.

Ernest nodded. "It was then I finally wised up to the way things are. All those jerks understand is the trappings of wealth. It has to *show.* You might say that I built that estate to benefit the whole area. And by God, it's working! Or at least, it was, before Helga died . . . ."

She was beginning to understand. "So primarily you need a hostess to entertain the lawmakers—or keep their wives occupied while you wheel and deal."

He didn't deny it. "How many successful men get by without a woman?"

After dinner they retired to the front room, but she had soured on offering him a liqueur with his coffee. Maybe she could return it if she didn't open it. Or else she'd just drink it herself.

She watched him fill her tidy room with cigar fumes and tried to think of something to talk about besides investments. She found herself picturing him on his elbows and knees hovering over her, red-faced, huffing and sweating. The thought made her ill.

When he tired of his cigar, he took out his watch. "We're missing Letterman." He looked over at her television.

"It's broken," she said quickly, not knowing she planned to say it.

She was sure he knew she was lying. "Then maybe I ought to be going along."

But at the door he surprised her by taking her hand. "This has been a rare treat. Maybe you'll be my partner at the Rotary Club buffet next week. We play Forty-Two afterward. Helga and I used to go every month. It was our way of staying in touch with the locals."

A carking irritation warned her to refuse. Ernest's cool wire-framed eyes looked through her, mirroring his confidence. She felt a sharp defensive ire protecting her, reminding her that custom is a straight-jacket. She gagged at the idea of a Rotary Club buffet once a month, but instead, she snapped, "I don't care to play second fiddle to the dead."

It was too late to bite her tongue. He looked as if she'd slapped his face. He reared back, snatched his coat off the hall tree and gave her a stiff nod.

He sulked down the walk without another word. Adrian sighed. She was too old to play the game, no matter how much money was involved. She would have done better to go after Mobeetie.

She gave the carefully coiffed hair a murderous yank. It was a waste, all that money for a stupid hair style. She peered in the mirror. She looked ridiculous. Ernest must have lied when he complimented her. He wasn't blind, after all, and neither was she.

If he weren't so stupid, she would suspect him of having an ulterior motive. And yet he'd openly admitted what his interest in her was. Could it be as simple as that? Why did she doubt him?

16

A two-inch snow had sweetened the grazing land on the Bar-G, and a little of it stuck to the harsh branches of the mesquite. Poke had brought the pickup around to the main house where Calvin Huddle, recovered from his near-death bout of nose-amputation, waited on the front porch. The boys had decided, as a Christmas present, to drive Calvin to Amarillo and present him with a bus ticket to Hollister, Oklahoma. He would be home in time for Christmas.

Calvin's hand still shook when he tried to light a cigarette. He had quit chewing tobacco since he lost his nose, because chewing was too painful.

The boys had kept him from a mirror for weeks, insisting on shaving him long after he was able to do it for himself. The jolt of seeing the extent of his disfigurement, when he finally insisted on a mirror, had sent him plummeting into depression. For several days he didn't speak. Then, ignoring his protests, Mobeetie told the hands to put him on a horse and take him out to ride the fences. In a week's time, Calvin, still non-communicative with the men, was confiding guardedly to his horse.

Calvin knew good and well why he was being ushered off the ranch. A couple of days before, Mobeetie had rounded the corner of the barn and overheard Calvin tell his horse how he was going to get his money from Snider one way or another. Mobeetie walked up, took the reins from Calvin, and said, "Sounds to me like you're well enough to go home, buddy."

The men presented him with a well broken-in Stetson that he could pull low on his forehead, so that if he kept his head down, the nose, or lack thereof, wasn't so noticeable.

As the pickup rumbled past the east side of Snider's property, Calvin muttered, "I'll be back, Greene. That's a promise." He didn't care whether Poke heard or not.

At the Pucketts', Momma was delivering her annual Christmas warning. "Isn't no use to commence getting your hopes up. Isn't going to be a tree this year, elsen the church women bring a leftover at the last minute. Isn't going to be any stockings. You're too big for that. Isn't going to be any turkey. Probably isn't going to be any presents, either."

Elsie wasn't sure. At school there had been a Christmas program, and Tommy Jo, with the flossy yellow curls, sang "Up on the Housetop," and Elsie's eyes misted up just from the joy of it. Miss Quattlebaum read "Twas the Night before Christmas," and Elsie watched the breathless way her much younger classmates listened and was infected by the magic. Then the principal, in a red Santa cap, passed up and down the rows with a candy cane, wrapped in cellophane, for every student. Elsie's cane was broken in two, which she somehow expected. She tore open the paper and ate the bottom half, sucking it slowly, watching the color disappear by degrees, seeing the stem grow slimmer and more pointed until finally it simply dissolved between her tongue and the roof of her mouth. The curved part of the cane she took home to hang on the tree. She was sure a tree would come.

Sometimes she ached for things. In the room she shared with Mozelle and Sael, among her treasures was a thumb-worn copy of the Penney's catalogue which Miss Adrian had thrown out several years back. For many seasons, Elsie had dreamed of the princess doll on page 172, but of course, she would never get it. In the past year, when she had been discovered with her shabby doll in secret, Mozelle had grabbed it from her, shaming her for playing dolls at her age. Now Elsie kept the doll hidden, afraid someone might throw her out or give her away to a poor child.

She was certain there would be a Christmas. For one thing, Miss Adrian always had presents for everyone, in case Santa forgot. For another, it had snowed, like it did in books. But Momma said it would be melted before Christmas day. Elsie would look at the snow, settled on all the crevices of Miss Adrian's fine home so that it looked like a great castle glistening in the sun, and she would suck in her breath and hold it as long as she could. If she could hold her breath long enough, Christmas would be here and the snow wouldn't have a chance to disappear.

The snow brought with it a profound silence. Elsie noticed that on cold days, she could hear sounds far away, like Snider's old rooster or the court house clock, clanking the hour.

This day, the last school day before the holidays, Elsie had been the target of a pelting by the boys, so that she arrived home wet with melting snowballs clinging to her coat and numb with cold. Momma skinned off her clothes and toweled her down while she delivered her Christmas warning. But Elsie knew that, no matter what Momma said, Christmas would come. And there would be chicken and cornbread dressing. Momma always fooled them like that.

Tomorrow she would take the pie that Momma baked over to Miss Adrian's, and Miss Adrian would have a sackful of things to send back with her. There would be presents for each of them, and more candy.

Elsie wasn't sure she wanted more candy. Maybe there was something wrong with the candy cane. Of a sudden, she didn't feel so good. She put on dry clothes as fast as she could, and as soon as Momma left the room, she went out onto the front porch, leaned over the railing, and threw up onto the fresh new snow.

17

It was during the holiday season at a time far removed when Adrian had last looked into the withered face of her mother, had plunged deep into the wisdom of her great grave eyes and pulled back with the certain knowledge that her mother was already beyond recall. As she did not often allow herself the luxury of touching upon that trauma, having wrapped it securely in its cerements years ago, she usually chased through the weeks from Thanksgiving to New Year's grappling with business problems, manufacturing them if none existed. But a week before Christmas, Adrian decided to buy a small tree, because dating Ernest had thrust her back into the stream of convention.

Things were tight enough without added expenses, due to the rash automobile purchase and her recent assumption of the huge ranch loan. Christmas bonuses to the ranch hands, her tenant farmers, and the Pucketts, would not be pared down, regardless. Briefly she considered asking Ernest for a small advance from her trust, but she dismissed the idea. She wasn't reared to ask for favors, even though her dependence would probably delight him. It amused her to perform these small nuances of courtship. But she would not go so far as to ask for a loan.

She had begun practicing certain fetishes, such as eating an apple every day and drinking three cups of green tea. She had been careless about staying out of the skin-aging sun, and her mother had considered her savage because of her disdain for gloves. Now she decided Dianne Keaton might have it right, and she dug out Mother's old gloves. Time was running out. All too soon she would be wading across that invisible barrier separating the adept from the inept, and Ernest would recognize the fact.

Since Grandfather was gone, she was not likely to receive a Christmas present, except the pies Sarah and Miz Puckett invariably sent over. Snider celebrated the same way he passed every day, and the last thing he would do is invite her to share his inebriation. She had come to greet the onset of the holidays with a fierce animosity, claiming privately that myths of the church, borrowed, she presumed, from Persian Mithraism, were responsible for many of the woes of modern life. The church had not treated her kindly. She would tell anyone who would listen that the church only promulgated guilt upon a gullible world. Thus she was able to get through the long days of the season wearing a mantle of disdain.

She kept insisting that she didn't expect a gift from Ernest, even though they were seeing each other regularly. He had heard often enough her reproof of religion and its rites, so he had ample excuse to ignore the occasion.

Thus she could feign surprise when Floyd from the drug store delivered the gift-wrapped box of cologne and bath powder. She snatched off the paper with shaking fingers even before Floyd could get off the front porch.

"Now who in the world could be sending me a present?"

"It's from Banker Vogel," Floyd said. "She wrote up a card. It's in there somewhere."

"She?"

"Neva Craig. Ernest's secretary. It's the brand Missus Vogel always liked." He grinned and waited for her reaction.

Adrian felt her blood simmering. She looked at the scented package. "Honeysuckle. Anything I can't stand, it's honeysuckle. Somebody doesn't have a lick of taste." She shut the door and dropped the package on the hall bench. For this she bought a Christmas tree. Neva Craig probably paid less than twenty dollars for it.

Was Ernest losing interest? She couldn't let that happen. Not everyone gets a millionaire dropped in her lap, but so far she'd done a piss-poor job of keeping him interested.

She decided to postpone payment of her taxes one more month, thus forfeiting her one-percent deduction for paying before the end of the year. She felt more reckless. This year, without Grandfather to caution her, she had extended herself further than usual. It was the restless turmoil that prodded her on. That, and the determination to maintain appearances in front of Ernest. And to get Snider's goat.

Maybe she ought to reciprocate: give Ernest a present. But she could think of nothing tacky enough. Probably he had no idea what his secretary had bought, and for all he knew, it was a good choice. Still, it would give her great satisfaction to out-spend him, make him blush at the shabby gift Neva had picked out. A costly bottle of bourbon ought to do the trick. Too bad she couldn't ask Snider to get it for her, but she had *some* dab of pride left. He had shunned her for so long that she wouldn't think of asking for another favor. Unless she just happened to see him.

On impulse, she decided to pay a visit to Madam, to see if she would make a special rum cake for New Year's Eve. That ought to get Ernest's attention. Ordinarily, she would have asked Miz Puckett to bake it, since the poor woman always needed the extra money. But Miz Puckett wouldn't dare have rum in the house, not with Old Man Puckett about.

No, this time she would ask Madam to bake it, even though she didn't know the woman. And she might as well do it right now. Maybe, if she happened to see Snider as she drove by, she might still ask him to run the errand. But she wasn't going to see Madam just as an excuse to pass by Snider's. No.

As it happened, there was no sign of Snider as she cruised slowly by his place, so she headed the Mercedes up the hill beyond his house and down the caliche wash behind. There, about a half-mile from the property line of the ranch, two barely-visible ruts cut off to the right. The old weathered shanty dugout, partially gouged into the ground, was sheltered in front by two large mesquite trees about twenty yards from the road, and a hand-painted sign advertised "Fortunes Told." A scraggly, non-descript stray hound announced her approach, and Madam came out onto the low-slung porch at once. Adrian parked on the perimeter of what she judged to be the yard.

She looked up to see a regal virago waiting, bangled arms on broad hips. The Madam was almost six feet tall, well-proportioned if heavy, and not unattractive. She wore a flowing purple rayon caftan with large sleeves drawn in tightly at the wrists. Around her neck hung a long strand of antique garnet beads of apparently good quality. Adrian wondered if they were stolen.

Adrian got out and took a few steps forward and smiled, realizing that she'd forgotten what Sarah called the woman. Now that she had a better look, she wasn't sure she would want to eat anything she cooked. Her dark hair, streaked with gray, was drawn up into a jackdaw's nest of a topknot, which sprouted stiff, dissenting sprigs on every side.

"Ah, the new owner of the Bar-G." The woman's voice was rich, guttural, with intimations of Eastern European grandeur.

Adrian couldn't hide her surprise. "How did you know?" But of course, Snider must have told her.

The big woman's eyes glittered, like the bright black eyes of a large rodent. "Have you not heard that I am a seer?" As she pointed to the sign, Adrian noticed that her broken nails were lacquered black, a theatrical indicative of the desperation of her position, no doubt.

She couldn't resist saying, "Then you must know why I'm here." She'd already decided that she'd made a mistake in coming. She had not anticipated drama.

"You are not the type to come for a reading. You have heard that I am a good cook. Perhaps you want a special dessert. What do you have in mind?"

Shaken, Adrian said, "I—don't know. A rum cake, maybe. Or something more exotic. I thought maybe you might have something—"

"Bubbling in my cauldron?" The Madam threw back her head and laughed, sending still more tentacles of hair flying. "Then come along and we will see what is brewing." She swept open her door and beckoned with a flourish.

The pungency of something like musk hung heavy over the little cabin, which was neatly if sparsely furnished. The entire house consisted of one sunken room, half below ground level, so that the windows were high and narrow and let in little light. To one side a sleeping alcove had been curtained off by a shalloon tacked to the low ceiling. A bucket of water with a dipper stood on a small table by the door. In the back of the room a rickety stool held a magnificent copper samovar. An ancient wooden stove beside it was obviously poorly vented to the outside, for smoke had blackened the wall.

A round table occupied the center. It was covered by a maroon shawl and held three items: an oil lamp, a deck of cards, and a tiny crystal ball nested in black velvet.

Madam dismissed the trappings: "Window dressing, to give my patrons confidence. You think I need them? I could tell just as much with only—your palm." And before Adrian could draw back, she had caught up her hand and turned it palm up.

Vexed by the woman's audacity and her theatrics, Adrian grunted but didn't pull away. Madam was tracing a line in her palm with a broken nail. "Ah. Your life has not been without tragedy, either. In that, we have something in common." Her brittle black gaze met Adrian's. "But fortunately for you, your parents left you something to build on."

Adrian nodded, aware that Madam would know all about everyone in a town the size of Attebury. She felt resentful that the woman had pointed out her obvious advantages and had given her no credit for her own skill. She pried her hand loose. "Let's get on with my order."

Madam dismissed it with a flop of her voluminous sleeve. "You'll have it. Forgive me, lady, but you are so transparent. With this one I don't even need a palm." She studied Adrian with an intensity that made Adrian's cheeks flush. "You are so dissatisfied. Restless. Perhaps you are thinking of taking a mate at long last, eh? Ah!" She expressed satisfaction at how easily she had hit her mark, for Adrian ducked and squirmed, disgusted by her own artlessness.

"So. Yes. I can see you are a remarkable woman: driving, striving. You have made enemies, yes? It is not easy for an ambitious woman to avoid collecting detractors. Still, one must collect something, eh? When we are left without our men and find that we are but a shadow, we must collect something to give the shadow substance, eh? Ah. And perhaps one of these enemies of whom I spoke, perhaps he is your own true love, eh? Could that be?" Madam's voice had taken on a sing-song quality as if she were in a trance.

Adrian was breathing fiercely. Her head was buzzing with the words that filled the room and hung there, accusing. "I know of no true love."

"Indeed? Perhaps you will recognize him if you go tonight—to the roadhouse in Jericho. I'm certain he will be there."

At that, Adrian laughed, feeling a rush of relief at the preposterous idea. "Well, maybe he'll be there, whoever he is, but I certainly won't. I'd almost rather be seen in church than in that honky-tonk. Let's get back to why I'm here." The spell, whatever it was, was broken.

Madam shrugged and indicated a straight chair for Adrian, scratching at a small tubercle near her eye with a ragged nail. Adrian shuddered. *I don't have to eat the cake*, she thought.

But her impression changed rapidly as the big woman began to lay out her suggestions for much more than just a rum cake. They were not those of a back-woods charlatan. Adrian detected a veneer about the woman now which hinted at good schooling, proper upbringing.

She leaned across the table and studied the woman's eyes. "Where did you come from, anyway? How did you get here? You're no country girl."

Madam smiled, a wistful shadow dimming the dark eyes. "You are mistaken. I am a country girl. I was reared far from the city, on the family estate, as befitted a young girl of my station. I was reared to give parties in my country, at that time behind the Iron Curtain."

She laughed softly, and Adrian caught a glimpse of the maiden she must have been. "Giving parties was all I was prepared to do. But there were upheavals, and I married for love and came to California. One night, passing through Amarillo, I lost my husband in a terrible wreck on the highway. After that . . . . one does what one must to survive. Surely you know that."

"And so you tell fortunes," Adrian said, thinking, *all women do what they must.*

"Or bake tea cakes. Or tend the sick. Society requires every woman to have a secret life."

A thought occurred to Adrian. "Tend the sick. Then maybe you were the one who . . . ."

Madam nodded. "You are thinking of poor Elsie. Yes. I kept the little witless one here as a favor to your cousin."

"Why should anyone do him a favor, of all people?" She couldn't keep the scorn from showing, remembering her days of numb vulnerability after Mother died, when Snider seemed to gloat in her grief.

The woman shifted in her creaking chair. "Oh come. Snider Greene is no worse than any other man. In truth, he can be very kind. He gives me this house rent-free, after all."

It was hard to believe. The house, on the back of Grandfather's property, had belonged to Grandfather until he had deeded it to Snider. Surely that must have been recently.

Madam went on. "To prove that he is not a greedy man, he told me I could live here for as long as I wish, in return for such help as I am able to give him from time to time. Unfortunately, there is a narrow limit to the things which I was trained to do."

"Are you aware," Adrian said coolly, "that this property was not Snider's until our grandfather died?"

The woman was silent for a moment before she burst out in a bitter laugh. "Ah, Snider my love! What other surprises are still in store for me?"

"So you're his lover." Adrian put her hands in her lap to hide their trembling.

Madam sobered at once and narrowed her eyes. "What is this? You are jealous? Is not one man enough for you?"

"I'm certainly not jealous! I'm merely interested in what kind of favor . . . . Anyway, it's of no consequence."

It wasn't a very large favor, Adrian decided, looking around the shanty. As if anybody else would want the place. But she doubted Grandfather had ever given the property to Snider. She suspected that Snider had found himself some cheap household help—or possibly even more than that, if he wanted it. But then, why had he hired Elsie?

They completed arrangements for Madam to prepare several desserts, which Adrian would pick up on a certain date. Adrian emptied her wallet of what few bills she had "to purchase ingredients" and promised to pay the rest owed upon delivery.

Dusk had whipped up a wind which caught her coat tail as she left the small hut. Automatically, she clutched at it, as if it mattered. Except she was reared a proper lady. Which is why she would never go near the Jericho roadhouse, just to see if Ernest was there.

Madam seemed to read her mind again. "Take my advice," she called into the wind after Adrian. "Go tonight if you want a look at the face of your true love. Better to know who our enemies are, eh?" She took a step forward, as if to be sure her words were heard. "Think about this: whatever it is, a secret will tell itself sooner or later."

18

The gusts which had caught her coat tail as she left Madam's were the front whiskers of a blue norther that tore into the town, drew back just at dusk and crouched for a respite, but, according to the weather forecast, was due to pounce again within a matter of hours. Adrian returned to her car and had barely reached the main road when her cell phone rang.

"Mister Vogel's been trying to reach you, Miss Craddock," came Neva Craig's high-pitched voice. "He said tell you to expect him over after a while. He said it's important. Probably wants to tell you about the overseas call he got today."

Adrian didn't ask who the caller was. The prattling Craig woman had already overstepped the bounds of secretary-employer confidentiality. No telling what she had told the rest of the town about her and Ernest. She drew a long breath. She was too weary to entertain Ernest, but she was grateful for the forewarning. Now she would have to postpone a stop at Snider's as well as the trip to Jericho, and Ernest would just have to wait another day for his Christmas present.

By the time she had fixed a quick meal of cornbread and buttermilk, the wind was rattling panes and scranneling under doors with a melancholy and tedious constancy. How awful this must be at the Puckett household. As the pitch of the howl suddenly rose, she bustled through the house, securing it against the buffeting that was sure to follow, dreading as she always did the terrible desolation of the north wind.

Remembering Ernest, she hurried to her bedroom to put some color on her cheeks. Why did she feel compelled to entertain him when she felt so rotten? She sensed a hidden pattern here.

He wasn't long in arriving, looking a bit like storm flotsam. His sparse sandy hair feathered about the large head. The perpetual cigar had gone out, a fact he discovered as she was ushering him in. He snarled at it as if affronted by an indignity and then glared at her as if she were somehow responsible before he turned and tossed it out the front door.

"Ernest, not on my front lawn," she said.

He stumped past her, bull-neck rigid. "It sank into the snow. You're too damn particular."

"The snow will melt, and there it'll be."

He shrugged. "If it'll make you feel better, I'll pick it up on the way out."

She followed him into the front room, reverting to her mental hand-wringing that once again she'd started off badly. "Tea? Or, I think there's something stronger left."

"No time." He plopped down on the couch and patted a spot beside him. "Come sit here. I have something to ask."

It was hardly sufficient warning. She lowered herself on trembling and suddenly unreliable underpinnings, wondering that he could not hear the thrumming in her temples. Oh, why hadn't she paid closer attention to Madam's prognostication?

He took her hand in his, and she did not understand her own irresolution at not pulling away. Now that the Moment had come, she wanted with a palpable desperation to halt this melodrama before it proceeded to its mawkish conclusion. But he was relentless.

"We've known each other for many years. There's no use to waste words. I want you to become Mrs. Ernest Vogel."

That was it? She was choking on its abruptness, on her own surprise and disappointment. She had expected more: some hint of affection, a word of ardor. Something, only a moment before, she had dreaded to hear.

So apprehension had dissolved, with languid indifference, into the unavoidable.

The mantle clock prodded quietly. She could feel his spectacled anticipation as she cast around the room for a lifeline, coveting her surroundings fiercely for the first time in years. Inhaling with exaggerated labor, she managed to lift her free hand to pat his meaty one, which held her other one imprisoned. "How you flatter me, Ernest." Her voice, dry and reedy as the wind caught against the locked vanes of an abandoned windmill, sounded far away. "I—I'll have to think about it."

He was obviously offended. Then he seemed to rethink his reaction and forced a hard spare smile. With his free hand, he reached into his inside pocket and brought out a snapshot. He cradled it in his palm with a tenderness which had been lacking in his proposal. "You remember my mother's family was from Bavaria," he began with patience. She nodded, feeling her palm grow clammy within his. She fidgeted in her silence and tugged timidly at the incarcerated hand, but he clung on.

"My nearest of kin on my mother's side still lives in Germany. Her brother Otto Theiss is all that's left, and in the past decades, especially since the advent of the European Union, Uncle Otto has become immensely wealthy. He has been able to gain control of several plants in Mainz that manufacture heavy equipment." He let this soak in, to impress her. She nodded dutifully.

Revived by a fresh draught of self-importance, he warmed to his story, bringing out, like a jeweler his velvet tray, the animation reserved for discussions of money. He dropped her hand—mercifully—and got up to pace around the border of her Oriental carpet, placing his toes precisely on the same repeating pattern. Again the preening rooster came to mind. "Uncle Otto can't possibly last much longer. I'm told he has no offspring. The time is not far away when all he has accumulated should rightly come to me. And I can tell you, the figure is astronomical."

He returned to sit beside her, offering the photograph. "This is my Uncle Otto and his wife Minna. She's dead now. He's all that's left."

She studied the tumescent version of Ernest. "I see the resemblance," she murmured, repelled by this glimpse of Ernest in futurity.

He adjusted his glasses, which he had begun wearing more often, and glowered at the likeness, weighing the compliment or the insult. "Possibly. So much the better, then." He leaned back and his hand traveled to his expanding middle in imitation of his uncle's pose.

Ernest had yet to make his point, if there was one. She had the sensation that she was observing a small boy living out his fantasies. A gnawing envy that the richest man in the county should someday become even wealthier lent him an obscene fecundity, in her estimation.

"Do you even know this man, Ernest? Have you ever met him?"

"I made it a point to stop over in Mainz the last time I was in Europe. Unfortunately, he was taking baths in Switzerland at the time. Since then, we have been in contact by mail. I sent him a photograph of my house and invited him to visit. He is too old to travel here, I imagine."

"How can you be sure you'll inherit all that stuff?" she asked crossly. "Besides, for all you know, there may be a law prohibiting a foreigner from inheriting in Germany."

He smiled. "My attorney assures me that someone very well placed has sanctioned it."

What was the point of this boasting of high-up connections? "So? Germany didn't support us when we invaded Iraq. Anyway, globalization can be sanctioned only so far. When it begins to look like profits from Mainz factories are being siphoned into American pockets—"

His annoyance showed in his quick dismissal. "You are bothering your head with something you know nothing about. I'm going over in the summer to see him, if he lasts that long. He's a hardy man, but he holes up at a warm spa until Germany thaws out, so it will be hard to find him until then. We can make it a honeymoon trip. That would please him."

She ignored his jibe, figuring she deserved it. As a school girl, she'd once imagined herself the chatelaine of a Bavarian castle. She couldn't fault him for his fantasies. Now he was enticing her with the only thing he knew to give; there wasn't going to be any talk of undying love in this proposal. She would have to get it out of her head that love alone could give her full stature. That had been another of her fantasies. *Money* conveyed stature.

Still, there were those words she longed to hear. No, not longed, exactly. Expected to hear. She would never ask him to say them. That wouldn't be the same.

Anyhow, if he said them, she might be expected to answer, "And I love you, too." Then her situation would have lurched into a predicament. *But I am fond of his money,* she thought.

He was still waiting for a response, but his self-assured smile told her that he had already taken too much for granted. He had wooed her in the only language they both understood.

"I don't know," she said, knowing that she did indeed know. "It's a tempting offer, but I'd have to get used to the idea. I've been independent for a long time . . ."

She fell silent, hoping he would back off for a while. Still he waited. She squirmed. "Besides, to go to Europe, when all these terrorists are . . . ."

The argument sounded lame, even to her. She could see that he was unimpressed by her excuses. Ernest, having already acquired enough money to last several lifetimes, was on a power jag. He would continue to ride the same horse, no matter what she said or did.

He slapped his knees and stood, as if she'd made his point for him. He had neither heard, nor wanted to hear. "All right, if you must think, think fast. There are many things to settle before the trip. That's why I've mentioned it in plenty of time. Now I'd better be off."

She looked at the mantle clock. It was a little before eight. She asked politely, "So soon?"

"I have another appointment, and I'm already late," he said. "I'll drop by tomorrow." He hurried past her without so much as a peck on the cheek, forgetting, once outside, to pick up his discarded cigar from her lawn.

She watched as his big Bentley pulled away, trying to imagine standing beside him at the altar. Moving her belongings into that garish monstrosity. Lying beside him in his bed, trying to conceal her pouty breasts, the flaccid thighs. She shut the door and fastened it and followed the whistling wind back to the kitchen. The buttermilk looked unappetizing, so she put on water for a cup of tea. Back to reality, for crying out loud.

Where was he going in such a rush? What had Madam said? ". . . Better to know who our enemies are."

He wouldn't dare. Surely he wouldn't rush from proposing, to meet that secretary of his at a honky-tonk. No. It was absurd to put faith in a fortune teller's words. She poured her tea, grinning at her own gullibility. But if only she could figure out what Ernest *really* wanted—

A blast of wind socked the house broadsides, and the lights dimmed momentarily. She hated it when the electricity failed. It was the time when she missed Mother the most, the time when she hated being alone in the house.

Of course, she reasoned, sipping her tea in the gloom, Madam might have inside information, might have learned from Neva Craig that she was meeting Ernest tonight. Neva might be a regular client of the seer's, might confide in her. Might have laughed when she told her of the stingy Christmas gift she had bought for her boss to give to Adrian.

Neva might also know exactly what Ernest hoped to gain by marrying her.

That must be it. Madam had been trying to warn her. Adrian took her tea to the sink and poured it out. She turned out the flickering lights and headed for the bedroom.

But even as she undressed, she knew she'd never sleep, never rest until she knew. Even if she had no intention of marrying Ernest—and she wasn't sure yet—she must know who he had an appointment with. Madam had been right: she must go to Jericho tonight. The woman had specified the roadhouse. She obviously knew something she could only hint at.

Anyway, there was still the Christmas purchase to make. She had legitimate reason to go.

Adrian shook out the pattern of her life so she could examine it in its entirety, like a patchwork quilt, because the time had come to own up to her shortcomings. She had perennially avoided confrontation, and where had it got her. Still, it wasn't her habit to be out after dark; so many things could happen to a single woman. She might have a flat or a breakdown, even if Madam hadn't predicted it.

She hadn't lied to the fortune teller about not going to honky-tonks, but it hadn't always been so. Back in high school, a group would go over on Saturday nights to catch the band and take a turn around the wooden hall. She knew the place well.

She went to her closet and pushed through all the stodgy old clothes. Seemed like she used to have better looking things. In resignation she chose a woolen pantsuit that ought at least to be warm. Everything she owned had the look of a hearse-rider.

No, it wasn't her habit to be out, but she would go, even if she had no illusions about Ernest. Because if he was seeing Neva Craig, there had to be some other reason that he wanted to marry her, and she'd be greatly interested to know what it was. Perhaps she was hoping to find them together. Then she could, with understandable indignation and a clear conscious, give Ernest the heave-ho, him and his off-hand proposal. But that would mean goodbye to a Bavarian castle. Then what, in heaven's name, did he *really* want of her?

The heavy Mercedes was almost buffeted off the road by the norther, for the road to Jericho and Maggie's Roadhouse led directly into the mouth of the wind. "I'll be in a pickle if it starts to snow again," she said aloud.

Out of the dusty haze ahead she could make out the neon sign announcing Maggie's Roadside Inn. The shambly building was without windows, but she could tell from the number of pickups parked in front that the place was open and doing its usual swift business. On one side was a separate entrance to Maggie's Package Store, but that was obviously closed at this hour. It would be necessary to enter the roadhouse to make her purchase. Briefly she wondered why she hadn't either made this trip earlier in the day, or waited until morning to come, when she could have bought the bourbon without having to enter the honky-tonk.

But then, she would never have known whom Ernest had come to meet.

As she pulled up, she could hear the raunchy throb of the band: the bass, guitar, fiddle, pedal steel guitar. She felt a shudder of expectancy as she bundled her coat tightly about her and ran from the car to the battered screen door with the tin Coca Cola sign tacked across the middle.

Before she could touch it, it flew open, barely missing her, and the last person she wanted to see stumbled out, carrying a box of bottles: Snider blinked as if he couldn't believe his eyes.

"What're *you* doing here? Slumming?" he said with obvious contempt.

When she found her tongue, she said, "I need some bourbon for a Christmas gift. Since you never seem to be available anymore—"

"So you just *had* to come out on a stormy night to get it." He turned to glare back inside. "Who're you meeting in there? Old Ernest?"

Her breath caught in her throat. "Is he here?"

"How should I know?" That was all. He stomped off into the gale.

"You could at least go back inside and buy my—" But her calling was lost in the storm. As she watched him go, tiny shards of sleet pricked her skin. She'd better hurry, make her purchase, and get home before the road turned icy.

Smoke rolled out to meet her as she stepped into the poorly lit dance hall. She batted back tears and fanned the smoke until she could make out the band members on the stage to her right. Dust rose from the wooden floor and mingled with the haze above the oilcloth-covered tables. Along the walls were high-backed booths, the bar and grill occupying the end of the room to her far left. She edged in as unobtrusively as she could and stood near the cash register, hoping Ernest wouldn't notice her. She only wanted to see who he came to meet.

When the waitress came, she ordered a bottle of their most expensive bourbon—"for a gift," she explained hastily. While she waited for it to arrive from the package store next door, she peered cautiously around the room, examining the crowd. Most of the revelers were cowboys. She spotted several from around home: the service station attendant, a man from the Hedley cotton gin, the little clerk who waited on her at Hopping's Dry Goods. A couple of tables of cowboys across the way. But no Ernest Vogel. She was a gullible fool.

The band slid into a pulsating stomp, a thrusting coital rhythm, and the crowd gathered around to watch two dancers: Maggie, the owner of the bar, and her partner. "Enough of this," Adrian muttered and turned her back on the mob. The waitress returned with her bourbon, packaged in a foil gift box that would be perfect for Ernest. Adrian paid for it and headed for the door. Then she heard her name bellowed.

"Miss Adrian? You can't run off before I claim my dance."

The crowd parted and one of her cowboys, Nasty Baines, stepped forward. Beyond him, on the dance floor, she recognized Maggie's partner: her ranch manager, Tom James: Mobeetie.

The sight of him, the pivot of the frenzied crowd, while as usual she skirted the edges of life, gave her a profound feeling of mortification.

Suddenly, the blast of the norther swatted the roadhouse so hard that it shuddered. Or maybe it was the Earth that trembled. Maybe hers was only the echo of a larger grief, the consuming anguish emanating from deep inside the earth, and all the frenzied dancing in the world wouldn't keep it at bay. Maybe it was a deep affront to Mother Nature, because they were all of the earth, destined to act out its grief like puppets.

The thought was strangely comforting. It was enough to help her drag herself up to the light again, to hear the music, to become part of the idiocy, to put out of her mind the silly admonition of Madam.

19

Adrian hesitated. She didn't want to appear stand-offish with her employees, but neither did she want to dance. She held up the package for Nasty to see, yelling to make herself heard over the music. "Might break this."

He came forward and took it from her, leading her by the arm. "That's a lame excuse. We'll set it on our table, and I'll cold cock any sucker that touches it!" He dragged her across the dance floor toward a booth against the back wall.

"I hope you notice how piss-poor this place is of women. If you don't dance with me, I might end up having to dance with Puny, and wouldn't that be a sight!"

He placed her bottle on the table with the admonishment to the others who were eating to guard it with their lives, then he steered her onto the floor, ignoring her protests. He grabbed her loosely, elbows held high, and jounced her backward across the floor. After her first timid stumble, Adrian saw it was the same old Panhandle stomp she'd done all her life. She cast off the vague foreboding and fell in with the beat, feeling its seductive throb in her bones. Caught in the anonymity of the dance, she didn't have to be different. The music, blaring over the speakers, was almost drowned out in the drumming of the dancers' feet.

She needed to explain. "I came to buy a Christmas gift. I don't come here as a rule."

Nasty laughed over the top of her head. "Do tell." He whirled her around, drawing her close enough to avoid colliding with another couple, but just as quickly swinging her out again.

The dance ended, and the crowd whooped its approval. She managed to grin and say, "That was fun. But I ought to go. There's a storm coming." She fanned at the fog of smoke and floor dust, desperate to escape before Mobeetie joined them.

Nasty's thick brows contracted in mock concern. "Afraid you can't make it in that bucket of bolts? That old Mercedes that rolled off the assembly line about a month ago?"

She was heading steadily toward the table, determined to get her bottle and leave. "I'm not afraid of a breakdown, but I'm not good at driving on slick roads."

But at that moment, the band struck up "The Cotton-Eyed Joe" and she quickly found herself arm-in-arm line dancing between two men. One was Mobeetie.

He yelled close to her ear, "Tell you what: Let me finish eating, and I'll drive you home and the boys can follow in the truck. We ought to leave too, if there's a storm blowing in."

She started to refuse, but he went on. "It'll give me a chance to sell my new boss on chain-dragging that pasture down by Samson's mill to get rid of the white brush." That was Mobeetie: always working the ranch.

She wavered, not that she cared about the chain-dragging, except at the moment she was short of working capital. As the music ended, and she could make herself heard, she baited him. "Any idea how much it would cost?" She watched his slow grin of triumph. He believed he had won, but he'd be in for a disappointment. She would save that news until she got home safely.

He and Nasty guided her to the table. He pulled up an extra chair and said, "Pass the pitcher down here, Puny. Miss Adrian looks thirsty."

They scooted around to make room for her, and someone poured her a beer, but nobody stood, nobody removed a hat. They greeted her warmly and respectfully enough, but they kept on eating. It was like coming home, being a few minutes late for supper. She was swept with longing to fit in. She claimed her beer and settled in with a hopeful grin, almost missing the glance that passed among them. It was a signal, she knew, and she had a pretty good idea what would be coming next.

Poke, the cooky, who sat to her right, seemed to be the designated leader. The grizzled old waddie waved a barbecued rib for emphasis. "You talk about poor, let me tell you about poor. By the time I was grown, I'd eat so many collard greens, my momma had to tie kerosene rags around my ankles to keep off the cutworms."

They roared him down, and Nasty slapped his mug on the table. "I've had about all of you rich boys I can tolerate. Down at Muleshoe, we had being poor down to a fine art. We stuffed our mattresses with collards instead of cotton, and we lived on rutabagas."

They had stepped into their parts. Did they live in them, or only when she was around? Joking seemed to be the only way they could relate to her.

"Man, now I know why you're so damn skinny." This from Puny Sykes. "You been eating too many rutabagas. Don't you know them things'll rot your toenails?"

Nasty shot back, "The hell you say. Rutabagas is pure vitamins. They make you so healthy, about the only way to die back home is to get bit by a rattler."

"Oh, if you're talking healthy, you're going to have to move over," Poke put in. "Everybody knows Hereford's the health capital of the world. The only way you can possibly die in Hereford is to get so old and shriveled, you finally just dry up and blow away."

Mobeetie shoved his plate toward Adrian. "Help me with these fries."

Poke was still at it. "Back home the land was so sorry, we couldn't raise bind weed. We even had to spread steer manure around the outside of the house just to raise the windows."

Mobeetie passed the pitcher over to Poke. "Drink up. You've got to increase your consumption. When your fifty-dollar raise comes, you'll be in trouble. You're already having a helluva time drinking up the salary you make now."

Now she understood the point. She had forgotten about Poke's raise. It was always something. And Christmas bonuses were due all around; that's what this whole performance was about. But how would she manage it? Of course, if she were married to Ernest . . . .

"Godamighty!" Poke said. "You trying to kill me, raising my pay? I'll be dead, trying to drink up that much."

The banter had another purpose, she realized. It was their defense against closeness. Despite that they shared a bunk house, what did they know about each other? They hid behind jokes and boasts to maintain a measure of privacy. Now she was acutely aware that Mobeetie's sleeve brushed hers every time he lifted his beer. Each time, the hairs on her arm came to attention. She used to be the boss's granddaughter. Now she was the boss.

She pushed away from the table. "I need to get out of here. You yahoos are beginning to make sense."

She got to her feet shakily, wondering if it was the beer or the smoke thick as gravy that was getting to her. Mobeetie caught her elbow, and she wondered if he had noticed.

"Lord! Did you spike that beer?" Then she remembered she'd had no dinner. She handed Mobeetie her car keys, picked up her bourbon, waved to the boys, and tottered toward the door. He shoved against it and put a protective arm around her shoulder as the wintry blast hit them.

In the fight to get to the car, her head cleared at once, but she saw no need to burden Mobeetie with that information. He helped her solicitously into the passenger seat then went around and squeezed his tall frame into the driver's seat.

"Just you lean back and relax and don't mind the storm," he said. "And I'll fill you in on the chain-dragging deal." The fatherly benevolence was transparent.

She knew his technique of old, from watching him manipulate Grandfather. They both knew very well she needed no soothing words, but he would play any game—whore, if necessary—to get what he wanted. *Well, let's see if it works this time,* she thought. She too knew a thing or two about manipulation.

She speculated on life's injustices. Here was Mobeetie, must be almost fifty by now, lean, virile, prime sirloin. Over the years, he'd only become better looking—a fact that obviously hadn't escaped his attention. His weathering smacked of potency; her own thirty-seven years already hinted at decay. Yet Mobeetie was married to the ranch which he cared for like a perpetual lover, thought more of it than even his horse. He presented his case for chain-dragging with the fervor of a lawyer pleading for his client's life, while she nodded and managed not to give him a solid answer, just to keep the thing alive as long as possible. She could not, of course, afford the expense now.

She said lamely, "I've been meaning to come out, ever since I signed the deed, but . . . ."

They strung it out all the way home, as if they'd rehearsed their lines. She speculated on the differences in the threatening trip to the ranch house through the blizzard and this trip to her house which was taking on catalytic properties, drawing them for mutual solace having nothing—or very little—to do with appetites.

It was a zone she and Snider had once occupied comfortably. In the darkened car she felt close to earth; knew a kinship with the Adrian of her childhood on the hill. As sleet pelted the windshield, she hummed to the tires' turning, throbbed with the engine, was in tune with the whistling wind, with the earth's rhythms and her renewed fecundity. She was accepting, giving; she was earth, holding at once the living and the dead, one to her bosom, one in her womb. She was nascence. She was also slightly tipsy. It took very little to unlock the room of her kinship.

Too soon he eased into her driveway. He put the car away while she opened the back door and hurried in to light the gas logs in the front room fireplace. What luxury, not to enter a cold house alone. She heard him stamp into the kitchen and, without asking, fill a saucepan with water for ranch-boiled coffee. She joined him, noticing the kitchen's pristine aseptic-ness. He dipped out spoonfuls of coffee, enough for the boys, who would welcome a cup for the road. She broke an eggshell and poured out its contents, washing the shell under the faucet before handing it to him to crumble into the pot. Their hands brushed, and she swallowed an unworthy infant panic. Quickly she retreated, went to the pantry and brought out the Scotch Ernest had rejected, muttering something about warming their bones—rushing on, despising the cowardice which gave the gesture overtones of seduction.

He grinned in surprise, but she felt his sudden wariness. She backed off and stood by with hands clasped behind her back like a child, watching the master at work. He took down her fragile tea cups and laced their coffee with whisky.

"No sense letting this fresh coffee go to waste waiting on the boys. If I know them, they're washing down the barbecue." He handed her a rattling cup and saucer, and she led the way into the somber front room, drafty and chilly despite the fire. The place was like a museum, she saw. Too perfect, too formal. Whereas, with Ernest here, it had just seemed shabby, dreary.

They settled before the sputtering jets, which fought the wind from the chimney for their flames: she on the sofa, he in the chair opposite. They avoided looking at each other by staring into the fireplace. The mantle clock ticked away like a time bomb. *The boys ought to be along soon,* she told herself. She took a sip of coffee and fought off a grimace.

"Good coffee," she said.

"One thing I know, is making coffee. Been at it all my life, pert-near."

The gas jets popped and spat, and the panes rattled behind the lace panels and damask drapes. Years ago she'd considered getting wooden blinds; she shouldn't have put it off.

There was no let-up, not an instant, from the wind. The smell of dung on his boots began to overpower the smell of Scotch and thick coffee. She thought she might gag. She caught his eye, and they both shifted uneasily and raised their cups, staring back to the fire. He smacked noisily.

Why don't they come, she thought. She and Mobeetie should have stayed in the kitchen, where they could have leaned on the table, a physical barrier between them. The clock struck the half-hour, and they both started. Their gazes met and they grinned. *He's dying*, she thought. *I ought to make some effort.*

"So you learned to cook," she said. "Guess that's why you never needed a wife."

He shook his head. "Never considered it. All I wanted was to run cattle. It's kindly of a disease. Once you know the feel of a good horse under you, and you get you a piece of land and a few head to work, nothing else can compete. Punching cows and courting don't mix. When's the last time you saw a married cowboy?" *He must reinforce the myth*, she thought.

"Grandfather was a cowboy."

"He was a rancher," he said with finality. He divided things so neatly.

She felt the silence weighing heavy as a bag of wet sand. Finally he got up and set his rattly cup and saucer awkwardly on the mantle.

"Maybe I ought to go check on the boys. They might have had trouble after we left, got into a fight or something. You got a book that I can look up Maggie's number?"

"In the hall. On the telephone table." Actually, it would be a relief to get him out of the room, because she was desperate to empty her bladder but could think of no excuse to leave. She fled to the tiny cubicle in the laundry room designated for Mozelle's use. Maybe he wouldn't be able to hear her from the hallway if she didn't flush—

She stole back into the living room to find he'd already returned. He appeared unaware of her gasp of horror as he swiped his dirty boots in the center of her carpet.

"Maggie's Roadhouse isn't listed. Maybe she only has the pay phone. Puny doesn't answer his cell phone. He probably didn't take it. So I guess they ain't nothing to do but wait."

A dull, heavy tiredness dragged her down, just from the tedium of stringing out small talk. Do you suppose they had car trouble?"

"Like as not. That old truck don't always want to start in cold weather. On the other hand, they might of just got to drinking and lost track of time. Maggie's pretty loose about curfews."

He swung his long arms two or three times, snapping his fingers in time to the clock, looking around, thinking hard. He walked back over to his chair and sat with a look of resignation. She flipped on the television and was greeted by snow. The cable must be out again.

"Oh well, I don't watch much, anyway," she said.

"Me neither."

"I know: I'll scramble some eggs. If we're going to be up all night, we might's well have breakfast." She jumped up and bustled off to the kitchen, not waiting for a reaction, glad to be out of there. Anyway, she was badly in need of food.

He followed her and leaned against the kitchen door jamb. "I'm still stuffed from supper. But I'll sit and have a decent drink while you eat."

She couldn't hide her perplexity, and he laughed. "I bet you don't know how to make one that has a good kick. Here, I'll do it." He scuffed over and got the bottle, and she marveled at how he filled her kitchen. He was an invader, she suddenly decided, remembering Madam's warning about an enemy. She would give anything to be rid of him.

"Well, no use fixing eggs for one. Just—make me a weak one, too." Actually, she had never craved a drink more fervently in her life. She was poised on a ledge, holding on tight.

"I already have." He handed her a glass and followed her back into the living room.

They took their appointed seats again and both sighed. Why hadn't they stayed in the kitchen? This was unbearable.

Mobeetie took a hefty swig. "Not bad. One thing Snider knows is good hootch."

She sniffed. "It's his most noteworthy accomplishment."

He took another slug. "Snider Greene's all right. Got his good points and his bad ones, same as anybody else."

"Why is everybody always telling me how wonderful he is?" She heard her own irrational whine as if it belonged to someone else. She took a sip of her drink. It hit the pit of her stomach and bounced back to her head.

"I never said he's wonderful. Sometimes, he's pure-dee weird. But I guess you'd know much better than me." He said it without much conviction, just making conversation.

She thought about Snider and Elsie, Snider and Madam. "Weird. You got that right."

They lapsed into another interminable silence. The clock struck the hour slowly, like a dirge: twelve o'clock. Could this endless vigil have lasted only a half-hour? Mobeetie drained his glass and clanked it onto the side table. She hoped it didn't make a ring.

"Have another," she said, hoping he wouldn't, only hoping that he would pick the wet glass off her mahogany table.

"Believe I will." As he went off to the kitchen, she jumped up and wiped the table with her napkin.

The wind moaned much louder once he was gone, and she was aware of a cricket chirping noisily in the vicinity of the foyer. Mobeetie clattered around in the kitchen, making more racket than was necessary. She hoped he didn't chip her glass. And still the mantle clock ticked leadenly. She felt a sharp pain between her shoulder blades from holding her back so stiff.

If they don't come soon, I will pull out my hair.

She watched him drag back in and reluctantly fall into the chair. She could tell by its color that this drink was much stronger. Good. Maybe he would pass out before she did.

He sampled the new concoction and smacked his satisfaction. "Now that's one your cousin would approve of. Old Snider can flat drink you under the hog trough and never even get a buzz on. I remember one time . . . ."

She downed her drink with one heroic effort and stood up. "If you don't mind, let's not talk any more about drinking in this house. My daddy . . . ." She trailed off. After all these years, her father's alcoholism was still a sore spot.

He shot her a perplexed look. "How come? I wasn't going to lay a hand on you."

Heat flooded her cheeks. She would gouge his eyes out if she could. Instead, she tried to laugh. "Lord. What a thing to say! It's only that I wasn't brought up to sit around drinking." Her tongue was getting dangerously loose. The booze was catching up with her in other ways, too.

She made a sudden decision. "I'm going to have to call it a night. You can bed down on the couch until the boys show up." Given the amount he'd had to drink, she didn't offer to let him take her new car home.

"All righty." He eyed the damask upholstery. "But I'm mighty grubby."

She hesitated. "Would you want to stretch out in the spare bedroom? You could take off your—boots, if you like."

He looked dubious. "Maybe I'll just prop up in here and wait."

She couldn't go off to bed and leave the gas logs burning, not with the wind gusting. A sudden downdraft could blow out the flame and maybe leave the gas escaping while she slept. As she bent over to turn out the fire, she almost lost her balance. "I never leave the fire burning overnight. You'll be warmer stretching out under the covers."

She hurried into the hall before he could argue and flipped on the light in the guest room, calling back to him, "I'll turn on the porch light, and when the boys come, you can lock the door behind you." She was aware of a high level of propriety in her tone.

"All rightsy." He ambled into the hall, listing precariously to one side. She'd never seen him abandon himself so completely to alcohol's effects. Abandon did not beget precaution.

She went into her room and shut the door, hearing her own breath, loud as her heart. It was the alcohol that caused her pulse to race, her cheeks to burn. She pulled on her flannel pajamas and flopped into the big four-poster bed. Jesus Christ, the night would never end.

She couldn't sleep, couldn't even close her eyes, because everything swam when she tried. She focused on the cobwebs on the light fixture, straining to hear the sound of the pickup, of Mobeetie dropping his boots, shifting on the mattress in the next room. Maybe he couldn't sleep, either, lying there in a spinning room, his jeans and shirt draped over the bedrail. Maybe he ached, too. He might be staring at the ceiling, eaten alive with desire, waiting for her to come. It was her house. She was his boss. She should make the first move.

The thought propelled her to her feet in a kind of crazed logic. She wove down the hall and threw open his door so hard that it banged against the wall. He reared onto one elbow as she flung herself onto the bed. She was wild with want, rabid to get on with it, but he fended her hands off, catching them in his own.

He didn't look at her. "Nothing's going to come of this, ma'am. I'm much too drunk. Anyways, even if the ranch wasn't my first consideration, I couldn't do anything with you. You're—my boss."

Humiliation stung her cheeks, pressed like a weight on her rib cage. There was no graceful way to get out of the room after making such a complete ass of herself. Somehow she managed to stumble out and make it to the kitchen, find the bottle and down one more stiff shot so that maybe she could pass into oblivion.

But it wasn't only the present she fought to blot out: from a back corner of her memory flashed a small crystal moment of pain, strongly connected with the last time she had lain in the arms of her adored Daddy. Soon after the Night of the Gun and her personal indictment of Momma. In her child mind she'd given herself responsibility for him, and she had not protected him, had not prayed aright or enough. She had authored her own anguish, decreeing a standard for them all, expecting a story book family, refusing, even at age eight or nine, to compromise or forgive. And so she had lost him, and she had borne that loss afresh with each subsequent one.

One thing was certain: She would have to fire Mobeetie. She could never face him again.

The next morning he was gone, and her brain was too big for its case. She couldn't look into a mirror, not because she feared resembling Snider with a hangover, but because she despised the fool she had been. It must never happen again, for she lived by a strict code that forbade pain. She didn't answer the telephone despite its persistent ringing, didn't bother to check Caller I.D., nor did she go to the door when Ernest Vogel came. She knew it was Ernest because she recognized the roar of his Bentley as he sped away. But when he'd had time to get home, she called him.

She considered that what she was about to do would serve as a sort of penance for her everlasting impulsiveness, but its primary purpose was protective. She tried to sound chipper, but she did not have to fake a measure of relief. Ernest was a safe port, and it was easy to tell him, "I've made up my mind. I accept. Let's get on with it."

20

Elsie got it mixed up. She had thought Valentine's Day was going to be Thursday. Thought that's what the teacher said. Instead, it turned out to be Tuesday. So Elsie went to school just like always and was caught unawares.

It had taken several years before she could remember, from one year to the next, how it would be: how Miss Quattlebaum would appoint someone—but never Elsie—to open the big decorated box on her desk, take out the valentines one by one, and after a breath-taking pause while everybody wondered, read aloud the names. It was fun to see who got the most valentines and who had a secret crush. Sometimes Elsie enjoyed it for a while. It did not hurt so bad until the very end, not to get a single valentine, ever. But this year, she could be sure that she would get at least one, because last year Miss Quattlebaum had started giving everyone in the class a valentine. Elsie's name would be called, and she would receive a red heart pierced through by an arrow. She'd puzzled about it last year and had finally decided that it had a special meaning: that love might be painful.

Besides, valentines from teachers didn't count, especially from Miss Quattlebaum, whom Elsie had suffered for two years already. Before that, she'd had the other fifth grade teacher, Miss Prince, who was pretty to look at. But maybe Miss Prince had got tired of her.

Just before the end of the day, Elsie sensed an undercurrent of excitement, and she heard Miss Quattlebaum say, "All right, class, settle down or we won't have our party this afternoon."

That was all the warning she had. She looked at the wall clock and saw that the little hand was on the two and the big hand was on the twelve. Always before, when the big hand got down to the six, the party began, she was pretty sure. Anyhow, she knew there wasn't much time left. She raised three fingers and the teacher nodded. Elsie was excused.

She tiptoed past the restroom and down the hall to the side door, afraid to venture to her locker for her coat. She hoped she wouldn't get in trouble for leaving it at school, hoped she wouldn't get a licking for skipping school. Seemed like she didn't on the last Valentine's Day she'd missed.

Once out of sight of the school, she scudded aimlessly along, swept by a perishing haunch-of-winter gale, knowing her discomfort was her due. She squatted down beside the road to get out of the chill for a few minutes and was watching the wind tear a winter-stiff goathead from its stubborn stalk, when Snider Greene's old Chrysler rumbled past, stopped, and backed up.

"Elsie Mae Puckett? That you? Get in here, girl, before you freeze your heinie off."

Elsie peeked through the window at the perpetually damp Snider, who sweated even in the dead of winter. He smiled and waited. She looked back in the direction of the school, wondering if she had made a mistake to leave. Finally she opened the door and got in, as she had been told.

"I don't mind," she said, although she did really, a little. She settled back uneasily against the stiff seat. It wasn't nearly so nice as Miss Adrian's car, having a torn and sagging ceiling, and it jounced something awful. But now she felt grateful for the ride. Of a sudden she could admit to being cold and weary.

"How you been feeling?" Snider yelled. He always yelled when he talked to her.

She shrugged and watched the houses go by.

"Eh? Cat got your tongue? I say, *how you been feeling?*"

She thought about it. "Poorly," she said in a tiny voice.

"What's that? Poorly, how?"

She nodded morosely. "Puny," she elaborated. A queasy wave rose upon her, just thinking about it.

He began to hum and so she was relieved from further attempts to talk. He had closed her out, and she returned to her protected solitary world and watched the houses and people though the clouded glass. While he was singing, she felt safe; she felt safest when she was ignored.

He pulled up in front of her house. She fumbled for the door handle, found there was none that she could see, and looked at him in helpless confusion. Snider opened his door and heaved himself out in a profusion of grunts and huffing. Then he swept around to open her door, bowing low. She didn't know what made him tease her so. She climbed down, not looking up, and scurried for the house. "Much obliged," she said over her shoulder.

But Snider Greene didn't get back in the car; instead, he followed her up the walk. She started when she turned to find him there, the tiny hairs rising on the back of her neck. He carried a paper that she knew instinctively had something to do with her. Now she felt grievously sorry that he had offered her a ride. Maybe he was going to tell Daddy she ran off from school.

"Run in yonder and see if your momma's home," he ordered. But before she could obey, he caught her arm and squeezed it until it hurt. "Not your old man and not Sael and not your gabby sister. Won't nobody do but your momma, hear?"

She did not know why her chin began to quiver. But she always did as she was told, so she hurried inside and returned shortly with her momma, who was drying her hands on a cup towel.

"Afternoon, Mister Greene." Momma smoothed the bun on her neck and looked proper.

"Afternoon, Miz Puckett. Could I have a moment of your time, do you suppose?"

Elsie stood behind her momma and watched Snider Greene slip into one of his grins that displayed many, many tobacco-stained teeth. Momma opened the screen door and let him inside. Elsie did not know what else to do, so she went into the kitchen and stood behind the door, chewing her hangnail and just waiting. She was afraid Snider Greene had come about her, afraid she would soon be in big trouble.

Snider usually talked so loud when he talked to her, but now he was barely mumbling. And Momma was mumbling back. Elsie pressed her ear against the door, straining to hear. She could tell by the oily way his words came out that he was talking Momma into something, and she could tell by the way Momma sighed that she didn't like it one little bit. Elsie held herself between the legs and waited.

There was no clock, but Elsie could tell that a long time passed before he left, because she heard the Johnson boys hollering insults as they passed, like they always did after school. The Johnson boys were in junior high school, which let out even later. So she knew it must be drawing near to supper-time, and still Momma didn't come. Elsie sucked blood where she had bitten off the hangnail and leaned against the door, feeling her feet prickle from standing so long.

At last she heard the screen door slam and listened to Snider Greene curse as he tried to start the car. When it finally roared away, Momma came into the kitchen and did an uncommon thing: she put her arms around Elsie and drew her head down upon her shoulder. "My poor baby," she crooned softly.

Elsie didn't not know exactly why, whether it was the missed valentine party, whether it was how hard she'd worked cutting hearts out of notebook paper, folding the paper in half like the teacher showed her and cutting it in the shape of a chicken breast, and coloring them with the broken crayola she'd found and hidden for weeks, then turning them over, licking her pencil point carefully, copying each name off the health chart, knowing but not wanting to admit how they would all snicker and roll their eyes when they saw who it was from—whether it was that, or something else, she wasn't sure. But she felt big saved-up tears forming and plopping down onto Momma's shoulder, slowly at first and then more rapidly until she was retching uncontrollably. Momma just patted her head.

"Cry it all out, lamb, God love you. Precious lamb. Cry it out."

Presently the back door banged and Sael stomped in calling for supper. Elsie quickly dried her face and, still heaving and gasping, tried to gain control. Sael leaned over and peered into her face, his nose almost touching hers.

"What's going on?" he demanded. "Somebody hurt Elsie?"

Momma pushed Elsie aside. "Nothing's going on. Go wash up, Elsie Mae, and help your momma fix supper. Sael, Snider Greene interrupted the washing. You'll have to go out yonder and finish wringing out them sheets and hang them on the line, hear? Careful you don't drag them in the dirt, you hear me?"

Sael grumbled but minded Momma, but Elsie lingered, knowing she didn't have to go wash up just yet. Momma was fixing to tell her something. She couldn't bear to hear it, so she said it first. "I'm going to have to go work for Snider Greene some more, ain't I?"

Momma took a wadded tissue from her apron pocket and blew her nose. "I guess you might say so, Lord help."

Elsie thought about the skating rink. Maybe this meant the skating rink would come back to town. "Am I going to get another ticket to skate?"

Momma shook her head and looked sad. "Won't be no pay this time. Mister Greene's going to take care of you. That's all the pay you get."

Elsie often didn't understand things except by the sound of them, and she didn't like the sound of this. "I ain't going back to Madam's, am I?" She began wringing her hands at the idea.

"No, you'll have a room in Snider Greene's upstairs."

Elsie shivered. "I don't never go up there. Spooky up there."

"It won't be so bad. You'll get used to it. I'll come around every few days and see he's treating you right."

Elsie tried to get it straight. It sounded like she might not get to come home at night to sleep. She tried to think what to ask. "Do I got to spend the night?"

Momma set about stirring the hash, turning her back on Elsie. "It can't be helped. Us Pucketts has got to be able to hold up our heads, else what have we got left?" She stopped what she was doing and turned to study Elsie closely, so that Elsie had to lower her eyes and hang her head to feel safe.

"You don't know, do you?"

Elsie looked up defiantly, wanting so much to make Momma understand that she wasn't stupid. "I know a whole lot."

"Of course you do," Momma said. And she went back to her stirring and said something that sounded like what in the world was she going to use to make into a wedding dress.

21

Now that Adrian had consented to marry him, Ernest should feel immense relief, but he couldn't shake off a sense of doom. He sat in his office with his hand on the phone, unable to decide which of several matters was the most pressing.

His foreboding had nothing to do with the dour predictions of the IMF, although he monitored the fomenting international situation closely. He tended always to take the conservative view, which of late meant the pessimistic one, but he did not entertain a gloomy forecast for the commerce between Germany and the United States. Trade relations advantageous to both nations most certainly would be maintained, regardless of how riddled with ambiguity were U.S. foreign policies. As a precaution, Ernest had conducted most of his international transactions through intermediary Swiss banks for more than a decade, and he could do so indefinitely. But the Swiss were a greedy lot, and now he leaned more toward the Caymans. So long as American-German relations remained intact, he could only view any unrest in the Middle East as ultimately good for business.

No, the source of his apprehension focused nearer to home; it concerned the bemused state of his son's marriage. Puzzling fragments dropping into place over a season were forming a disturbing picture of Bobby's domestic life. First was Inge's withdrawal from the family circle, maintaining undeflected her reserve. Then there were the telephone charges to California, which he'd had Neva investigate. She had traced the number to a film producer. According to Bobby, Inge had been star-struck for years. Maybe she had been trying to work a deal to get into pictures, which was especially inappropriate for a mother-to-be.

More recently, there was the fleeting figure he'd seen at the end of the hall entering Inge's suite, and Bobby's absolute denial that a man could be in her rooms. There was Bobby's refusal to investigate, or to question her, almost as if he were afraid of what he would find.

Ernest was now convinced that Inge hadn't married for love, that she had been disappointed on reaching Attebury to find that the Vogels were not as prominent as she had hoped, that she lived in a perpetual fantasy spawned by the movie industry about what a rich American girl ought reasonably to expect, that in her boredom and total rejection of the local citizens, she had taken a lover and might even now be planning to run off with him, baby or not.

This last thought chilled Ernest. It might be possible that she planned to have an abortion, and this he would not tolerate. Inge could go or stay as far as he was concerned, but she would not deprive him of an heir. If she left, she would have to leave the child behind.

It further occurred to Ernest that, with enough fabrication about the extent of her influence, Inge might have lured something much larger than just a Hollywood lothario into her bed. This Ernest would not stand for, even if Bobby would. If he found this were so, that Bobby was indeed being cuckolded in his own house, then Inge would be smartly dealt with, and he would not hesitate to move her to the other end of the globe—once the baby was born.

Ernest determined to do some covert investigating immediately. He must bring Inge's peccadilloes to an end quietly so as to allow Bobby to save face. Attebury was too small to abide scandal, and Great-Uncle Otto would not like a divorce. Otto Theiss was the kind of man who would instigate a thorough investigation of the whole clan before he made such a healthy bequest; as it was, it would be hard enough to justify Bobby's misconduct prior to his marriage as merely wild oats.

It would be easier to monitor Inge's activities once Adrian moved into the mansion, which was another good reason—one among many—for setting the wedding date soon, before Adrian had a change of mind. She was an impetuous female—always had been. If he said the slightest thing to irritate her, she might call it off. That's why, much as he deplored the expenditure of time and money, he would have a formal engagement party quickly. Then it would be too mortifying to back out. Even a woman must reach a point when it is too late to change her mind.

He sat at his desk contemplating these matters when Neva poked her head in the door and said, "Roger wants to know what he should do about the overdue loan on Parsons' place."

"Tell him to foreclose," he said without hesitation, irritated by the interruption when he had more urgent things on his mind.

"Sell it at auction?"

He assented, then a thought struck him. "Where's that list of the assets on it?"

"On my desk. It's the usual stuff. Nothing out of the ordinary."

"What about rolling equipment? Any kind of van?"

"I'll have to look." She disappeared and returned with a sheaf of papers. "Yes, there's an old delivery van in the shed."

He slapped his hands on the desk. "Sell everything but the van."

She looked puzzled. "What should I tell him to do with it?"

"I'll send someone around to pick it up tomorrow."

Simplicity. The best plan was always the simplest.

22

Once the decision was made, Adrian did not allow herself any doubts, although for a week she woke in the middle of the night with tears on her pillow. Only in the darkness did she admit this wasn't how she had envisioned her marriage. It wasn't how a bride-to-be should feel about her fiancé.

She had expected no thunderclap of elation when she accepted Ernest's proposal, and she had not been disappointed. He had taken her acceptance as a matter of course, acknowledging it with an affable, "Good. We ought to work it in soon, but we'll have to postpone the honeymoon until Uncle Otto returns to Mainz."

"Work what in?"

"The wedding ceremony. By the way, I've already arranged the trip over. Confirmed reservations came this morning."

Adrian marveled at how he had apparently taken her acceptance for granted from the beginning. Without so much as consulting her, he had already decided when they would be married. She accepted his imperious dismissal of her because she carried the guilt over her conduct with Mobeetie, for which she'd suffered a storm of the spirit ever since.

To compensate, during her waking hours, she concentrated on the many signs that she *needed* to be married, because she could no longer function on her own. Recently, for instance, when she approached a four-way stop, regardless of who should have the right-of-way, she yielded to the man in the business suit, no matter his age or what he was driving. By the same token, in the past she usually felt privileged to traverse the intersection before a middle-aged woman or a person of color or someone in a jalopy. Now she was nearing middle-age, and with a pang, she knew this sense of non-entitlement was what Miz Puckett and Elsie lived with every day of their lives. Adrian had recently felt intimidated by entering a place of business such as the car dealership or computer store, as if she should apologize for being there, taking up people's time when they could be dealing with a person of importance.

Perhaps it had begun with Grandfather's death. While he lived, she had a champion. His demise wrought a change in her relationship with Snider, and she was only just now realizing why. Grandfather had kept Snider in check. She had never really dominated her cousin; it was the team of the two of them, Grandfather and she, who had bullied him into submission. So she had lived her entire life with a sense of false security. It was no wonder she only half-heartedly pursued a career, never married, never even had a serious love affair. Snider and Grandfather had answered all her needs, and she had presumed the situation would last forever. Now that Grandfather was gone, Snider was an unfettered jackal. There was no telling what he would do.

Maybe he'd stored up venom against her all his life, for all she knew.

There were other reasons why marrying Ernest was the right decision, the only one open to her. That she was a good manager had been another of her illusions. She knew nothing about ranching and had no interest in learning. The annual payments to the bank for the ranch loan would be steep. The fact was that the ranch had been declining steadily in Grandfather's waning years, and once those payments were made and yearly expenses were met, she would probably be in the hole. Now, the burden she'd carried since she'd inherited the ranch would be behind her; she would turn over her financial matters to Ernest and play the helpless wife: "I don't know how I got things in such a mess." He would lap that up, and he'd see that there would be ample funds for Puny's raise, despite her recent foolish excesses.

She saw now that her folly of paying cash for the Mercedes had been an attempt to raise her esteem in the eyes of the car salesman. What had gotten into her? What did she care about what he thought?

The trigger to her acceptance of Ernest's proposal still stung and she had been unable to put it out of her thoughts. As lagniappe, with any luck, hearing the news of her upcoming marriage might cause Mobeetie to doubt that her actions had been attempts at seduction after all, and her humiliation at his hands could be forgotten. But he would still have to go. She never wanted to see him again; in fact, the very next day after his rejection, she'd made inquiries at the Farm Service Agency about someone to replace him, because much as she would like to dismiss him at once, she had the ranch to think of. She had extracted a promise from the director to be discreet and to let her know if someone came to mind. Meanwhile, she would avoid Mobeetie.

That unfortunate encounter had not been motivated by a desire for love or even by lust. It was a desperate reaching out for human warmth, she knew. This yearning had happened before over the years, dating back to when she and Snider were small children, tucked in on the day bed on Grandmother's screen porch on hot summer nights. Adrian would wake to the sound of night creatures close-by, and stiff with fright, she would lie very still and pray for daylight. Then Snider would shift in his sleep, or poke her with a chubby elbow, and she would begin to breathe normally again, soothed by the warmth of that inadvertent touch.

No one wants to die alone, she thought.

As for Snider, well, he would be amply paid for ignoring her. He probably never dreamed that he could be so easily replaced.

Even as she was accepting Ernest's proposal, she had been imagining Snider's reaction when he found out: the look of incredulity as he realized she was lost to him forever.

She still harbored illusions that he cared something for her.

He had to learn it from her, and there was no use phoning him; he'd only let the answering machine pick it up. Besides, she had to see his expression: his shock and yes, his grief. He might hide it from everyone else with brusque sarcasm, but she knew him too well. She would be able to read his feelings if they were face to face. So she couldn't break the news on the phone. But she needed an excuse to see him.

The following morning, when she had given him time to get up and have his coffee, she left Mozelle working and drove out to the hill. She marched up to the house and dug his house key from her purse, figuring he probably wouldn't come to the door. But before she could use it, the door opened, and there stood—

"Elsie Puckett! What're you doing here?"

"I come to clean."

"Clean?" Inconceivable. *What is it this time?* Adrian wondered. She swept past Elsie and said, "Where's Mister Greene?"

Elsie pointed to Grandfather's old room, which was now Snider's office, among other things. The door was slightly ajar. Adrian didn't bother to knock.

She found her cousin still in his skivvies, sitting at Grandfather's desk, a cup of steaming coffee at his elbow. She called over her shoulder, "Elsie, would you bring me a cup of coffee?"

She flounced over to Grandfather's rocker and sat, realizing belatedly that his back would be to her. "I've come for Grandmother's tea service. I'm entertaining more frequently now that—"

He didn't turn around. "Just be sure you bring it back."

"I—have something to tell you that might affect our relationship."

"We don't have a relationship."

The words stung, but she went on coldly. "We still have joint interests in Grandfather's elevator shares, which you seem to forget with regularity."

The desk chair swiveled around. The bloodshot eyes were little more than slits under the puffy lids. She concentrated on the small points of blue, which would telegraph his reaction to what she was about to tell him. In the past she had controlled him through those eyes.

"Ernest and I are getting married." She realized that her heart was pounding as she waited for the stunning news to register.

The blues glinted, and small crinkles appeared among the folds. Snider was smiling! He seemed almost gleeful, and a part of her died. Or perhaps he was simply amused, which was too infuriating to contemplate. But his words were cautious.

"Your inherited property remains your private estate and not part of community property, you know."

"But Ernest will manage my affairs. He has the expertise. Why shouldn't I avail myself of it? Besides, we'll be traveling at lot. We're going to Europe soon." Rub it in. *Wipe that stupid grin off your face, you sonofabitch.*

Elsie tiptoed in sloshing a mug of coffee. Ernest didn't take his eyes off Adrian but spoke first to the girl: "You can take that coffee back. Miss Adrian's not staying," then to Adrian: "Get your tea set and get on out. I've got work to do."

The words didn't sting, exactly. They'd frequently hurled abusive barbs ever since they were old enough to talk. Ordinarily she would have shrugged off his rudeness and thought no more about it. Except he was all she had.

He had turned back to his desk. She rose and tried to think of a graceful exit line. Finally, cursing the tremor threatening her voice, she said, "I just thought you would want to know, since I'm your closest relative."

She waited but he said nothing more, so she started toward the door. Just as she left the room, she heard him mutter, "Maybe not."

"What did you say?"

"Nothing. Take the tea stuff and let me get back to work."

Which was ridiculous. How long had it been since Snider had any "work" to do?

She drove home in a funk. It wasn't the reaction she'd expected. But maybe he was hiding how he really felt.

She found Mozelle in the kitchen, scrubbing the oven with feigned alacrity. This was a chance to find out what Snider was up to.

"I was hoping you'd bring Elsie to help out," she said. "But I was out at my cousin's this morning and was surprised to see her there." She waited.

"I'd just as soon be here," Mozelle said. "You never know what kinda mess you'll get into out there."

Adrian left the talkative Mozelle still rambling. No use trying to pump information from her or from Sael, either. Adrian was convinced that whatever it was, they knew nothing about it.

Passing the hall mirror made Adrian uncomfortable, for she was aware her attributes were fading. Maybe that was why Snider had cut her out of his life, why Mobeetie was so cool, why she allowed the car salesman to fluster her so. It was harder for a beautiful woman to grow older than a homely one. A beautiful woman who loses her looks is no woman at all. Her looks had once been legendary, and she was still surviving largely on that myth. She would be on display at the engagement party as Ernest's wealthy friends looked her over, so she had to be spectacular. Even her own friends—what few she could count—would judge her in a new light. She thought of Mobeetie, who would receive an invitation. Let him see what he'd missed.

And Snider. But he probably wouldn't bother to come. He had ceased to care; that much was obvious. Adrian swallowed past a lump every time she thought about it.

Ernest had suggested coming over that evening to discuss plans for his announcement party to be held toward the dusty tail-end of planting season, but she pleaded a headache and went to bed early. Her attention had been wrenched from wedding plans, ever since that first night.

The following morning she decided to take the unused tea service back up the hill, hoping for a friendlier welcome than she'd received on her previous trip. But she hadn't realized that she would not see Snider again. He wasn't home, so Elsie told her, and Elsie was incapable of lying.

No, now that she thought about it, it wasn't Elsie; it was Miz Puckett, who was also there. Elsie had opened the door, but before she could say a word, Miz Puckett had materialized behind her, nudged her daughter aside and took the tea set from Adrian's hands. Now why would Snider require the services of both mother and daughter?

"I'm surprised to see you here," Adrian said.

"I just come by to check on Elsie," the woman said. "She'll be living here until after canning season."

Adrian found this highly peculiar—even though she knew Snider's passion for apricot preserves and his niggardliness in keeping every single apricot for himself—because those apricots would not be ripe until mid-summer.

Something more was afoot.

Miz Puckett had already shut the door. As Adrian stepped off the porch, she had the strangest sensation, as if she had just presented the woman with the last symbol of her past and as yet had nothing with which to replace it. She had entered a liminal space again: a vestibule between past and future with all its attendant distortions. If she squinted, might she almost glimpse two barefoot children scampering about the side yard? Or if she lifted her gaze to the far west, might she see the rooftop of the mansion she was soon to occupy?

No, she could see nothing in either direction. She was captured in limbo, like a zombie with no life at all.

23

In her closet, Adrian went browsing through the past, looking for an appropriate gown for the engagement party, but her figure had subtly changed. Finally, after another trip to Amarillo to try on a dozen off-the-rack so-called "designer" dresses, all intended for twentyish women, she retreated to a fabric store, where she chose a pattern with simple lines. For a fabric, she selected a heavy silk in salmon, reminding herself that she was marrying the richest man in the county and deserved the best. She took it to the finest dressmaker in the city.

I'm not up to this, she thought more than once, when she tried to picture playing hostess at Ernest's parties. She'd never liked to give parties, but she could bluff it through—and she would, considering it the penalty exacted for marrying for the wrong reasons. Then again, marrying for love was a recent notion not practiced in most of the world. *At least I won't have to grow old alone*, she thought again, which was more than Snider could say. Or maybe he thought he wouldn't last that long. And at the rate he was going, he'd be right.

As for Ernest, he had left his secretary Neva to make preparations for the announcement party. She hired an Amarillo caterer and instructed Precious to arrange for a little extra help to pass champagne. And there was one other item: he had commissioned an ice sculpture of their wedding date for the banquet table.

Adrian discovered the date upon which she was to be married on the night of the party, at the moment Ernest threw open the doors to the dining room to reveal the sculpture to the assembled guests. It read "May 30." Adrian gasped as the guests applauded and crowded around to shake Ernest's hand. He turned to her and raised the bushy eyebrows as if to say, do you like my surprise? She tried to force the corners of her mouth to twist into a smile. How could he spring this on her?

Her neighbor Sarah squealed, hugged her and teased, "Are you going to forget me when you move into this big ole place?"

Adrian swallowed her shock and shook her head, unable to speak. Other well-wishers crowded around, and she acknowledged them vaguely. Ernest, beaming and flushed with pleasure, handed her a champagne flute and said something she didn't understand. She accepted the glass gratefully, then noticed a ring in the bottom. At first she flushed with pleasure at this sign that Ernest had an ounce of romance in his blood. But she took a second look and knew she had seen this ring before.

While the crowd oohed and aahed, she turned to him and mouthed, "Helga's ring?"

"My mother's," he said behind a benign smile and hard eyes that warned her not to make a scene. He took the glass, handing it to Precious with instructions to wash the ring. Adrian accepted a second flute and took a sip, glad for the diversion while she looked around at what would soon be her new home.

The house, only seven years old, still had the neoteric sheen: sleek and sophisticated like something off of a movie set. Adrian admired the uncluttered effect, but she wondered if she would be able to live in it. She couldn't seem to keep from collecting things. Sometimes she thought that if her things were taken away, she would have no identity left.

Not that it mattered. Somehow, her life had gotten away from her. She was being swept along on a current too swift to battle.

24

It was Ernest's established routine to arrive home about four-thirty on weekday afternoons. He never left the office unattended, unless Bobby was in the outer office. Everyone knew that. Inge certainly knew. On occasion, since his suspicions about Inge's lover began to grow, he had slipped away during the day to try to catch her in the act. He never had, but it occurred to him now that Bobby had always known he was leaving, and if he were trying to save face, he might have alerted Inge his father was on the prowl.

On this day, on the pretense that he wanted to surprise Bobby with a gift, he talked Adrian into coming in one morning to baby-sit his office without Bobby's—or even Neva's—knowledge. He even suspected his own secretary might be protecting his daughter-in-law.

"Bring a book to read," he told Adrian. "Just sit there and don't open the door to anyone."

As soon as Adrian arrived, Ernest stepped into the outer office and told Neva they were not to be disturbed. He returned to his office and locked the door. Then he left by the custodian's entrance and drove to the edge of the Vogel grounds, where he parked his Bentley in the shadow of the front gate. He left his cell phone in the car and walked up to the house, staying close to the edge of the horseshoe drive in the shadow of tall junipers.

The excitement of the escapade had left him breathing hard, and his heart thumped audibly by the time he reached the side door. He leaned against the jamb and caught his breath, waiting for the tightness in his chest to subside. It was only April, yet the air seemed stultifying. He looked across the grounds toward the tennis courts, where dandelions were beginning to sprout in the cracks. The trees he'd planted seven years before had sprung pale bright young leaves. Scraggly trees, already leaning permanently with the wind. In Great Uncle Otto's country, such trees as these would have been torn out by the roots.

He chose the side door because he was almost sure to miss seeing Precious, and also because he wanted to stop in the library. One wall of the room housed his gun collection, which included a number of pistols. He kept a small one loaded at all times, in case of emergency.

He did not take the back stairs, nearest Inge's rooms, again for fear of running into Precious. He tried to quiet his breathing, still unduly labored. With what stealth he could muster, he made his way on tiptoe down the immense length of the house to the front stairs. God knows he needed the elevator, but he didn't dare. Very slowly, he climbed the broad front stairs to the second floor. Then once more he had to traverse a long hall to reach the wing Bobby and Inge occupied. He stopped before Inge's door and found his hand was shaking as he tried the knob.

It probably should have been locked, but it wasn't. He crept into her sitting room and stifled his breath at the sound coming from the bathroom: a man was humming. He felt the blood rising, storming his head as he rushed across the room, into the small hallway and threw the bathroom door wide.

His worst fears were realized. In one moment the bright future he and Helga had envisioned for their son, after a tumultuous adolescence, vanished. It was Bobby's marriage to Inge that had pulled him out of a downward spiral, and made it possible for him to return to Attebury, the earlier scandals forgotten, or at least fading in the memories of townspeople.

But Ernest hadn't reckoned on this: A tall handsome young man, his chin and cheeks covered with lather, his slender frame swathed in a short silk robe that showed his well-muscled legs, stood before Inge's bathroom mirror. On second glance, he couldn't have been too young; light glistened on the forehead of his receding hair. Ernest should not have been surprised. He always suspected Inge of being shallow, of marrying Bobby for his money.

The intruder started in terror as he looked into the barrel of Ernest's pistol. His eyes darkened and became pinpoints of fear. The razor fell from his hand with a clatter across the marble counter, and he backed away, looking around for some escape.

"Don't try to run, you bastard!" Ernest, still panting, waved his pistol and looked past the man toward the door leading to the adjoining bedroom. "Inge, whore, get in here!" He would scare her, but he would never kill her. Not while she carried his grandchild.

The young man seemed to read his mind and relax to a degree, and the shade of a grimace—or a smile—threatened at the corners of his mouth. Ernest felt his rage pulsing against his temples at the man's obvious insolence. There was something familiar about him. Was this the chauffeur he'd hired when visiting dignitaries came in town? One of the extra waiters brought in by Precious? But before he could question him, a sharp pain gripped him in the chest, and he felt the breath squeezed from him. He could see surprise in the man's eyes as his gun hand went limp and the pistol crashed to the marble floor. Ernest gasped and backed away, feeling behind him for the door, never taking his eyes off the man. With his left hand he clutched his chest; with his right, he explored along the sitting room wall, trying to reach Inge's chaise lounge and telephone. He was near to unconsciousness, he knew, but he must reach the phone. Otherwise, the sonofabitch in the silk robe would let him die.

25

Since mid-February Snider Greene had suffered a growing apprehension. At first he feared only The Man, because no one knew what had become of him since the incident that deprived him of his nose. It was possible that Calvin might hold him responsible, or at least liable, for his medical expenses.

But gradually that dread burgeoned into an amorphous terror and mistrust of almost everyone, except his cousin Adrian. She was obligated to make monthly payments to the bank for his part of the ranch, but otherwise, she could no longer profit from his death. Besides, in his wildest imaginings, he couldn't picture Adrian doing him harm.

But there were others—legions—who had reason, or so it now seemed. He scarcely left his study these days, except to make a frantic trip over to Jericho to replenish his whisky supply.

By April he'd begun buying it by the case so as not to make the trip so often, even though he had to hide his stock from himself to keep from drinking it all in one night. Yet something had happened to his tolerance. Lately he could have no more than a jigger or two before sinking into helpless oblivion, a vulnerable state for someone with so many enemies. He began to believe, when he came to, that he had been deliberately drugged.

So Elsie became his chief suspect. If it wasn't Elsie, then it must be Madam, who stopped in several times a week to bring the mail and a few groceries. He suspected collusion between them: Madam supplying the poison and Elsie, only feigning stupidity to throw him off guard, slipping it into his drink.

Maybe neither of them masterminded the Plot against him. Maybe they were only the henchmen. Someone from the outside pulled the strings. Here his list of suspects grew daily as he recalled past deals. He never used his cell phone anymore, in case someone was monitoring his calls. He stopped even turning on his computer, because of spyware that had been planted by his enemies. He kept the blinds drawn against a hundred pair of spying eyes out on that expanse of prairie in front of the house.

Eventually it got to the point that when he heard Madam coming, he would lurk just out of view, hoping to overhear an inadvertent slip about the Plot when she passed the mail and groceries to Elsie.

It was inevitable that he would be found out, but not before learning what he needed to know. It was late April, and Madam hadn't been around for almost a week. When he heard her coming, Snider wedged behind the dining room door and waited, peering into the kitchen through the crack.

The big woman swept in the back door, flipping the flowing purple sleeves out of the closing door with an expertise born of long practice. She set the sack of groceries on the table and looked around for Elsie.

"Where are you, *rocnoxa? Gospodjo.*"

The side porch screen creaked quietly and the girl crept in, head hung low, as usual. She bobbed and pointed to a scrap of paper on the table.

"He done left a list for next time," she said, the pride in her voice giving away her obvious pleasure in being able to remember.

"Well, you can tell him Clabber Watson says no more credit until something is paid on the bill," Madam said. "Can you remember that?"

Elsie fidgeted, showing signs of distress, and Madam's indifference seemed to dissolve. He watched her pat the girl. Then her gaze moved to the pan of rolls on the counter top.

"Ah. There is what smells so delicious. So. You are not quite the helpless mite which he makes you out. It takes a clever girl to make bread."

"Momma done that," Elsie said.

The fact struck Snider so violently that his knees buckled, knocking against the door and giving away his hiding place. He wondered how often Miz Puckett came poking around in the early hours before he woke. That Elsie had been bathed and provided with fresh-ironed clothing hadn't occurred to him until now.

"Is that you, Mister Greene?" Madam advanced on him and flushed him out, her gold filling flashing in an undisguised smirk.

He stepped out as gracefully as he could manage. "I was killing a daddy longlegs in the corner. Elsie never runs the dust mop around the baseboards." He spoke as if Elsie was nowhere around. He wished to God she would stand up straight.

"Then you heard what I said about Clabber Watson. He has cut off your credit. I was just telling your—you *did* say she is your wife, no?"

He cleared his throat at great length, gargling the loose phlegm in a way he'd long since discovered to be intolerably offensive, and pretended he was choking. "Excuse me, Madam. I am troubled with catarrh. As I was about to say, I'm no longer satisfied with the quality of Clabber's produce, which has obviously been in cold storage. It rots overnight. From now on, I'd be obliged if you'd pick up our supplies at Jim Hurley's."

He turned and scuttled to his study before she could answer, closed the door and turned the key. He must have time to think.

He should have known it was Miz Puckett: She had more reason than most. He must watch over Elsie more closely from now on. If anything happened to her, Miz Puckett would sic that idiot boy Sael on him. Perspiration popped out on his brow. Sael Puckett had the strength of a buffalo and the brains of a stump. What to do. What to do.

In the meantime, he opened his desk and took out the only friend he could count on, uncorked it, turned it up and drained it. Then he stumbled off to the adjoining bedroom—he could not bring himself to sleep in Grandfather's old bed—and climbed in, clothes and all, and pulled the covers over his head.

Elsie was going to remember to tell Momma tomorrow about how Madam always called her a wife. She had been troubled by this for a long time, but she could never remember to ask when Momma was about. She was so happy to see Momma, whom she missed with a consuming sickness, that her rememberings were driven clean away.

Elsie didn't see many people anymore. Always shut off by an invisible barrier she did not understand, she was now locked away on the hill besides. When Snider Green first brought her here, she used to get up early and, because it was cold then and she knew how sound carries on cold days, she would listen for the school bell. The sound gave her comfort and told her that back in town, there was still order.

Snider Greene didn't care what time she got up as long as she was quiet. Her chores were easy enough: she fed the chickens and gathered the eggs. She turned the windmill on and off. She did up the dishes and sometimes swept. Momma had taught her how to make his coffee. Momma came by several times a week, but not often enough to keep the ache away.

Still, she was not always unhappy. She had given the chickens names, and they liked her, she could tell, for they followed her every time she walked out the back door. Now there were the small things that came in the spring: the sparrows and road-runners and scissor-tail swallows. Soon she would see grasshoppers and red ants and horny toads and lizards. And there was the enemy, the cat, who belonged down the hill but acted as if he owned the yard.

The cat was sneaky. If it suited him, he rubbed against her legs and pretended he believed she was as good as he. But other times he stalked the chickens or toyed with an unlucky lizard. She could never trust him.

She wasn't too unhappy, until the sun went down and the chickens settled in the coop and Snider sent her out to stop the scranel cries of the windmill. The old lever was stiff, and she would swing her full weight against it for an eternal black nightmare, closeted in the dark with only the howl of the biting wind to remind her of the real world, until finally the lever gave and she could pull it down and fasten it with a wire. Then she'd gallop across the chicken yard with her heart pounding, and sometimes she would bite her tongue and not know it until she got inside and tasted the blood.

In the house things were no better. Unless Snider Greene was already too drunk to notice her, he sent her straight off to bed, up the dark stairwell into the fusty dormer bedroom whose closet opened into the black eaves of the attic. The mice, who had not been bothered for years, talked aloud to each other. Elsie could hear them through the wall.

She would climb into her bed and shiver with grief for her momma. Often the aching of her spirit would make her nauseated. She even wished for Mozelle and Sael and Daddy, dismissing how they had misused her at times.

Often, though, Snider Greene would drop off early, leaving the TV blaring. On those nights, she didn't go to bed, but sat on the floor in the hall just outside his study and listened as long as she could. Then she slid into a heap right where she sat and slept until the rooster began to crow and the early news was on. Sometimes she was so stiff she could hardly get up, but it was better than climbing the stairs to the dreary room with its cavernous closet.

Every day when Elsie woke, she hoped this might be the day Momma would take her home.

But on the morning after Madam found Snider Greene hiding behind the door, he got up earlier than usual. He came into the kitchen where she was having a piece of bread and jam. She was surprised to see him. She hadn't even thought about making coffee yet.

"Elsie, is your momma coming out today?"

She hung her head, caught with a mouthful of food, not knowing what to do about it. Finally she was able to gulp it down. "I ain't sure."

"Don't give me that." He jerked her to her feet by one arm, pinching it so tightly that a pain shot clear up to her armpit. "She comes out all the time, doesn't she? Pert near every day, isn't that right?"

All she could do was sob and nod. She had never seen him so angry, and she remembered her terror of Daddy when he got mad. Snider dropped her arm and stalked to the back door, turning the key.

"I don't want you letting that woman in this house again, you hear?" She could see that his hooded eyes were flashing and that his breath came in quick spurts, like snorts of a bull. She didn't know what to ask about feeding the chickens.

And so, when Momma came to the door and knocked, Snider Greene held Elsie behind him and waited her out. But Momma wouldn't give up, just as Elsie knew. Finally he yelled, "Go away, old woman. You can't see Elsie any more, so don't come back."

Momma rattled the knob a few times and Elsie, for one brief moment, thought Momma was going to break it in.

"Get away from my door." Snider bellowed so hard that he shook. "Else I'll call Flop Pyle and have you run in for trespassing. Hear?"

Things got quiet for so long and finally, with sinking heart, Elsie heard Momma close the gate. A tear trickled down and hung on her lip, and then she burst out wailing, trying with sheer volume to give vent to the enormous anguish of her soul.

"Oh shut up," he snapped. "You're going to be with your momma before long, and good riddance."

She wasn't sure she heard right. She sniffed and ran her wrist under her nose as she followed him back into his study. "When? When?"

"Probably about the time you get the canning done. You *can* put up preserves, can't you? Any idiot can do that. Yes, I'd say that's about right. You can go home to your momma when you've finished putting up the apricots."

A wave of relief washed over her. She ran back to the kitchen and looked out the window at the apricot trees already heavy with tiny green knobs. She did not know how long it would take them to grow and ripen. She would try to remember to ask Madam. Madam would tell her how to put up the preserves, maybe even help.

She felt the hard knot in her stomach turn slowly, like a doorknob, and she settled down beside the window to watch the apricots grow.

26

Adrian learned of Ernest's hospitalization in an off-hand manner, as if she were no one special. When Ernest didn't return from his mysterious errand in an hour, she unlocked the office door and announced to Neva that she had errands to run and would return when she finished. She headed for the Farm Services Agency to remind the director she was still looking for a replacement for Mobeetie. Then she got a sandwich at the City Cafe before returning to the bank.

She dreaded going in, because bank employees would again stop work to peek at her left hand. To keep them from recognizing Helga's ring, she turned it diamond-side in. Anyway, the whole thing put her in mind of Grandfather saying that people have a tendency to focus on the nouns of life, when verbs are the only reality.

When she asked if Ernest had returned, Neva only shook her head. Bobby wasn't in, either, but this didn't surprise Adrian. He probably presumed his father was on the premises and had gone to lunch without checking.

Something about the secretary's grey-lipped silence struck Adrian as peculiar, and she prodded further. "He said he wouldn't be long. It's been three hours."

For the first time she noticed Neva's sullen pout and the two bright spots of color on her cheeks. "Nobody tells me anything. Bobby got a call and rushed out, and with no one else in the office, how was I supposed to take a lunch break?"

Very strange. Adrian persisted. "You have no idea where Ernest is?"

Neva hesitated. "Well I do *now*. He's in the hospital." She turned back to her computer.

Dumbfounded, Adrian waited, but it was obvious she'd get no more information from Neva. She left her cell number and told Neva to phone if she had news. Then she drove out to the mansion where she found the Vogel housekeeper sitting in the kitchen drinking a glass of tea.

Precious' loquacity, verging on hysteria, told more than words. "Mister Vogel keel over up in Miss Inge's sitting room. I didn't know nothing about it until Bobby run in right past me up the back stairs yelling his dad's had a spell and for me to watch for the ambulance."

Precious took a noisy gulp of iced tea before she went on. "Don't know how he come to find out; don't know how come Mister Vogel be in Miss Inge's room in the first place, when he ought to be at work. Except that Miss Inge's s'posed to leave for her confinement today."

Adrian was unaware that Inge was going away so soon, although Ernest had said she wanted to have her baby under the care of a German-speaking doctor. But the fact was unimportant now in the rush of unreasoning guilt at realizing that Ernest had been ill for hours without her knowledge. If she had stayed at her post—but she dismissed that line of speculation. Feeling guilty would be putting too much importance on herself. After all, if Ernest and Bobby had wanted her to know, they could have told Precious to call.

Adrian spoke evenly. "What kind of spell? Do you mean a heart attack?"

"Might be. They put a breathing mask over his face. Don't know how Bobby knew. I be right here the whole time. Mister Vogel might of hollered, but I didn't hear nothing. Blamed place is too big, uh huh."

She patted Adrian's hand, and her voice grew comforting. "He didn't look too sick to me, honey."

Adrian lost interest after that. He was apparently not dying. Surely. Not yet . . .

His "spell" would probably postpone the wedding, scheduled for only a few weeks away. Maybe she should feel relieved. Instead, she felt a certain distress to think that she would have more time to deal with her money worries.

She could share with no one her ambiguities. Her feelings were seldom appropriate. What was it Madam had said? Society demands that a woman have a secret life. Maybe that was because so many of her feelings were inappropriate.

She learned Bobby hadn't accompanied the ambulance to Amarillo, which was no surprise. Bobby was singularly lacking in sentiment. In that respect if in no other, he resembled his father. Adrian could imagine Ernest's insistence that Bobby go back to the bank and stay until closing time. Ernest had the notion that things would fall apart if a Vogel weren't on duty. When Helga was alive, she often had to forego her own plans to warm Ernest's chair when he left town suddenly. This, apparently, was to be one of Adrian's duties as well.

Bobby had her cell phone number, she thought with building resentment. He should have had the decency to perform that courtesy, no matter how he felt about her marrying Ernest. It didn't take much to get her dander up where Bobby was concerned.

She avoided him when possible as, she suspected, he did her. But this time she felt obliged to squelch her pride and exhibit appropriate concern. Conscience and propriety required it.

She left Precious with her tea and went back to the bank, wearing her mantle of righteous indignation. Neva informed her that, after a brief absence, Bobby was now back at his post.

She didn't wait to be shown into his office. He rose hastily as she stalked in.

"Adrian." His smile was bland as he indicated a chair. If she had expected some show of remorse that he hadn't thought to notify her, she was disappointed. "I guess you've heard," he said. He sat on the corner of the desk, folded his arms across his chest and swung a dangling leg. He might have been discussing a loan application.

"I should have thought you'd let me know," she said crisply.

He shrugged, not looking at her, but studying the toe of his Gucci instead. "It's probably only gas. He's never had any trouble with his heart."

She wrestled with the suffusive atmosphere of so much that was brashly Bobby's: the blatantly erotic posters, Art Deco rugs, the mixture of Jacobean furniture and Eames chairs were hostile, clashing. He had always been an insufferable boy, forever antagonistic. The good people of the town had felt sorry for Helga, to have mothered such an unruly spiteful son. Some said his early escapades ultimately killed her. No one knew how Helga felt, for she had borne her grievances in silence.

Adrian sat feigning interest in Bobby's story, careful not to betray the slightest irritation that he hadn't informed her sooner, determined not to give him that satisfaction As it was, he would tell her only what he wanted, which might or might not bear any resemblance to the truth.

"Dad came home unexpectedly, found Inge's brother there, and became livid that he hadn't been informed of his visit," he said with a shrug. "Dad likes to be in charge. But you must know that by now."

She nodded, feeling her chest contract. It was the longest conversation they'd ever had. She tried to imagine marching down through the years exchanging pleasantries with him on holidays. But of course, it would never happen. He would be moving once the baby was born. Inge was obviously anxious to leave. Surely they wouldn't stay once she and Ernest married.

She brushed the thought away like a gnat.

Having made the obligatory inquiries about Ernest's condition, she left Bobby's office with a lame "If there's anything I can do . . ." and decided she ought to drive up to Amarillo to see about Ernest herself. Maybe tomorrow. Or the next day. Give him a chance to rest. He wasn't alone, after all. He had many business "friends" in Amarillo. Still she ought to do something.

"Ought" is a very tacky word, she decided.

She went home and phoned his hospital room, realizing that he probably didn't know that she had left his office untended. Now he need never know.

He answered on the second ring, and she said, "What happened? Did you faint, or—?"

His voice was gruff, gravelly. "Nothing happened. Nothing I can't handle."

Why wasn't she surprised? "Well, that's good," she said. "I thought the least I could do is assure you that I don't mind that the wedding will have to be postponed."

But Ernest wouldn't hear of it. "There's not anything wrong, I tell you. I've got things to tend to. I'm coming home in a few hours. Aren't I the picture of health?"

"Oh, you're a fine specimen," she said, at once weary to the bone.

"This won't alter our plans," he insisted, as if she'd had any part of them.

Her exasperation got the upper hand. "Did you know it's possible to change your mind about something and be no worse for it? The doctor will want to do some tests—"

"Dammit, who's paying his bill? I'll leave when I want, and I'll decide when I'm ready to marry. No doctor will tell me what to do."

She started to argue, then bit back her words. She recognized the panic and sensed what he was feeling. Ernest Vogel had had a brush with death, and he was running.

Perhaps they deserved one another, after all.

27

As Adrian predicted, the wedding had to be postponed. Tests indicated that Ernest had suffered a heart attack, and the catheterization that followed, once his condition had stabilized, revealed two blockages which the cardiologist was able to clear with stents. But such was Ernest's agitated state that the doctor was reluctant to dismiss him until a psychiatrist could be consulted. Apparently there had been some sort of confrontation with family members which was likely to be repeated, and possibly a tranquilizer would help him cope more rationally.

She pondered on this state of affairs, admitting with reluctance that she and Ernest were more alike than she had realized. Whatever the problem—doubtless with Bobby and Inge—non-violent discussion would have been a more effective method of achieving results than her usual habitual headlong attack. It seemed to her now infinitely more courageous, as well, she thought, still mulling over her confrontation with Mobeetie.

But instead of the elation she expected for this welcomed marriage reprieve, for the next few mornings, a heavy lassitude held her in bed for a hours until she finally rolled out by degrees, aware that the act of combating something gives it power. And what she was combating was a shortage of funds.

She had no strength to offer to help Neva Craig notify the wedding guests. Now, with marriage plans on hold, her immediate financial worries loomed again.

She made the trip to see Ernest daily, considering the visits investments against the time when she would need his financial help. He took her presence as a matter of course, greeting her with a list of errands that she was to perform. Often these required her going to his home, to fetch his favorite slippers, or a book.

Since the night of the engagement party, she had spent little time in the mansion. The place looked as if it needed a good haircut: the yardmen had apparently been dismissed or had quit. Inside, Precious shuffled from front to back at a doddering pace; surely she didn't have to keep the whole place by herself. But on examination Adrian discovered that many of the rooms had been closed off, probably to save the housekeeper work.

Or to save on heating and cooling costs.

Maybe she would get Mozelle and Elsie and Sael to put the house and grounds in order before she moved in. The prospect lifted her spirits for reasons she didn't try to analyze.

Some of the rooms, she discovered quite by accident, were almost bare. She wondered where everything went, but since most of it was not to her liking, she felt relief that she wouldn't have to contend with it. Maybe Ernest had given it to Bobby and Inge. Good riddance. She considered decorating a few rooms with her more traditional treasures.

Ernest remained in a state of agitation, tranquilizers notwithstanding. "Bobby promised he would send that brother packing, now that Inge's gone, but I don't trust them. You've got to check their rooms, check the garages, see if there's an extra car parked there or around behind."

It was hard to imagine that Ernest wouldn't know what was going on under his own roof. It was more than awkward to do as Ernest demanded without confronting Bobby outright. It meant she had to prowl around the house, question Precious obliquely, listen at doors before she knocked.

Bobby caught her one day, lingering in the upstairs back hall. He glared with open contempt, his malevolence tangible and frightening. "Is this what we are to expect once you and Dad are married, listening at keyholes?"

"Certainly not." Her ire was partially pretense, for she was so flustered at being caught that she had to hide her shame. "I'm only trying to put Ernest's mind at rest that your—houseguest—has been sent away as he requested."

"He's gone," Bobby said darkly. "Now we have to find another doctor who speaks German. I won't have Inge's health jeopardized by someone who can't understand her."

Adrian was puzzled. "Doctor? I thought it was Inge's brother who was here."

"It was," he said quickly. "He's a doctor."

"But surely her own brother wasn't planning to deliver her baby. I thought doctors didn't treat members of their own family."

Bobby's face grew a livid red. "Why don't you butt out? Who asked you, anyway?"

Adrian's sympathies would have been for the young couple were it not for Bobby's overt animosity. Although she felt Bobby was right in wanting to choose his wife's doctor, she sided with Ernest out of wounded pride and said with sarcasm several layers thick, "Delivering a baby isn't brain surgery. It wouldn't be the first one our local doctor has delivered."

She was gratified by his look of irritation. Still, she knew better than to antagonize him. Why did she do it? Just as with Snider or Mobeetie, she seemed unable to help herself. Again, the sense of a well-trampled path hidden by undergrowth.

But his mood took an abrupt turn as he studied her as if gauging her receptivity before drawing her near, glancing toward the back stairs. He lowered his voice and gave her a tentative smile. "I'm sure you must have been told that this is to be a special child."

She was too startled by this confidence to do anything but nod, although she wasn't sure what he meant.

"Inge must have the best, you see," he went on. "If Dad wouldn't allow me to bring a doctor in, then I had to take her where one is. But I should be with her, you understand?"

She did indeed. In spite of herself, she patted his arm. "Of course. You should be together." It wasn't necessary to add that Precious had already apprised her of their plans, but the elation at securing a period of uninterrupted grace during the early weeks of her upcoming marriage was hard to mask.

He grinned. "Then see if you can soften up the old man. He insists that some member of the family be at the bank at all times. Says I can't desert the bank while he's bedridden."

She realized that she was being manipulated into taking up the slack, to fill his hours at the bank. She cast around for an alternative. "Can't you can find a good nurse to look after her during the week? You can drive up to be with her on weekends."

The shocking cold returned to his eyes, which she read as an attempt at intimidation. She patted his arm once again and said cheerily, "It'll all work out. You'll see." Then she walked away and headed rapidly for the stairs.

Bobby was so hard to understand. What if Ernest never fully recovered? Bobby would take over at the bank—he would eventually be sole heir—and what a disaster that would be. Despite his title as vice president, he knew nothing about the business.

He could hardly be expected to grieve for a father who had held himself aloof, managing to put a hemisphere between them for years. Ernest was such a pretentious toad, always had been. He and Helga hadn't meant for their son to fit into Attebury, or else they'd never have arranged to send him to Le Rosey. And it had taken monumental arranging, she recalled, including the intervention of the influential Delattre family. For although Helga could claim ancestry among the Austrian Battenburgs, and her wealthy Great-Uncle Otto in Mainz, still, to that most elite of Lake Geneva boarding schools, Ernest was only a small town Texas banker.

Helga had once confided to Adrian how young Bobby detested the town of Rolle, despised the school and his shoddy treatment by its snobbish masters. It wasn't long before his rebellious attitude and—more than likely—the fact that no one there really considered him Le Rosey material, caused the head master to summons them to fetch him home.

Helga had suggested an English school and following that, a French one. One by one he had been thrown out of the best Europe had to offer, before he was brought back to the States. Never, in all those years, did Adrian ever see evidence that either parent missed their son. Eventually Ernest could think of nothing but a small Lutheran school in Missouri which a distant cousin had once endowed. Why he was asked to leave that one, Adrian never knew.

Eventually Ernest had thrown up his hands and said he wasn't wasting another penny on the boy. He could come to Attebury and go to public school, sink or swim, or he could take off on a west-bound freight train. Bobby elected to come home. Despite more hinted-at scandals he stuck it out long enough to graduate from Attebury High. Ernest sent him off to a small college in Colorado because, "It's the only one I could buy him into."

Helga never confided about what happened to him there, but somehow he fell in with a crowd at last where he seemed to fit. But before long they had to stir things up, had to stage an orgy which reached the attention of the Dean, who claimed that nothing of this sort had ever happened before. All participants were summarily ejected from the premises, having to move to a hotel until their parents could claim them. Helga was in tears for weeks, but Adrian never learned the sordid details. Nor did she care to.

Helga had reenacted what happened next; Ernest had presented Bobby with a plane ticket and remanded him to the employ of an old friend in the Foreign Service, with the specific instructions: "Don't come back until you've married and made a man of yourself. Otherwise, you can kiss your inheritance goodbye."

In just one year, Bobby was back, with a wife. But did that make him a man?

28

Ernest had told her that he expected to be dismissed after the doctor made rounds on Tuesday, so she drove up to the hospital earlier than usual that day. But to her surprise, although he was dressed and sitting in a chair with his packed bag at his feet, he didn't want her to take him home. He had called Neva and asked her to send his car and driver.

Adrian said, "But you knew I was coming."

He glanced toward the door of his room. "I want to get a good look at the driver."

"Why?"

He hesitated. "I haven't told you about the night of my heart attack. There was a man—"

"Inge's brother. Or doctor, whatever. I know. Bobby filled me in," she said.

He went on as if she hadn't spoken, and she could see from the sudden rush of color on his neck that he was becoming upset. "Tell me this: If you were a doctor, and you saw someone obviously having a heart attack a few feet away, would you disappear in the opposite direction?"

She was dumbfounded. "You mean that's what he did?"

Ernest shrugged and rubbed his forehead. "I may have passed out at some point. I don't remember him being there. I do remember calling Bobby. He claims the doctor stayed until the ambulance came, but I don't recall seeing him."

Strange, she had to admit. "Maybe he had an emergency of his own."

"That's what Bobby says. But wouldn't you think he'd have stopped by my hospital room to check on me? Surely he must be here every day. As for Inge . . ." He leaned forward and she could see how bloodshot his eyes were. "If your father-in-law were in the hospital, and if you were only a few miles away, wouldn't you visit him?"

Not if I were Inge, she thought. But she said, "Sometimes women in their third trimester have to be very careful about getting up. Sometimes they have to stay in bed entirely. That may very well be the case with Inge."

To console him, she patted his arm, but another thought struck her. "Now what does this have to do with your sending for your own car? Are you trying to impress the hospital staff because not every patient has a chauffeur-driven Bentley?"

He scowled at her, and she immediately regretted her sarcasm. "I'm almost sure I've seen that man before. And I've never laid eyes on Inge's doctor. *Or* her brother."

She still didn't see the connection between the doctor and Ernest's Bentley. Unless . . . "You think it might have been your driver you saw in Inge's rooms?"

He stared off as if trying to call up an image, then shook his head. "I can't be sure. He had lather on his face. He had a high, receding hairline. I've never seen the driver without his livery and cap. Never noticed anything about him. I just know I've seen that man before. I just can't place where."

The nurse came in with a sheaf of papers. "The doctor left some instructions. Told me specifically to wait until I saw you here, Ms. Craddock."

Puzzled, Adrian took the proffered sheets. As she examined them, she could see why she was entrusted with them. If Ernest had received them, he wouldn't have mentioned them to anyone. She smiled.

"You're to report to Cardiac Rehab three times a week for the next three months. Starting tomorrow." She breathed in deep relief. Now he would *have* to put the wedding off until July.

There was no further opportunity to discuss the man who had been the catalyst for Ernest's attack. At that moment an aide arrived with the wheel chair to transport him down to his waiting car. Adrian kissed the top of Ernest's head and promised to stop in to see him later.

For most of the ride home, she felt freer than she had in a long time. Mobeetie would soon be history. She had almost three months to get ready for the move to the mansion, and to lose a few pounds before the wedding. By the time she reached her own garage, she realized with a groan that with Ernest out of the office every other day, even if she didn't have to drive him to Amarillo, she might have to fill in for him at the bank. Bobby couldn't be expected to sit glued to his chair every minute, not with Inge in her third trimester.

What a silly notion, that one of the Vogels must be on the premises at all times. Monumental hubris is what it was.

29

During the weeks that followed, Adrian and her neighbor Sarah grew closer than they had been in years. The prospect of Adrian's move and change in marital status made them both sentimental about their friendship, which never had been anything special to begin with.

They stood by the back fence early of a morning, before the awful heat set in, and gnawed on the news of the day, including speculation by some commentators that backroom Washington finagling was drawing the country closer to another war. But when Adrian repeated this to Ernest, he blustered and assured her that the politicians didn't want war any more than he did.

Townspeople stayed out of the midday heat, hurrying between sheltering shades to keep the sun from baking their brains. The parched air was sluggish. Folks augmented their overworked air conditioners by fanning the sweat dry with folding fans the grocery store offered as a giveaway with bottles of sports drinks. The ground cracked, and even the horned toads disappeared. People began to wonder if the back of the drought might not be broken, after all. Bagworms invaded Adrian's catalpa tree while she was running back and forth taking Ernest to Amarillo or warming his chair at the bank.

Adrian had intended to swallow her revulsion and question Bobby obliquely about the brother's whereabouts. She was certain Ernest hadn't told her the whole story. But each time she went to the bank, Bobby was on his way out, and she could think of no way to detain him.

Ernest was gaining in strength but Adrian vetoed a June wedding date, pleading she'd feel ridiculous being a June bride. How Snider would ride her for that!

"What's the hurry, anyway?" she asked him, figuring the bout with his heart had made him obsessed with living every moment.

"We have those tickets to Europe," he said. "We have to wrap this up before the twenty-fourth of July."

"It doesn't have to be a church wedding. We tried that, and sent out all those invitations. I'd feel silly doing it again. We'd be just as married standing up before the Justice of the Peace."

She could see them all now, good Christian women in careful pleats and proper shoes, gawking and simpering behind their hands about what a "lovely bride" she made as she walked down the aisle. No, it would have to be a simpler ceremony, even if she was a first-timer. Few in Attebury would have taken her for a virgin, anyway. There had been too many rumors about her and Snider for years. She suspected he had begun by bragging around the schoolyard years ago.

So a big whoop-la with a bride in white? She'd be the laughing stock of the town.

"We have to have a church wedding," he told her. "People'd be insulted, not to get an invitation this time."

"We can send announcements," she said without much conviction. "Since your heart attack, they would understand."

When he didn't answer, she said, "Anyway, if it is in a church, I'll never walk down the aisle like a lamb going to slaughter. I'll come in like all the others and sit in a pew. When the time comes, I'll take my stand in front of the minister in my ordinary Sunday clothes. I'll do that and nothing more. And afterward, you can have your big reception."

It was reluctantly agreed that the wedding would take place in Ernest's Presbyterian Church but according to Adrian's restrictions. Ernest set the date for July 23, so that they would have ample time to get to Dallas to meet their NetJet the following day. It meant missing the last two weeks of his rehab, but she didn't argue. Truth to tell, she would be relieved to get an infusion of cash for the ranch, which she would do as soon as they were married. She would, after all, have to offer Mobeetie severance pay when she dropped the axe.

Although Ernest planned on Bobby's serving as best man, Adrian harbored the hope that the baby would arrive and Bobby would beg off.

To fend off a hovering apprehension over the approaching event, she ground pride underfoot and struck out one bleating afternoon for the ranch. She was overdue in inspecting the results of the chain-dragging. It was probably foolish to have removed the troublesome brush, even if it did vie with the grass for water, since rangeland dirt was piling up like snow around the fence posts in drifts she hadn't seen in her lifetime. Yet, after almost a decade of drought, the wildflowers were returning. She wondered where the seed came from, after all those years.

Mobeetie must have seen the dust of her car coming up the road. He met her on the front porch and made no move to invite her into the house. His flinty eyes flensed her of her self-possession. Some things never changed.

"I thought I'd drive out to see how the dragging went," she said.

"Well, you seen most of it on your way in. They only done the two front pastures."

"That was a lot of money for just two pastures," she snapped.

She had calculated on raising his ire, yet she had no right to complain. She'd told him in a high-handed way to get it done and not bother her about it. It was too late to quibble now. If only he would cool down and invite her inside. She leaned against the step rail, one boot tentatively on the bottom step. Perspiration formed at her temples. "The new tank ever fill up?"

The tank, still referred to as "new," had been completed in the unfortunate congruence with the worst of the drought, when dust storms were so bad that the cowhands wrapped themselves in wet sheets at night to keep off the dust. She knew very well the tank had not filled, but she couldn't stop herself from goading him. It was his idea, after all, presented to Grandfather during one of his lucid moments.

But he surprised her. "It's about as full as any of the others."

"Is that a fact. Well, I'd like to see that."

"All righty, I'll get one of the boys to carry you out in the pickup."

"You can't see doodly-squat from a pickup, and you know it." She turned and stomped toward the stables, where a young poke was currying the seldom-used horses.

"Saddle Babydoll," she told him. She called over her shoulder to Mobeetie. "See if you can find Nasty to ride down with us. You can ride a little ahead and open the gates, and Nasty can come along behind and close them." She didn't add that tomorrow morning she would be too stiff to move if she had to get off and remount a horse a half-dozen times.

"Whatever you say, *ma'am*."

She could only guess at how much it must gall him to be at her every beck. It gave her a measure of satisfaction to watch him stalk across the yard to the bunkhouse with shoulders held stiff, chin jutting.

Even as she waited for the horse to be saddled, the sun fried the top of her head. She hadn't thought to bring a hat. No use thinking Mobeetie would offer her one. She wondered what possessed her to insist on such a ride in the heat of the day. It was just that sometimes she felt she was losing control of the whole thing, relinquishing her claim to the land by default, by lapses of attention. She stood on the outside of the stable and smiled in at the young hand, feeling like an interloper, as if it were Mobeetie's land, not hers. She must reestablish her territorial right to rule.

The horse was led out, and she mounted with difficulty, grateful that Mobeetie was not around to see the young man help her up. She gave the reins a jerk and headed for the first gate, confident that Mobeetie would mount and overtake her before she reached it.

The snorting, ill-tempered horse was no happier to be out in the heat than the rest of them. She didn't have anything to shade her eyes, and only the perpetual scarf tied like a rag around her head kept the wind from sending shooting pains into her ears. Tears filmed her vision; she'd even left her sun glasses in the car. *Probably just the wind,* she thought, as Mobeetie passed her at an easy trot without flanking her way.

Much of the time she rode alone, listening to the whir of an occasional scissor-tail swallow and the monotonous buzzing song of the cicadae. She held the reins loosely, letting the palomino follow the cow trail, sending grasshoppers flying out of the way with each step. She glanced behind to see Nasty lagging several dozen paces in the rear. He touched his hat in salute. She was so grateful for this crumb of acknowledgment that a sob escaped her throat.

"Damn emotional female," she said, shaking away a tear. She didn't have a clue why the experience was taking such a toll. The horse was jouncing along now on more uneven ground. Her rib cage welcomed the heaving she'd held in check.

As her horse approached the edge of the wilderness, a doorway opened before her. She recognized that her life had entered another liminal space, between what she had been for over three decades, and what she would be in a few weeks. She held her breath and plunged through the doorway into the thicket.

Presently they emerged from the wall of mesquite to the other side of a bare slope, the beginning of the Cedar Brakes, where the land dropped off the Cap Rock from the High Plains. The space ahead felt ethereal. The earth's quiet energy pulsed from the ground. In that moment of surrender, she almost felt the universe shift. From here on it would be steep going. There was no turning back; the door had closed. The world from which she had come no longer existed.

She neglected to gain firm control of her mount before they reached the Brakes. Her stupid horse plunged down each embankment head-first instead of at an angle, so that it was difficult to keep from sliding forward in the saddle. It was also as if he were trying to dump her over his head. She almost went astraddle the fork, gripping it tightly between her thighs to keep from pitching over the pommel. As the dumb beast continued to jounce down head-first, a curious sensation, almost forgotten, shot through her groin. *I am still alive*, she thought with certain wonder. Snider had known that pleasure spot well, back in better days.

The dirt tank, completed so long ago, was about a third full of brackish water. Little actual digging had been done, or could have been done in the rocky terrain. A small gulch had been diverted so that it emptied into the low-lying crevice between two bluffs. The stream bed was completely dry.

She made no attempt to hide her sarcasm. "How much did this cost?"

At first he didn't answer. At length he spat and said, "I reckon you've got the figures somewheres, *ma'am*." If he didn't cut out that mocking *ma'am*, she was going to scream.

"And how many more years do you think it'll take before I see some return on this investment?" Goading. As if he knew. But she had to build a case for dismissing him eventually.

He flicked a grasshopper off his sleeve with great deliberation and said, "Reckon you'll have to ask Madam. Fortune telling's not my department."

Even though she knew his blasé attitude was meant to irritate, she couldn't hold back. "Seems to me you're much more indifferent than when you're trying to get me to sink good money into this ranch."

His voice became caustically polite as Nasty rode up to join them. "Oh, I ain't never indifferent, no matter what the situation, *ma'am*; you ought to know that. I just can't always perform miracles on command. Like, all during this drought I ain't been able to fill this tank for you. You got to wait on the rain, just like common folks do. Lots of things can't be demanded, *ma'am*. They got to be sidled into."

Now she understood. "People who can't perform shouldn't lay their pride on the line." She allowed herself the luxury of a sneer. "If it doesn't rain, the cattle can always quench their thirst at another tank. There are other places to drink, I'm sure you're aware."

As Nasty looked perplexed from one to the other, she reined her horse around and started up the bluff. Once atop the Cap Rock again, she let the palomino out at a full gallop, fanning the hot wind, until she came to the first gate. Fuming, she waited for Nasty to catch up to open it. She refused to admit that she might be waiting to see if Mobeetie would follow.

He made his way back slowly and didn't catch up until they'd passed through the last gate. Then he trotted up, grinning amiably. "I heard about your wedding. Too bad about Ernest Vogel getting sick like that."

Stab and turn, you sonofabitch, she thought.

"Actually, I could use the extra time to get ready for our European honeymoon," she said coolly, dismounting stiffly, hiding her aches. She fled, cursing him all the way back to the car, all the way to town. *Something's wrong with me*, she thought. *I should be over this hate by now.*

The ranch road forked off not far from Madam's place, and on impulse Adrian veered over. Maybe she'd order something special from Madam as her contribution to the reception.

The place was locked up tight, with no sign that Madam had been around recently. Adrian, still chafing at Mobeetie's needling, took it to be an omen.

"Who needs her?" she muttered, roaring away from the little half-dugout. "Why should Ernest scrimp? We ought to have the biggest, finest church wedding this burg has ever seen, and we ought to throw a blow-out that stews the whole town."

She could hardly wait to confront Mobeetie with the *fait accompli* of his dismissal. This time as never before she had felt intimidated on her own land, like a trespasser. Wouldn't he be surprised to learn that nobody is indispensable.

Not knowing why, something that Meister Eckhart had said came to mind: that the more one thing is like another, the more it pursues it.

She was due to spell Bobby at the bank so he could drive to Amarillo to see Inge. They'd have to take her in riding clothes and smelling of horse sweat. She parked at the curb, on the corner of Main and the highway, in front of the bank.

Coming down U.S. 287 was a scraggly family of four. They had the look of illegals trucked in from Mexico. The man, bone-thin and par-boiled, was pushing a rusty garden cart piled with the family's shabby belongings. A squat, gaunt woman and two black-mopped urchins straggled along behind. The smaller tyke, who looked about two, stumbled and began to balk, and the woman hoisted him onto her hip. The father glanced back at the older boy, who was perhaps four. With a look of pity, he set down the cart, picked up the child, and deposited him in the cart. The little fellow perched precariously atop the heap and clung to the handles behind him as the couple proceeded. Adrian had seen dozens in recent months: dregs from the bottom of the migrant labor pool, although usually they traveled in a caravan of beat-up trucks crammed to the maximum. Today, maybe it was a coincidence that she felt a clutching pain at the sight of them. It might be fear, some intuitive alarm, vying with her intent to show Mobeetie, vying for her attention, perhaps, even back at Madam's.

For a moment she was transported to a time long before she was born, when Okies traversed this part of the Panhandle on their way to California. People were as disregarding of their plight then as the townspeople were now. She watched the pitiful little group shamble down the sizzling highway toward some cardboard barrio out on a God-forsaken stretch beyond the wavy cloud of dust, and she ached to warn them that it was futile, that there was nothing better ahead. Fall harvest would be light this year, and besides, it was months away.

They brought to mind Elsie, stumbling expectantly through adolescence toward—what? She recognized a common, mindless stamina they possessed, some strength to drag one foot in front of the other, to keep going one more day.

Maybe it was because none of them could believe that things could get as bad as they were going to get. Or maybe, she thought wryly, they were too dumb to know when they were beaten.

30

The air smelled faintly of geranium. Towering fierce thunderheads studded the tall July sky. Earlier in the month, townspeople had labored in a renewed spate of patriotism, decorating floats, hand-cranking freezers, packing beer and watermelons in ice chests in preparation for the community picnic after the parade and prior to the Fourth of July Rodeo.

Now that the annual festivities were behind them, citizens could settle down to wait out the rest of the sweltering summer. Adrian especially coveted the surcease of the latent wind, which would quicken again in less than two months. It occurred to her that it might be her last summer ever to be part of the traditional celebration. From now on, she would be trapped like Rapunzel in that castle west of town. Already people were beginning to treat her differently.

So it was a time, maybe the last, for savoring the full fruits of summer, for taking an idle hour to loll on the shaded porch glider and suck on a fresh peach, for swatting flies and listening to the clacking of Sael's push mower on the thin Bermuda grass—he was too unreliable to trust with a motorized one—and to the chatter of children who had no better sense than to play hide'n'seek out in the ripened sun.

When Miz Puckett dropped by one afternoon to bring the wash, she held out an enormous sack of apricots. "I was by to see Elsie this morning. She give me these for you."

Marveling at Elsie's way with Snider, Adrian snorted. "Usually, if I'm lucky, I can talk Snider out of a handful." She took the sack into the kitchen and emptied it into a large bowl. "Here, let me divide with you."

"No, no. I got me a sackful too. I couldn't hardly get home with all them apricots."

Adrian could think of several questions she'd like to ask. For a while, according to Mozelle, Snider had refused to allow Miz Puckett visit Elsie.

It liked to have worried the poor woman to death. Now that had changed, but it wasn't like Snider to be so generous. Maybe Elsie had donated the apricots behind his back.

Too, she'd heard the ridiculous rumors that Snider had married Elsie, but she couldn't bring herself to ask. Miz Puckett answered the question as if she read her mind.

"Elsie and I are about to begin canning. She aims to be home to stay soon as it's done—maybe by next weekend."

Adrian didn't like to think about the following weekend, for it would be her wedding day. She put it out of her mind and determined to make the most of the present.

The arrival of the apricots gave her an idea. She picked out half and took them next door to Sarah and invited her to the movies. She could see Sarah's reluctance, so she added, "This may be my last night on the town as a single girl."

Sarah fixed her face in a resolute smile and consented. They left for town right after supper and found perfect seats in the theater, but halfway through the feature Sarah whispered, "I'm sorry, but my head is killing me. It's been bothering me all day. I shouldn't have come."

Sarah wouldn't hear of Adrian's leaving, too, so Adrian fished into her purse for the keys to the Mercedes. "Then take my car. If I can't catch a ride with someone, I'll walk. I think I can make it five blocks without rupturing something."

So she was able, for the last time, to have Kevin Costner to herself. In recent years, Adrian had often had such dreams, more lurid than she cared to admit. At times in her dreams, she confused Costner with Mobeetie, who had the same sensual imperativeness.

She dreamed her way through the movie and drifted out of the Pastime when it was over. She had already vetoed the idea of looking for a ride home, preferring to return to reality gradually during the solitary walk. But as she stepped into the light, she heard a familiar honk. It was the pickup from the ranch. Poke was at the wheel, and Mobeetie was beside him. They wheeled in, barely missing Bobby Vogel's car, parked next to them.

"Hydie, Miss Adrian. Want a lift?" It was Poke who asked. Naturally.

She hesitated, then stepped off the curb, ignoring glances of bystanders. It was, after all, her last weekend single. Mobeetie unfolded and climbed out so she could sit astraddle the gear box, an honor always awarded to women. As she settled between them, she caught the strong odor of beer. Maybe it wasn't smart to entrust her safety to them.

"Been over to Jericho, fellas?" she said, hoping Bobby hadn't seen her.

"Yes ma'am," the cooky said. "We got sick of my chicken fried steak. Got us a craving for some good barbecued ribs."

"And beer." She fanned the air, pretending disapproval.

"So you noticed." Mobeetie nudged her, and it occurred to her that he bore not the slightest resemblance to Kevin Costner. "How come a nice little filly is gadding around on a Saturday night by herself? Don't Ernest Vogel ever take you anywhere?"

"Ernest is still recuperating." She pursed her lips, feeling the irritation building. It never took long. Mobeetie was only surface friendly, and that was induced by Budweiser, and because Poke was there. He was easily the most resistible of men.

Poke wove the five blocks to her house, singing "Violate me in the violet time in the vilest way that you know," although there was a time when Mobeetie wouldn't have allowed his boys to sing a dirty song in her presence. She sat rigidly upright, hoping to God she made it home.

She needn't have worried: once they turned off Main they didn't meet a single car. Poke jerked the pickup to a stop in front of her house, and Mobeetie rolled out with great ceremony and solemnly helped her down. He even escorted her up the walk whistling softly, and it seemed to her that he wasn't as drunk as he first appeared. She could think of no small talk. She opened the door, stepped inside and waited.

Mobeetie leaned against the facing so that she couldn't possibly close it. It was too dark to read his face, and she congratulated herself on her indifference.

"If you want another chance, I could come back later," he said.

She considered this only the briefest of seconds. "I think not, thanks."

She hoped he was offended, but his tone sounded derisive—she couldn't be sure.

"Could be you're afraid to cut loose and be just an ordinary woman."

"Not at all," she lied. "Just indifferent. As you pointed out coming home, I'm a 'nice little filly.' That—other time was just—alcohol."

"Which other time was that?"

Maybe he was thinking of that time down on the ranch, when she was so unsure of herself, when she needed a man's steadiness—or so she thought. He was a fool not to read her mind then. "There was a time, maybe, when I might have offered you a—permanent arrangement. You could have owned that precious ranch if—"

She hadn't meant to say it, but now that the words had escaped, she'd as well be able to flag down the wind as hold them in. "You've never cared for me as a person. I was just your boss's heir. God forbid that the great Mobeetie James could look upon a woman as an equal."

With that she gave the door a hefty shove so that he had to jump to keep from getting hit. Then she wheeled and stalked into the kitchen, hating herself more than she hated him.

Lord, what a fool she could make of herself! She brushed away a tear of frustration.

Why go on? I've lost the fight. And I always end up sweeping up after myself.

The telephone interrupted her dramatics. She felt immediately foolish, chiding herself as she bustled back to the kitchen phone. She snuffed back her tears, ashamed of her histrionics. She was *proving* her own inferiority. She was so much better communicating by e-mail. She could afford to give more of herself and still keep her distance. Too bad her entire relationship with Ernest couldn't be conducted online.

As she anticipated, Ernest was on the phone, with good news. "It's a boy. I've just had a call from Amarillo. We'll name him after Uncle Otto, of course."

She felt relief. So they wouldn't have that hanging over their heads during the wedding, and maybe that meant Bobby wouldn't even attend the ceremony. And surely, by the time she and Ernest returned from Europe, Bobby and Inge would have moved out of the mansion.

For a moment she remembered Bobby's car at the movie a scant thirty minutes earlier and wondered why he wasn't in Amarillo with Inge. She meant to ask about it, but Ernest diverted her. "I've been thinking. I want everyone to see my grandson. We can go ahead with the wedding as planned and have a small reception at the church. Then, by the time we come back from Europe, Inge will be home, and we'll have one tremendous celebration at the house. Invite everyone we know to meet Baby Otto."

So her one and only wedding was to take a back seat to the new baby. "If that's what you want, I'll see to it," she said in what she hoped was an icy tone—as if she really cared a fig.

Her disapproval was lost on him. "Don't bother. I'll have Neva take care of it."

That's how it was to be? Bobby and Inge still hanging around? And she wasn't allowed to plan her own parties; he had Neva for that. What in God's name was left for her to do?

31

On the twentieth day of July, the daybreak, encountering nothing to obstruct it on that everlasting sterile plain, spread across the prairie in one swift flash around five o'clock. The transition from dark to day was so abrupt that Mobeetie, who happened to be looking out the window, witnessed a polecat strike out between the main house and the bunk house, passing so close that sashes banged shut in both buildings. The soft breeze fell rapidly away, and hot wind bit into the day with the determination of a noonday gale. A scissor-tail swallow dove for a grasshopper which had paused in its morning dance, and thus breakfast was taken care of for both parties.

Once the skunk had left the area, Mobeetie stepped onto the porch to assess the day. The wind brought the acrid sweetness of mesquite smoke to his nostrils, as up toward Snider's a faint ribbon of dark gray unraveled into the clear horizon. Mobeetie smiled. Maybe Snider was smoking a side of ribs to take to Adrian as a wedding gift. Or, more likely, he'd forgotten this was her wedding day.

By nine o'clock, the locusts' song had escalated to a raucous shout, and Miz Puckett had put up ten jars of chow chow to the music and shelled a mess of black-eyed peas for supper. By her calculation, Elsie ought to have finished canning the last of the apricot preserves and would be gathering her things to come home. As soon as Sael had eaten his breakfast, she would send him to fetch Elsie in the new van Mister Vogel had given him to use to run errands for him. But Mister Vogel wouldn't mind if Sael made this one extra trip, surely.

Down at the bank, Ernest was giving Neva last-minute instructions about the shipment of a large crate to Switzerland, and instructed her to see that

Sael Puckett picked it up as well as Adrian's baggage and delivered them, along with his own, to the local airport freight office.

The time of the wedding had been scheduled around the closing bank hours, so that Bobby and the other employees could attend. A small reception in the church basement had been hastily arranged with the understanding that once the newlyweds returned from their honeymoon, a large party at the mansion would welcome them home and, more importantly, introduce young Master Otto Vogel to his public. The new mother had begged off attending the wedding, so immediately after performing his duties as best man, Bobby would drive up to Amarillo to bring her and the new baby home as soon as Inge felt well enough to make the trip.

The morning seemed interminable for Adrian, who hadn't slept well. She had an appointment at the hair salon for a last minute once-over of hair and nails, which didn't eat up as much time as she had hoped. After dawdling over lunch and thinking nostalgic drivel about its being her last meal in her girlhood home, she took a protracted bubble bath. Despite her sluggish pace, she was ready at a quarter to three, wearing her new salmon dress and her pearl ear studs. She had nothing for her head that seemed appropriate, and she chided herself for giving so little thought to it until now. It was as if a blank spot invaded her brain whenever she thought about the wedding. Surely she could have picked up something if only she'd thought of it this morning, even. Hurriedly she tacked a scrap of net to a comb and pinned a silk rose over it. It didn't look half bad on someone who never wore anything on her head if she could keep from it.

Her suitcase was packed with the few things she would need for the one night they would spend in the Vogel mansion before they left for the honeymoon. She may have slighted her wedding attire, but she'd made a special trip excursion to Amarillo weeks ago to pick out lingerie and nightwear. She'd be damned if she'd have the local clerks down at Hopping's Dry Goods chipping away about her frivolous choices. The cotton pajamas that had served the year around for as long as she could remember would no longer do. She needed all the help she could get. She had splurged on a brown satin gown and wrapper.

Shortly after Sael Puckett ambled by to pick up her large bag, Adrian turned the key in her front door, loaded her smaller case and her matron of honor, Sarah, into her new Mercedes and took off for the Presbyterian Church.

At precisely four o'clock Irene McNabb struck up a Hayden march—Adrian had vetoed Lohengrin—and Ernest entered from the vestry with Bobby and the minister. Adrian and Sarah, seated on the second row of pews, stepped forward to meet them, and Adrian suddenly wished she'd had the forethought to ask Snider to give her away. It would at least have guaranteed that he would be there, and maybe even sober. She had searched for him when she came in and realized with an ache that he hadn't come, unless he had staggered in late.

She cast a sideways glance at Ernest and felt something akin to fondness. He wasn't bad looking; with the loss of a few pounds, he would be almost handsome. And look at him: fresh haircut—a bit too short, as if it happened ten minutes ago—and all decked out in an Italian silk suit. He tried so hard. *He did this for me*, she thought.

A niggling mouse reminded her: *And he's rich to boot.*

The dry-mouthed ceremony took less than seven minutes and was terminated by Ernest's hurried, arid peck at the corner of her mouth. But had he ever kissed her any other way? *Given the company, it's only proper.* She turned to smile at the assemblage, which, she noted, was everybody in town who could ride, walk, or crawl to get there. Except the Pucketts, of course.

And Mobeetie.

And Snider, whom she missed most of all. An empty spot settled in the pit of her stomach. In all her years, she'd never imagined his not being on hand at the important junctures of her life. *Which had usually been celebrated in bed*, the same mouse reminded.

It had been decided ahead of time that no one would accompany them from the basement reception to the Vogel mansion. Bobby had slipped out as soon as he had made a token appearance to offer a toast to the happy couple. So the new Mr. and Mrs. Vogel accepted the crowd's congratulations, ducked the shower of rice, and rode away in Ernest's Bentley, polished to a fare-thee-well for the occasion by the chauffeur, who was nowhere in evidence.

Ernest, behind the wheel, broke the long moment of awkward silence by clearing his throat. "Sarah taking your Mercedes home?"

"Yes. Yes, she is. Yes." *Shut up, Adrian.*

"You'll need it tomorrow. We'll have to go over and bring it back to my house."

"Our house," she corrected him with some satisfaction.

"What? Oh. Sure." He sped up and whipped into the circular drive at such a speed that she was thrown against the side. He screeched to a halt and leaned across her to open her door. "I'll get your case from the trunk. You'll find your room up the front stairs and to your left."

"*My* room? Or *our* room?"

He squirmed and pulled his bull neck tight into the stiff collar. "Now Adrian, you'll have to think in larger terms from now on. You're now a woman of *real* means—not that you don't have—I mean, you've never lived in a manner as befits your station. But you must begin to think of yourself as more than a bank officer. You must behave like an international heiress."

"Hold it. Back up and begin again with 'bank officer'."

"Why yes. Like Helga was. A member of the team. It's strictly a legal matter. Has nothing to do with how you occupy your days. You won't be needed, unless I'm out of town."

Interesting that he hadn't mentioned this before. Or perhaps he had. Sometimes she didn't hear what Ernest had to say. "All right. I'll think bigger. I'll think of myself as an officer of the bank." It amused her to make him uncomfortable, and she could see the hair follicles on the back of his neck turning red, as if something were about to escape from his very pores.

He swallowed and tried again. "What I'm trying to say is—Helga and I didn't—she had her own sitting room and bedroom, you recall. It's the civilized way to live, the European way. You and I are both accustomed to having to ourselves a whole—entire—"

"Bed," she supplied.

"A whole room to ourselves. Rooms, in fact. I'm a restless sleeper, myself. We're both set in our ways, remember."

She expelled a weary breath. "Don't remind me."

"It would be difficult to readjust now. And people of our station shouldn't have to." As if at once relieved of a burden, he sprang out of the car with a light, carefree step.

Her cheeks stung as if she'd been slapped. Rejected already, and she hadn't even made it to the bedroom. Still, putting her romantic and impetuous notions aside, she admitted, reluctantly, that Ernest made sense. If she were more realistic, which she seemed loath ever to be, she would own up to cherishing her privacy. But the moment called for dramatics.

Hell, she thought, stalking into the foyer, *I may as well have brought my cotton pajamas.*

But maybe not. She did love a good challenge.

She had plenty of time before dinner. Ernest went upstairs to take a nap, and Adrian shooed Precious out of the kitchen. She would put her own touches to the wedding supper that Precious had prepared: ignoring the hospital nutritionist's guidelines, she set aside the salmon steaks and popped a hearty T-bone under the broiler, then stirred up her special peach cobbler with cinnamon and sugar. It was her first real attempt to please Ernest, and her actions also seemed to gratify Precious, who retired beaming to her quarters. Adrian worked with a fever to finish her preparations, then went into the large drawing room to wait for him to come down.

The furniture was still draped in sheets. A musty smell lingered, and she discovered the air conditioner vents in the twelve-foot high ceiling appeared to be closed. The windows were stationary; there was no way to let in fresh air. She made a mental note to get Sael over with a tall ladder to open the vents and to have Precious bring in some fans to air out the place.

She crossed the foyer to the grand dining room and found it ghost-draped as well. So the only rooms on the first floor that were currently in use were the small library at the back of the house, the morning room, and the kitchen. *That's a bachelor for you*, she thought. Well, things would change now. But for tonight, she would be content with serving his wedding supper in the morning room, where the air conditioning was working fine.

His illness had taken its toll; until he sat across from her at the table, she hadn't noticed the gauntness of his neck. He had opted not to dress for dinner and wore a gray knit exercise suit. Apparently he'd been working out while she fixed their wedding supper. Still, he attacked her efforts with relish, and his color seemed to improve as the meal progressed. She didn't want to spoil the mood by saying the wrong thing, so she said almost nothing, and neither did he.

But he was obviously warmed by her small attentions. Or maybe it was the fact that he'd not had a bite of beef since his heart attack, and his routine hospital dessert had been Jello. As he finished his cobbler, he nodded his approval and smacked noisily. "Excellent," he said, patting his midsection. He got up from the table and came around to award her with an awkward tap on the shoulder. "That was some meal."

He toddled off to the library, abandoning her to the meal's remains. She considered ringing for Precious, but on second thought, she wanted to make a good impression on them both. Or perhaps she only wanted to punish herself. She sensed she might be onstage performing a role she didn't realize she knew, reciting her lines perfectly, with what appeared to be feeling. Maybe, in the unseen audience, Snider was sitting in the front row.

She cleaned the kitchen, taking her time, scouring spots that had been around for six months, doing the sort of dirty work she'd been above doing in her own home. Finally she went to the library door and smiled expectantly. Ernest was sprawled in a large leather chair watching an old movie. Good Lord, it was only eight o'clock. He seemed not to notice her.

She crept in and sat on the edge of the sofa, resigned to waiting until the program was over. Then, before another began, she turned to him. "We don't want to overdo on your first big day out, do we? Hadn't you better turn in?"

She didn't miss the fleeting frown or fail to detect a swift surge of rage, which he masked quickly by taking another sip of brandy. He stretched his legs onto the footstool, settling in. "I usually take in 'C.S.I. Miami' before I go to bed."

Well, maybe that was best: she would need time to get ready. She climbed up to her suite, noting its gaudy furnishings indifferently as if it were a hotel room. She'd do something about them in a few weeks. She ran a hot tub and sank in to soak; it was her second bath of the day. Her skin would itch to high heaven when she got out.

She lathered with the scented lemon soap, examining herself as she imagined Ernest would. Was she still lithe and reasonably desirable, or was she becoming as gnarled and weathered as an old fence post? It was hard for her to gauge. In the dark, would he know the difference? Or care?

She got out and dried briskly, then took great pains to lave in lotion from her neck to her toes. She daubed discreet drops of perfume in every fold and brushed her hair one hundred strokes. So much for that salon hairstyle. She slipped into the new brown satin nightgown and satisfied herself in the mirror that the results were good. Her large gray eyes glowed with expectancy, or perhaps dread; her skin was flushed from the excess attention. Smug, she arranged herself on the bed and flicked on the television, waiting for the program to end and fantasizing Mobeetie's remorse at this moment.

Or Snider's. He probably figured she'd never go through with it.

She had enough time to get into the proper frame of mind. By the time the familiar theme signaled the end of "C.S.I. Miami," she had worked herself into such a state that she was convinced that making love to Ernest was the most important goal in her life. Maybe, or so she hoped, sex without love, being always forbidden by her standards, would be so daring, so stimulating, so *hot* that it would stir her to new heights.

Which is why sex with Snider had been so delicious.

She flicked off the television and breathed deeply.

His rooms were across the hall from hers. With a start she heard the toilet flush, and she realized she must have dozed off. She plumped up her pillow and waited. It wouldn't be long now. She moistened her lips, wondering if she should have put on some lip gloss.

She heard the water running: Ernest was taking his shower. Of course. *Rats.* She settled down to wait a bit longer, lulled by the sound of the singing pipes.

When she opened her eyes, the sun was streaming in.

32

Ernest wanted to go to Amarillo early the next morning to see his new grandchild, but to save him the trip, Bobby sent a cell phone video that satisfied his curiosity. He was noncommittal about his new grandson, who was the usual scrawny newborn with wandering eyes that reminded Adrian of Sael Puckett's.

To console the disappointed Ernest, she said, "By the time we get back from Europe, Baby Otto will have plumped up and filled out and will look much more like what you expected."

She had no chance, nor any inclination, to confront Ernest about his conduct the night before. Preferring to be a witless romantic, she hoped his explanation would be that, by the time he finished his bath, he had found her asleep and decided not to disturb her. On the chance that he hadn't come to her room at all, she decided not to risk questioning him.

They ate a hurried breakfast, aware that in two hours Ernest's man would drive them to the local terminal, where they would board their NetJet flight to Switzerland.

On the way to Attebury Municipal Airport, as they passed the shacks fringing the cotton gin, Adrian sat up with a start. On the stoop of a house not fifty feet from the highway, looking directly at their car was—she was certain—Madam. The big woman was wearing the familiar flowing purple tent, making her impossible not to spot. Adrian would know that wild black hair anywhere. Impulsively, realizing that the woman couldn't see her through the tinted glass, Adrian rolled down the window and called, "Madam—"

Ernest caught her hand as she waved. "Adrian! Close that window, for God's sake!"

"But it's Madam. I'm sure of it. You know: who used to live out by the ranch."

His eyes narrowed with contempt. "I didn't know you two were such great buddies."

Adrian felt her cheeks flush. She swallowed. "She's a marvelous continental pastry chef. Recently she moved, and I'd lost track of her." She paused, regained her composure and a certain amount of hauteur. "It takes a woman to understand the importance of maintaining a relationship with a good caterer. You never know when an emergency will arise."

This seemed to mollify him and he returned to his reading.

At the airport, the driver saw to the small bags. Ernest bustled inside to check on the luggage and crate that Sael had picked up earlier, leaving Adrian to climb out of the car by herself. She fluttered along late in his wake. It occurred to her that since the arrival of the baby, he had tuned her out, like muting a television. He hadn't the slightest notion that she was anywhere around.

The NetJet hadn't arrived. Like a snorting bull pawing the ground, Ernest began to kick at the floor. She ought to try to calm him, because his volatility wasn't good for his heart, but a strange lethargy overtook her. The small waiting room was steaming hot, and he stormed back and forth across the narrow wooden boards, stirring up even more heat. Adrian looked for a chair near the ceiling fan and waited for him to settle down. Eventually he found a newspaper on a seat by the open window and flopped down heavily, burying himself behind the paper. She read into his actions an intolerance not just of the delay, but maybe of the whole situation in which he found himself. Or maybe she was just being paranoid.

He regrets it already, she told herself. *I am an outcast again, even in my own marriage.*

A small dark boy with his tin shine box came in from God knew where and grinned expectantly at the man behind the paper. "How 'bout a shine, mister?" he said to the newspaper, but Ernest made no indication that he heard.

"Shine, ma'am?" The boy now stood before her, his wistful eyes wide with hope.

She looked him over. He was a scraggly mite with sweat popping out all over his wooly head. He had probably walked from the shanties a good mile away. His shine box, much too large for such a tot, was filled with scraps and dabs of old polish, discards from some barber shop, no doubt. On impulse, she stuck up her foot. "Why not? Just give 'em a dusting."

This brought Ernest from behind his paper, and he glared at her in shocked disgust. *Mercy, see what I've done*, she thought with satisfaction.

The boy gave her shoes a few licks, and she awarded him with a five dollar bill. "That's enough. Better run along."

The boy skittered out throwing thanks over his shoulder. Adrian continued watching him until he was out of sight, then pretended that she could still see him, so she wouldn't have to meet Ernest's disapproval. The two were left alone in the sultry waiting room with only the barely audible emanations from CNN on the wall-mounted TV and the whirring overhead fan.

Ernest eyed the man behind the counter and moved over to sit beside her, leaning close to her ear so they couldn't be overheard. "What makes you do these things? A lady doesn't have her shoes shined in public like some cheap tart."

She set her teeth and spoke through them. "You are mistaken. I just did."

She batted back moisture of rage and turned her attention to a pair of dirt daubers assiduously constructing a nest on the eave above the open window. Didn't they know someone would only come and knock it down?

She recalled the days immediately following her father's death, when Mother was still trying to come to terms with it, deliberately complaining of her married life as a way to console herself. Adrian listened as her mother tried to remember how long she'd eaten chicken backs and necks, saving the juicy pieces for the man of the house, how long she'd cleaned urine from around the base of the toilet. "That's over now," Mother had said with a sigh, and Adrian wondered if Mother had ever loved Daddy.

Adrian puzzled about what had brought that to mind now. Of course: it was the all-pervading mephitic odor from the adjoining men's room, their trademark. She'd forgotten it so easily. In only two decades.

The NetJet soon landed. The pilot and an attendant appeared with profuse apologies for the delay. Ernest got up and followed them as they checked out the baggage. It wasn't until the attendant threw open the passenger bay and lowered the steps that Ernest seemed to remember Adrian, came to the door and motioned for her and, with sudden courtliness, escorted her to the gangway.

Onboard, the attendant brought coffee and reading material, and Ernest put on his glasses, attending to his *Wall Street Journal* with fierce devotion even before they began to taxi away. Perhaps he felt awkward. Adrian absently leafed through her magazine and watched the countryside glide by as they taxied down the runway.

She studied the rows of cotton plants, could almost make out the stunted leaves. She had learned, slowly, about dry-land farming, learned that it was a losing affair, especially if the wind got up during plowing and blew away good portions of the topsoil. There used to be a windbreak on the ranch until Reagan had all windbreaks torn out on the premise that they used too much water. Now that that insanity was behind them, maybe she'd replant some low-lying arborvitae or juniper along the north and west boundaries of that sandy little farm on the east corner of the ranch—soon as she raked up the cash. It was something she had intended to do ever since she acquired the ranch, something Mobeetie had lobbied Grandfather for. Too bad he'd never know about it. He'd be long gone by the time she got around to it.

"Ernest, what would you think of planting a windbreak on the ranch farm—and maybe later, putting down an irrigation well on that portion?"

He looked up, focusing on something behind her, just over her head. "Whatever you want. I don't plan to interfere with the running of your property."

She returned to staring out the window. It didn't seem a propitious moment to suggest that he help finance the improvements. The plane left the ground, circling low over a cotton gin, where cotton litter stuck in the weeds along the side of the road and even hung from telephone wires year-round. As they passed low over the nearby houses, Adrian saw Madam run out into the street, look up at the plane and gesture excitedly.

"Ernest look!" Adrian said. "It *is* the Madam. She must have seen me in the limo. She seems to be yelling at us." She glanced around and was astonished to find that Ernest hadn't bothered to lower his newspaper.

The plane gained altitude, leaving the retreating shacks a gray blur in the distance.

"Why didn't you look?"

He said blandly, "I didn't see her. Not sure I'd recognize her if I did."

"She was there; I'd know her anywhere. Strange . . . She was motioning at us, I'm certain."

He returned to his reading. "Not likely."

"Funny she'd move off to that dismal little hovel, of all places. If anything, it looks worse than the one she left. Maybe Snider threw her out . . ."

"Probably so. Yes. No doubt about it. Snider threw her out."

Adrian's warning devices were on point. Something was peculiar. She thought about it for a while. Finally she said, "I'm astonished at you."

He looked up over the top of his reading glasses. "Huh?"

"I fully expected you to say, 'Oh no, Snider would never do a thing like that.'"

"Why should I?" He acted it as if he weren't particularly interested.

"Because you've been taking up for Snider for months now, coming to his defense every time I made the least criticism of him. Now, you seem so anxious to get off the subject of Madam that you're willing to agree—"

He scowled, pulling off his glasses one earpiece at a time and polishing them with slow, deliberate circling motions of his forefinger and thumb in his linen handkerchief. His sigh was long and deep; he seemed very weary. "Why must you blow everything out of proportion? I merely agreed that Snider probably turned her out so we might end an inconsequential matter, in the hope that we could drop it so that I could read in peace."

It was the longest speech she'd ever heard him make without drawing a single breath. He replaced his glasses, passing his fingers behind his ears to be sure the shanks were properly in place. Then he gave his paper a snap and retreated behind it.

Oh yes. She'd almost forgotten how important it was not to interrupt their reading. She sank back, seething, and watched the fields below, reaching up to run her fingers through what was left of the hair salon hairdo. She wouldn't forget Madam. When they got back from Europe, she would drive out by the cotton gin, and she would prove to him that she was right.

The stop in Dallas was prolonged: the flight was delayed by some security flap, although it was routine for Ernest to take a NetJet out of Dallas. When she asked him why, he explained, "I'm acting as courier delivering securities for the bank. I have to present my papers to security." His tone warned her not to ask so many questions.

They had a tasteless meal in one of the terminal eateries. There was nothing to do but wait until Ernest and his crate were cleared. Several times he excused himself, taking his cell phone with him. Finally, he returned, too livid to speak coherently. His words were almost strangled.

"We have to go back to Attebury," he barked.

"Whatever for?" she asked.

His face was dangerously red. "Those damned idiots failed to load the crate onboard. It's still sitting at home in the airport."

"Can't they just send it along on another flight?"

"I'm the courier of record. The crate can't go anywhere without me. Don't you understand what courier means?"

"But if we have to do that, we can't possibly—"

Ernest exploded with such fury that heads turned all around the restaurant. "Will you shut up and do as I say? I've already contacted my pilot. We've got to get home before—"

A startled look of shock darkened his eyes at the same moment that he clutched his arm.

"Ernest, are you all right?" She rushed to prop him up. "Is it your heart?"

He lowered himself into a chair and handed her his phone. "Flag down a cart and get me on it. And call for a wheel chair at the gate. If it's my heart, it'll have to wait until we get home."

33

Elsie sat on the bedroom floor watching the whirring mica wings of a bee trapped between the window pane and screen. Its fat hairy body crashed against the glass as it thrashed around in search of the hole through which it had entered. Maybe it was in pain.

The tight little box of a room was steaming hot, but Momma had pulled down the sash because the bugs kept crawling through the hole in the screen. Sweat trickled down Elsie's temples and joined the rivulets of tears along her jaw.

She had been overjoyed to be coming home, had dreamed of nothing else the whole time she was at Snider Greene's. Maybe she had just forgotten how it would be at home. She could stand Mozelle's taunts and Sael's jabs, accepted the cruelty of her daddy. But what kept her in line was Momma's anger. This she took as her due and when it came, it sank to her core. She would retreat into deep self-punishment, feeling the sky, the air, the walls choking off her breath. A swelling anxiety boiled up to meet her black sadness. She became frantic, knowing that she had, by some misbehavior, lost Momma's love. Without it, she could not survive. A frenzied desire to win it back took hold of her, but she was paralyzed to act because she couldn't move past loathing her own worthlessness.

She heard the front screen slam, heard Sael clump into the front room where Momma and Mozelle were watching television.

She heard Momma say, "Well? Did you putten it right back where it belonged?"

"Yes ma'am."

Elsie had never been so torn. She wanted to please Momma always, but she had only taken what belonged to her. She would have explained that, had tried hard to explain, but Momma was too angry to listen.

"I don't know what got into that girl," Momma went on, and Elsie's misery heaved in her breast. Elsie could never talk when Momma got mad, because she always cried too hard.

"You should of tooken a switch to her," Mozelle said, and Elsie could hear her spite.

Momma sighed. "She never taken something that wasn't hers before. I'm not right sure she knew what she was doing, elsen I would of."

Sael opened the bedroom door and stepped inside, closing it carefully behind him. Elsie only glanced at him, then returned to her tearful study of the trapped bee. Sael tiptoed over to her, a nasty grin on his face. He had a few whiskers on his cheeks nowadays, making him look even more hateful. "You know where I been, Elsie Mae?" he whispered, squatting beside her and pinching her thin arm. "Know what I saw?"

Elsie let out a shuddering whimper. She thought her heart was going to break. "Let me alone," she said in a high whine which she hoped would carry into the front room.

"Sael. Leave her be." It was Momma calling.

"I just want to tell her what I saw out at old Snider Greene's place," he said, "out yonder where I putten his salt box."

"Come away and quit tormenting her."

"You're missing 'Fear Factor'." This from Mozelle.

Her brother left her willingly after that, and Elsie turned her attention again to the hapless bee. She felt an overwhelming pity for it and wondered desperately how she could help it find the hole in the screen.

"Elsie Mae?" It was Momma again. "You want to come on in here and watch television?"

Elsie's spirits brightened. The heavy dark weight on her soul began to lift. Maybe Momma was through being mad at her. Maybe she loved her again. She put her head down near her knees and dabbed her face dry on her dress, taking a deep, cleansing breath. Then she jumped to her feet to go and join the others.

But a tap against the window reminded her of the plight of the bee, and she made an important decision, the type of decision she had seldom made before in her whole life. She returned to the window and raised the sash just enough to get her fingers inside so that she could unhook the screen. Then she took the stick used to prop up the sash and wedged it into the space between the sill and the screen, knowing that Momma would be mad all over again if she found out, and then she would have more bad feelings.

But she couldn't help it. There were some things she was just going to have to do, no matter what.

Besides, some people didn't understand things. Maybe nobody understood her, not even Momma. They didn't give her credit for any sense. They talked about her like she wasn't even there, like she couldn't hear what they said.

Anyways, she whispered, *even if Sael did put it back, it's mine.*

And one of these here days, when it had been long enough, she'd go right back out there and get it. And she would keep it with her always.

34

They left Dallas amid rumors of heightened security. Apprehension was rife among passengers and personnel at the airport, but Ernest seemed strangely above it all, as if the whole affair were of no importance to him one way or another. For her part, Adrian couldn't wait to get home, but she worried about Ernest's brief "spell" even though his symptoms had quickly subsided.

She felt some guilt that she couldn't worry more about Ernest's health, or Bobby's taking his family out of the country during a new terrorist threat. Maybe these new warnings would influence Bobby and Inge not to leave. She shuddered at the thought. How could she and Ernest build any kind of marriage with them under the same roof?

Ernest was so agitated about his precious crate that he waved aside all concerns about his chest pain. So much for day two of her honeymoon.

As the plane began the approach into Attebury's airport, she peered out the window, trying to spot Madam's house. She had forgotten that all the little hovels looked the same. But she thought she spied a hand-lettered sign stuck in one yard. Maybe it advertised Madam's services.

"One of these days, after all this flap is over, I'm coming out here to see if I can find Madam," she said. "I'm certain she was signaling us."

"That old fake?" he groused. "You don't want to see her again. Anyway, I've got to get to Zurich. Don't bother me with trifles again."

She turned back to the window, amazed that she was able to control her rage. He wouldn't get away with such dismissive conduct for long, but she wouldn't make a scene here. She was out of the mood for a honeymoon. Let the old toad have his way for now. Let him traipse across the Atlantic alone, for all she cared.

She had a full schedule, anyway: Providing Ernest's chest pain proved inconsequential, there was moving to do, not that she planned to transport every single thing she owned across town to Ernest's place. She couldn't imagine giving up her home completely. And there was business to attend to: overdue taxes, a payment on the ranch note and other ranch expenses. Now that she would have access to Ernest's checking account, she meant to clear away the obligations which had been weighing heavily upon her, due to her own stupid impulses. His condescension was the price she would pay to become solvent again. It was her right, really, her retribution for his patronizing attitude.

By the time they touched down in Attebury, news was out that now both Germany and Spain were under terrorist watches. Bobby, grim-mouthed and jittery, met them at the airport with a copy of the *New York Times*.

Adrian, who had crawled into the back seat, read over Ernest's shoulder. "Well, that settles it," she muttered. "You can forget about going until things cool off." Seeing his jaw line harden, she regretted that it had sounded so much like an order.

He brushed the paper aside, hardly scanning the headlines, as if the whole matter was of no consequence. He motioned to Bobby, who was still standing beside the car. "Take me around back to the lading office and hurry."

"You forget this is Sunday." The younger Vogel made no move to get behind the wheel. Bobby did not take orders well.

Ernest's neck darkened to a dangerous crimson, and he pounded the dash with such vehemence that Adrian jumped. Bobby began a nonchalant slouch toward the driver's seat, but she saw his small-boy fear. Ernest wasn't just angry. She had never seen him in such a state. It was a side of him that was new to her.

"*Scheist*! The whole world is trying to thwart me. Drive by anyway. He might be there."

"Ernest, your heart—"

Bobby threw the car into gear and gunned to the back, stopping with a screech, allowing the flurry of their own dust to settle around them. Off to the west, where the town petered out and gave way to the unforgiving land, she could see intimations of a summer electrical storm.

Bobby looked triumphant when they found the lading office locked tight. Adrian watched the roll of angry red fat on the back of Ernest's neck thrum and thought that maybe they should have changed to a joint checking account before now. He ordered Bobby to take him to Bubba Calhoun's house, wherever it was, punctuating his commands with guttural curses.

"Don't you think you ought to call the doctor first?" Adrian said, but Bobby, having finally filtered the situation through his own sensitivities, interrupted. "You mean that box you packed at the bank a couple of weeks ago?"

Ernest spoke almost under his breath, certainly through clenched teeth. "I need it today. Calhoun must open this office and supply me with new customs papers now."

"I don't know where Bubba lives," Bobby said, returning to his usual recalcitrance.

"Then get us home. I'll look him up in the phone book."

The car spun off in a burst of flying pebbles, flinging Adrian against the back of the seat. She fought for her balance as Bobby whipped onto the highway like a madman.

"Oh for crying out loud! This is insanity!" she said. "Your crate isn't going anywhere tonight. You need to call the doctor."

Ernest twisted in his seat so that he could glare at her, blanketing her with a livid ultimatum. "Now get this straight right now, Adrian: you will refrain from comment of any kind about my affairs, now or ever." He faced the front again and spat out the words over his shoulder like grape seeds, nodding his whole body to emphasize them. "You will benefit as much as anyone from the things I do. Your job is to tend to your own business, run the house and take over at the bank when I'm gone. If you do those simple things—*simple things*, Adrian—without questioning my decisions, you will live out your days in comfort. Do I make myself understood?"

He turned once more, and his gaze bore down on her with frightening intensity. She might have lashed out, fought back, but for the glimpse of Bobby's glittering watchfulness in his rear-view mirror. *He loves this,* she thought, slumping back in resignation to stare out the window, keeping her tight-clenched fists buried in the folds of her skirt.

As soon as Bobby had come to a stop in the portico, Ernest bolted from the car, ignoring Precious' greeting that the president was "fixing to address the nation."

"Hang the president. I've got to find the phone book."

Bobby and Adrian hurried to the library and hovered close to the television to hear about the latest terror alert. Precious lingered timidly just outside the door. Inge was nowhere in sight, but it might be supposed that she waited somewhere upstairs for Bobby to translate to her the meaning of the president's words.

Bobby looked at Adrian and sighed, drawn into the human family by shared anxiety. "I think it'll be safe enough to go to Zurich."

"Oh surely not." Adrian muted the sound and motioned for Precious to leave them. "Anyway, Ernest was having chest pains in Dallas—"

She wasn't prepared for his sudden malevolence. He chortled. It was a dry, chopping sound. "Ah me. You might lose your lover so soon, dear Adrian?"

His caustic tone, full of loathing, startled her. It came to her that she had never faced her detestation of this wayward, spoiled boy. It was a pleasing sensation, this naked hatred; it was invigorating. Still, war is more safely fought when undeclared. She forced a wooden smile.

"Bobby, Bobby, how can you use a word like 'lover' with me? Nobody could take Helga's place with your father, least of all someone like me."

His contemptuous glare traveled her length, but she could tell he was mollified. "That's obvious, dear Adrian." He stalked out, and she heard him taking the back stairs two at a time.

It was just as well that Bobby would soon be gone. Otherwise, she might slit his throat.

She heard the thud overhead, a heavy crash, like a body dropping. "Ernest!" she screamed, racing up the front stairs toward Ernest's apartment. "Bobby! Come quick! Oh, my God." *Not now, Lord. Not yet.*

Ernest lay in a mound on the floor, the telephone receiver still in his hand.

35

Once a grey-faced Ernest was safely inside the EMS vehicle, his weak voice summoned Adrian. He was on the edge of unconsciousness. "Adrian. My crate—"

She went to the door to soothe him. "I'll see to it. Just rest." As he raised a hand and fought to protest before he dropped off, she felt a smug satisfaction that his plans had been thwarted.

She was much too exhausted from the long flight home to accompany the ambulance to Amarillo, and for once Bobby seemed willing to take on the chore without a fuss. He seemed genuinely concerned about his father's condition. As soon as they were gone, she shuffled to her rooms, refusing Precious' offer to send up a tray. She fell across the bed without undressing and slept all night without giving Ernest's condition another thought.

The next morning, after talking to the charge nurse on Ernest's station and being told that he would be undergoing another catheterization, she took his car out to the lading office. But the laconic Bubba Calhoun ignored her as she walked into the office. He pushed back the green shade on his narrow head and bent lower over his desk several feet behind the counter.

"Didn't you hear me come in?" she said finally, knowing good and well that he did. "My husband sent me for the crate he called you about."

Calhoun squinted up at his computer screen as if in deep concentration. Adrian was not used to this kind of service. Sullenly, reluctantly, he looked up, his frown of irritation warning her of her intrusion into man's territory. "That box has been nothing but a pain in the butt to me. It wasn't even sealed good and it didn't have proper documentation. I had to get Neva Craig to locate a copy of the customs papers. Then yesterday I got your husband's phone call chewing me out. I don't have to take abuse like that, even from a big shot like Ernest Vogel."

Now she understood. "I'm so sorry. Ernest can be cross when he isn't feeling well. He was ill when he called—he had a heart attack a few minutes later."

Calhoun appeared to be grudgingly appeased, but he added, "I even had to go over to the hardware store and get some straps to hold the thing together, or it would of got about as far as Lelia Lake before it come apart."

"You'll be compensated for your trouble," she said, fighting the outright relish she heard creeping into her voice.

"Well, anyway, I can't give it to you. It can't be released to anyone but the courier."

As she drove toward town, she tried to summon Ernest's face, to conjure up his pompous exasperation when he found out that his crate was being held prisoner. Once again he would suffer because of his own compulsiveness.

She stopped in at the bank, which was almost empty, except for Neva at her desk. Adrian asked her to add her name to Ernest's household account, but she was disappointed to learn there was less than a thousand dollars in it. She had hoped to clear out some bills right away, to ease the building tension over her temporary insolvency. And she would have to refrain from calling to Ernest's attention the need for a cash transfusion until he felt better.

At that moment Bobby appeared in the doorway. Adrian concealed her consternation, simply because he seemed to be studying her, looking for a sign of it, perhaps hoping for it. "No matter," she said lightly. "I'll tend to things from my own account for a while."

Bobby grinned as he stepped aside to allow her to pass. "I noticed yours is a little undernourished."

She was infuriated to think that he had been prying, although in his position, it would have been difficult not to know her financial situation. She lied. "I have other accounts, of course. Larger ones in Amarillo. I'll just handle things from there."

Her creditors wouldn't mind waiting. The Vogels were good for any amount. And the mood of the town, now that the initial scare had subsided, was one of optimism, although the heightened terror alert precipitated a spate of panic-buying in Attebury. Rumor had already spread that there might be food shortages due to hold-ups within the shipping industry. Infected by the scare talk of people in the bank, Adrian went back home to take a careful inventory, with Precious, of her new pantry. Maybe she should lay in some bottled water; their supply was dangerously low. Ernest's enormous kitchen had been too long neglected. There was little of anything, except frozen pizza—Bobby's favorite—and yoghurt—Inge's. She would put in a word with Mobeetie for a side of beef. Maybe, under the circumstances, she'd offer to share a steak or two with Snider.

There was no answer when she phoned her cousin, and she suspected he was behind on his bills again and was hiding out. She supposed, now that she was married to Ernest, the whole town would come to her, expecting her to pay Snider's debts, which she might do in a weak moment, just to save the family pride. And to make him beholden to her again.

It occurred to her that his drinking must be getting worse. Her suspicions were heightened when, at the grocery store, Clabber Watson stopped bagging her purchases to tell her, "I'm worried about Snider not eating. Used to, he'd run up a big bill every single month, but that Madam person that buys his groceries hasn't been around in several weeks. I reckon that package store in Jericho gets all his money now."

In self-defense, Adrian drew up and glared. "Have you ever considered for a moment that he may have decided to take his business to Piggly Wiggly?"

Clabber shrugged. "Hardly likely. Jim Hurley at Piggly Wiggly doesn't give credit."

She wasn't through. "No? Well just maybe Jim Hurley knows how to mind his own business. Maybe Snider prefers to pay cash for that." And she flounced out, leaving the flustered grocer still bagging her groceries.

She was tired of living in a vestibule, having left her old life behind but not yet having begun her new one.

Surely, once Ernest was well and Bobby and Inge were gone, she and Ernest could begin to develop some degree of intimacy. There was no denying the desolation left by Snider's dismissal—or had she cut him off? Did they both know, that afternoon after Grandfather's funeral, it was the end of way of life that had satisfied both their hungers for years?

Now, it wasn't the younger Vogels' presence she found intimidating. Precious had again assured her that they were seldom around for meals; Inge and the new nurse Gretchen ate in her rooms, and since the arrival of Baby Otto, Bobby often ate out. It was just that, with them in the house, she couldn't imagine lying in Ernest's arms.

After lunch she finally got up the nerve to phone Amarillo, dreading having to tell Ernest that the crate would have to remain where it was until he could see to it. But to her relief, the private-duty nurse informed her that he was sleeping and that he was scheduled for a quadruple by-pass early the next morning.

"Then please don't disturb him," Adrian said hastily. "Just tell him when he wakes that he can rest easy: everything is taken care of. He'll understand my message." When she hung up, she rationalized that there was no reason to drive up to Amarillo that day. He needed his rest, and since she would have to spend the next day in the hospital waiting room, she could use the afternoon to get the mansion in order.

The house was a dismal mess. Precious explained that Mr. Vogel had let the other servants go a while back. It was just as well. Adrian would feel more comfortable with the Pucketts than with a corps of strangers. The prospect of satisfying her curiosity about the welfare of Elsie would have been enough in itself. Since the Pucketts still didn't have a phone, Adrian headed out later that afternoon to speak with Miz Puckett.

She met Elsie on the way, stumbling up the dirt street in the opposite direction. The child had put some flesh on her bones, Adrian noted with satisfaction, although she was still more shoulder blades and hip bones than padding. Even in her moments of sharpest dread, Elsie had invariably worn a light of sweet innocence about her eyes, but when Adrian got closer, she could see that now her face was wooden. She stared blankly ahead, as if a shield blocked her vision.

She is taking on the look of poverty, Adrian thought in alarm as she slowed the car and rolled down the window. "Elsie! Want a ride?"

The girl, stooped as ever, scratched the toe of her hand-me-down oxford in the dirt then shook her scraggly head. "Going out to Mister Greene's to feed the chickens."

It was none of her business, but she asked, "Does he pay you well?"

Elsie squirmed and looked confused. "I don't think I get paid."

Just like her chintzy cousin, conscripting the poor child into free labor. When he was into one of his drinking bouts, he was even more devious than usual. During some past binges, he'd let the chickens die. Sometimes he let them freeze to death. It was probably easy enough to talk Elsie into caring for them. She seemed to have an affinity for the creatures, anyway. God only knew she had little social exchange outside her family, pitiful waif, finally budding into reluctant womanhood, and not a soul to share her secrets. Adrian knew. She swallowed and looked in her purse for a few bills, thinking that she mustn't put Elsie in Baby Sister's place.

"Come here, child." She put the money in the girl's thin palm.

"When you see Snider Greene, tell him Miss Adrian plans to bring him some steaks. Can you remember that?"

Elsie's pinched little face screwed up in concentration. Adrian could see that she had given the child more to cope with than she could handle. The weight of the extra burden seemed to make her sink lower into herself.

"Oh never mind. But Elsie—that money is for *you*, not for Mister Greene, understand? Put it in your pocket."

Elsie stared at the bills in her hand as if they were alien before finally following instructions and tucking them in her jeans. "But the skating rink's done left," she said.

Adrian tried not to be impatient. Why she ever fooled with the child escaped her. She put the car in gear and started off again, glancing in the rear mirror as Elsie scuffed on down the street. Then she saw three young boys jump from the bushes and surround Elsie, taunting her, yelling insults. Miraculously, the girl continued her shuffling pace, head down as if she were being whipped.

What courage it takes to keep plodding on, Adrian thought. She swallowed hard and batted back a surprising tear.

One day soon she would run out to see Snider. There was no reason to avoid one another, just because their relationship had changed. Events on the national scene could not measurably affect their lives in Attebury. The football team was shaping up better than any they'd had in a decade. The cotton crop was looking good, if rain would just hold off until after harvest.

The *Attebury Advocate* had announced that school would be dismissed the second and third weeks in October for cotton-picking. Adrian would tell Miz Puckett this would be the ideal time to schedule the party, for—providing Ernest survived his surgery—he would surely feel up to it by then, and he would still insist on returning to Switzerland as soon as the doctor allowed. Bobby and Inge ought to be able to be ready to move if she announced the party now.

Yes, cotton-picking put people in a festive mood. Maybe they harked back to their Druid ancestors, as she did in the fall. In a frenzy of expectation, she hurried on to the Pucketts' house.

She thought no more about Snider Greene, and apparently neither did anybody else, until the skating rink returned to town.

36

The Man, that migratory Lord of the Plains, was back in town.

Even though no one had forgotten his previous year's assault upon Elsie Puckett, there was never any question of legal accountability. Adrian heard the same excuse time and again: Elsie was, after all, a half-wit who probably brought it on herself, surviving, as she must, by her animal instincts. People figured her conduct probably incited the natural urges which could be anticipated of a man of Calvin's healthy young appetites.

After what happened, nobody had the heart to consider further punishment.

Calvin Huddle was no longer the dashing stud who'd quickened the pulses of female skaters and a few old watchers as well. His skating was as spectacular as ever—if anything, even better. But Calvin was a prize to look at no more. Word spread quickly that his nose really had been severed halfway up, and the remaining nub had scarred over so that it looked like an angry rosette planted between his eyes. Those who'd seen him first hurried to the Dairy Queen to describe it to others. They claimed the red blob seemed to draw his eyes closer together so that he looked like a simpleton.

A very enraged simpleton.

Calvin sped around the rink with a defiant and raging glower which dared anybody to look him square in the face, so nobody ever did—not while he was watching. After Adrian heard the description repeated several times, she had driven by to take a look, secretly hoping that whatever damage Elsie did to him was permanent.

She was surprised, considering the pains Snider had taken the year before to protect Elsie from Calvin, that he didn't now insist that she move back into his home until the skating rink left town. But Miz Puckett assured her that as soon as Elsie had fed Snider's chickens each morning, she would be free to come over to the Vogel mansion to help get the house ready for the long-postponed farewell party for Bobby and Inge.

"Just so she's through in time to go up of an evening and lock up Snider Greene's chickens," Miz Puckett said.

Adrian made an instant decision. "Tell you what: let Elsie stay over in one of our spare bedrooms till the skating rink leaves town, and I'll drive her out to tend the chickens." It would offer Adrian an excellent excuse to try to mend fences with her cousin.

Miz Puckett agreed with obvious relief, and Elsie reported to work the following morning toting a paper sack containing her pajamas and a few clothes.

Adrian was particularly glad she'd made the decision after her trip to the grocer's that afternoon, for Clabber Watson had some alarming news. "You know that skating rink fellow with the funny nose? He was by here today, asking after Snider. Funniest looking guy I ever did see. Put me in mind of a clown whose red nose had popped. Wanted to know if Snider Greene still lived out on the hill. Claimed Snider owes him some money. Now ain't that a news flash? I told him to get in line."

Adrian was not amused. She straightened her spine and lifted her chin, feeling herself importuned on every side with regard to Snider. "Has it ever occurred to you," she said coldly, "that I might get tired of you always throwing my cousin up to me? What do you talk about to your other customers? The weather? Or do you wash our family linen with them too?"

She left the store feeling a measure of satisfaction for having spoken her mind for once. So Snider owed Calvin money. She wondered whatever for. Well, Calvin was learning how hard it was to collect; that ought to divert his attention from Elsie for a while.

Still, there was Snider's safety to consider. He was so helpless when he was drunk.

Adrian seemed to find more and more reasons to stomp out mad from Clabber Watson's grocery store. The Vogel bill now rivaled Snider's, and until Ernest got well enough to transfuse their account, she was powerless to pay. Bobby would probably help if she'd stoop to ask, but Bobby never showed his face in her presence if he could keep from it. He even avoided seeing her when she came into the bank, and the only time he visited his father was when she was gone.

She found many excuses to be away, and so she welcomed taking Elsie out to Snider's to tend the chickens. She rather hoped it was an unnecessary precaution, but on the very first trip, she was to be vindicated for her fears.

No sooner had they pulled up in front of Snider's place that morning than she spotted Calvin Huddle heading up the hill on foot.

While he was still a long way off, she pushed Elsie out of the car and dashed out behind her. "If we're going to get this done, we've got to work fast. Looks like the Man from the rink's headed this way."

The wonder was that Elsie seemed to grasp their predicament at once. She scurried around back to unlatch the chicken house, then ran to the feed bin and brought out a bucket of grain which she thrust upon Adrian. "I'll fill up the water trough while you spread the feed," she said with surprising authority.

Adrian emptied the bucket with one great sweep among the squawking birds and slung the bucket back into the bin. She looked up at the house. The old goat was probably cowering inside, hung over, tickled pink to see his uppity cousin out doing his barn work. Maybe she ought to warn him the Man was coming. No, it'd serve him right if the Man took out what he was owed in hide. At once she recognized her old turncoat pattern.

"Hurry up, Elsie," she called, and she ran around front to see that Huddle had now progressed halfway up the hill. "Come on right now, unless you want to meet him head-on."

Elsie seemed to waver a moment before she came running. It occurred to Adrian that the girl might still entertain ambiguous urgings; might even consider her drubbing by Calvin only her due; might still, God forbid, be enamored of him. Adrian snatched Elsie by the arm and shoved her into the car.

"We'll take the roundabout way home to keep from running into him," she said, heading out south toward Madam's old place.

Elsie clutched the dashboard with pearl-knuckled hands, and her words were ejected in little paroxysms of terror. "We ain't going to stop, are we?"

Adrian reached over and patted the small trembling shoulder. "At Madam's? No, don't worry; we won't stop. She's moved on, anyhow, didn't you know? You won't ever have to see Madam again. Or Calvin Huddle, either." She added the last as a direct order.

"Or Snider Greene neither," Elsie said firmly.

Puzzled, but not surprised, since sooner or later Snider antagonized even the most insensitive, Adrian said, "No, not if you don't want to."

She drove along in silence for a while, picking at the various corners of the girl's fears. Presently she came to a firm decision. "Elsie, I don't want you coming out here alone ever again, hear? I'm going to call Snider and tell him he'll have to care for his own chickens from now on."

The knuckles relaxed and the hands fell into Elsie's lap, where they twisted her shirt tail into a wad. Adrian wished she could read the child's mind.

Finally Elsie said, "Will the chickens be fine?"

"They'll be fine," Adrian said, smiling to herself at the girl's simple concerns.

But of course, Elsie had so few friends. She would miss caring for the fowls. Yes, that was why she was twisting her shirt: she wanted permission to keep coming but was afraid to ask. Well, she'd just have to wait until Calvin Huddle left town.

PART II

Skewed Justice

37

But for a freak accident, Adrian would have found the body sooner. She often thought that, in light of all that followed, justice might have been better served if she had, providing the shock didn't kill her.

Ernest's hospital recovery had been complicated by the onset of a chest cold, so that it was the second week in October before the doctor eliminated the sedatives and gave him cautious permission to sit up.

Adrian made the short drive to Amarillo that afternoon and was immediately called into his presence, into a room thick with the hovering ghosts of Vicks Vaporub, to face a pasty and docile version of the old Ernest.

He lifted his puffy eyes to hers. "It's a haze, that day we got back. I was going over to see about the crate. I didn't make it, did I?"

She answered with caution and a swift, meager smile. "No, no you didn't. The crate's still at the airport. But it's just as well, what with the terrorist threats."

He lay back against the pillows; remorse seemed to have shriveled him. "I was hoping that was a dream. God, what a mess!"

"Not really. Bubba Calhoun has it in his office. There's no problem."

One thing at a time. Get Ernest back on his feet so he could do something about the mounting bills. There would be time enough later to figure out how to keep him from kiting off to Zurich again. Why couldn't Bobby see to this, anyway?

"I need to get that crate out, but I can't seem to do anything but sleep," he grumbled.

She made the unnatural gesture of patting his shoulder. "That's what the doctor intends, to keep you from fretting over things you can't do anything about."

She would be forced to dip into her own resources a while longer. In a few weeks the crop on the ranch farm would be in and she would be solvent again. Otherwise, the only expedient was cashing in some of her grain elevator shares, for which she would need Snider's signature. She decided to pay him a visit early the next morning, when she was sure to catch him before he had a chance to get soused, escaping into his private delusions of eminence.

That is how she happened to be out early enough to meet the Man, Calvin Huddle, running toward town from Snider's place. She savored her satisfaction at the grotesqueness Elsie had wrought on his face. So he, too, had learned the wisdom of catching Snider early in the day. She wondered if he had collected from Snider. Probably not.

She parked in front of the house and was overcome with melancholy as she heard the wind rise, as if it had been waiting for her. It was always windy on the hill, and the sound ground away, beating her down. She had defied it with the sheer optimism of childhood, her innate capacity for joy butting the wind's depressive ravagement, feeling even back then that in the very dichotomy she was standing on the rim of some truth. As if the rim were a liminal space. Now the elusive inconsistence slithered away again.

If this place—or Snider—was so detestable, why did she miss it, or him, so much?

Except for a time in adolescence, when they'd lollopped around the barnyard learning the forbidden art of dancing, they'd been natural enemies: she the pampered and pretty one and he the scurfy scamp on perennial report. Later he nurtured open envy of the success she enjoyed, yet none of his envy vanished when she came home to sacrifice her life caring for her dying mother. When the townspeople began to look to her to straighten out the messes his drinking caused, his resentment pyramided, as did her own.

Now she must ask him to help her and endure his gloating when he learned she needed money. If she could think of another way, she wouldn't give him the satisfaction. Maybe the time had come to be charitable, though, to make peace, admit that she hadn't always despised him; give him that crumb, at least. But no, he would only sneer and gloat that she had saddled herself to a man who was turning out to be an invalid.

So she would continue to wear her despite for Snider; it might be her talisman. They both fed on it in some measure. She stepped out of the car, still tied in her own resentment, and forgot to put it in gear.

She reached the porch before she remembered—too late—and turned to see her car moving.

She chased down the walk and out the gate, calling to the Mercedes as if she could persuade it to stop, but the car was rolling now, picking up momentum as the road gave way down the hill. She cursed her thin-soled shoes as she stumbled on the gravel, all the while watching the car move farther ahead. In the beginning it kept to the well-defined ruts which prevented it from veering off into the gully, but ahead the road curved at the bottom of the hill, and she knew it would not make the turn.

Then with dismay she saw that Calvin, still sprinting down the long hill, was directly in the path of the silent runaway car.

"Look out!" she screamed, and she could almost see her cry carried on the wind, for he turned just in time to jump out of the way.

As the car shot past him, he grabbed the door handle and clung there until he managed to dive inside and grab brake. The car wobbled and jerked to a stop just short of the ditch.

Gasping, Adrian sank by the road and held her side, which streaked with the pain of exertion. She watched Huddle take command of the car and back it up the hill toward her. He pulled alongside and got out, averting his disfigured face. She was still bent over in pain.

"Thank you. I thought you'd be hit."

He helped her stand, guiding her around to the passenger side and handing her in. "I'll take you home," he said.

She started to demur, to go back to Snider's, but her ankle hurt. She had twisted it, hadn't noticed at first because of the stitch in her side. Maybe she wasn't meant to have to see her cousin. Maybe there was another way to get cash without having to ask him to co-sign the elevator shares. Meantime, because she'd felt uneasy about Snider after she saw Calvin leaving his place, she'd ask Sael to come up and check on him after work.

"Take me to the bank," she told Huddle, dismissing for the moment how much she despised him for what he did to Elsie.

The Man drove her to town and parked at the bank. She thanked him again, limped inside and headed for Ernest's office. His secretary was used to her visits by now and followed her. "Looks like you hurt yourself," she said in a tone which in no way indicated that she was sorry.

"So it seems," Adrian said shortly. "Bring me my account records, please, and call my house and leave a message for the yard boy. He ought to be there by now cutting the grass. Tell him when he gets through, to stop by here and see me." She enjoyed ordering the young woman around;

thought that perhaps it might not have been a bad life to have been a businesswoman of some sort. Maybe it wasn't too late. Maybe she should have her own office permanently.

She had neglected seeing to her own assets and liabilities much too long. An examination of her records showed that she owed a staggering amount, what with mortgage payments on the well, the balance for chain-dragging on the ranch, a sizeable note on the ranch and an outstanding feed bill. She ought to have more to cover the debts. She went over the figures again, sure she had missed something. She spent the entire morning at it.

There was no way around it: she would have to ask Snider to co-sign the shares.

At mid-afternoon Neva Craig came in without knocking, looking around proprietarily. Behind her was Flop Pyle, the deputy sheriff, who didn't do much except arrest drunks, marry indigents and even grant a few divorces. He took off his straw Stetson.

"Hydie, Miss Adrian. Have you been out at Snider's lately?"

Now what, she thought. "I was there today, but I didn't see him. I had a runaway car. Sprained my ankle, chasing it down the hill. If it hadn't been for the Man from the rink—"

"Beg pardon?"

"The Man, you know. With the nose. He happened to be going down the hill and caught the car for me. What's the matter, anyway?"

"Nothing, probably. Thing is, nobody's seen Snider lately, and this here Man keeps hounding me about some money Snider owes him. I went out there day before yesterday, but wasn't nobody home. I got to thinking . . . well, you know how Snider drinks. He might of fallen and knocked hisself out or something."

At this, she felt a stab of real alarm. She should have checked on him earlier.

And that is how she came to be out at Snider's at dusk and how she stumbled onto the nightmarish sight of the corpse, gutted and drained and rendered, smoked to a perfect turn, hanging in the smoke house. Just like that. Gone. No warning.

Or had there been?

She was obliged to sit down on the back steps and put her head on her knees before she could make it back to the car. She tried to jab in some numbers on her cell phone, but she was too incoherent to make herself understood to the 911 dispatcher. She kept calling as she shakily drove home, finally phoning Sarah and asking her to call the sheriff. She asked

Sarah to spend the night with her. Without a second thought, Adrian had returned to her own home, not the Vogel mansion.

She clutched her neighbor all night, shivering and crying out in her restless sleep. Each time she woke, the corpse danced before her closed eyelids, and she knew she would never waken again without that gruesome image before her. It could not be Snider, please God, not Snider.

Flop Pyle came around the next morning to get her statement and to report that, out of courtesy to her, he had asked Mobeetie to come in and identify the remains. She started to protest but quickly realized that if the body were not Snider's, then Snider must have put it there, and she preferred to believe anything but that. Besides, Flop had already solved the case to the satisfaction of everyone by taking into custody the Man from the rink, whom just about everyone had heard threaten Snider. And still she kept praying, *It can't be Snider, please God, not Snider.*

Word of the tragedy had engorged the town, and everybody who could get there had gone out to view the scene, so that Flop was obliged to deputize a few of the ranch hands to stand guard over the property. Adrian, who remained in shock for the next two days, refused to see anyone but Sarah and continued her ceaseless prayers: *Please, no.* But remembering Daddy and the gun and Baby Sister and even Mother, she knew prayers were useless.

Snider, she said over and over, *what have you done? What have I done to you?*

Even after Mobeetie came and forced his way in to her bedside and held her hand and told her point-blank that Snider was dead, she continued to say it, as if Snider might answer her, might forgive her for a lifetime of condescension.

Eventually, of course, she came to hate him for leaving her. He had won, at last, for he had beaten her to the grave. And only then did she realize that she couldn't live without him.

38

A prodigious number of Snider's former detractors turned out for the funeral, which, despite Adrian's best efforts, took on the atmosphere of a carnival. Adrian rallied somehow and drove herself to take charge of arrangements, considering it a sort of penance she owed Snider. She wished to her soul that Rathjen's Funeral Home had facilities for a quiet cremation; the remains were hardly more than ashes anyway. As it was, she could scarcely believe the morbid curiosity of several, including the mortician, who expressed disappointment that the coffin wouldn't be open for viewing. They were ghouls. They seemed to have forgotten that the coroner's autopsy had destroyed what the smoking had not. How Snider would have enjoyed the irony. She had not felt so close to him since they were children.

Ernest, who had been dismissed from the hospital but was still confined to bed because of the lingering cold, pleaded doctor's orders and stayed away. But Bobby dutifully sat with Adrian in the family section, as did her neighbor Sarah and even Mobeetie.

On other occasions, she could now admit, she'd pitied Snider, but never more than now, for she had won: she had outlived him. He couldn't win against her, she could almost hear him say, even though she wished it otherwise. She now understood the injustice he'd always felt. At this point, feeling some empathy, allowing herself to admit to having feelings for him, she found that she would rather believe him dead than a murderer. For if by some monumental error of the coroner's office that wasn't Snider in the coffin, then he must have put the murdered man there.

"He was a good man," Sarah said righteously, echoing what Adrian had heard a dozen times by others who had no use for him before.

The funeral had been delayed until the coroner could establish the probable cause of death: apparently a blow to the head. Although, with so much of him missing, it was hard to tell. A more definitive verdict would be delivered once samples were analyzed by the crime lab in Amarillo—but they were months behind. It was the work of a vicious butcher, all agreed. And that butcher was obviously the Man.

Since Snider had been a Mason, albeit a poor one, he was accorded the honor of a full Mason funeral, just as Grandfather had. The local chapter provided six pall bearers dressed in those little white aprons that had afforded Vivian and Snider so much mirth at Grandfather's service. Another apron draped the coffin.

Following a ridiculously effusive eulogy by the Methodist preacher, the congregants trooped up to the bleak, wind-swept cemetery where the Masons did the burial honors. At the end they sprinkled sand on the coffin and recited a passage that promised everlasting life to Snider Greene. The idea of his hovering forever nearby, plaguing her in death as he had in life, was enough to jerk her from her momentary sentimental fantasies about his good qualities.

As the first spadeful of caliche rattled onto the coffin lid, people began to turn away. Bobby, acting as her escort, pulled at her arm, but she remained stolidly until the hole was filled.

Following the graveside services, Adrian and the others went back to Snider's house, where a party was already in progress. People had been bringing food for two days, and now the city of Attebury showed up for the feast they had prepared for themselves. With a set jaw, Adrian waded through, greeting them.

Earlier in the week she had brought Mozelle and Sael out to clean up the place, to make it presentable for callers who came to pay their respects. Mozelle had been reluctant, protesting that Sael could do it without her. But Adrian had no desire to be alone under such gruesome circumstances with the unpredictable boy. And she didn't have the heart to ask Elsie to come.

As soon as she and Bobby arrived, she stationed him in the front hall to great the callers, and she set Mozelle to work carving ham and serving the guests. Mobeetie and the boys seemed to have disappeared. She was startled, when she retreated to the kitchen to wash dishes, to find Elsie and Miz Puckett already hard at work. She felt a warm surge of gratitude.

"We come to help," the woman said. "Mister Greene was such a fine man."

Elsie stood on tiptoe looking out the window toward the chicken yard where, Adrian saw with dismay, the dead birds were still lying about. The

girl sucked in her breath and pointed. "Oh, I should of fed them." She ran
out the back screen, and Miz Puckett only clucked and shook her head.

Adrian watched as Elsie scampered from one bird to another, bending
to pet a dead fowl, crooning over corpses. Then she went into the chicken
house and came out with a few grains of feed, which she tried to force down
the gullet of an obviously dead bird. Revolted, Adrian nonetheless felt the
child's grief, felt the first tears of the day course down her cheeks. She
turned to Miz Puckett, removing the woman's apron and telling her, "Take
the child home. I can't stand to see her suffer another disappointment."

Elsie's conduct with the chickens provided an early kernel of doubt of
Elsie's ignorance concerning what had happened to Snider. Had she known
that if she stopped feeding the chickens they would surely die, perhaps
because someone had already killed Snider? Because of the condition of the
corpse, the local coroner had been unable to determine the time of death.
He might've been dead for several days, for all anyone knew. Anybody,
except possibly Elsie, who could have seen something. And of course, the
Man, who had been taken into custody once he was found to have Snider's
Masonic key ring in his possession.

But if Elsie had seen anything, it was probably already buried deep in
her muddled brain, and Adrian hoped nobody thought to question the
child and cause her renewed trauma. Much as she wanted to know every
fact, she couldn't bear to wound Elsie.

Still, there was a nagging suspicion, and it was reinforced later in the
afternoon, as Mozelle stood over Snider's sink doing up the last of the
dishes while Adrian dried and put them away. She opened the cupboard,
noting with approval the clarity and color of the apricots Elsie and Miz
Puckett had put up back in the summer. *Row upon row of perfectly beautiful
preserves.*

The import of what she saw didn't strike her full-on.

She had almost forgotten about Sael, whom she'd sent to dispose of the
fowl carcasses. She called through the screen for him to finish quickly so
they could leave. Her limbs trembled with the effort of remaining in this
house.

Bobby had remained faithfully at the front door all afternoon. The last
of the callers had been gone for some time, yet Bobby had not joined them
in the kitchen. Adrian went to investigate. She found him in the study,
sitting at Grandfather's desk. He started when she entered, and she was
sure a guilty flush spread over his face. She looked at the tumble of papers.
It looked just as it always did.

"Are you going through Snider's papers?" She regretted saying it immediately, regretted sounding so shrewish. But he didn't appear angry.

"Are you nuts? What could that old sot have that would possibly interest me?"

Her proprietary feeling about Snider had become irrational, and she seemed unable to keep from lashing out. "Then what are you doing here?"

Bobby, the perennial storm center, slapped the arm of the chair and leaped up as though he might tear into her. She felt his malevolence with a startling clarity, felt she had played into a trap he'd set. *He'd like to throttle me,* she thought.

"I was resting, you got that? Resting. And now I'm going home. If you and those two dunderheads don't want to spend the night here, you'd better hitch up your girdles and come on."

He stalked out into the hall and bellowed for the others. Adrian took another look around the desk. Bobby Vogel didn't fool her for a minute.

39

Although it still consumed Adrian's every waking thought, Snider's death apparently didn't concern Ernest too closely, obsessed as he was for getting his crate to Switzerland. But for propriety's sake—or so he said—he asked Bobby and Inge to postpone moving out for a few days. Adrian conjectured that he wanted to travel with them as soon as the doctor gave him permission to go. By now he had succumbed to most of the doctor's wishes without argument.

As Adrian passed Ernest's sitting room the morning after the funeral, Bobby was pressing his father to allow them to get on with their move. "We've given you what you want," he said. "Now give us our freedom."

Ernest groused from his easy chair, "Are you so anxious to get out from under my roof that you can't wait until I regain my feet?"

Adrian was beginning to suspect they didn't want him as a travel companion. She stepped inside and spoke up quickly. "There's no need to postpone anything because of Snider. That would be hypocritical. We've detained Bobby and Inge long enough." *And you, too, you greedy old toad. Go on to your Swiss bank without me. It was only a sham honeymoon, anyway.*

He looked from one to the other of them and sighed. "I know when I'm outnumbered. But I'm feeling stronger every day. If you're sure you and Neva can manage at the bank while I'm gone, then . . ." He turned to his son. "Yes, it's best to make the trip as soon as possible. Get Neva to arrange our reservations."

That Bobby showed some reticence at that point didn't escape Adrian. She followed him into the hallway and hailed him quietly.

"What is it, Bobby? For a minute, I thought you were going to back down."

The younger Vogel's face twisted in anger. "He takes so much for granted. Who said we'd like to travel with Dad? We never once said we wanted to go to Europe. And Inge—well, this'll send her into the stratosphere."

"Have you tried to tell him that?"

"You don't tell him anything. He doesn't hear what he doesn't want to hear. I've told him over and over that Inge wants to try to get into show business in Vegas, maybe. But Dad wants somebody to oversee his interests in Europe. He'll never let go of us."

She watched him stalk off down the hall and felt the first affinity she'd ever had for him. For that brief moment she almost forgot to ponder what had led to Snider's mutilation. But in seconds the dark cloud descended again. Snider was gone. Had he been tortured to death, or had he died quickly and then burned?

No. Not burned. *Smoked.* Why smoked? She shuddered. *Why?*

She forced herself to think of something else. *Keep busy,* she reminded herself.

During Ernest's most recent illness, Adrian had reflected on their marriage arrangement. So far they might as well be living on different continents. She had considered for days exactly what she had expected to get out of marriage. She had concluded that as a woman she had anticipated marriage to offer her a safe haven—from want, from fear, from hurt. In return, she should offer Ernest comfort and eventually, she hoped, love. But how would love develop if they were seldom in the same room, much less the same bed?

There was no way she would ever be willing to settle for the sterile relationship that would apparently satisfy Ernest. Too, she felt bound to show Mobeetie that she meant business about this marriage; that she no longer cared beans about him. This was not a matter of pride, not a desire to wound him. No. Every marriage should be consummated. And now with Snider gone, that desire took on a special urgency, since they had always handled stress by coupling.

She went downstairs and told Precious not to expect her for lunch. She had decided to drive out to the ranch that morning.

She avoided the back road, which would have taken her by Snider's house and instead went the long way around to approach the front entrance from the highway.

Mobeetie was in town when she arrived, but she left word with Nasty that she would take a ride around the north pasture, up by the old homeplace, and would be back in an hour.

It was the first week in November, and the raw, bitter wind bit into her face bringing instant tears. Cattle hovered together under the scant protection of a small mesquite grove, the same grove that shielded them from the relentless summer sun. Her horse, grown fat and lazy by her neglect, behaved badly, snorting with indignation at being rousted from her warm stall to satisfy a mistress she did not remember. Adrian prodded the stubborn beast, jerking the reins savagely to prevent her from turning and heading back to the barn. *I am only marginally in control*, she thought, *everywhere in my life.*

Years of disuse had reduced the original homeplace to a hovel, and her distress at seeing it thus was acute. Here is where her mother had begun her own childhood, and where Adrian and Snider had often played as children under Grandmother's watchful eye. Her skin encased a lorn, hollow void, not completely divorced from the death of Snider. Everything came back to Snider.

They were not the idyllic years she'd later fantasized them to be. She hadn't forgotten the long weeks alone on that yawning prairie when the men were off on a drive, or the days upon end when Snider spoke oftener to his horse than to her. Now she smiled bitterly at the revelation.

What a fairy tale she'd make of things, forever expecting some man to make her happy. She was unable to exclude Snider, which might explain why she'd detested him so. Maybe he'd never been as bad as she thought.

She found the admission comforting, and she reined the horse around and gouged her flanks, riding free across the open pasture into the face of the cold wind. It occurred to her that there were some cold winds she simply could not back into. She made up her mind—again—to quit fighting, to face her fate with a good grace. She was by-God going to grow old without Snider. And unloved. Period.

Mobeetie was waiting on the porch when she rode up. "I've made coffee," he said, helping her off her horse.

Her teeth were chattering, her nose running. She followed him gratefully through the house into the kitchen. She pulled up a cowhide chair, which smelled good, like home. So did the coffee. Mobeetie handed her a steaming mug and poured one for himself. He was still standing, shifting. With her boot she shoved a chair toward him. "Sit down. You're making me uncomfortable. Like a guest."

He sat. They drank in silence. She was sick of this; there wasn't time to fence.

"I really ruined things between us, didn't I?" she blurted, without realizing she'd intended to say it. But it was as if he hadn't heard. Once begun, she had to continue. "We used to have such an easy partnership. Then I started acting like a fool . . . ."

He coughed noisily. He was looking out the window, flushing furiously.

"But I'm over that. Can't we just forget it and move on? We need to be able to work together . . ." She finished lamely. Maybe she sounded guilty. Maybe he suspected she had planned to replace him as soon as possible. Now she could scarcely remember why.

He cleared his throat the way Snider used to when she would beg him, "Talk to me. Just talk to me." She couldn't be sure Mobeetie had even been listening. He appeared to be studying something in the distance, and only the knotting of his jaw gave her a clue to his discomfort.

"Well?" she said finally.

"Well, I'm doing my best, *ma'am.*"

She gave a false little laugh. *Get me out of here,* she prayed. Instead, she heard herself say, "Now, is this any way for two old friends to be?"

He tried to smile, but only one side of his face moved. She could see that she was failing. Things would never be the same. Abruptly she stood up and started for the front door.

He had risen and was following her through the house, driving her, almost, as a cutting horse drives an errant yearling. "I've been wondering. Now that you've moved over to Ernest's, what about your old house? Going to sell it?"

She hadn't expected the question, any more than she had faced what to do with her house. She thought it peculiar that Mobeetie should be interested, but she was grateful for any conversation between them.

"I don't know," she said. "I'm not sure I could give it away, a place that size. It's funny how many houses I have on my hands: the homeplace out here, my old house, Ernest's house, and now maybe even Snider's. We don't know about that, though. I have to look for a will."

"Yeah, you're plenty rich, all right," he said with what sounded like a touch of bitterness.

She bit her lip, holding back a storm. He was baiting her. She could never seem to say the right thing.

She drove back to town in a morose frame of mind, stopping at the post office just to have something to do, just to keep from having to return to the mansion quite so early. She found one letter in her box, hurriedly scrawled on the legal stationery of Bryan Manly, a young attorney whose mother had been her high school English teacher. The letter sucked her back into her unexpelled grief.

Dear Ms. Vogel:

Forgive me for being among the last to offer my condolences on the death of your cousin. I learned about the tragedy while I was in Austin attending hearings. I was in town briefly but was unable to reach you by phone before I had to leave again. I was urged by my client to contact you. I am the court appointed attorney for Calvin Huddle, who has been arraigned for the murder of Snider Greene.

Mr. Huddle believes he can clear himself with your help. I will return to town Tuesday afternoon. Would it be possible for you to meet with me at my office around 2:00 p.m. on that date to discuss the matter?

Adrian wadded the paper and whispered an oath. From the first of the grisly business, she'd vowed to detach herself from it for the sake of her peace of mind. Snider couldn't just keel over like other drunks, or succumb to cirrhosis. She despised him for causing her the pain of unwelcome grief. And the horror, the unmitigated horror, of his death. Now even the killer's lawyer was drawing her into it. That was too much.

Still, it was Tuesday, and she had no real excuse not to see Manly. Anyhow, she didn't want to go home yet. It lacked an hour being two o'clock, but she walked across the street to the store-front office anyway. Bryan Manly himself ushered her in, his fresh face flushed with pleasure. His office was furnished with shabby leftovers from his mother's attic. She thought back: *Why, he must be in his mid-twenties by now.* Her own life was slipping through her fingers, and sometimes she forgot to fight. Why hadn't Snider fought? But she knew why.

"Here's the situation, Miss Adrian—uh, Mrs. Vogel," Manly said. "Calvin Huddle claims he didn't kill your cousin; that he never even saw him alive."

Alive. The word struck her with force. She was remembering the day she saw the Man running downhill from Snider's place; belatedly she now recognized his terror. "But he saw him dead; is that what you're saying?"

The forehead furrows smoothed away magically as he smiled. "That's his story. So what he told me about seeing you that day, about running away after he found the body, about stopping your runaway car—that really happened?"

"I don't know what he told you, but yes, I did see him running from Snider's, although it wasn't the first time he'd been near Snider's place. That particular day—I think it was the same day I found the—Calvin wasn't bloody, but that doesn't prove he's not guilty." She tried to contain her pounding heart. Because of what Huddle did to Elsie, she wanted him punished, and she only just now realized how much. And somebody had to pay for Snider's death.

Bryan Manly rose from behind his desk, grinning. He looked nowhere near old enough to defend a murder client, but then, Huddle didn't deserve any better. "No, it doesn't prove he's innocent," he said, "but it'd make the judge willing to listen to the rest of his story, if you would testify in a deposition to what you told me. Look, I know this is a delicate situation. Huddle's not anyone's favorite person. But you'd want the *right* person punished, I'm sure, and Calvin may not be the one. So before you say no, will you come with me over to the jail and at least hear him out?"

This was highly irregular. She wanted to refuse, but more than that, she wanted to appear unbiased. She had made up her mind that, one way or another, the Man needed to suffer for what he did to Elsie. Maybe she was the only one who could prevent his going free. She got up and followed the lawyer out of the office and down the street to the jailhouse.

40

The young Romeo of the rink had lost more than every semblance of glamour: he had also lost his rage. Even excusing the rosette nose, he was a pitiable sight: greasy, filthy ginger hair; sparce, scraggly beard he constantly scratched. About him, the scent of man scat. The angry light had faded from his eyes. He looked up listlessly when Adrian, still in her riding clothes, entered the visitors' room behind Manly, who had apparently arranged the meeting ahead of time with the sheriff. How had he known she would agree to come?

Once they were seated at a wooden table facing Huddle, the attorney started to speak, but Adrian broke in, fastening the Man with a glare.

"Let's hear your story," she said, bristling with detestation she couldn't conceal, "People keep telling me Snider owed you money. What for?"

Calvin gripped the edges of the table until his chapped knuckles were bled of color. She was important to him, she knew, feeling a pang of conscience which she quickly dismissed. Bryan Manly, apparently viewing the man's tautness with alarm and misinterpreting it, cleared his throat, a warning to Huddle. But Adrian felt no threat. You can't be intimidated by someone in urine-stained khakis.

Manly spoke up. "I wouldn't go into that part, Calvin. It might prejudice Mrs. Vogel, and it has no pertinence to the charge, anyway."

She fought to contain her annoyance. "Let me be the judge of that." She had, after all, known this pipsqueak of a lawyer all her life. She figured she could intimidate him.

Manly shook his head, smiling his patience and condescension. "No ma'am. Too much hangs on your cooperation. And women being emotional about these things, I can't let my client risk getting you upset where you can't think rationally."

She held onto those parts threatening to crumble in rage, weak with the effort, weak with her need to push Calvin Huddle past civility, sensing he was working hard to disguise the feral streak which had goaded him to rape poor Elsie.

"Go on and tell her what you told me about Snider's key ring," Manly said.

Huddle began earnestly, looking her directly in the eye. It was a disconcerting look of desperation. "The key ring was a signal. I was to send it back to him every day until I thought I'd done the job he hired me for. Then I was to keep it. That would let him know the contract was completed. Then he was to come after the key ring and pay me."

"Only that never happened," Manly put in. "Calvin was injured—"

"That girl went crazy!" Calvin's face flushed with anger. He touched his nose. "She *mutilated* me. I nearly died."

"So you left town with Snider still owing you money," she said.

He nodded. "I never had the chance to collect it until the rink came back this year."

"But Snider refused to pay this time, is that it?"

"He hid out. I could never find him. I left word for him all over town, went out there several times. I got the picture that he planned to lay low until the rink left town, so I made up my mind to break in early of a morning, catch him unawares—"

"And that's when you found Snider's body," Manly supplied hurriedly.

The Man shuddered, and she was dismayed at the genuineness of his reaction. She felt her own revulsion well up to meet his; did not want to hear what was coming. "Hanging with a rope looped under his arms. Body so black, I didn't know for sure—it didn't even look like a human. But when I got up close and saw the face—I never saw anything like that in my life."

Her insides churned, her head felt light. She didn't want to believe him. But if he didn't kill Snider, if she allowed his conviction anyway, then someone else would go free, somebody walking loose on the streets of Attebury.

Calvin went on, lost in the scene he was relating. "I ran out of that place and down the hill, just about hysterical. I almost flagged you down when I saw your car, but I got to thinking you might be suspicious of me for poking around out back."

Manly put out a restraining hand on Huddle's arm and said, "Well, Adrian, what do you think? Will you testify about Calvin's appearance when you saw him? Will you tell them he wasn't blood-covered?" He paused. "And would a murderer stop and save your runaway car?"

"I don't know," she said, knowing, in her heart, that she did know.

She left the jailhouse deeply depressed, for if Calvin weren't guilty of murder, he would never have to pay for Elsie's rape if he went free now. A possibility had occurred to her that might explain some of the missing facts, but it was too monstrous to contemplate. Elsie could tell her, but she couldn't ask Elsie, not Elsie. One other person might possibly know.

She made plans to drive out by the cotton gin the following morning.

41

There was not much except a couple of gas pumps and the cotton gin. Somewhere off the main road was a shopping district that had dried up when the highway was rerouted. It was a half-hour trip from the Vogel place, and Adrian reached the city limits shortly before eleven. The sky was a peculiar cobbled grey, promising some change in the weather, so she sped in the direction of Madam's house.

The gin and its shantytown across the tracks were a shade dingier, a fraction more run-down than the several other scattered dwellings and buildings on the main thoroughfare. It was a tough-looking neighborhood. She cruised slowly along the dirt street fronting the tracks until she spotted the familiar sign advertising Madam's trade. She stopped in front, gathered her courage and went up to the door. Now she could admit the real reason she was compelled to see the gypsy woman again. Today—now—she must know: Had Snider married Elsie? Not that she cared one way or another . . . .

The big woman must have seen her coming, for she was waiting at the door, rodent eyes flashing, beads set in motion. "Ah, you found me. I put out the sign especially for you." She unlatched the screen and ushered Adrian in.

The odor of slop jar temporarily overwhelmed Adrian, although Madam had sought to disguise it with incense. The little room was even darker than the old one, but the familiar trappings were there: table covered with oilcloth, the cards, crystal ball. The samovar sat on a shawl-draped box in rear.

"Didn't you leave your old house rather suddenly?" Adrian asked, more to make conversation than to glean information.

"It was not so sudden," Madam said. She motioned for Adrian to sit at the table. "I heard about Snider Greene. I am sorry. It is too bad. They have arrested the Man, I hear."

Adrian studied the fortune teller for some indication that she knew more than she was telling, but the woman sat placidly across from her and didn't bat an eyelid as Adrian said, "He says he didn't do it."

Madam shrugged the thick shoulders, setting her beads clicking. "What would you expect? Myself, I never knew him, although I staunched his wound once." She got up and moved to the bed in the corner of the room, lifted the thin mattress and drew out an envelope. "I have something for you."

Adrian caught her breath as she recognized Snider's handwriting.

To Adrian Craddock in the event of my death.

"Snider Green gave it to me many months ago," Madam said, "as you can see by the use of 'Craddock' instead of 'Vogel.' It is a will, I presume."

Fingering it evoked the pain of proximity. Adrian noted that it had not been opened, and put it in her purse to read when she was alone. Now she turned her attention to the lagniappe she could never have anticipated: a connection between Madam and the Man. "You say you took care of Calvin Huddle?"

"No, I only helped stop his bleeding then sent him on his way." Abruptly she changed the subject. "He was a fine man, your cousin. He always told me he liked having me around. He called me his 'insurance policy.'"

Adrian didn't understand, but she let it pass because something else puzzled her more. "Then why did you leave?"

"I had a good offer. I had to accept."

Adrian looked around the room again. It did not appear that the good offer had significantly improved the woman's fortunes. She returned to the subject of Calvin Huddle. "Did Snider ask you to care for Calvin the way he did for Elsie?"

"No. Why should he? Snider Greene did not know the Man, as far as I know."

So. If Madam was telling the truth, she knew nothing of a deal between Snider and the Man. Then again, maybe she was lying. Adrian searched her face, trying to gauge her truthfulness, while the woman pursed her lips and played with her bracelets. Adrian allowed the lapse of what she hoped was an uncomfortable pause, but she seemed to be the only one made uncomfortable. At length she broke the silence. "Is that all you can tell me about the Man?"

"What else? If you wish to know more, ask your ranch hands. I sent him there. I saw one of them pick him up."

Strange that Mobeetie never mentioned it, unless he never knew about it himself. The hands may have hidden Huddle in the bunk house, but there would be no point in concealment.

She sensed Madam was growing restless, so she came to the point. "I came to ask you about Elsie. Now that Snider is gone, there's no one else to ask." She still had trouble saying, *Snider is gone.*

Madam's dark eyes clouded and she rose from her chair to indicate the interview was at an end. "I know nothing of that one. I am sorry."

Adrian knew that to ask a point-blank question would mean to receive no answer. She would have to sidle into it. She took a stab in the dark. "It's her health. I worry about her. She's never been strong since—the delivery."

Madam's eyes showing obvious concern, so Adrian hurried on. "Maybe you can tell me: Did she lose a large amount of blood during labor?"

The woman turned her back and crashed around at the metal cupboard which served as her kitchen. "How should I know? You think I delivered it? Am I a fortune teller?" She laughed at her own joke.

Adrian heaved a triumphant sigh. Madam did not appear surprised at the mention of labor. "So there was a baby!"

A fraction too late Madam realized her error. She wheeled and waved her floppy sleeves toward the door, openly snarling. "Fine lady, you fish for information that is confidential. Ask Snider Greene's widow, if you want to know more."

The word *widow* jolted her. Painfully.

Adrian already knew the answer to her one remaining question. "The baby: Where is it?"

"I know nothing," Madam said. "And that's the god's truth. Go now, Mrs. Vogel. We have nothing more to talk about."

Adrian rose, but she had to try once more. "Did someone pay you to move? Is that it?"

The veiled black eyes told her nothing. Madam said levelly, "Please go."

Adrian left quickly, suddenly chillingly aware that the big woman might be capable of desperate action to keep her secret. She drove back home slowly, sorting out Madam's words from their potential hidden meaning, casting around for explanations for her refusal to say more. Maybe she would have talked had Adrian offered her money. Why hadn't she thought of it? It was almost as if she didn't really want to know what Madam might reveal.

She had never seriously considered the possibility that Elsie and Snider had married, but she could imagine a scenario where he might make it legal to act in Elsie's behalf after Calvin raped her. He might have had a marriage on paper. It was probable that he had arranged for an abortion at the hands of Madam, and then paid her to leave to keep her quiet. But why would he go to that much trouble for an idiot girl? Had Adrian ever truly understood him?

42

The will was of scant interest to Adrian now. She opened the envelope, satisfied herself that it did indeed contain a lengthily worded will. Snider had always been a man of many words where a few would do. She put it aside to read later that evening.

The doctor, a family friend, was just leaving when she returned to Vogel mansion. "Good news, Adrian. Ernest is as good as he's going to get. He can do anything he's man enough to do, if you catch my drift."

He laughed wickedly, and Adrian wondered what the penalty was for choking a man with his own stethoscope. Then he took her by the arm, as if to emphasize the seriousness of what he was about to say. "I don't think he ought to travel yet, but I have no real reason to keep him from it. He's highly emotional, you know. I leave it to you. When you feel it's right, you can tell him I give my permission."

So.

Ernest had no excuse now. Tonight would be the night. She would soon know if this was ever going to be a marriage. What is hard to get is greatly prized. The idea of seducing Ernest at once took precedence over Elsie, Snider's death, even getting rid of Bobby.

She hurried up to her rooms to unearth the brown satin gown and peignoir. By God, it would see duty yet. She bathed before dinner and felt her spirits lifted for the first time in days.

At dinner she elected not to mention the visit to Madam, which he would like no more than having her shoes shined in public. For the same reason, she also elected not to mention the Calvin Huddle affair. Imagine the snit he'd throw if he knew she'd gone to the jailhouse.

He was in an ebullient mood, so she was not required to talk. The doctor's pronouncement had brought color to his cheeks. Already he was making plans to go to Switzerland. She saw how she could use his anticipation to her advantage.

"I spoke to the doctor on the way out," she said. "He said we would see how you do with your regular activities first. How you perform—well, the normal duties you might be expected to perform." She peeked up from her plate to see if he was taking the bait. "If you do well, then he said it might not be too long before he'd allow you to travel."

"Oh, I'll get along fine."

Adrian called for a little brandy after dinner, and the two of them spent a companionable hour with the television in the library. When nine o'clock finally arrived, she rose.

"We want to get plenty of rest, don't we?"

"By all means. To bed, then." He got up heavily. "You go on up. I'll turn out the lights."

She took her time giving him ample opportunity to get ready. It wouldn't be like two young lovers, of course; no sense fooling herself it would be sensuous, or even rough and tumble, as it might have been with Mobeetie. But it would be her due. It was a matter of pride, if nothing else. She pushed aside momentarily the thought that pride once drove her to leave home.

With a start she heard the toilet flush; she had missed his step on the stair. Maybe he was trying to sneak off to bed. She gave him a few minutes longer, wondering if he would come to her. Apparently not. She crossed the hall and opened his door, snorting in her anger now.

He was sitting on the side of the bed, startled by her unannounced appearance, gaping up at her in her flimsy nightclothes. She took a deep breath and gathered her courage, her well-rehearsed entrance completely forgotten.

"Ernest Vogel, do have any plans to consummate this marriage?" she blurted.

The color drained from his face, with the exception of his eye sockets, which were scarlet-purple. His anger was a palpable wall several feet thick. "Adrian, for God's sake. Act your age!"

And with that, he turned off the bed lamp, plunging her and the room into darkness.

She backed out the door and stood in the hall, too mortified to move, and heard a door close down the south wing. Bobby or Inge must have witnessed her expulsion. Right now they were snickering over her humiliation. *Rats*, she thought. *I've done it again.*

As her natural resilience returned, she began to fume, turning her anger not upon Ernest but upon herself for getting into such a degrading situation. She stalked back into her rooms and threw on her old camel's hair coat. The night was much too cool for her thin slippers, but she didn't take time to change. Maybe she would punish herself and catch pneumonia. She was leaving, maybe for good. Sleep in her own bed again. Never spend another degrading night under this roof stripped of all dignity.

She gunned out of the drive, noticing that, for a second, the light had come on in Ernest's bedroom. Then the house was dark again. She drove away, hoping he would lie awake worrying.

It would be a relief to be home again where she wouldn't feel so disenfranchised, so out of place. She knew exactly what she intended to do as soon as she got safely inside: she'd run to her room and throw herself across the bed and cry her heart out.

But once again she cursed her impetuosity: she'd gone off without her house key. She stood shivering on her own front porch and fumbled in the pocket of her coat, hoping by some miracle she was wrong. How mortifying to have to skulk back to Ernest's house now.

A motor rumbled in the driveway behind her, and she thought Ernest had followed her to take her home, until from behind the glaring head beams, she heard the driver growl, "Better get away from that door, friend, before I blow you to kingdom come."

43

Adrian recognized Mobeetie's voice and stepped down off the porch. She could smell his beer breath even before she reached the pickup window. He was easier to deal with after a trip to Jericho. He opened the door, chuckling.

"What brings you over here this time of night? You and old Ernest have a lovers' spat?"

He had forgiven her. He forgave everything when he was tight.

"I came over here to sulk, if you must know. But I left my door key at the other house." She saw no point in lying. "What are you doing here? Coming to see me?"

"Just cruising by. Hunch, maybe. Got some pictures here of a bull I'm thinking we ought to buy. But we can't look at them out here in the dark." He pulled them from his shirt pocket and handed them over. He couldn't just apologize like anybody else. He never apologized.

She held them up to the bright autumn moon, but she could see nothing.

"Wait," he said. "I got a flashlight rattling around in the back somewhere."

She followed him to the rear of the pickup and watched while he dug through the loose hay until he found it. They sat on the tailgate and he held the flashlight while she examined the pictures, pretending interest. No reason to tell him that she had no spare cash to buy anything at the moment.

"My, my," he said, and she noticed that he was beaming the light not so much on the snapshots as on her satin-covered belly. He swallowed audibly and took the photos from her and put them in his pocket. She pulled her coat around her, trying to think what to say.

"You going to drive somebody crazy, running around dressed like that, little lady," he said in a hoarse murmur. She caught the scent of male in rut—and dropped into a liminal space.

A sudden fire leapt in her groin and she remembered, maybe from another life: *this is it*. She meant to resist, initially anyway, or maybe to suggest they break into the house through a back window, but she yielded even before he caught her arm. He bore her gruffly back against the hay and slipped his hands under her coat, clumsily, like a school boy. They were like two adolescents in the back of a van. She could feel the roughened, chapped fingers snag the slippery fabric, pulling it along as they roved over her. The calloused hand bared her breast; it was like the first raw and hairless boy who ventured into her T-shirt behind the schoolhouse, whose awkward warty fingers had wandered across her sensitive surfaces and sent her writhing to her knees. Now she moaned and pulled him closer, incensed by the rank animal smell. *Like Snider.*

"Easy now, easy," he said as if gentling a horse.

There was no time for easy; something might happen and he would be gone before she could have him. She ripped at the buttons on his jeans, tearing a nail to the quick, and drew him to her, wrapped around him, squirming with frenzied insistence to get on with it, do what Snider had done so anxiously.

"Whoo—ee! Ride-em!" Mobeetie was dangerously loud, but she couldn't be bothered. She was laboring, working as hard as if she were ridding herself of child. *Strange*, she thought, *how I finally always have to bare my backside to the world to get what I want.*

The ultimate power, the final courage, maybe, is in vulnerability. So Snider was the most courageous of all? *Leave Snider out of this*, she commanded.

When she was spent and sweating and Mobeetie had dropped like a leaden weight upon her, she pushed him aside and lay in the prickly hay studying the harvest moon. *I ain't had no lovin' since January, February, June or July.*

Mobeetie groaned and sat up on the side rail, fastening his clothes. "Man oh man, I'll sure as hell tell you one damn thing, missy: you actual sure as hell don't act thirty-seven years old."

Rage flew over her like a douse of coal oil. She sprang to her knees and pushed him backwards over the rail, sending him crashing heavily on his back to the ground.

"Damn it, I by God am, you sonofabitch! And in case you forget, you're ten years older'n me! And there's not a damn thing you can do about it." She jumped off the truck bed and kicked him roundly in the side, sending excruciating pain shooting through her slippered foot. He had always imposed some sort of barrier to intimacy. Was that the best he could come up with?

"Get out of here, you bastard. And while you're at it, pack up and get off my ranch! Go off somewhere where 'old' won't offend you so much, you cotton-mouth rattler! Anyway, with you, as far as I'm concerned, it's a case of too *little* and too late—and you can take that any way you want."

She was past caring that her shrieks probably carried to kingdom come. She stormed over to her car, close under Sarah's window, hot tears blinding her. *To hell with them all.* She flung open the door, ground on the ignition and, wheeling around his pickup, tore great ruts in her Bermuda grass lawn. Mobeetie, still propped on one elbow on the drive, rolled over quickly to keep from being hit. He'd been just an actor on a stage, like Ernest.

In the sullen silence of the moonlit street, Adrian felt the waters of the ages rise in her blood. She was aware of a connectedness with a vast servanthood stretching back to some primal goddess, with all the darling daughters of the ages. Beginning with Grandfather, she had tried to fulfill the expectations of men. *The rulers dictate the virtues, invent the myths,* she thought. *The serfs try to fill the skins of the mythological inventions. And if, like Snider, they lack the substance to do so, they attack themselves with the club of their own reproof.*

The pain gripped her like a birth pang, and she came to understand that any pain is birth pain. It reached down and scraped the bottom of the womb of earliest woman. She felt connected, grounded, knowing she had chosen her pain. *But Snider? Had he?*

She wasn't Adrian Craddock, grieving cousin, and even if Ernest had died, she wouldn't be Adrian Vogel, widow. Widow would never be her role, only a statement of her trauma. There was no accurate appellation for her role with Snider.

Lacking love growing up, she had settled for pity, try to deny it as she could. If she hadn't wanted pity, she wouldn't have clung to the role. Back then, she had not been rooted to her womanhood, so she had not been rooted in reality. She had been a role; a role isn't human; it has no compassion. She felt human now; the pain verified it. She wanted, like Rilke, not to stay folded anywhere. Whether she liked it or not, she had to plumb the depths of her pain, sensing that it was inexorably tied to Snider's. But they hadn't shared their pain; they had buried it.

She had been like a cat, burying its wastes. *Civilizations are lost because they bury their wastes,* she thought. Because within the wastes lies the power. *Vulnerability is strength, maybe.*

She determined to dig up the wastes in whatever time was left. No wonder Mobeetie had never loved her. She had concealed her neediness, but he had sensed it anyway and had despised her for it.

The clock struck eleven as she opened the front door of Vogel mansion. Good Lord, could all that have taken less than an hour? She crept up to her room and eased the door shut, then felt her way into the bath and closed that door, too, before she turned on a light. Then she let her coat slip from her shoulders before the mirror.

Maybe she expected some sign of renewal. But the ravages of almost four decades of living were still there. She turned off the cruel light, feeling the fecund exudate like a sensuous caress that she might never feel again; not wishing to bathe it away. She needed to sleep.

Mobeetie James had no intention of sleeping. Gingerly, he had crawled to his feet and brushed the dust from his back, cursing the bitch who had got the best of him again. If he had any demur about what he was about to do, it had now evaporated. It was fate, almost. Almost as if she had handed him the invitation on a silver tray to do what he was about to do anyhow.

He backed the pickup into the street and headed for the all-night truck-stop out on the highway. There was a telephone on the wall that anybody was welcome to use, so long as they put a quarter in the cigar box on the counter. Mobeetie had reason not to use his own cell phone for this particular call. Before he went inside, he fished into his wallet for a scrap of paper.

Then he walked in and rang Bobby Vogel's private number.

It was the best quarter he ever spent.

44

Adrian woke late with a guilty start, remembering a hair appointment at ten, chiding herself for not bathing the night before. She had her senses now: with the moon had set some long-standing, clement, romantic myth that had guided her life like a star.

More than her slatterliness, she regretted the impetuous firing of Mobeetie before it was time. There still was no replacement on the horizon. Surely he hadn't taken her seriously; he seldom did. She would make light of it. Apologize, if necessary.

Ernest spent the morning in his rooms, preparing for his first visit to the bank. Inge remained secluded with Baby Otto, doubtless celebrating the end of her confinement. Bobby went to the bank as usual, but on his way out, he apparently dropped a memo from his pocket. It caught Adrian's eye as she entered the breakfast room. Actually, it was the name "Mobeetie" that caught her attention; she wondered what business Bobby had with him.

Knowing that she must eventually confront Snider's last message to her, Adrian called down to Precious for some coffee, then steeled herself and settled on her chaise lounge to read it. On closer examination, she found the will to be relatively short. She put it aside for the moment and turned to the other pages, a personal letter to her:

> *Dear Adrian,*
>
> *You have not had much love for me, and that is the main reason I have felt no obligation to come forward with this information before. Your looks have always made making money come easy for you. And you got one idea about me and kept it all your goddam life. So I'm not writing this with the intention of saving your fortune for*

you. In fact, the only thing more entertaining for me than British comedies is watching you gradually being drained dry.

I'm writing this, with copy to Ernest, so that if anything ever happens to me, you will know under precisely what rock to look to find the worm who killed me. Ernest, you see, has been caring for your estate as "trustee" with more care than you ever imagined, dear cousin. He has, I'm happy to state, stripped you clean. Those "grain elevators" in which he invested your principal do not exist except on a piece of paper.

When this first came to my attention—while I was searching county records on another matter—I confronted Ernest with the suggestion that he have a good explanation or else a reason why I shouldn't come to you with my information. Ernest assured me that he was soon to come into a large fortune of his own—so vast that it would completely obliterate any deficit in either your funds or the bank's. (Yes, he has borrowed from Peter to pay Paul ad infinitum.) You'll be interested to know that the true balance of your investment account at the time of this writing is very near zero, although the statement which you receive probably shows otherwise.

Then there is the matter of the mortgages. Everything you own is mortgaged, courtesy of Ernest and me. You'll recall giving him power of attorney during your period of grief. This cash was urgently needed at the time for an overseas venture of Ernest's—to cover some overextensions of an uncle, he said. He plans to redeem those liens when his ship comes in, if it isn't sunk by Al-Zirqawi. At any rate, apparently due to certain genes of longevity in his uncle's family, Ernest's great fortune has been slow in coming, so slow that he has become a desperate man. Desperate enough to offer me a small share of his wealth in gratitude for my legal expertise and for my discretion concerning his imprudences. And even desperate enough to take another wife.

Didn't you wonder why Ernest, who never seemed to have the slightest interest in women, suddenly became so enamored of you? It was just about the time that I came to him with my knowledge. Wives can't be forced to testify against their husbands, you see. Furthermore, husbands are often given free rein to manage their wives' affairs. So even if you learned the truth from me, you could

do less damage to him as his wife, unless you were stupid enough to expose him to the law and bring about your own ruination.

But if I'm found dead before you, take this letter straight to the law. Ernest will get his copy in the mail shortly hereafter.

Adrian felt no surprise, felt instead a certain vindication. She batted off angry tears and picked up the will, a crudely scribbled note:

Being of sound body and mind, I, Snider Benson Greene, do make the following bequests upon the event of my death:

To my legally espoused, Elsie Mae Puckett Greene, I leave my house, free of liens, since in accordance with the homestead law of the State of Texas, one's homestead cannot be attached for payment of other debt. In addition, I leave her all my worldly goods: the contents of aforementioned house and my 1999 Chrysler.

To my only living blood relative, Vivian Greene Craddock—soon to be Vogel—I leave my "debts," with my blessings.

She could hear Ernest's shower running. She moved through her routine and waited, applied a dab of lipstick with shaking hand, retouched her hair. Then she crossed the hall and took a rigid vigil in a chair by his bed.

He peered out of his dressing room, half-dressed. "All ready? How much time do I have?"

"Not much." She didn't try to hide the irony.

"An hour?" He had returned to his dressing, humming softly.

"I wouldn't think so."

He stopped humming and stuck his head around the corner again. Her expression must have said it all, for his florid face went ashen in moments. *Don't die yet,* she thought. *Let me do it for you.*

"You guessed it," she said. "Snider's letter. You must've paid Madam to leave town, hoping I'd never get my copy."

He was flustered, denied it with "no, no, no," but she saw that he was straining to control the tremor in his voice. He drew on his trousers and left the dressing room door ajar.

"Anyway," he said, "it isn't the way that idiot tells it. He had delusions."

"*He* had delusions." She was holding in, battling to maintain her composure. There was plenty of time. Maybe he was insane. Maybe he planned to kill her, too. She would be careful not to let him get between her and the door.

She needn't have worried; he remained in his dressing room. She hung onto the arms of the chair for support as he continued to speak through a crack.

"In the first place, I had nothing to do with Snider's death. God, woman, do you think, knowing he'd written such a damning letter, I'd kill him?"

She wanted to believe him. "But you took the money, didn't you?"

There was a pause. "'Used' is a better word. I have charge of your trust. I made what I thought would be a good investment for you. I borrowed it for a while—to expedite Uncle Otto's production capacity."

He came back into the room and sat on the side of the bed, trying to take her hand. "Adrian, this war on terror will make us billionaires. We'll live like royalty. We'll *be* royalty. Isn't that worth the risk?"

"Risk? I thought your inheritance was a foregone conclusion." She pulled her hand away and wiped it on her skirt. He was serious. He believed he could get away with it.

"It practically is. How much longer can Uncle Otto live? You should hear him wheeze. These donations I've made, they're the best investment I could have made for you—much better than phony grain elevator shares."

She could almost admire his gall. It had thrown her off balance. It was like trying to condemn somebody like Sael, who had no notion of guilt. It was like talking to the wind.

"Ernest, what you've done is embezzlement, and it's grand larceny. You'll go to the penitentiary for this, don't you understand? Quit talking royalty and start thinking convict."

"And who's going to turn me in? You? A wife can't testify against her husband."

"You're wrong," she said quietly. "A wife can't be *made* to testify, but I can testify if I want to." Her thighs were shaking. She covered them with her hands.

His flat German face remained placid, but he shook his head. "What judge would take the word of a hysterical, over-sexed woman against a Presbyterian elder—the banker who holds his mortgage?"

She had misjudged his cunning and the degree of her helplessness. "But there's Snider's letter," she said lamely.

He got up grandly, pishing and toshing, strutting, fastening the shirt button against his fleshy neck. "The word of a drunk? Who would believe him? The man didn't have a friend; he owed everyone in town." With a pang, she realized he could be describing her on both counts.

The doorbell sounded the arrival of the chauffeur to take Ernest for his first visit to the bank since his illness. Adrian got up, uncertain how to leave this, unwilling to let the matter rest.

"We aren't through with this discussion. I'll decide what to do about you." It was a high-handed technique she used often with Snider, whom it had invariably cowed.

He smiled benignly into the mirror at her. "Keep two things in mind. First, there's not a judge in this state who would convict a man for managing his wife's money in the manner he sees fit, even if it is foolishly managed.

"And second and more important: the only way to recoup your money is to let me complete this deal. When the inheritance is mine, I can repay your accounts and the bank's as well. No one will ever be the wiser."

"And if I turn you in?" she said.

He turned to face her, his eyes red-rimmed and blazing. "If I am deterred from making this delivery to Zurich, then your entire estate is gone. You'll be virtually penniless, my dear—in fact, as things stand, you are so at this moment."

45

Common sense told her to hold things together, give no hint of financial problems to Ernest's influential friends. She might need contacts later if she had to start all over again. It didn't sound like a bad prospect. But Snider's treachery had badly shaken her will to fight.

The seed of a plan was germinating. She dismissed the notion that she must divorce Ernest at once. No, providing he wasn't guilty of Snider's murder, she knew what to do about him. She would use as she had been used, but first she must know exactly how much he owed and to whom. Without arousing Neva's suspicion, she would find out that morning. She must be practical. Just as she would avenge Elsie's rape by refusing to help the Man, now her passions cried out for revenge against Ernest. But she hadn't survived by cutting off her own nose, and no rash act would undo this disaster.

She and Ernest rode the elevator down together. He instructed the chauffeur to wait until he'd had his coffee, then went into the morning room. She took a detour by the kitchen.

She found Mozelle alone, standing over a sink, washing crystal by hand. Adrian picked up a cup towel and dried a few. Mozelle, glad of an audience, began her customary grumbling.

"Seems like I spend my life with a bottle of dish soap, even though there's a perfectly good dishwasher right over yonder. But no. Precious says we don't put the good crystal in the dishwasher. So here I am, slaving away, and Elsie not doing doodly-squat but whining around the live-long day."

Adrian felt her heart turn over. The child had no comfort from anyone. She'd been left to pine away. "Poor little mite. She must be homesick." She recalled her own first bereft days out on the hill so long ago.

"Naw. Over at the house she used to cry all the time."

"Why does she cry?"

Mozelle pursed her lips. "I ain't supposed to say."

This was her chance. Adrian had to ask. "Does she miss her baby?"

Unable to contain herself, Mozelle nodded eagerly. "I figure Elsie Mae has flat gone pure-dee crazy. First everybody—even Momma—is saying her and Snider is married, but Elsie claims it isn't so. Then she commences claiming she had a baby and somebody taken it off. Now she's commenced with a new one that don't make no more sense than turnips in the chow chow."

Prickles rose on the back of Adrian's neck. "A new one? What's that?"

Mozelle shrugged and slopped dishwater over the edge of the sink onto the floor. She wanted so badly to tell, Adrian could see. "Momma told me to be careful else somebody might believe Elsie's stories was true."

Adrian picked her way carefully. "Elsie is a good child—"

"Not all the time," the girl said with a tinge of querulousness. Adrian had seen her envy of her younger sister creep in before. "At times Elsie just flat sins. She committed fornication."

Adrian smiled at Mozelle's four-bit word. "But Elsie can't be held accountable for what happened with the Man."

Mozelle shot her a contemptuous glare and slopped the water more vigorously. "I know what I know. She started the whole shebang. Broke into his motel room, she did. Told me so herself."

Adrian considered this, decided she had to hand it to Elsie. She herself hadn't fared as well the night she broke in on Mobeetie. "I don't want to hear this," she said. "That's her business."

Mozelle snickered and wiped an itchy nose with her forearm, dribbling suds across the cabinet and sending a spray against the blinds. "Betcha Flop Pyle thinks otherwise."

"The deputy? Why do you say that?"

Mozelle said with certain pride, "According to how Elsie tells it, she's the one responsible for Snider Greene being dead."

Adrian surprised herself at the swiftness of her counter-attack. She spun the girl around, gripping her roughly, feeling her nails dig into the fleshy arm. "Don't you ever say that again! Not even to me, you hear?"

Mozelle squealed and Adrian released her abruptly. She left the kitchen and hurried to the morning room panting, astonished at her own investment in Elsie's welfare. Elsie couldn't be held accountable for what she said. She didn't see things as other people did. Like as not, she trudged through life bent with imaginary guilt, she'd been blamed for things so often.

It occurred to Adrian that, although it would have been physically impossible for Elsie to murder a man the size of Snider and string him up to the rafters, she might have seen something—perhaps she had gone back out to feed the chickens again—which in her own mind made her culpable. The child might very well have witnessed a nightmare. If, in the course of the upcoming trial against the Man, either attorney tried to question Elsie, Adrian would do her best to prevent it so that the child would be spared reliving such a horror. A lawyer could twist whatever she said to mean anything he wanted.

She left Mozelle and went into the morning room, where Ernest was putting away a hearty breakfast. She tried to eat, but she hadn't anticipated the random interruptions of her own stray thoughts. She couldn't put the apricots out of her mind: They kept squatting there: row upon row of fresh-canned preserves. Snider usually had consumed the entire lot within a few weeks. Had his drinking displaced his eating entirely?

Ernest rose abruptly, tossing down his napkin as if he were late. Possibly he planned to leave the house before she could harangue him. She wouldn't, because she could see nothing to gain by it. She couldn't afford the luxury of making him angry: he might have another heart attack and leave her a destitute widow. She jumped up planted herself determinedly between him and the door. "I have something to say."

Glumly he sat down again and made a production of tying his shoe, the square German jaw fixed in obstinacy. It was clear that he expected a scene.

"I've been thinking," she said. "I suppose, if I was used, it was only because I allowed it. Maybe I asked for it. So I accept my share of the blame, and now I want to help us both. I have no desire to tear you down—that I plan to act on. You were right when you said my only chance of recouping my losses is to let your deal go through."

Relief flooded his face, and the locked jaw slackened. He looked up and grinned all the way back to his gold-capped molar. "I'm glad you're behaving sensibly."

"But first I want the details from the beginning. What is this 'deal' about? What 'contributions' did you make?"

He glanced toward the kitchen, the ravages of his recent illness still evident on the sallow cheeks. Eventually he glared up and said archly, "I don't see that it's any concern of yours." Before she could protest he held up a warding hand and added, "But I see no harm in telling you, if you have your head set on it."

"You damn right I do. No concern of mine, indeed!" She checked herself before she lost it completely. "Never mind. Go on."

"Some time ago, Uncle Otto approached me for a contribution. A movement was emerging in the Middle East to unseat a certain government, and it was important that Otto's oil interests be safe-guarded. So I did what I could. I—ah—happened to be short of assets at the time—"

"What about Otto? Why didn't he kick in, if he was so hot about it?"

He hesitated, and she knew he must have asked himself the same question often. "He claimed he had to remain neutral. Anyway, I'm certain he was using every cent he could scrape together to retool his factory to make munitions. It had to be done secretly, of course."

"Did you take this money from the bank?"

"Not at first, but later there were other expenses. Tremendous sums are needed to unseat a sitting ruler. And it's coming, Adrian, whether we participate or not."

He was on his feet now, striding about, lost in his dreams. He had retrieved the stub of a cigar to gnash against while he almost goose-stepped, chest welling, hands clasped behind his back. "It's a lifetime opportunity. Can you imagine the possibilities of getting in on the ground floor of a new regime? Why, think of the size of those army contracts alone."

She felt his contagious excitement, because she knew a business deal when she heard one. Now that she was sure of the crate's contents, she understood the urgency in Ernest's returning to Zurich. She mustn't stand in his way, mustn't do or say anything to jeopardize his health. It was clear that if he dropped dead now, she had nothing.

Still, she couldn't resist one dig. "Need I point out that you should have stopped when your resources were gone? All right, so in your mind you were only 'borrowing.' And what has Bobby to do with all this? Did he embezzle, too? Has he had his hands on my money?"

"No, no. He's not clever enough." He leaned against the window casing, staring morosely out over the seeding grounds. "Once I began to shuffle funds, I couldn't risk being away from the bank. That's when Helga began to help. She was the one, incidentally, who came up with the idea of borrowing from your estate by selling you shares in nonexistent grain elevators."

She felt a stab of betrayal. Helga had been her trusted friend. "What makes you any different from Billy Sol Estes or Bernie Madoff?"

"Because I intend to pay everybody back. I'm not trying to *steal*." He made it sound so plausible. "It was for your own good. But if we'd told you what we were investing in, you wouldn't have allowed it. Yet you stand to make much more now."

She pressed on. "Get back to Bobby. What's his role in this?"

"None. A warm body protecting the books that he has no clue are rigged. I could never trust Bobby. He cracks under the least stress. But when Helga died, what choice did I have? Someone had to safeguard the books on the rare occasions when I was gone from the bank. I couldn't just up and remarry right away. But he has no idea why he's protecting the books."

She moved closer, perching on the edge of her chair, closing in for the kill. The matter of the baby, of whom Ernest seemed genuinely proud, had repeatedly intruded. "You have doubts that Bobby's the father of Inge's baby, don't you? You think she's been having an affair—"

The velocity of his reaction rendered him brittle as only a rigid man can be when asked to change directions without warning. She thought he might strike her. "You're suggesting Bobby was cuckolded, and I won't hear of such an imbecilic thing!"

Mentally she retreated. She'd been so sure, but now her theory faltered. "It was just a hunch. It seems—well, that Bobby is so indifferent . . ."

Ernest sank down heavily in his chair. Talk of Bobby invariably took so much out of him, leaving him featureless, his voice toneless. "I don't know why those two have ignored the obvious fact that family is the core of life. Maybe it's because Bobby was so difficult that we couldn't have him at home, and he missed the importance of family. But he'll learn. They both will as more children come. He used to be so wild, and look at how he has settled down already."

A new ironic thought occurred to her. "Did you have to buy him a wife with my money?"

"Ridiculous! I never 'bought' Inge. He was unruly—surely you remember. I knew a wife would settle him. So I sent him packing and told him not to expect another cent until he found a good woman. You make it sound as if I made free-wheeling use of your money. That's not so."

Of first importance was to know just how depleted her finances were. She had skirted the problem as if it were a lump in her breast, needing to know and yet not daring to face it. Still, no matter how bad things were, she could survive. Grandfather had done it often, when the cattle market got so bad, they were shipping cows for their hides and tallow. He'd hung on then, had squeaked by without laying off a single hand; had, in fact, taken on a few down-and-out waddies from neighboring spreads. He had incurred few risks even then, for land could be had for next-to-nothing. He'd grasped every opportunity to enlarge his holdings, and even had allowed the former owners to stay on as share-croppers. She was made of the same stuff.

They sat over the breakfast dishes, each lost in plans. At length she said, "There are two stipulations to my cooperation. First, I must see the *real* records. This morning. If I'm legally culpable, I deserve to know what you've done."

He did not acquiesce but asked, "And the other?"

"Rescind your order that Madam not speak to me about Elsie and Snider's death."

His look of puzzlement couldn't have been feigned. "I don't know what you're talking about. I don't care what that old gypsy says—I've never had anything to do with her. What's your fascination with that idiot Elsie?"

Relief washed over her like a warm bath. Ernest's indifference cleared him of any involvement. She would like to think that, bestial as she had come to view him to be, she hadn't been completely mistaken about the man she married.

He went on. "If you're thinking that moron might know something about the killing, you're giving her credit for more sense than she has. If she had stood there and watched the whole thing—which she may very well have done—she wouldn't comprehend it. You don't understand inferior people, Adrian. They're less than human. They're like animals."

But then what fantasy had gone through Elsie's head to inspire her ridiculous confession? *If there were only a way to unlock her mind.*

Too, there was the matter of the apricots, *the uneaten apricot preserves.*

46

Despite Ernest's grumbles, Adrian drove him to the bank to go over the books and show her exactly what he took and how he covered his tracks. The amount surprised even Ernest, but it obviously filled him with inordinate pride. The amount took Adrian's breath away. He was cleverer than she'd imagined. *The spoils of the earth belong to the self-disciplined,* she thought.

She was certain, given his reputation as a wealthy banker and civic leader, she could convince her creditors that, due to the merging of their interests, their accounts were temporarily in limbo. She could get extensions or make arrangements to pay only the interest for a while. Surely she could manage that much money somehow.

Nothing much could be done about the Hedley cotton farm or the Hereford place. The crops had been sold for the year and the money had already reached Ernest's pocket, for she found no indication that it had ever been deposited to her account. She was faced with paying taxes and making mortgage payments on two places almost immediately.

When she'd seen as much as she could stomach, she rose to leave. "Tell the driver to come for you when you're ready to come home."

"I fired him," he said. "He was just one more expense."

She raised her eyebrows. "So you're satisfied he wasn't the man you saw in Inge's room?"

"Not even close."

As she drove toward the mansion, she mulled over her options. Her chief concern was the ranch. She might, if her creditors called her in, forfeit the other parcels, but she would never put the ranch in jeopardy. The bank held the note, due in January, so it would be simple enough to get an extension. But she must be cautious; she mustn't weaken Ernest's house of cards. If the bank's true condition were discovered before he could make good his machinations, her own chances of getting back her trust money were nil. Much as it pained her to see the house her father had built go, she decided to put it on the market.

But when she got home and called the newspaper, Slick Naylor had a surprise for her. "Now is this ad to substitute for the one your husband gave me, or do you want two ads?"

"Ernest gave you an ad? About my house?"

"Yes ma'am. Last Thursday. It'll come out in this week's paper."

Sonofabitch. It was a good thing she was shipping him off to Zurich, before he could filch another dime. *No wonder Ernest admired Snider: they were so much alike,* she thought with a pang almost like longing. Strange how often her thoughts turned to Snider. *Damn him for dying.*

When she heard Ernest arrive by cab in less than an hour, she hurried to the back hall, ready to give him what-for. Precious was nowhere in sight, happily, so they would have the privacy she needed to bless him out. But from the small den he called to her.

"Adrian . . . dear . . . come and sit for a minute." He said it far too kindly.

She caught her breath. *Dear God, not more bad news.* She went to affirm her fears. His gray-sandy brows were drawn close, an inverted V over small sorrowing eyes. It was possible that he was acting again, but she doubted it. He motioned to a chair with the jerky festinating gesture of a doddering old man, frightening authentic, if indeed it was a performance. The usually poker-straight shoulders slumped in—what? Defeat?

I have played this scene before, she thought, the panic rising in her like a black tide. But nothing could ever be as bad as that time again.

For one tunnel moment she thought he might be about to confess to Snider's murder, and then what would she do? Keep quiet about that, too, just to give him time to recoup her money?

But to her surprise, he took her hand. "Adrian, if I could undo the past months, so help me, I would; I'd do things differently. I don't regret the 'donations,' but I wouldn't have left you completely stripped." He drew away and clasped his hands between his knees, as if to keep them warm. The little match boy, commanding pity. "You know there's a ranch note coming due."

"I hope to cover that by selling the house. Which reminds me: why did you—"

"I . . . thought we could hold onto that note with no difficulty. But something has gone wrong. The bank doesn't hold that note anymore."

At the mention of the ranch, she had placed herself at a remove from which she could listen as if she were Elsie willing unconsciousness while being raped.

It was time to regain consciousness. She leaned back and brooded. Since she could remember, she'd been making concessions for survival. She didn't cross her father, not seriously, because she was his dependant. Then her mother's death had left her bereft, ignorant of the simplest practical skills required just to function. But Ernest, as her trust officer, had stepped in to offer support, and she'd leaned upon it, thankful to be relieved of the burden of having to learn the impossibly complicated minutiae from which she'd always been shielded. Oh, she had picked up a lot over the ensuing years, but she had left too many details to Ernest and to Snider.

And still she was making concessions. Must she remain silent about Ernest's thievery while her own small empire crumbled? She cried out, "How could you let the note go?"

"I didn't. It was Bobby. There's not a dime on the books to show for it, either. He's been doing a bit of embezzling on his own, I suppose. But your property! The imbecile! It's like cutting off his own leg. I told you he was stupid. I can't leave him in charge for twenty minutes."

She felt queasy and empty in her new enlightenment. *There's always some vulture poised on a limb, waiting for you to stumble.* Uneasily she thought of times when she had done the same thing. She said, "Maybe, if we go to whoever bought the note and offer a much larger payoff later, he'll back off and give us a few months of grace."

"Exactly my thinking. He'd never take the ranch from you, as loyal as he's always been."

Startled, she jerked her head up. "You know who holds the note?"

"It's Mobeetie James."

A pain, quick like a rattler, darted across her heart. First Snider and now Mobeetie, who had conveniently closed his eyes to her relentless longing as she had Snider's. His pride was a sore unhealed, waiting, deeper even that she imagined.

She couldn't believe he meant to take the ranch. This must be only a ruse, a weapon to get some leverage. He always claimed, and rightly, that he was only a cowboy. Surely he didn't really want to own the place, for God's sake. Where would he get the money to run it? For that matter, how had he scraped together enough to buy the note? Assuming that money had changed hands at all . . . .

Now that she thought about it, she suspected that Bobby and Mobeetie were in cahoots. Bobby's antagonism over his father's marriage supplied the motive. She'd never detested Bobby Vogel more than at this moment. She could strangle him with no regrets.

She jumped up. "Stay right here until I get to the bottom of this." Meekly, he nodded.

She barreled out to the ranch, breaking a crust of early-forming frost already covering the dirt road, giving it an old, hoary look. The temperature was dropping dangerously. A norther must be on the way. She should have dressed more warmly, but no matter: her adrenalin would keep her warm. She thought of how often she had been witness to and partaker of the vast repose of prairie and heaven. Yet other times she had stood at the window and watched with leaden dread as the rolling blue norther took its toll of the livestock and their spirits.

She met Mobeetie at the main gate emptying the mailbox. He pushed back his hat the better to stab her with his hard, brittle gaze. His voice kept an affable lift, like honey coating a jalapeno pepper, but he spat over his shoulder. "Out for a ride? Or did you come to run me off?"

"Neither. We need to talk business." She gunned on past him, stirring up a wall of dust which he was forced to ride through. Not a good beginning, she chided herself ruefully.

He parked beside her and kicked at the regiment of mongrel dogs that had taken up residence in the protection of the house's outer wall. She followed him inside. He didn't offer her coffee, but she went on past him into the kitchen, threw her coat over a chair back and sat. He leaned against the door jamb and crossed his arms. She didn't expect him to make it easy.

She asked him to sit down. He shrugged and straddled a chair backward and waited, but she blurted it out, forgetting her resolve to be diplomatic. "You know why I'm here."

"Why don't you tell me?" He was rigid, determined to make it more difficult. She felt her power draining off, sluicing away to him. He was sinking her. She was listing like a ship.

"Okay, I guess I deserve this groveling," she said evenly. "I've come to tell you I acted foolishly the other night." When he feigned puzzlement, she added, "That night in the pickup."

He feigned trying to remember, wringing every drop of her patience. Then he looked up quickly and shot her a grin. "Foolish hardly covers it, lady."

"Well, it's the best I can do, and it's the best you're going to get," she said heatedly. "Now, are you going to accept my apology for pushing you out of the truck, or not?"

He got up, kicking his chair out of the way. "Yeah, I do—for pushing me out of the truck. But not for firing me. You should never have done that, lady. This ranch don't run without me."

"I know that," she said, quietly submissive. She held onto the edges of the table, not willing to relinquish the chair as he opened the back door, holding it for her. "I didn't mean it. I was hurt. Terrible hurt." *God.* She sounded like Mother.

Still he held the door, not looking at her, the knot along his jaw working hard, gnawing a distant resentment. He had dismissed her.

Finally she said, "Am I being ushered out of my own house, then?"

His look of amazement warned her she'd said the wrong thing again. He spat out a rapid, mean laugh, like bullets. The skin around his agate-black eyes had taken on a choleric flush as if the red stuff in the thermometer had risen to the top. "Your house? *Your* house? This was once your grandfather's, and now it's mine. You never belonged here."

She jumped up, ready to fight, but a sudden fear quelled her. Belatedly she took note of the gravelly menace in his voice, a muffled rumbling undercurrent like lava. He was holding himself in check with great effort. A visible vein throbbed in this neck. His hands clenched and unclenched with impatience just to be shed of her. He could as easily wrest control of the ranch with no more feeling than when he was castrating calves. But he never considered them hers.

It finally dawned. "I've just figured out—why we've had so much trouble communicating. You never thought of me as a person. To you, I was Grandfather's toy." As Snider was hers?

If she expected a denial, she was disappointed. His silence was consent. Shaken, she fumbled past him, not sure when the balance of power had shifted, sure only of defeat without a fight. Her lack of identity in his eyes made her an unworthy adversary. She felt her way down the steps. The years of debasement that had formed the structure of her life-struggle were illuminated as brilliantly as the frosty light. It had been a delusion that the women of the family were partakers of the human experience. She'd been a by-stander, even though he had let her hold the reins on a short stretch of even road. In his estimation, a woman without a man is without substance, and maybe he was right. He had bought himself insurance against intimacy.

A chilling wind hooted around the corner of the house, biting into her legs, almost sweeping her feet from under her. The pulley on the old cistern whined in protest. She made her way with tortured, plodding steps toward the car, accepting the wind's buffeting as just punishment for her life-long gullibility. She closed her eyes against the dirt. Many a night she'd wrapped up in a wet sheet to keep the sand off. Along with Grandmother, she and Snider had lowered sheets into the cistern and dragged them through the snarling wind to the bunkhouse, so the boys could breathe in them. Believing all the time that she was one of them, that she mattered. Maybe she'd not mattered much even to Snider. She was as big a fool as Elsie, except that Elsie had grown up *knowing* that the spoils of the earth were reserved for somebody else.

She tore across the prairie at a treacherous speed, daring an obstacle to loom up through her tears. Never part of the ruling class after all. Born into the serving, faceless mass of crones who clean the toilets. The world's foot soldiers. *I have perpetuated the myth of my existence. Like Elsie Puckett.* The fleeting thought of Elsie, of her vulnerability in this perverse place, kept Adrian from careening off into the jutting rocks in the gulch. Or it could have been the kernel of rage burning like a pilot light at her core flaring just long enough to get her through the brakeland and out on the other side. She passed the half-dugout where the Madam had once lived. First dwelling of valiant settlers. They had been no more than cavemen then, surviving on little more than their wits. Things hadn't changed all that much.

She drove in a state of despair, casting for solutions. There was Snider's estate; no one knew yet that he had willed the house to Elsie. Adrian was torn between ethics and survival. There were valuables of Grandmother's, things that were rightfully hers. She was executrix of his estate. She had yet to assess what might be sold to satisfy his debts—and possibly a few of her own. She refused to think of this as dishonest; Snider had helped Ernest milk her estate. And shouldn't she have shared in Grandfather's personal possessions? Now it was unthinkable that an outsider, even Elsie, should inherit her grandmother's things, especially her silver, at long last.

Elsie would never know the difference. And old man Puckett would squander everything.

Despite that Ernest was waiting, she turned off in front of Snider's citadel, now stark and moribund on it own wind-swept Golgotha. Eventually her old key turned in the lock and admitted her into the fusty-smelling house, a place she'd never again be comfortable entering.

It was dark and cold. The electricity was disconnected, so she moved through the rooms pulling up the crackling shades, letting the chilly sun strain through dirty panes. She returned to Snider's study and Grandfather's pigeon-hole desk, still piled high with papers. Not knowing what to look for, she sifted listlessly through them, trying to shuck off her leaden sense of loss.

Once before, the house had been this quiet. It was when Grandmother lay in state and she stood alone beside the wasted corpse in its coffin. The same eerie apprehension crept over her now in the waning light of the old place, beset with groans and creaks every time a gust buffeted its ancient timbers. Repeatedly her attention left the papers and roved the room, coming to rest on the hallway door. With growing surety, she sensed a presence somewhere near. There was no sound other than the whistling wind through a thousand crannies and her own quick breaths through her parched lips. She got up quietly and stole to the door, peering around the corner into the cavernous hall stretching darkly to the back of the house.

The light from the oval glass front door streaked only dimly to the back reaches of the hall. She took a tentative step into the hall, startling herself with the click of her heel upon the echoing hardwood floor. Swallowing to quiet the pounding in her throat, she heard her own voice resound against the hollow walls. "Who's there?"

A scrape on the stair landing brought tingles between her shoulder blades, a cold shock in her chest. She stood her ground, fists clenched, too terrified to run. Someone was waiting just out of sight. A minute more she stood while her bravado disintegrated by degrees. Then panic seized her. She wheeled back to the study, grabbed her purse, and clattered out the front door to her car.

Once inside with the doors locked, she fumbled for the ignition, not daring to look back at the old house. Someone was more surely watching. She felt it. *Snider!*

"My God, maybe the place is haunted!" She sped away, churning up a cyclone of dust before daring to turn for one more look at Snider's house.

Perhaps she imagined the shadow that darted from the chicken yard to the smoke house.

47

Ernest was waiting in the cavernous kitchen, expecting an accounting for her long absence. The alcohol-induced petechia on his nose and cheeks had grown more pronounced since his illness. Instinctively she withdrew in a sort of purdah as she sidestepped him and went over to the coffee maker. He pulled out his handkerchief and sneezed into it, watching her over it like a bandit.

"Well? Did he back down?"

She didn't care for his abruptness, which left her no room to protect herself. "Actually, we didn't discuss it." She shook her head tiredly; felt stray wisps of hair fan the air.

She wanted to go off by herself like an old cat, to die. But she was chilled to the marrow—partially from shock—and the kitchen offered the only solace in the house. They both had decided not to turn on the furnace until absolutely necessary to save on fuel bills. She sat at the table and wrapped her hands around her warm cup.

He hawked and spat into the sink while she cringed, ignoring his mutterings that Mobeetie wasn't cut out to be a landowner. "You should've let me take care of it. I can deal with him."

The kernel of rage pulsated, flared again, but she concentrated on keeping her tone even. "You will not go to see him. You will *not* beg that man on my behalf."

He snorted. "What's more important, Adrian, the ranch or your pride?"

He turned on the water to wash the phlegm down the drain, and she moved her chair so she wouldn't have to watch. He had asked a loaded question, like offering a choice of poisons.

"I feel driven to make you understand how I've always felt about *things*," she said. "Objects, I mean. I guess I've clung to—like, for instance,

Mother's belongings—to make me know who I am." She hurried on past his frowning and detached discomfort. "I realize you're not the slightest interested. That's what I've learned to live with: nobody has ever been interested. But I'll have my say all the same. I've clung to *things* to give myself an identity, and that's the meaning of the land to me."

He leaned against the cabinet, staring out the window into the bleak winter afternoon. Only a thin ribbon of rosy haze streaked the western sky.

"Ernest?"

He didn't turn around, apparently nailed to the wall of his own indifference.

"Ernest, you have no idea how important security is to someone who has no responsibility for her own. Now that I think about it, that's why I've been so greedy for land. It got to be a disease. The more I got, the more I needed. But it never helped a goddam bit."

"Adrian. Watch your language. My God, you sound like a guttersnipe." With a snort, he stalked out of the kitchen, pretending disgust, a ploy he used often. He didn't fool her; he just didn't want to be bothered.

It was futile to try to make him understand. She went into the drafty back hall to retrieve her purse, took out her cell phone and called the ranch. Mobeetie answered immediately.

She was unable to keep from sounding like a chiding, waspish harpy. She took a deep breath and plunged in. "I don't know how you finagled Bobby into giving you the note. I suspect you blackmailed him, and I'm fairly certain I know how. But that no longer matters. The ranch is yours, if you're big enough to raise the money to keep it operating. I can't redeem that note, and I don't even think I want to try."

She wasn't sure he had heard. She couldn't hear him breathing.

At length he said, "Well now, ma'am, that sounds sensible. Anyhow, you've got old Ernest Vogel to take care of you."

She disconnected before she screamed at him. Maybe the life would drain out of her. Maybe collecting things was all that had kept her alive. But instead, she felt a curious release, and with it, a new surge of fury. Fairly panting with outrage, she stormed upstairs, daring her weakness to surface, and slung open the door on a startled Ernest examining his passport. "I am going. Somehow I'd come to believe that without a man, I was homeless. But I have a home, and I'm going back to it. So don't *dare* try to sell it out from under me."

He regarded her with indolent amusement as he pocketed the passport. The longish sideburns on his slack cheeks twitched like the hind end of a feisty kitten. "And what is this little tantrum about?" he asked with merry indulgence. "Do you think walking out solves anything?"

He got up to pat her on the shoulder, but she drew away. He appeared not to notice.

"Anyway, what you said isn't so. You have a home, but it is here. While I was at the bank this morning, I persuaded Earl Rathjen to take your house in exchange for some cash and some those same worthless elevator shares he'd also invested in. It will be his new funeral parlor."

She shrieked out, "Earl, too? Did you chisel money out of everybody in town?"

Ironic that it would soon house the dead. As if it hadn't been doing that for years, if she were honest. She wondered if he thought he could actually sell it without her permission.

"We're lucky to find someone who'll take it," he said. "A place that large could stand vacant for years in a town like this, especially with the economy the way it is. Luckily, it's available at just the right time. Earl wanted to cash in his 'elevator shares' and enlarge his present location. I had to do some fast talking to get him to take the house instead."

He had already dismissed her outburst. He took a strutting turn around the room. "This deal with Ratjen is a bit of luck. Now I won't have to worry about him rattling the bars at the bank wanting his money when I leave. This gives me some breathing room."

The weight of her anger and frustration left her weak. "How dare you dispose of my house without so much as consulting me! Why, I ought to—"

He shrugged. "I had no choice. Anyway, I've decided it might be wise to be prepared to stay in Europe for a while. I'll need someone to take care of me, so you and I—"

She couldn't believe it. "You haven't heard a word I've said. I'm through with this shoddy pretense that I'm your wife; that I have anything to gain by staying." She hated becoming shrill and strident, so she swallowed and tried again. "I'll still cover for you, but for no other reason than to get my money back. I don't know why, but I want to keep trying to hold things together."

He showed a moment of genuine concern, but he dissembled quickly. "All right. I may as well tell you. I've taken an apartment in Mainz that will be my headquarters until I'm sure my investment is safe—in other words, until Otto's estate is mine. In time, he might even invite me to move into his mansion. I must oversee everything to keep some greedy outsider from wresting control." He had forgotten about her.

"I've been worrying about how I could cover my commitments at the bank. But now that this house deal has come along, with Ratjen out of my hair, plus even a little cash in the deal, we'll be able to make a clean break . . . ." He was again lost in his own plans, rubbing his freckled hands together with the cupidity of a gypsy peddler.

She snapped to. "Wait a minute! I've got taxes due and mortgages and a twenty-thousand dollar payment on an irrigation well. That is *my* house and *my* money, and it will go for *my* commitments. What's the matter with me? I'm letting somebody do it to me again!"

"Yes, yes. Well, well." He wiped his mouth, muting his greed for the moment. "The fact is we're not going to need those farms. They'll only be a bother in years to come. We've outgrown that sort of thing. We've become international."

She sputtered in helpless exasperation. "You really think, after this, I'd leave town and run off with you to Europe? Listen to me!" She jabbed him in the chest, pushing him backward until he landed on the bed. "I was born in this mongrel country, when there were only a few towns. Just think: my great-grandparents were pioneers, modern-day pioneers. While the east coast, and even other parts of Texas, were in the middle of the industrial revolution, this was still Indian country, right where we're standing. This isn't ancient history we're talking about."

He studied her for a moment. "You're saying this land means as much to you as Germany's thousands of years does to Uncle Otto. I get it. But even if you won't come with me, I'll keep my end of the bargain. You'll get your investment back, if you cover for me at the bank."

Her composure was shredded. She was only minutes away from violent shakes, although she couldn't analyze what bothered her most. She threw up her hands and headed for the door.

"I simply can't answer that now," she said. "I don't know . . . maybe I've rounded a corner. Maybe I can't ever go back to things the way they used to be."

Snider used to plead for a return to the past, after she'd betrayed him, turned on him for some minor infraction of her spur-of-the-moment code. "But yesterday you said . . . ," he'd whine, but her retort was generally, "Will you never learn that I'm not the same twice in a row?" To be the same was to be trapped. To keep bobbing with fancy footwork was to remain free. But she had damaged Snider, broken his spirit, trained him into mute obeisance, degraded him for no reason other than her need to take out on someone her unacknowledged rage over Grandfather's treatment of her as a mere girl. She had helped author the role he played, delineated to the town the myth of his ineptness, to which even he subscribed. She couldn't make it up to him now. It was hard to put that out of her mind.

48

A fresh norther cut across the plains that night, a wind raw as a rope burn, tearing into the hides of the cattle and rattling its way into snug homes through chimneys and flue pipes. Adrian had slept under covers so heavy her toes hurt, listening to the wind's rasp through the bare branches of the Chinese elm outside her window. Yet she was oblivious to the cold, because she was on fire with an idea at once appalling and thrilling, and she was frustrated because she had no time to investigate now. Still, the prospect propelled her out of her warm bed at first light.

First, she had work to do. Bills were beginning to pour in, but she was able to stall most of them. "We're in a period of transition since I married Mister Vogel," she must have said a dozen times in that matter-of-fact, imperious manner which had been her defense for years.

There was no reason for alarm, as far as most of their creditors would be able to tell. She and Ernest were reckoned the two wealthiest people in the county. Too, the general economic mood was hopeful, which ought to buy them a little time.

"It'll be a disaster if somebody calls in a loan," she told Ernest at breakfast. "Word'll get around, and there'll be a stampede."

Ernest had nothing to say. He had groused around ever since he got up, finding fault with everything. Now he had changed his tactic to silence.

She threw down her fork with a clatter. "You know, for somebody who needs help, you're the most arrogant man I've ever met."

He got up and helped himself to a toothpick, turning his back on her. She supped her coffee in seething silence, watching its steaming tendrils disappear in the unheated breakfast room. Her life-long sense of plenty had melted and slid from her like ice off a roof, leaving her feeling as deprived as a Puckett. She had just given Precious notice to look for work elsewhere, but she told her she could continue to live in the quarters above the garage indefinitely. She dreaded dismissing the two young Pucketts, as well, for she knew how much Miz Puckett depended on her patronage.

Besides, they were her link with Elsie.

Bobby stuck his head in the door, dressed for the bank. "Precious tells me she's been canned. What's the deal?"

"The deal is, there's no money to pay her," Adrian snapped. "So you and Inge won't be enjoying room service anymore. You'll have to wait on yourselves, like the rest of us."

Ernest motioned to him. "Come in. I want to talk to you."

Bobby stepped just inside with shifting reluctance. "Can't it wait?"

Ernest glared. "That's an arrogant stance from someone who has just disposed of your step-mother's ranch note without leaving a sign of paperwork."

Bobby paled but kept his cool. "If there's no paperwork, what makes you think I had anything to do with it?"

Adrian couldn't keep still. "Can it, Bobby. We both know you did it. Mobeetie as much as admitted it, and I know why he was able to talk you into giving it to him."

"You don't know what you're talking about." Bobby wheeled and headed for the door.

"Wait, young man. I'm still your father." Ernest's tone was enough to stop Bobby in his tracks, but when he didn't run around, Ernest said to his back, "I'm leaving tomorrow. I—could postpone it a day if you and Inge are ready to go. But no longer than that."

Bobby wheeled, his face flushed with the effort of defying his father. "We can't leave, Pop. Inge isn't strong enough. Anyway, maybe I should stay on at the bank until you get back."

"That's not necessary. What do you think Adrian's for?" Ernest caught himself and turned to smile at Adrian with a defensive shrug.

She could see the boy needed help; besides, if she were ever to get the note back, she would need him nearby. "I don't think it's unreasonable," she said. "I've hardly been at the bank enough yet to know the routine. I haven't the faintest idea what to do."

"To hell with it. The two of you are in cahoots." Ernest, seeing himself outdistanced, stalked out, leaving them alone.

Bobby said grudgingly, "Thanks."

She was too cross to be pleasant. "What for? I meant it. You certainly can stay until I learn what I'm doing, at least."

"Are we to continue to charm one another by living under the same roof after Dad leaves?"

"I have no choice. Ernest has sold my house out from under me." It wasn't quite the truth. Obviously she'd have to sign the sale papers. Otherwise, Rathjen would find out he held phony elevator shares, and the whole thing would unravel for all of them.

Bobby broke into laughter. "I hope you're not planning to stay long," he said, "because if Uncle Otto doesn't kick the bucket soon, you'll be trespassing. Dad never owned this place. The bank owns it. And probably owes more on it than it's worth."

"I should have known. Well, that's not my headache," she said as she stormed out. She was bluffing, of course. She still planned to get to the bottom of whatever hold Mobeetie held over Bobby.

For the time being, she dismissed it from her mind. She had decided that when Mozelle and Sael came to work that morning, she would take them to Snider's to help her clean and sort, a chore that had taken on urgency in the light of their straitened circumstances. Not that she was frightened to go there alone. She had overcome her terror. By the light of a new day, it seemed clearly a silly fabrication of her agitated imagination. The sound she'd heard was probably the scrape of a tree limb against the roof. It could not have been the ghost of Snider Greene. But still she saw that body hanging in the bleak shadows every time she closed her eyes.

Daylight was mired in an eerie orange haze. The norther had churned up a cloud of dust, and when the wind quieted, a suspended fog was left shimmering in the cold sun. The old house on the hill stood surrounded by a nimbus, an unearthly halo, which even the Pucketts commented on as they drove up.

The windmill groaned in the unnatural stillness which lay over the hill. She must remember to send Sael out to turn it on. While the Pucketts got boxes from the trunk, she took the lead up the front walk, her bravado surprising even herself. She felt for her key, then remembered her hasty getaway the last time. She tried the door, and it gave way. Stupid of her not to have locked it.

The two Pucketts plowed in ahead of her, yammering about who was to do what, complaining about the dark and the smell. She took a deep breath and plunged across the threshold, ashamed of her absurd fright. As usual, she manufactured the necessary resolve, hoping it would carry her, hoping it was evident in her voice.

"Mozelle, you begin in the kitchen," she said, following them down the long hall to the back. "Box up all the edible food, which we'll share. You can take your half to your mother." She threw open the cupboard and was confronted by those rows of apricot preserves.

The gawky Sael danced beside her, eager to be shown his chores, and now that she was satisfied that she and Mozelle would be safe alone in the house, Adrian was eager to get him outside. She led him out the back door and past the smokehouse. The scent of fitch hovered over the yard.

"Turn on the windmill. Then clean out the smokehouse. Snider usually smoked meat in the fall," she said. "I don't know what he'd done before he—but you might find some—" The thought of eating meat that had been smoked along with Snider's body made her gag, but the Pucketts might not be so particular.

"Oh yes ma'am, plenty meat. Leastways, there was last summer."

The shock wave hit her and bolted her to the ground. She walked to the smokehouse and held the hasp in her hand, too weak to pull open the door. She hadn't realized Sael had been in the smokehouse until recently.

"You open the door," she said, overcome by a new fear.

A murid odor struck them in the face. The rats had spoiled what meat had been left hanging. Adrian grimaced and backed out of the dark shed, remaining to survey it from the doorway, calling up some degree of amnesia as protection against the memory of the day she found Snider's corpse. She would have dismissed the contents of the smoke house entirely if meat weren't so expensive . . . Or maybe some insatiable morbid curiosity drew her back.

On the far wall was the blackened fireplace, vented to the outside as well as the inside. When Grandfather wanted to smoke meats, he could build a fire in the outside fireplace and vent the smoke to the inside.

On the floor against the wall to her right sat the wooden salt box, where Grandfather often cured pork, burying it under a layer of salt. Snider hadn't used it since the doctor told him that too much sodium was bad for his blood pressure.

Overhead was the traverse beam from which several small rat-spoiled carcasses hung. Sael pointed to a piece of leather tied loosely around the beam.

"Right there's where he was. Rope went square over that piece of leather. Tied under the arms, And the other end tied to this here anvil." His voice had taken on authority as he indicated a badly rusted iron block which Grandfather had used back in his horse-shoeing days.

The body was not suspended by the neck. How could she have forgotten?

She looked up at the piece of leather on the beam. "Hanging across the leather? I wonder what was the significance of that?"

"I purely remember that," he said, boasting. "It don't seem like he was gutted whilst he was strung up. Seem like he was gutted right about in front of where you're standing."

She gasped and jumped back, noticing the concrete floor in front of the door for the first time. A black circle, the source of a lingering putrid odor, covered a six-foot area of the floor. The police hadn't mentioned it to her, but then, why should they? She retreated beyond the sheltering eave into the sunlight. "Let's forget that place. Go turn on the windmill, and then clean out the chicken house. Get a shovel and bury the remains of the dead birds."

It was a relief to escape to the house. She went up front to Grandfather's old room in hopes of finding something of value in Snider's desk. She found the strong box almost immediately, but it took almost an hour to locate the key, stuck down in the corner of the top drawer. The room was too dark to see the contents well, so she took it into the hallway and dumped it out onto the floor in front of the oval glass door. Her original anticipation changed to disappointment when she saw that the documents were blanks.

"How strange," she muttered, puzzled that Snider would save blank forms like marriage licenses and birth certificates. *Maybe he had used one to fake a marriage to Elsie.*

A possibility came to mind at once, or course, and the appalling idea which had kept her awake all night became less implausible by the moment. It was a terrible thought, one which caused the hairs on the back of her neck to prickle, but one which she could voice to no one.

49

When the insistent pounding invaded her consciousness, Adrian attributed it to Sael nailing something outside. Eventually she realized that someone was banging the huge brass knocker on the front door. She looked at the clock, saw it was only a little past nine.

It had already been a long day. She had heard Ernest get up at six but had ignored the noise as he pottered around downstairs in the kitchen. It was the day of his departure for Zurich, but he could fix his own breakfast, or he could do without. She listened as he tiptoed past her door a half-hour later, obviously making his way down to tell Bobby and Inge goodbye. It irritated her that he hadn't waked her, so she got up and stuck her head out into the hall. He was slipping a letter under Bobby's door. She felt better. At least he wasn't telling Bobby goodbye, either. But she condescended to give him the briefest of goodbyes as he passed her door. By the time his Bentley roared away, she was back in bed.

Now, reawakened by the knocking, she went out to the railed landing which fed onto the curved stairway. From there, she could lean over and see the feet of her caller through the foyer glass. It probably wasn't Mobeetie, and she didn't want to face a bill collector. Even if it was Mobeetie, she wasn't sure she wanted to see him. *Dear God, let it be Mobeetie.*

They were not the feet of a man: the length of the hem was the giveaway: Madam waited outside. Sensing this might be the break in her fortunes that she'd always come to expect in hard times, Adrian fastened her robe as she hurried down to open the door.

The *bruja* eyes dissected Adrian, commanding entrance, taking charge. Without speaking, Adrian stepped aside and allowed the big woman to sweep past like royalty, her voluminous dress trailing like a train, and turn directly into Ernest's elegant drawing room as if she knew where to go.

Madam sucked in her breath, probably surprised to find the furnishings draped in sheets. She walked over and picked up the cover of a magnificent side table, touching a heavy crystal dish, fingering a Chiparus figurine before she dropped the cloth back upon them. She looked around, spending several minutes in proprietary examination of the room's appointments while Adrian waited uneasily near the door, certain of her vulnerability in respect to the woman but ignorant as to how she came to feel beholden to and at the mercy of Madam. Taking on Elsie had rendered her vulnerable, somehow.

"Nice," Madam said at length. She dropped down on the shrouded sofa in a jangle of beads. "Come, sit, lady; we have things to discuss."

"What sort of things?" Adrian eased tentatively onto a straight-back chair, poised to take flight if necessary.

Madam's face was hidden in shadows, but Adrian didn't think of pulling the drapes. Often, as a small child, she had been so weak with anticipation by Christmas morning that she couldn't rise from her bed to join the family around the tree. She felt a similar weakness now. She couldn't see the woman's expression, but she could detect her appalling gall from her tone.

Madam expelled an exaggerated sigh. "I find myself in embarrassing circumstances. Business has not been good in my new location. I find I must move on."

Relief mixed with disappointment flooded Adrian. She lied easily. "That's too bad."

"Indeed. It's especially unfortunate since I do not have funds to make a move to the west coast as I'd planned. I must ask you to help me."

Adrian expected that. *Everybody wants money eventually.* She stalled for time, hoping to pump information from her before she admitted that she had no money. "But why so far away?"

"The terrorists are coming," Madam said darkly. "You Americans do not believe it, but the terrorists will not stop. Ever. I am getting out, maybe to Canada. Everybody hates Americans, but Canadians, not so much."

Adrian suspected that what Madam feared was much closer to home than the terrorists. *Or maybe,* she thought, *every old woman in the world is paranoid.*

Madam went on, urgently. "You are wondering why I should come to you? I don't come for a handout. It is because I have something to sell that you want very much."

Adrian shivered involuntarily. "What's that?"

"My silence."

Adrian regarded her with amusement. "You're wrong. I'm not the least interested in my cousin. You can tell the world anything you want." She was lying again, hoping to extract more by feigning disinterest.

Madam's heavy eyebrows shot up; she was clearly surprised. "Is it possible that you remain ignorant of the situation in which you are living? It is clear I've come to the wrong person." She rose and crossed the room with her Cossack strides, but Adrian leaped from her sentinel post and caught the big woman's arm.

So it wasn't about Snider. In that case, it must be about Ernest, and Adrian needed to know. "Don't go," she said. "Maybe we can make a deal, after all."

"For instance?"

Adrian groped for bait. Damn Ernest Vogel. If ever she needed cash, it was now. "I—find myself in the embarrassing position of being without ready funds, but I have furniture to sell. I'll have the money in a day or so. I'm willing to pay a reasonable amount—not to keep silent, but to talk. To me. To tell me—whatever it is."

Madam's face brightened and she broke into a cackle which Adrian feared would carry upstairs to Inge's rooms. The woman slapped her head. "Oh Lord, I have backed into my exit! Why didn't I think of it? Of course, you would be ignorant. All right, that's fair. We have always been friends. I am willing to wait—but only for a short time. You will contact me? I'll be in the little chicken coop I call home."

Adrian nodded. "I'll come when I have the money. But we haven't discussed how much."

"That will depend on you. My price today is five thousand dollars. Each day I delay endangers my life, because those mongrels are coming from the Middle East, make no mistake. I saw it in my crystal ball. So each day I stay over will cost you an extra thousand."

It was more than Adrian had expected. That amount would take a healthy hunk out of what she could get from the sale of her furniture, but she knew haggling was useless. "I'll get it as soon as I can. Fortunately, Ernest has left town, so he won't have to learn anything about this."

It was as if Madam already knew about Ernest. She smiled darkly as she leaned toward her and whispered, "Ah, Mrs. Vogel, you think it is your husband I fear? Pah! It is the other Mister Vogel who has a black heart. Why do you think I waited until he left the house? I value my life so I have left instructions to contact the sheriff to pick up Bobby Vogel if anything should happen to me. I warn you, if you must continue to live under this roof, take every precaution."

Adrian sensed the truth of this, but her logical side remained in command. She was cooling to the proposition. She didn't care to pay to hear of Bobby's shenanigans, if that's what this was about. Besides, she could guess what Madam intended to reveal. She waved the woman aside. "Bobby is capable of many foolish things, but violence is not one of them."

"You would be surprised, Mrs. Vogel . . . ." She swung through the door almost gaily.

For the briefest moment Adrian wondered if Ernest was responsible for the woman's visit. Maybe he was making a last-ditch attempt to throw suspicion off of himself by implicating his own son. Maybe she should call the sheriff then and there, but on the off-possibility that Elsie might somehow be drawn into any new investigation of Snider's death, she decided to wait.

Because in her mind, Elsie's fate was now inexplicably tied to her own.

50

Ernest did not tell Adrian exactly when he was to fly to Switzerland, because he had no intention of going to Dallas and risking a repeat of the last security flap. No questions would be asked if the crate was loaded onto its final carrier from the local airport, so he had made arrangements for a smaller NetJet to pick him up in Attebury and take him directly to Zurich. As far as Adrian knew he must leave early in the morning in order to make a plane connection in Dallas, but his real reason for leaving so early was to make a quick trip to Amarillo.

They said a frosty goodbye at about seven-thirty. He told her he would be gone a week, two at the most. She might have been suspicious had she known that he carried extra suitcases, for Ernest had as many valuables as he could comfortably transport, primarily jewelry. That some didn't belong to him was of no consequence. He had extracted them from lock boxes at the bank on the same night that he took every bit of cash and negotiables he could find. Anything he wasn't planning to dispose of in Amarillo had already been put in the box which Sael had built a crate for inside his van in the dark alley behind the bank. With the proper papers attached to the crate, it wouldn't be opened until Ernest himself opened it at his Swiss bank. He would act as the bank's courier. No one would question that arrangement.

As for the contents of the suitcases, he planned to leave them with a reputable broker who was willing to pay in advance—at fifty cents on the dollar—and wire the payment directly to his Swiss bank. After the transaction was completed, he would drive back to Attebury airport and dump the Bentley. It was another item that he owed more on than it was worth.

As for Bobby, well, he had been warned. Even that morning he had tried one last time to urge Bobby to take Inge and get out. But without giving away more than he dared—for he couldn't trust his own son any farther than he could drop-kick him—he could only plead with him to get out for his own good. But the little prick was too much his mother's son. He was dragging his feet about leaving Attebury just to be contrary. The kid had never fitted in here. He had nothing to hold him except his stubbornness. Well, so much for trying to help. Ernest had washed his hands of him.

In the lengthy letter he had composed to Bobby, he left instructions outlining those household furnishings and paintings that were mortgaged and which ones were free and clear, which Bobby could either sell or keep. Ernest was through arguing. If the brat didn't want to come to Switzerland, nobody was going to beg him. He was a grown man now. If he believed he could make a living, let him try. But when the money ran out, then he might be willing to listen to reason. Eventually, Ernest counted on having his grandson nearby.

He had left many loose ends. It wasn't a tidy departure, not one he could be proud of. He hadn't intended it this way, hadn't meant to cut himself off from Attebury. But the people would get what they deserved. For a year now, since the election that swept his party out of power, sentiment had grown openly against the former Speaker. It had spilled over and tainted people's estimation of Ernest as well. He wasn't an insensitive oaf. He had noticed the abrupt silences when he entered a room, had overheard snatches of conversation about his being in the former Speaker's pocket. His strong party affiliation was an indictment of him wherever he went.

Then there was Adrian. If he'd realized he'd be leaving so abruptly, he could probably have figured another way out. She'd been more than he bargained for, poking into things that were none of her affair. Siding with Bobby about moving to Switzerland. A woman could often come in handy, but no woman defied Ernest Vogel, especially his wife. She should be punished, but the authorities would do that. He took a grave satisfaction in the outworking of justice.

As he pulled out of the drive, he took one last look at his beloved mansion. Then he turned toward the southwest, the opposite direction from the airport. He glanced at the dashboard clock and realized he was running late. He had intended to be on the road before sunup, before anybody was awake to observe.

As he entered the gates of a townhouse development a few blocks away, he broke out in a grin of relief. At least one thing was going right.

Neva Craig waited on the curb, suitcase in hand.

They flew into Zurich and boarded the bus into the city, where Neva would go to the hotel while he went directly to the bank. He wanted Neva to know as little as possible about his business; she already knew too much. That's why it was safer to bring her along. It was a grueling schedule. He needed sleep badly, but as his own courier, he must attend the crate constantly until it reached its destination.

The usually punctual tram was late in pulling out. He settled back, grateful for the chance to rest, but he became unnerved when he heard a passenger ask the conductor about the delay.

"We have been ordered by the police to remain in the terminal, Madame," he said. At least that's what Ernest thought he said; his French was rusty.

Before long, two Swiss policemen boarded the car, obviously searching for someone. Ernest closed his eyes and pretended sleep, but his heart pounded so loudly that he was sure they could hear. They marched up the aisle and snapped to attention at his side.

"Herr Vogel? Be so kind as to follow us, please."

So the money had been discovered. But they couldn't prove anything. He was transporting it to the Swiss bank for safekeeping because . . . because he'd got wind of a terrorist bombing back home. He was preserving the bank's assets; that's all. He had even brought his secretary; she could verify his story. He took a deep breath and straightened his tie as he got up. He must watch his heart, not become upset. Carefully he composed an expression of surprise.

"What's this? Where are we going, officer?"

"There are some questions the captain would like to ask."

So it was the money. No longer able to hide his agitation, he cried out, "You have no right to confiscate that crate. It is the property of the Attebury State Bank in Texas. I am an American citizen."

But they took him off the conveyance and drove him to an interrogation room to question him about the corpse the customs X-ray had revealed.

Adrian was notified of Ernest's arrest by a hysterical Neva Craig, who reached her at noon the next day. What Neva told her made no sense—in fact, Adrian hadn't been aware that the secretary was to accompany Ernest. As soon as she hung up, Adrian phoned the American embassy, trying to get answers from the young aide who promised to call her back.

Within hours he reported in. "The American officials have probably started extradition proceedings, but I must caution you: it doesn't look hopeful. Your husband refuses to give any explanation about the body, except to point out that it passed customs at the Attebury airport with no questions. He has engaged an attorney to fight extradition, as if he anticipated prosecution if he is returned to the States. I've spoken to him, but he is too distraught. He claims the Swiss stole his money, planted the corpse and are holding him on trumped-up charges."

Whatever the truth of it, this incident probably sounded the death knell for her hopes of regaining her "investment" in time to redeem her holdings. She did not believe for a minute that the charges against Ernest were anything but bogus. Ernest might be many things, but he was not a murderer. His family was here, safe, under this very roof. Nobody in town was even missing. But she despised his perfidy to her: taking Neva Craig with him. What was that about?

He wasn't coming back. She couldn't think beyond that. He was leaving her to get out of her financial difficulties the best way she could. Maybe he'd planned this from the beginning.

The surge of adrenalin the revelation brought carried her high. For the moment she was living again. She was late getting to the bank. Not even Neva could be counted on now to do what needed to be done. She would have to call an emergency meeting of the bank's directors, all the while berating herself for having remained silent about his dealings for this long.

The immanence of her own physical deterioration brushed her with its despair. She could not die penniless. If she'd never had anything else, she had always had money. But now even what Snider had was to be denied her. She would have to live long enough to die a wealthy woman somehow.

The urgency clamored to be let in as if it had never been far away. It had long since become her bed fellow. It was to the urgency that she was truly married. The wonder was that it hadn't been a companion since childhood, when she first realized that she was not immortal.

She had planned, prior to the call from Zurich, to give Snider's last will to Bryan Manly. It was a good thing the appointment had already been made; otherwise she might be tempted to destroy the will naming Elsie as his beneficiary. At some level, though, she had the certainty that to deprive Elsie would be to drain the last dram of life from her own body.

Before she left the house, she knocked on Bobby's door, but he was in the shower; she could hear water running. There was no sign of the note

Ernest had left earlier, so she scribbled another telling him of his father's arrest, feeling some retributary elation at the dismay it would cause. She harbored no slim hope that Bobby would fly to his father's rescue and bring him back to her. Not unless there was something in it for Bobby.

She drove directly to Manly's office. He had no clerk, no secretary, no receptionist. He needed the business. She hoped there was at least money for his fee.

"You handle wills, of course," she said to him. "I mean Snider's??"

He said. "I—wasn't aware there was a will. But of course, Snider being a lawyer . . . ."

She handed it to him. "I just came across it. Somewhere in all that mess, there ought to be a little money. I'd collect my fee off the top, if I were you."

He barely glanced at it. "Mrs. Vogel? What about Calvin Huddle? Will you testify in his behalf? You're the only hope he has."

She hesitated. She never knew who might hold the key, who might bring her the potion, the elixir of life. Maybe justice for Calvin was the key. Or better yet, justice for Elsie.

"I'd like to see him again," she said.

She asked to be left alone with Huddle. It was a little town; surely they would grant her that. The jailor and the attorney reluctantly backed out of the visitor's room, leaving the door ajar.

Adrian wasn't satisfied, but she leaned across the table and whispered into the contorted face, smelling his putrid breath and his filthy body. She almost changed her mind, he was that repugnant to be near, but she must look at this from Elsie's point of view.

"I have a proposition," she said, taking care not to let her voice carry to the outer room. "If I get you out of here, would you be willing to take responsibility for Elsie's upkeep?"

"Elsie? The moron?"

"*Hush.* Snider did pay you to impregnate her, didn't he?"

There was no need to wait for his answer.

"You raped her, didn't you?"

He rose from his seat. "She asked for it!"

She shushed him and motioned for him to sit. "Okay, maybe from your standpoint it was a tough call. But regardless, somebody has to take care of her. She's been abused at home in the past by both her father and brother. The old man will make her life a living hell if he learns about her pregnancy—and Elsie won't be able to keep a secret forever."

She leaned even closer and studied his eyes, ignoring the rosette nose as best as she could. "What kind of person are you? Would you—do the honorable thing by Elsie if I helped you get off? Would you provide for her, in other words? Get her out of town?"

He ran his hand through the unkempt ginger hair and fingered the stub of a nose, hatred growing dark in his eyes. Then he smashed his fist against the table so suddenly that she jumped.

"By God, nobody's going to blackmail me into anything! She may've ruined my looks, but she'll never pull me down to her level. I'm not like her or any of you yokels in this friggin' burg. I'll get plastic surgery, and then I'm going to be a star again—"

The outburst brought Flop into the room. Flop grabbed Huddle by the arms from behind. "Come on, buddy, don't nobody yell at Miss Adrian like that." He hustled the Man toward lock-up, while Adrian tried to hide her sudden satisfaction.

In a sense she felt sorry for Huddle, for she had seen his fear. His insistence on seeing himself as different was fear of what could result from allowing familiarity, closeness.

What would she have done if he had taken her up on her proposition? But she had made it knowing he never would, knowing he had no feelings for his victim—yes, victim, and knowing also that someone had to be Elsie's champion. She pursed her lips and tried to look disapproving. She blinked hard; her eyes had misted over, for some asinine reason. She sighed, feeling the weight of the burden she must now carry for the rest of her days.

Bryan Manly placed a tentative finger on her shoulder. "Mrs. Vogel? Do you have something to tell us now that would help me get charges dropped against Huddle?"

It wasn't a decision she'd come to easily. "Whatever gave you such an idea?" she snapped. "I can't tell you a blessed thing. For what he's done, the Man should be locked up for life."

51

They assembled in a room heavy with authority: The enormous mahogany table that dominated the space. Leather-lined walls. Velvet drapes, money-green, hanging most of the full height of the twelve-foot ceilings. A Chinese rug which Ernest and Helga had brought back themselves, years before. Several impressionist paintings which Ernest liked to brag he'd paid a fortune for. A perfectly atrocious hodge-podge of opulence designed to give the members of the board, who were the only ones who ever used the room, assurance of the bank's stability. Adrian found herself gritting her teeth as she took her seat at the head of the table—not from the dread of the task ahead, but from irritation at Ernest's appalling taste.

She'd known most of these men all her life, and more important, they had known her and Grandfather. She didn't approach the hour with apprehension; she expected that she was going to enjoy it, in some perverse way.

Two of the men were ranchers, except that both had chosen to remain on the land, and thus they assumed a superiority over her for betraying the land. Two men were merchants: the owner of the lumber yard and the owner of the dry goods store. The manager of the opera house, the judge, the superintendent of schools, and the president of the college. Bobby Vogel, sanctioned bank vice president and cashier since Helga died, was not present, a fact which surprised her not at all. Neva, who should have been sitting at Adrian's elbow, was also absent. In her place sat a young steno, laptop in hand, set to take notes on the meeting.

Their voices blended in the dull hum de rigueur their exalted office. She waited until they fell silent, until those who'd risen when she swept in purposely late, had taken their seats. She had the sensation that, rather than exposing Ernest, she was about to offer herself as vestal virgin; this was the first test before a council of elders to determine her worthiness to sacrifice herself.

But meting out justice to Calvin Huddle had empowered her. No one in this town would punish him for Elsie's rape and battering, but they would have to hold him accountable for Snider's death, so long as no one but Adrian knew the truth. And she wasn't through. There were others who would be made to pay, if not for their real crimes, then for something else.

So she took a deep breath and plunged in. "Gentlemen, your president has confessed to me that for some time he has been 'borrowing' funds and falsifying records—" She tapped the gavel and raised her voice above their outcry. "—about how the bank has been investing. My own nest egg has been wiped out, and even my ranch is in jeopardy. The note which the bank held has been stolen by my step-son and signed over to my foreman in an out-and-out extortion deal."

Again their voices escalated, and both ranchers, who knew Mobeetie well, reared up in protest. She banged the gavel and waited until they sat down, stunned by the wave of hostility she felt washing against her.

"I don't expect you to take my word for this. I'm asking your permission to bring in an independent auditor to verify what I've said. I don't think you can count on Ernest coming back; he's been arrested in Switzerland, and they've probably impounded the money he shipped out of the country. And Bobby's absence today leads me to believe he's leaving town as well."

A collective state of shock paralyzed the gathering. Adrian looked from one to another around the table: men who had respected Grandfather. Ranchers who tipped their Stetsons to her on the street, who inquired about her health when they met in the bank. She peered into their eyes, but they glanced quickly away, refusing to meet hers now. With a start, she felt their collective animosity as if it were a palpable entity. It was no new thing, she realized; it had been there for years, maybe always. They had resented having to treat her as if she were another man; had resented her money, her power.

It is a war that began years ago, she thought. *I give up. We have run out of foot soldiers.*

She could still win. She could still sit in the closed garage with the motor running. But no . . . they would win again.

She could withdraw. *It's an old avenue for us women; the trees have grown large along it since I was here last. But it's familiar, comfortable. There is comfort in the familiar even when it is painful.*

But there was great stress being a stranger in an enemy camp. It was bad for the health. She knew, too, that she had resided in the camp for a number of years without knowing it—at least consciously. She wondered if an unacknowledged awareness of hostility could make one ill. Her eyes stung from the bristling air. She swallowed and looked for comfort toward the steno girl, who kept her head discreetly ducked. She looked impossibly young. *God, I hate being the oldest woman in the room*, Adrian thought. Funny how, even at a time like this, it was so important. Important to all of them, perhaps.

She was completely alone. But then, hadn't she always been alone? If she had a soul, it must be weeping now. She subdued her own unexpected trembling and stood. "So now the cat's out, there's no need for me to continue this farce. You all have work to do, I expect." She handed over the gavel to the manager of the opera house, who sat to her left.

The opera house scion stared at the mallet in astonishment for a moment, then stood, turning to the young steno.

"Looks like we might be here most of the night, so why don't you bring us the books and then go make us some coffee."

Adrian had already reached the door when he added quietly, "I wouldn't plan on leaving town, if I were you, Mrs. Vogel. Before this day is over, I imagine we'll be planning to file charges against the whole Vogel bunch."

It was as she expected: Bobby was leaving. But the moving van from Amarillo, drawn up in the circular drive at the front entrance, couldn't have been arranged so quickly. He must have planned it for days, waiting for Ernest to leave town to gut the house. By the time she got home, it had been denuded of valuables. She could see the empty rooms through the windows.

She left her car in the drive and ran quickly up the curving stairway to the second level, where very little had been disturbed. She ran the length of the long hall to Bobby's rooms. The furniture was intact, but he was not there. She heard voices across the hall in Inge's suite. Without ceremony she opened the door.

A young man, blond, handsome, vaguely familiar, sat on the bed. Bobby strolled in from the bathroom. Inge was nowhere about.

"You're stealing from your own father, then?" Adrian didn't try to hide her contempt. The young man, of course, must have been the one wearing a towel Ernest had seen earlier in Inge's bathroom. Was he Inge's lover, rather than her brother?

"I'm taking no chances, dear Adrian," Bobby said with not a trace of fear. "If he ever comes home again, I may be penniless. If he comes home and you have ruined him, which I suspect you have done today, then I'll be penniless. I might even be indicted."

"I may bring charges against you for stealing my ranch note," she said.

He ignored her and went on. "If he comes home and you tell him about Klaus being here, I'll be penniless. I can at least live comfortably for a few years—maybe more—on the sale of that truckload."

She looked around. "Where's Inge? Where's the baby?"

Klaus snorted, but Bobby shot him a look. "Inge is gone for good. She fancies herself an actress, poor deluded girl. She has gone to Hollywood to break into the movies." He said it as if it were of no consequence.

The hair rose on the back of Adrian's neck. Inge had disappeared, and Ernest had transported a corpse to Switzerland. Had he done it knowingly?

She pressed on. "And the baby?" She held her breath, worried about his answer.

"Precious has taken him to her quarters. I thought that was best for now."

Relief spread through her bones. She looked at the two men. "And you're leaving today?"

Behind her she heard a shuffle and a familiar voice. "I don't think they'll be going anywhere. Or you, either, Miss Adrian. I'm holding you as a material witness."

She knew him before she turned around. She was looking into the barrel of Flop Pyle's Colt 45. "Oh please!" she said. "A gun? Really!"

It would fitting, she knew, were she manacled and led away to a dank dungeon where at last she would uncover the pearl of great price; would scoop it up in a handful of ooze and would be transformed at once into the fairest of Somethings she'd never dared to imagine. For the urgency that never slept dogged her yet and would follow her behind iron bars.

Still, mightn't she have anticipated that even this, perhaps her most dramatic moment, would be flawed by its ordinariness?

There was something illusion-flaking about the process of arrest, beginning with the ride downtown in the back seat of Flop's squad car, shared with the most detestable of men, Bobby. She wasn't actually manacled; Flop wouldn't dare. But he was cool, refusing to respond to her overtures at conversation with more than a grunt. With the tedium of the processing, reality began to assert itself.

Here she was, assuming liability again, this time, for Ernest. Why did it seem familiar, like a recurring nightmare? Hadn't she also shouldered the early burdens of Mother and Daddy, to say nothing of Baby Sister? And later of Grandfather? And hadn't she accepted ongoing responsibility for Snider for the whole of his life? Hadn't she relinquished the ranch to Mobeetie without so much as a bleat of outrage to the authorities?

And now, hadn't she somehow assumed a like role with even Elsie Puckett? Good lord, she had been a lifelong martyr. Some weakness in her makeup at birth must account for it, some monumental self-centeredness that she never outgrew. As a baby, perhaps, she believed the sun shone for her. Did she then feel she must do oblation for the rain? Predisposition it must have been, which became habit. She began to feel wiser in the process of unlearning. The pattern, the nebulous pattern, had revealed itself; it was the pattern of everlasting prostitution.

52

During the several hours that Adrian cooled her heels before Bryan Manly could find the judge, she concocted a possible scenario: The trial of Adrian Craddock Vogel would take less than a half-day. The prosecution would have a strong case, assembled on the spur-of-the-moment. The defendant would be shown to be in devilish financial straits, having by poor management, frittered away the sizeable fortune left her by her late grandfather. She had gained the confidence of her new husband, a banker of integrity and wide repute, used her waning wiles upon the still grieving widower, wangling the lovesick groom into diverting enormous sums of cash for their own use, possibly to pay off her wide-ranging debts.

Not many people would believe it. Sentiment against Ernest was already running high. Most people had a natural suspicion of his political cronyism, and nobody believed that Bobby wasn't also somehow involved, pervert that he was notwithstanding. But not a shred of evidence would be garnered to implicate Bobby. He probably wouldn't even be arraigned.

At best, Bobby would spend a few frantic hours in jail, trying to contact someone to post his bond. His buddy Klaus had vanished with the wind as soon as Deputy Pyle appeared.

It might be days before anyone thought to wonder what had happened to Inge.

But no: nobody would believe the prosecution's case, but no one would come to her defense, either. Her neighbor Sarah would recall her entertaining cowboys, going to lewd movies and engaging in obscene acts in broad view of her neighbors.

Gallantly, she would hope, Mobeetie James, who had cared for her ranch as if it were his own, would refuse to speak out against her. But the inference would be that he could tell plenty if he weren't such a gentleman.

And hanging over the proceedings would be the unspoken knowledge that the defendant was Snider's kin and sometime lover. God only knew how many people he had done in his life. And didn't he cause the biggest scandal the town had ever known, getting gutted and smoked?

Adrian winced under the realization that the undercurrent of town sentiment would run against her. She had ridden too high for too many years. She would have to prepare herself for the inevitable outcome. The twelve-man jury would make the verdict in a three-second voice-vote, stringing it out for looks' sake, deliberating twenty-five minutes before returning a verdict of guilty. Any other verdict would be a travesty.

But maybe the twelve good men would recommend leniency in deference to her gender. The judge would accept with relief, since Grandfather had been more than good to him over the years. Surely nobody would want to see her behind bars in one of those cells with a nasty toilet in one corner and no sheets on the urine stained mattress.

At the moment, Adrian considered her time in jail punishment exacted by the Universe for taking justice into her own hands concerning Calvin Huddle. He might never realize that he was eventually going to the penitentiary, not for killing Snider, but for what he did to Elsie. Maybe she would get the chance to tell him before Bryan Manly sprung her.

And if she were convicted of—whatever—her sentence of, say, ten years might be commuted to time already served in the county jail, the general feeling being that the poor soul had already lost everything, which ought to be punishment enough. The court would see fit to garnish her property as partial restitution to the bank and its depositors. The only exception would be the ranch which, it would be learned, was now owned outright by Mobeetie James.

"After all, she's not a criminal," she could imagine juror Nasty Baines saying. "Just a typical woman with very little common sense."

"Blood is thicker than water," came another voice in her head. "She took after Snider. Probably couldn't help herself."

Throughout her incarceration, her thoughts kept returning to Elsie. There was something about the pinched little face that tugged at Adrian, some common isolation, and some will to go on. It was as if locked up in that forever-child was the magic to Adrian's own overcoming, a shield against time. Adrian's mother used to say, "Beauty is your shield against poverty," and when her own beauty began to fade, she wanted to walk out across the prairie and disappear, like an old Indian. But Elsie always came home, hanging on, keeping on.

When Manly secured her release and she was assured that she was only being held as a material witness, she felt a strange vindication. She might eventually be plucked clean, but she would survive. Her freedom was connected with her consent to insecurity.

When she stepped into the sunshine, Manly had brought her car around. She gave him a motherly pat. "You're going to be paid. There's still the furniture. Abe Malmberg, the used furniture man, will buy it." *Most growth consists of relinquishing*, she thought with a pang.

He reached in his pocket and pulled out a folded scrap of paper. "I almost forgot. That old gypsy woman came by. Said you'd promised to pay her some money. Cash, she said, for information. I didn't have five thousand, but she settled for one thousand. She told me to give you this. She was in a hurry to get out of town."

She took the note without looking at it. Unless it pertained to Snider's death, whatever it contained no longer seemed important. "You'll be repaid, I promise. And I'll also see that the Pucketts pay you for probating Snider's will."

Despite her own predicament, Adrian had given much thought to Snider's death in the past few hours. She had it figured out now. The Madam's note would confirm it. As soon as she was out of sight of the court house, she drew the car over to the curb and unfolded the scrap of paper, turning it first one direction and then another.

"I ought to have known," she muttered. It wasn't written in English:

Maybe she could get a Russian translation from the computer at the library. Doubtless her own had been confiscated by now. Anyway, she considered the note another hopeful sign. The gods must not be too intent on punishing her.

Or maybe she shouldn't pursue these mysteries to their ends. As long as there was something left to discover, maybe she was safe from reaping the consequences of sending an innocent man to the penitentiary. Or maybe she would be spared to be Elsie's protector. She liked that idea better.

She went by the Vogel place, knowing, because Manly had told her, that the house had already been impounded by the bank. It would probably eventually be sold to Attebury College. Yes, it was better suited to be an institution. And Bobby would be ousted from it, just as he'd been kicked out of a half-dozen others.

Precious had already stored Adrian's personal things in gunny sacks and put them in the garage for her. She drove around back and activated the electronic gate. Such a meager little collection her life belongings now made. She put the sacks in the car, wondering where the photos of her parents and grandparents were. Had she brought them along or left them at the old house? Would the funeral director Rathjen have discarded them?

She climbed the stairs to the servant's quarters over the garage to collect the mail Precious had saved. The old woman shoved a box out to the way to let her in. Adrian noted that she was packing, and that she had only slightly more to show for her life than remained to Adrian. In a corner of the front room stood the crib where Baby Otto was sleeping.

Precious complained in a hushed tone, "Don't know how much longer Mister Bobby think I can keep that sweet thing up here. We all got to be moving along before long."

Adrian patted the frail black arm. "Dear Precious. What will you do now?"

A flash of broken teeth lit up the dark face. "You don't need to worry about me, Miss Adrian. Mister Mobeetie came by, time ago. Think he turn into a fine gentleman, now that he a big rancher. I be working for him from now on."

Adrian bit her lip, refusing to hear, took the mail and left hurriedly to keep from shrieking out in rage. She never looked back, didn't answer when Precious called after her. She had survived, she reminded herself. She would somehow make a comeback, and then she would settle the score with Mobeetie.

In her haste to leave, she hadn't thought to ask what was to become of Baby Otto, the innocent victim of this madness.

Ahead of her in the road back to Main Street, Sael Puckett sauntered as if he was going nowhere in particular. It was more than luck that she should find him now. She pulled up beside him and opened the door. "Get in, Sael. I need you to help me."

The boy climbed in compliantly. His uncharacteristic passivity was another sign that she was doing the right thing. She had discovered the magic.

They drove out to Snider Greene's and parked around back. She pointed the idiot boy toward the smokehouse, padlocked since the day of the cleaning. It was a shabby, stunted building that reminded her of an aging dwarf.

"I want you to get something down for me," she told him matter-of-factly, wondering if the boy had forgotten about the body that had hung there in October. Drawing herself up, she marched over, turned the key and threw back the hasp. As he followed her inside, she pointed to the black iron wash pot hanging in the fireplace. "Move that wash pot to the center of the floor."

The burly boy loped over and hoisted the heavy pot with some effort, dragging it to the spot she indicated, then stood back proudly, waiting for her approval.

"Good work. Now take that piece of leather down." She gulped it out, indicating the overhead beam and the leather over which the rope had been slung to hang Snider's body.

An old ladder-back chair with a cowhide seat stood propped in one corner. Sael pulled it over beneath the beam and climbed up on it. With his pocket knife, he cut away the string securing the leather and peeled it away from the beam, dropping it at Adrian's feet. Involuntarily she jumped. Gooseflesh crept up her back as she bent and forced herself to touch the hardened skin. She turned it over and found what she feared. With a welling horror, she let it slide from her fingers.

The shovel still lay on the floor. She knelt and touched the handle, thinking how she would have done it had she been the killer. Overhead, a rat scampered along the beam. She shuddered and stood up, controlling her tremors with effort. "Let's get out of this nasty place. I'll take you home now." She led the way, holding herself, forcing herself to walk, not run.

Sael picked up the piece of leather. "Can I have this?"

"I think not," she said sharply. "Put it down and come on."

The boy became mulish, his askew eyes glittering green in rebellion. "How come I can't take it? Snider Greene ain't going to use it anymore."

The momentarily forgotten fear of the unpredictable boy shot through her. She had always been careful not to cross him unless she was safely out of his reach. She took a deep breath and composed herself. "You're right. Maybe later you can have it. Put it down and I'll give you a dollar instead. Wouldn't you rather have a dollar for an ice cream cone?"

She had a great deal to do before five o'clock if she was to get to the slaughter house before it closed. She dropped Sael with his dollar off at the drug store and drove out to the ratty old tin building that housed the co-op slaughter house, all but closed down during winter.

A grubby butcher in a bloody apron showed her to a grey cubicle and offered her a weaving chair. "Now what can I do for you, little lady?"

"I've come to buy sowbelly, the fatter the better. And while you're about it, throw in some entrails. How much will that cost?"

He grinned, giving her an appraising once-over. "We give the stuff away. Wasn't for that stuff and dandelion greens, half the poor folks'd be dead by now." He left her, shutting her in the stuffy, rank little closet. She looked at her watch. If she'd brought a laptop, she could have been translating the letter now. Her main concern was the light. She would like to work in daylight.

The stench, bad enough for miles when the wind was right, was suffocating. She escaped the little room for the out-of-doors. The biting blustering wind was preferable to the intolerable bloody dampness. She pulled her coat tight against her chin and huddled close to the metal building. *What in thunder am I doing here,* she wondered. Maybe she was going mad.

The slaughterer soon found her and put the parcel of animal parts in her car trunk. She drove back to Main and stopped at Clabber Watson's store, where she unloaded the hog innards, took them inside and asked him to weigh them.

The grocer raised his eyebrows in astonishment. "You got a dog now? Well if weighing dog meat is all the business you plan to give me, I'll soon be broke. You hardly ever come in . . ."

She thought about making up some excuse about inheriting a stock of canned goods from Snider's pantry rather than admit that she'd been stretching the budget eating leftovers, but she held her silence. The sight of that row of apricot preserves flashed across her mind again.

He figured the weight of each package and wrote them on a piece of butcher paper for her. As she made some mental calculations, a slow smile formed that she could not contain. Life surged through her veins. Even with his insides gone, the torso of Snider would have weighed two hundred pounds. She said, "How much would you say the rink Man weighs?"

The grocer shrugged. "That skinny guy? No more than one-fifty, soaking wet, I'd say."

She was becoming adept at lying. "I have to buy a gift for someone about his size, that's all." She took the packages and left quickly. She'd already said too much.

53

She took a detour by the dumpster, discarding all but the sowbelly, then turned toward the town library, aware that she was confusing Elsie's welfare with her own again. But she was driven to follow her hunch to its conclusion.

In the library she sat at a computer, sorting the possibilities. She translated the letter and made some careful notations from a physics article. Then, noticing the time, she tucked the figures into her purse and left. She had to know, and the only way was to prove it for herself.

It was almost five o'clock. From her cell phone she called Troy Davis, a high school physics teacher, to ask about lifting weights with a pully. Then she stopped at the hardware store for some rope, a ball of twine, and a pocket knife: she planned to recreate the killing.

Only a rim of the sun remained by the time she pulled up at Snider's place, noting how quickly the sun had fallen. Maybe she ought to put it off until tomorrow. But the urgency egged her onward. The day was still bright enough to see.

Even so, she dreaded going into the house. She couldn't erase the sense of the presence she'd felt there once before. With the package of sowbelly in one hand and the hardware purchases in the other, she marched around to the back yard, postponing entering the house for as long as possible. Even the smokehouse was preferable.

The lone soot-coated north window filtered scant light into the smokehouse. The cowhide chair stood under the beam, where Sael had left it. Adrian unwrapped the sowbelly and, taking the string and knife from the hardware sack, stepped up onto the chair. The leather seat, although concave, was nonetheless sturdy, having lost its suppleness with the years. *This is the way with leather*, she thought. *And sowbelly.*

The beam was still above her head, but she could reach it without standing on tiptoe. She slung the sowbelly across it, fat side up, and secured it to the beam with the string. Even in the gloaming light, the fat glistened.

She climbed off the chair and moved it out of the way, taking her time, enjoying the drama. Then she turned her attention to the black pot that Sael had placed next to the chair. It was too heavy to lift, but she could drag it until it sat directly under the sowbelly.

At last she could put it off no longer. She was as driven as if she were going to save a life. Swallowing her dread, she crossed the yard to the back door of Snider's house.

The old wooden step gave slightly under her foot; several nails were missing and the wood was dry-rotting. The whole place was a rubbish heap, thanks to Snider. A lot of good it would do Elsie to inherit a shambling wreck unfended by paint through countless dust storms.

The hollow hallway was spared the gloom from rooms that led off it by light from the oval glass in the front door. The once proud and gleaming hardwood floor had lost its sheen under Snider's stewardship. She could feel the grit underfoot, despite recent Mozelle's dust-mopping.

Peculiar how sound echoes in an empty house, how the slightest wind off the prairie whines into every cranny. As if it were looking for something . . .

To her right at the back of the hall yawned the dark and forbidding stairwell which had so unnerved her before. She should have bought a flashlight at the hardware store, except that she would need both hands. But she knew the way by heart: The study was the first room on the east at the front of the house.

She could tell before she reached it that something wasn't right, for she could feel the breeze. With alarm, she realized how foolish she was to have come alone.

The window onto the front porch from Snider's study was opened wide, and the screen was unhooked. Adrian's heart thumped wildly, but she held herself in check. This might be the ultimate test, the one she must pass to atone to the gods for taking justice into her own hands. At the moment nothing in her life was as important as what she was about to do. Peering around the room from a timid step over the threshold, she could see that nothing had been disturbed, at least, nothing obvious. No sign of vandalism or burglary. It occurred to her that Madam had more than likely broken in and made herself at home for a few days.

She moved to the bookshelves and took down several of Snider's law books, all that she could carry. She'd have to make two or three more trips into the house to get enough books. She tried not to think about it. As quickly as she could, she carted them out to the smokehouse, dumped them into the black pot and returned for more, attributing her breathlessness to fright rather than physical exertion.

She made three such trips, then returned a final time to get Grandfather's old kerosene lamp and the kitchen matches. The sun had dipped suddenly below the horizon, and she would soon be working in the dark. Momentarily she considered giving up for the day and coming back tomorrow, but she might not live until morning. Maybe she would die in her sleep.

Anyway, now it was ready. The black pot was filled with Snider's heaviest tomes. Adrian tied the rope to the pot handle and climbed onto the chair again. After two attempts, she tossed the other end of the rope over the beam, working it along the rafter until it lay over the sowbelly which was tied fatty side up. She jumped down and moved the chair out of the way. Then, planting her feet securely and wide apart, she began to pull. The rope slid easily over the pork fat, and suddenly it was taut. She gave a mighty tug, and the black pot rose slowly from the floor, weaving only slightly at first, and then swinging in a wide arc as she leaned all her strength onto the rope. She was dangling from the rope herself, her feet no longer touching the floor. Willing the pot to rise. Gasping for breath, climbing the rope hand over hand, ignoring the sting as the rough jute tore into her palms until they seared and bled, she persisted. Slowly the pot climbed higher, propelled along on the pulley made of hog fat, and Adrian felt herself coming down until her feet again touched the floor. She leaned her head against the rope and clung, waiting for her thudding heart to subside. Intent on her own exertions, she hardly noticed the light had disappeared.

The blood throbbed against her ear drums at first so that she would not have heard a small noise. But as she secured the rope to the heavy anvil where the original rope had been anchored, much as she supposed the killer had done, she thought she detected a faint grating upon the hard ground outside. It might even have been a scuffling noise. She couldn't swallow. She was sure that Sael had come back. Or was it Madam? Prickles ran up the back of her head.

She remembered the lamp. Should she light it, making herself a visible target, or should she stay in the shadows and wait for the intruder to make the first move?

And then reason returned, and she did what she always did.

"I know you're out there," she bluttered in a commanding voice. "Don't try to run away or I'll shoot. I can see you plainly, even though you can't see me. Now step inside."

After a long hesitation, while Adrian scarcely breathed, the intruder shuffled forward, sidling just inside the door. Adrian's shaking hand felt around the wall, groping for the shovel.

"Stay right where you are. Now bend over and light that kerosene lamp that's sitting by the door." She put her hand in her coat pocket, pretending she had a gun. She fought the tremor in her voice, hated its quavering. "No funny business, or I'll blow your head off."

The intruder didn't say a word, just bent over and fumbled a long time with the lamp and matches, while Adrian wondered if he would try to use the lamp as a weapon. Eventually she began to breathe easier as it became obvious that the intruder was following orders. The bluff, like most of her others, might be working. She could actually make a citizen's arrest. Her cell phone was within reach, in her purse. She would call Deputy Pyle and hold her prisoner with her imaginary gun until he arrived.

The lamp sputtered, then began to catch hold. Adrian took a step deeper into the shadows.

"Hold it up near your face, and tell me what you're doing here," she commanded.

The wick burst into flame. The light illuminated large grey eyes, and she knew. Adrian caught her breath. She thought of Thoreau, reflecting on the eyes of partridge chicks: "All intelligence seems reflected in them."

54

"What are you doing here?" Adrian asked gently, for she saw that the girl was badly frightened.

"Lookin' for somethin'." Elsie lowered her head and played with the dirt on the floor with the toe of her shoe.

"What are you looking for?" Adrian decided to be bold. "Your baby?"

"No ma'am. I know where it's at."

Adrian summoned up the translation of Madam's words, an idiom she had looked up in the library: *Elsie: by her are two children.*

"Both of them?" she whispered.

A consuming grief clouded the sad eyes. "No ma'am."

The girl looked behind her, out the door of the smokehouse, as if she expected someone else to hear. Adrian felt real alarm.

"Is someone with you?"

"No ma'am. He ain't here—yet."

"He? Who?"

"My daddy. He told me to come up here and get the money. He said he was comin' too. Only he's too drunk. He fell down and cut his head." It was a long statement for Elsie.

"Money. Did Snider give you money?"

Elsie hesitated, but she could not seem to help telling. "I taken it," she said in a tiny voice.

"When?"

Elsie thought so long that Adrian was sure she had forgotten the question. Then she said, "I think it was last summer. Before the apricots."

Before the apricots. A possibility dawned, one so devastatingly obvious that it filled Adrian with horror and exhilaration at once. Could it be possible? She said, "Snider Greene was already dead when the skating rink came to town last fall, wasn't he?"

Elsie concentrated hard, then hung her head again and nodded.

"When did he die? Sometime last summer? Even before the apricots got ripe?"

Elsie nodded again.

"But you stayed here until you'd finished the canning." That explained why there were so many jars of apricots. Snider hadn't eaten a single one. *All that time he'd been hanging out here!*

Adrian never meant to confront Elsie this way. She didn't want to persecute the girl; she only wanted to find out the truth for herself, to prove what she knew all along. Adrian was drawing her stamina from the courage of the other survivors, Elsie being the chief one.

It was unbelievable. "He hung out here for . . . three months," she murmured, now almost beyond grief. Her cousin's smoked body had been preserved so well that no one suspected it had been there for so long.

She took the lamp from Elsie, gently, so as not to make her fearful, and set it on the hearth. "Sit in that chair and tell me about it, child."

The girl did as she was told, folding her small hands in her lap, apparently taking no note of the bitter chill that had stolen in on the wind as the sun went down. Adrian squatted on the hearth and thought she heard, from the recesses of some well of inner wisdom, the echo of a long forgotten maxim: *It is impossible, therefore it is true.*

"He treated us like dog meat," Elsie whispered without a sign of emotion.

The first pain gouges her while she is out in the chicken yard in the blaze of a July day. Snider has sent her out to the cistern to draw some rain water for his toddy. It must be all that pumping she did before he finally leaned out the window and bellowed, "Prime the pump, you silly sap!" That must be why she got the pain: it must be like the catch in her side when she runs too hard. Except this one is in her back and not like a side stitch, but she cannot say what else it is like. She leans against the pump and waits for it to go away. It makes her want to grunt, but she doesn't.

Maybe it is one more part of her punishment—for that is how she sees her stay in Snider's care. She isn't clear why she is being punished, unless it is for hurting the Man so long ago, when she bit him on the nose.

At times when Snider dozes off she steals quietly out to the windmill, now sentineled by Johnson grass, and she cradles down out of sight, puts her cheek against the pipe and feels the throbbing cool. She listens to the grasshoppers sing and the windmill complain. Once, when she found an Indian Blanket nestled valiantly among the weeds, she knelt to examine the tri-colored petals and wondered if it would cause pain if she pulled them off. And again, when the old cat caught a lizard, she watched, revolted, as the cat toyed with the hapless little creature, allowing it almost to escape in the high reeds before he shot out a lightning claw to drag it back and toss it into the air. At once she knew: *I am like the lizard.*

She has never understood why people like to hurt her, torment her, and now, why Snider is keeping her prisoner. But she begins to see that if she doesn't allow herself to think of the lizard as having as much feeling as the cat, it is all right for the cat to mistreat the lizard.

Maybe, then, it is all right to pluck the petals from the Indian Blanket, or even the legs from a grasshopper. She tries these things, to see. Yes, she can see that it must be all right. She can see how Snider Greene must think. And the classmates who make fun of her. And Daddy and Sael who do to her whatever they want.

So she decides that she needn't ever understand just why she is being punished, just as the lizard never will, or the grasshopper, or the wild flower.

In the past few months she has grown so fat that she can scarcely sleep more than an hour at a time, and that sitting up in the rocking chair. It has gotten to be almost more than she can do to turn off the windmill at night, for she can't lift her arms without gasping for breath. Her belly rumbles and rolls much of the time, sometimes thumping itself against her so hard that she jumps and cries out in pain and surprise. It is some kind of spell that Snider Greene has put on her.

Always she yearns for Momma to come and get her. She has never been away from home except the time the Man hurt her and she had to stay with Madam Dirty Feet to get well. That time she was too sick to miss Momma, and Madam kept her asleep much of the time with her magic. But now she is wretchedly lonely, and she cries in secret when the sun goes down.

She leans against the pump as a far rumor of thunder reaches her ears. Overhead mysterious configurations of thunderheads appear to converge over her, and she wonders if this is more of her punishment. Maybe, while she is paralyzed by her pain, a cloud of dirt will choke her, or a bolt of lightning will knock her flat.

The pain subsides and she straightens, not believing her good fortune, and draws the water. Then she scurries off to fix Snider's toddy.

But to her dismay, as she scuttles into his study, water begins to pour down her legs. She tries to hold it back, to escape, certain that Snider will whip her for this terrible thing.

Instead, he only says, "Godamighty, wouldn't you know!" and takes her by the arm and pulls her up the stairs himself. He turns back the covers and shoves her onto the bed, handing her a grubby towel. "Try to leak on this. Don't move. I'll be back directly."

She hears him go off in the car. She means to get up and clean herself, but the pain grips her again, causing her to cry out in surprise at its force. When it is gone, she is panting, wondering if Snider is even at that moment lurking outside her door to enjoy her suffering.

Shortly, she hears the old Chrysler backfire and then the back screen slam. As voices near, a new spasm seizes her; she squeezes her eyes tight, grimaces and prays that Snider is bringing Momma to help her. Timidly she calls out, "Momma?"

When she opens her eyes, Madam leans close to her face then looks around the room in disgust. "What a pigsty to bring a child into!"

"It's not my fault," Snider says sullenly. "Elsie's responsible for cleaning the house. Blame it on her."

Madam sniffs and, reaching into her bosom, brings out a few seeds which she forces between Elsie's teeth. "Chew on these, little one, and you'll soon forget your troubles."

Past experience with Madam's remedies puts Elsie at ease. She bites into the bitter seeds and feels her tongue go numb. In moments her head is swimming. She doesn't lose consciousness, for she can hear Madam's voice and can respond to her commands, but her spirit feels separated from the action altogether.

She hears Madam order Snider from the room, hears her yell repeatedly through the closed door, "Not yet, not yet! Leave us be, you old sot!" Madam soothes her with a pat and whispers, "He can't be all bad, taking in a poor tatterdemalion like yourself, love. He's only a man, after all. What does he know of these things?"

The spasms get worse instead of better, causing Elsie to grip the mattress and squeal for breath, but the pain and the squeals seem unconnected to her. Madam does not seem distressed by her dilemma, but urges her on with, "Good girl. Push down. You'll soon be finished."

Between spasms, she sleeps, dreaming that she is free, running across the buffalo grass plain, hand in hand with a faceless Someone, sharing secrets like other girls do.

"You're in luck, love: it's a boy." The big woman lays a tiny form upon her belly. Stuporous, Elsie doesn't recognize this creature as a human at first, but she takes great care not to let it roll off, all the same.

"Glory, there's another!" Madam exclaims, and Elsie hears Snider bellow outside the door as still another spasm hits.

"We're not through, after all, little one. Push again. This one's a wee runt and won't be much trouble to—Ah! As I thought. Only a mite, and a girl, at that. Pity about its foot, though."

Elsie accepts this new burden into the crook of her right arm and adores it instantly. Its tiny fingers are no larger around than a lizard's tail, and its face is about the size of the old cat's. But its scrawny legs are like limp twine.

Snider bursts into the room and thrusts a wadded bill upon the Madam, telling her, "You can go now. Take your money and get out."

The big woman ignores him once she's pocketed the money. She presses her lips firmly together and goes on with her work, kneading Elsie's stomach. "I will go when I am finished. This is part of my job."

"You heard me. The girl can take care of herself. And hold your tongue about this, or you can look for a new place to live. In Zimbabwe." He pushes the protesting Madam out of the room and turns to examine the two babies: the large howling one on Elsie's belly and the wee one cradled in her arm. A smile spreads across his broad face.

"It's possible this might be a break. I might get extra for two," he says.

He is gone before Elsie realizes it, leaving the door ajar. She hears him puff down the stairs, hears him rattle the receiver on the phone in the hall. An inner sense of alarm that the call concerns her compels her to strain to remain alert and listen. Even the tiny creatures shush their whimpering as if to hear.

"What would you think of two?" she hears him say. There is a pause. "All right, then, double for the same price, how's that? There's no other way. You couldn't have another one running around town. Good. The sooner the better. I'll get another certificate ready."

Presently he hollers up the stairwell, "Hey you! You can get on up and go home now."

Elsie lies there with her burdens, wondering if Snider is talking to her. Madam's seeds have not yet worn off. She closes her eyes and sleeps again, taking care not to move.

Some time later, she opens her eyes to find him glaring down at her. "You still here? I told you to go, didn't I, numbskull? Don't you understand anything? Now get on up—" He leans over and peers past her through the dormer window. She can see it too: dust from an approaching car. Hastily, he snatches up the babies, bundling them in the dusty old bedspread and hiking them under his arm. "Never mind. It's too late now. You stay right where you're at and don't make a sound, you hear? Stay until I come back and tell you it's okay to leave, hear?"

Unexpected outrage washes over her as she watches him cart the squawking babies away. She *knows* those babies are not like the grasshopper, not like the Indian Blanket, not like the lizard. She pushes herself up shakily and begins to clean herself with fevered haste, looking for a cloth to staunch the flow. Through the window she can see that the car has now pulled up in front and a tall man is emerging from it. He carries a covered basket.

On unsteady legs Elsie creeps into the hall and down the stairs to just above the landing, where she can sit and peek cautiously around the corner. There is nothing to see but the empty hallway. Snider has taken the man into his study near the front of the house. Elsie steals to the bottom of the stairs and peeps around again. She hears a brief, muffled conversation, and soon the man comes out of the study and leaves, carrying the basket with him.

But before Snider can retrace his steps to the end of the hall, the man is beating on the door again. He bursts in, not waiting for Snider to open it.

"What in hell are you trying to pull? I said *healthy* specimen. This one is club-footed."

Snider examines the contents of the basket. "So it is," he says. "Well, so what? A kid's a kid, and you got two for one."

"You promised me the best genes," the man says.

"A quirk of nature," Snider says. "Who can account for it, even in the finest of families? Well, you don't want it, then? You might need it later—what if the other one dies?"

But the man has taken Elsie's precious child from the basket and is thrusting it like a wad of garbage on Snider. "You promised a perfect specimen. Perfect specimens do not die."

"But what am I supposed to do with it?" Snider protests, again bundling the baby under one arm like a sack of feed.

The man has already turned to leave. "That's your concern. Just see that no one else gets it. The resemblance might give it away."

"I know, I know," Snider grumbles, closing the door.

Elsie expects him to bring the baby back to her now that he is through with it. Instead he goes back into his study muttering, "Jesus, always. Just my rotten luck. Like always."

Moments later he reappears without the bleating child and waddles down the hall toward the stairs. Elsie scampers out of sight and waits, holding her breath when he yells, "Hey girl! Get on out. Go on home to your mama. And don't come back any more, hear?"

When she screws up her courage, she takes a timid step around the landing corner. Snider stands below, glaring up at her as if she has done something wrong, and she knows it must be the water and the blood. He raises a fat finger and shakes it at her so she cringes down against the rail, peeking at him from under her arm.

"And remember, girl, you been disgraced, hear? Don't you ever go telling anybody what you did today, else it'll shame your poor mama to death, hear? Not only that, your old man would beat hell out of you. Beat you until you'd probably die. You know what I'm saying don't you, you little dunce?"

Frantically, she nods her head and skitters past him, fleeing out the back door into the chicken yard. As she rounds the house, she looks back and sees Snider watching her through the screen door; knows he'll move to the front and watch until she is all the way down the hill and out of sight.

New and powerful instincts propel her. Despite her weakness and the bothersome bloody flow, she speeds down the wind-ravaged hill like a jack rabbit, turning frequently to check if she is out of sight yet. At last she sees him close the door, and she whips around and races back up the hill, taking care to stay in the bar ditch and crouch low.

The baby's insistent squalling reaches her on the wind. She hears it from a long way off, and she flies against the gale, her lungs bursting with pain.

Elsie has learned caution as a small child, for when her daddy was drunk, he often slung things at her or worse, if he could catch her. She doesn't approach the house from the front, where Snider might see her from his study window, but edges up to it obliquely, coming up on a corner. Then, on her hands and knees, she makes her way up to the porch and to the window opening onto it. She hardly notices the splinters from the old porch floor which jab her knees in a dozen places. As she peeks above the sill, what she sees almost causes her to faint.

In a rage, Snider has picked up the crying infant by the heel. "Jesus, I'm going nuts if this doesn't stop!" He splats the baby's head against the door jamb with a crack, and the crying stops.

Wearing only his shorts and no shoes, he leaves the study, carrying the now lifeless little body by the heel. Elsie sinks back weakly onto the porch and tries to understand. It is like the cat and the lizard again. Like the grasshopper. But even after the grasshopper was maimed, still it staggered away. Often she's seen the lizard gamely try to escape again, after being mauled. Surely the baby will be all right after a while.

She spins off the porch and darts to the back. A sprinkle of rain strikes her nose. She looks up and sees that the clouds have turned black, and she takes it as an ominous sign. She stays out of sight, edging closer to the corner nearest the smokehouse, watching Snider poke around the yard, still carrying the baby by the heel, kicking aside the persistent chickens that flock at his feet. If he doesn't hurry up and go inside, it will rain on her baby.

"Where's that goddam shovel?" she hears him mutter as he passes the corner of the house.

Elsie knows exactly where it is: she's seen it leaning against the wall in the smokehouse. It occurs to her that Snider might be thinking of digging a hole to put her baby in. Sometimes people do that. She must get to the shovel first and hide it.

As Snider heads for the hasp on the smokehouse door, Elsie streaks across the open space to the building's north side. The sooty old window rises reluctantly, but she uses all her might, and although it is high, she shinnies up over the sill with ease, leaving a trail of her own blood. Her heart is pounding hard; she can hear Snider fumbling with the hasp.

The shovel is where she remembers. She grasps it like a mace with a strength that surprises and pleases her, and waits for Snider Greene to get the door open.

She lets him get all the way inside before she brings the shovel slamming down across his skull, for she wants to be sure to be able to catch the baby. Her first blow only stuns him, but the second fells him. He lets go of her precious baby, and she drops the shovel to catch it, for her eyes have never strayed far from that tiny form, even during the attack.

Now that its head has turned purple, it seems less human than she thought at first. Maybe it will get better, though, and begin to make noises again, and maybe its head will turn white again. She puts the baby in a safe place where it will cure, the way she has seen Momma do with things that she wants to save.

Then she returns to the problem of Snider, who sprawls on his back, his huge mound of belly rising and falling in labored breaths. She thinks how much like a hog he looks, how mean like a hog he is. If he gets up again, ever, he will get her baby and be mean to it again.

She runs out into the now-pelting rain and returns presently with the butcher knife. She has seen it done many times: animals gutted and drained. She does not know that it requires great strength to accomplish, to slice the belly so perfectly, so that the entire thing comes out as one clean sheaf of skin, layered with five inches of fat.

The organs are coated with fat. She carries them out and dumps them in the chicken yard. Then she goes back to the job at hand.

It is too taxing to sever the hands and feet completely, but she makes great slits across the arteries so that, once the body is hung, the fluid will drain out rapidly. She refrains from looking at the head, for it makes her want to bash it against the door jamb, the way he did her baby's.

A fraying rope hangs from a nail on the wall. She labors to tie it around his chest, just under the arms, lifting his shoulders as if they were no weight at all. The rope looks flimsy, and the beam overhead is rough. She needs something slick for the rope to slide on. The discarded fat from Snider's belly will do, she knows by instinct.

From the kitchen she brings a ball of twine and, perched unsteadily on the cowhide chair, she winds the string around the piece of skin, securing it, fat side out, to the beam where Snider always hangs his meat.

When everything is ready, she slings the rope over the fat and begins to hoist the carcass into the air. As blood streams from the limbs, the pulling gets easier. It takes several hours of constant toil to raise the body as high as it will go. Then she winds the end of the rope about the anvil and steps back.

The rain has long since ended, the moon has risen and is even now waning. Elsie has labored the night through. She takes one more look at her baby, then completely spent, she straggles into the house, creeps into Snider's room and falls across his bed into oblivion.

"And the next morning?" Adrian spoke heavily, weighted by an accumulation of griefs, haunted by her childhood loyalties to Snider.

"I come out and built the fire for smoking. And I threw the money away, only I forget where. Then I got mixed up and told my daddy—"

"Money?"

"It was on Snider's bed. I think it was from the man with the basket."

"And you stayed on in the house after that?"

Elsie nodded. "Had to tend the fire. Had to wait till the apricots got canned. Had to feed the chickens. And see about my baby."

Adrian felt the hairs rise all over her body. She tried to see Elsie's face in the flickering light. She must ask, even though she was afraid to know. "Where is your baby?"

The girl got up and walked over into the far shadows, where stood the old salt box. She tried the lid, then dropped down beside it and laid her head on it, crooning softly. "It's stuck. I can't get it open no more."

She came back over to Adrian and looked at her hopefully through twigs of unruly hair. "I seen Momma put things in the salt box to cure them. They always come out cured after a while, Momma says. The baby didn't cure right away, so I quit digging it up to look at it. Momma, she wouldn't let me keep it. She made Sael bring it back here."

Adrian saw in the pleading eyes that the girl was sinking into a sea of her own unshed tears, riding on a raft of hope.

"Do you reckon you can make it come to?"

Adrian felt her own eyes fill with warm tears, and she swept Elsie into her arms, holding her close and feeling the compassion drain the urgency from her own body. "Oh my poor lamb, my poor, poor lamb. No, dear one, your baby won't get all right. Your baby is dead."

They found the self-same shovel with which Snider had met his end, then lifted the heavy box between them, dragged it around front, hoisted it into her car trunk, and drove to the cemetery.

For want of care, the old burial ground had all but returned to its pristine state, especially in the back, where the older graves lay. It was to this area, beneath a clump of sprawling mesquite, that they came. There, with only a marginally cruel wind to their backs, they hollowed out a shallow grave by light of the moon, then hauled rocks from the nearby gulch to fashion a cairn.

Then she drove out to Ernest's house to do what had to be done.

55

Although the bank had repossessed the mansion and its depleted furnishings, including the vanload that Adrian had seen on the night of her arrest, she could see that Bobby had not yet been forced to move out. He had, in fact, been prohibited from leaving town.

Without knocking, Adrian burst into Bobby's apartment intent on a showdown, dragging Elsie along. She flicked on the overhead light in his sitting room. Open packing boxes stood everywhere. She called, "Bobby, get out here."

Bobby, disheveled, eyes rimmed red with outrage, stumbled in from his bedroom, looking at his watch. "My God, it's five in the morning. What in hell do you want?"

Adrian turned to Elsie. "Is this the man who took your baby?"

Elsie lifted her head just enough to see. "No ma'am."

Adrian felt as if the wind had been knocked out of her. She'd been so positive. "Are you sure? Look again, girl."

Instead, Elsie sidled near the door to Bobby's bedroom and pointed. "That's him."

Before Bobby could move to close the door, Adrian had a look, too. The young man Klaus lay feigning sleep. After the first moment of shocked disbelief, she knew it was true. All those stories about Bobby in the various prep schools, in college . . . he hadn't changed. She stalked in to the perfectly groomed head of hair and snatched Klaus by it, pulling him to a sitting position. "So. You're the one. What a despicable—"

"Where's my baby?" Elsie cried, showing sudden passion.

"Get her out of here," Bobby said. "She doesn't know what she's talking about."

Adrian hadn't taken her eyes off the man. "Who are you really?" she demanded. "Speak up. No need to pretend you don't speak English. Elsie has already told me that you do. She saw and heard everything that went on at Snider's that night."

The young man glanced at Bobby, still hovering in the doorway, raked a nervous hand through his blond hair, and punched up his pillow to make a backrest. He smiled and sighed, apparently glad the masquerade was over.

"My name is Klaus Hauptmann," he said with dignity. "I'm an actor and a fine one. Obviously I fooled Snider Greene."

"You don't have to say anything, Klaus," Bobby said, but Adrian interrupted.

"And what exactly do you think you're doing here?"

Klaus gestured around him. "What does it look like? I live here. Bobby and I've been together for a long time. We met in Germany, while he was staying with his uncle. I was doing a night club act as a female impersonator." His laughter was full of irony. "I never thought it would be my ticket to Vegas."

"You're not there yet," Bobby growled, "and if you don't shut up—"

"Shut up yourself, Bobby." Adrian had lost all patience. "You could both be held as accomplices in . . . ." She wasn't sure what they could be charged with. Unless quite possibly Inge's murder.

Bobby blustered, red-faced. She found it hard to believe he could be bluffing. "What are you talking about? My lifestyle is no crime. My entire life I've been backed into corners by my father, forced to live how he wanted. He tried to make me something I couldn't be; he as much as blackmailed me to marry. Luckily, I found the ideal mate to suit not only him, but Uncle Otto as well, and Klaus was only too happy to come to the States."

Adrian remained dubious. "And Inge approved of this arrangement?"

The two men looked at each other and burst into laughter. Bobby said, "Adrian, you goose, there's no more Inge."

"You . . . admit that you did away with her?"

Klaus wiped away tears of mirth and said, "We never dreamed Inge would have to be around for more than a day or two—"

Bobby cut in. "It wasn't until Mother died and Dad made me come home that we ran into trouble. If he had suspected the truth, he'd have cut me off without a dime. We came here, hoping to leave quickly, but time dragged into months. Dad had something to hide, and he had to have someone in the bank to protect the books from scrutiny when he needed to be away."

"I thought I'd go crazy," Klaus said, "in purdah all those months . . . ."

"I finally extracted a promise from Dad that if Inge and I had a child, we'd be allowed to leave Attebury," Bobby said. "I told Snider a German friend wanted to adopt a child. Then once he found a prospect, Klaus 'arrived' to see him. I couldn't have Snider Greene know the baby was for me. He'd have blackmailed us from now on."

Or until you murdered him, Adrian thought. A grey sick feeling crept over her. "So Elsie's baby was actually wanted by no one."

"Mein Gott!" Klaus pointed at the girl. "Das wast Elsie's baby? That is the perfect specimen we paid Snider fifty thousand dollars for? And Snider is the father, I suppose."

Bobby reared back and exploded with guffaws. "Either Snider or the Man at the skating rink. I know for a fact Snider paid Huddle for *something*. Christ, what a joke on Dad!" He sobered at once and touched Adrian's sleeve, almost reverently, as if it could heal. "Dad would cut me off without a dime if you so much as hint—"

"You forget," she said coolly. "Your father's not likely to get out of the mess he's in. Or I should say, the mess *you* have put him in. Your story won't hold up, Bobby. Ernest is over in Zurich with Inge's corpse."

"They think Dad killed Inge?" he said, as Klaus fell across the bed laughing again.

"And don't threaten me," she went on. "All I want is the baby. The poor little thing has been deprived of any love . . . ."

"Precious loves him," Bobby said with a hint of melancholy, and she thought with a pang of how deprived his own childhood likely had been.

"Besides," she said, "you have more immediate problems. What about the charge of embezzlement, along with your father? And what about giving Mobeetie the lien on my ranch? He knew about the baby, didn't he? And he blackmailed you. I'm surprised you were able to get out of jail on bond."

Bobby confronted her with the same leer she had come to know so well over the past few months, and there was no mistaking the venom in his voice. "You cannot possibly intimidate me. And nothing can hold us in this town if we don't want to stay."

"And what will you do for money if you skip out? Didn't the sheriff confiscate the contents of that van I saw the other night?"

"I doubt that you're seriously worried about my welfare," he said with a sneer.

Adrian shivered with the knowledge that, if he disliked her before just for marrying his father, he detested her now for knowing the truth. But on second thought, she wasn't afraid for her life. Bobby didn't have it in him to follow through on anything, even revenge.

But what about Inge? She studied Klaus, who looked harmless enough, but weren't lust and jealousy motives for murder? Which of the two had actually killed her? She suspected it was Klaus. What would he do to protect himself from being apprehended for his crime?

The air was suddenly ominously thick with threat. She shuddered and motioned to Elsie. They left quickly, the girl following meekly out toward the servants' quarters over the garage.

"In a way, Calvin Huddle *is* a killer, you see," she explained, as much to herself as to Elsie, hoping to absolve them both of responsibility. "Not of flesh, but of spirit. A wanton despoiler of spirit. He's where he deserves to be. And you might say that Snider is guilty of his own death."

Or I am, she admitted. She could have prevented it if she'd been more attentive.

This explanation seemed to satisfy the girl, who nodded complacently.

They climbed the stairs to the servants' quarters to collect Baby Otto, who had already begun to resemble Sael. With relief, Precious relinquished the child without question. "Now I can get on out to the country, to begin my new job with Mister Mobeetie James," she said.

Refusing to hear, Adrian took the baby and left with Elsie in her wake. She never glanced back. It had seeped in, like a gentle and persistent rain: *There is no peace without surrender.* She was at peace now that she had nothing else to lose. She and Elsie got into the car, and she carefully placed the baby in Elsie's arms. Adrian saw the stark terror dawn in the partridge eyes.

"Daddy gonna kill me," she said.

"No he won't. He'll never find you," Adrian said firmly. She put the car in gear and headed back to town, out Main Street and up the hill. Maybe they could stay in Snider's house until she figured out what to do. By now the town was teeming with the morning's activity. Elsie cringed low as they passed the court house hangers-on, but there was no sign of old man Puckett. Adrian recalled Elsie saying he fell and hurt himself.

Even before they reached Snider's place, she saw the crash, the spectacular collapse of one corner of the house. She sped up, heart pounding with dread of this new disaster, racing to a skidding stop at the front gate of Grandfather's home. To her astonishment, a small crowd was gathered to watch an amazing sight: Sael, under the direction of old man Puckett, was demolishing the place, an axe-swing at a time. Miz Puckett and Mozelle stood docilely by, watching. Elsie gasped and crouched on the floorboard, still clinging to the baby.

Adrian sprang from her car and rushed over to them, paying no heed to the buzz her presence caused among the onlookers. She grabbed Miz Puckett by the arm, shaking her savagely. It was as if a part of her own self was being violated; she didn't know until then that the house was a part of her.

"What in *hell* are you doing?"

The washer-woman pulled away, brushing her off as if she might contract a contagious disease. "This is our property now, Mrs. Vogel, and I wish you'd move on. If it wasn't for you—or your family—Elsie wouldn't of gotten pregnant and beat up and almost killed."

Adrian was keenly aware that, for the first time in her life, Miz Puckett hadn't used the title of deference, "Miss Adrian." She turned to Mozelle and assumed her old authoritarian manner. "Mozelle, what on earth is Sael doing, chopping down the house?"

Mozelle hesitated, looking to her mother for guidance. But her natural inclination to talk overcame her reticence. "Huntin' for the money. Elsie done told about the money some man paid Snider Greene for her baby. Only she can't remember what she done with it. Daddy, he's set on finding it—or her, one."

"But you're wrecking the whole house!" Adrian cried above the crowd's cheer, which rose as a large section of a gable toppled.

Miz Puckett bristled and turned to Adrian again. "We can't punish Snider Greene, but we can do the next best thing. I told you, get along, Mrs. Vogel. Don't come around here no more."

Sick with the sight of such destruction, yet hoping that what she'd denied about survival after death was folly so that Snider could see what a fine mess he'd made of things, she went back to her car and sped away quickly, before the old man thought to question her about Elsie's whereabouts. She swallowed her emptiness, for her roots were gone at once: the pictures, the mementos, even the place where she was reared. With Elsie still huddled on the floor, she drove on south and turned off the road at the half-dugout, former home of Madam, and all that was left that was Snider's. She patted Elsie on the head.

"It's safe to come up now, lamb."

The dugout door stood ajar, so they pushed their way inside. The shanty didn't need airing; it wasn't that air-tight. She took the baby from Elsie and laid it in a makeshift crib: an old apple crate that Madam had once used for a bed table. Elsie cowered in the corner while Adrian surveyed the place. Adrian forced a smile. It served her right to end up here.

"We'll be just fine," she said, affecting bravado.

She set about arranging the sparse sticks of furniture that Madam had abandoned in apparent haste. She placed the table, with one wobbly leg, in the center of the room. It was a worse table than the one Madam had used in that spot, but with a nail and a hammer—or rather, a rock—she could probably fix it.

"Good," she said with forced cheerfulness. "No mirror. We will live in this house with no mirrors. Then we can be whatever we like. And we can see our reflection in each other's eyes."

Elsie perked up. Obviously she'd figured out that she was allowed to stay.

A tremendous crash filled the air. Adrian closed her eyes, figuring that Sael had finally brought down the whole structure. On a cold day the sound carried easily across the plains. She waited and heard the chopping sound resume: He was reducing the place to toothpicks.

"It isn't so bad," she told Elsie. "Maybe we can salvage some firewood over there." As she thought about it, she realized that, since Elsie had inherited the house, in all likelihood the Pucketts would have moved in, forcing the girl to live in the place associated with much of her pain. It was just as well that the story came out and the building came down.

Madam had abandoned one old cowhide chair with a broken back and a rope-bottom chair whose ropes were practically frayed in two—of no use to a woman of her girth. Adrian placed these chairs on either side of the table, vowing to repair them in a day or two.

"I once heard a blind beggar on TV say that we each have an affliction that teaches us how to live." She spoke slowly, hoping Elsie understood. "I have one, too, you know. Mine is greed."

Suddenly an ironic idea occurred as to how to throw people off her track, should anyone come looking for her. She chuckled and took a scrap of cardboard and carefully lettered a sign.

Elsie stirred in her corner. "Miss Adrian? I done remembered about the money. It was in a big envelope. I taken it out by the windmill and threw it in the Johnson grass."

Adrian wasn't even tempted. "It doesn't matter. Let's just leave it there. It'll be a fine joke on them." She and Elsie could never profit from money paid for Elsie's baby.

She took the sign outside and stood for a moment listening to the lowing of the whiteface from across the fence on the ranch. She smelled the wind and decided a snow storm was on the way within the week. She'd have to weatherproof the door before then.

It was the first day of December. A winter sun had burst upon the big sky and across the silvery grassland the wind rose, carrying late seed of buffalo grass to settle in the ruins of Snider Greene's house up the way. Already the prairie was reclaiming its own.

She glanced around for a likely spot and found it near the main road. Giggling, she propped her sign against the stump of a dead mesquite and anchored it with a rock.

It read: "FORTUNES TOLD 50 CENTS."

At the sheriff's office, Flop Pyle received a directive from the DA, who had reached a decision over which he'd wrestled ever since he received the coroner's report. Pyle reluctantly picked up the phone and told the jailer to release Calvin Huddle: without Snider's innards, who could be sure he hadn't died of a heart attack?

EPILOGUE

Neva Craig had returned from Zurich immediately, but it was February before Adrian received details from the American embassy of charges against Ernest, with a description of his alleged victim. The latter confirmed what she already knew, but Adrian was in no hurry. She was waiting for the spring thaw.

Anticipation of the high adventure before them coursed through her in those weeks, making her feel younger than she had in years, a fact which she carefully hid from townspeople when, leaving her car at home, she shuffled into town for day-old bread and pork livers. A pitiful sight, she heard people say. And Flop Pyle studiously ignored her.

"I'll build a fine house someday," Snider used to say. "Smart kids like us, it's not right we have to be stuck out here in the caliche and mesquite. We'll get our due someday."

Adrian planned on it, was in fact willing it into being.

Some nights she and Elsie lay awake on the narrow cot, each mired in her own world, and Adrian wondered, *Are you dreaming me, or am I dreaming you?*

At times a vague restlessness troubled Adrian, which she recognized as her old greed and arrogant will to power. At first she lacked courage to keep her judgments from flying off like tumbleweed caught in a gale, but gradually, infected by the calm example of Elsie, the tendrils of her mind grew slack, and she gave assent to whatever she found in herself.

Near-dawn ushered in its own miasma: She would lie listening to the coyote's howl and to the dissonant wails of her own chorus of greed and lust and would reluctantly own them as her essence. Next to the still slumbering Elsie and her baby, with the prairie's waking she would come to terms with her own night trove. She learned to trust in the dark and relinquish even the audacious assumption of responsibility for how poor Snider had turned out.

Sometimes she strapped the baby to Elsie's back and they went foraging across back country, careful to stay out of sight, stopping to examine an insect or a blooming weed. Other times they lost themselves in plans, but first Elsie had to be taught to think of the future.

They plotted what they would do, where they would go, if by some magic they could. And in the darkness of their hovel, with only the baby's breathing to mark the passage of time, she would marvel at Elsie's innate wisdom and sense of wonder.

Once Elsie whispered, "I'd go to see the ocean."

Adrian remembered San Diego and said, "So would I."

Easter came early, toward the end of March. Custom placed Cemetery Day on the following Saturday, when plot holders gathered for cemetery clean-up and all-day picnic-on-the-ground. Adrian feared someone might find the unmarked grave on borrowed property, so that week, she prepared for excavating. A mid-week rain signaled that fortune was with them, for digging in the crusty soil would be difficult at best, even with the shovel, which Adrian could no longer bring herself to touch.

As they jounced up the hill to the cemetery, she prepared Elsie for what was to come. "We'll have to move the box before someone finds it. You don't have to help me, though."

Elsie's voice was full of anticipation, killing Adrian's own hopes that the dead baby had been forgotten. "You going to dig up my other baby? Will she be cured?"

Adrian pulled to a stop a few feet from the rock cairn and got out. "No, dear. Don't expect to find your baby the way you left her." She had almost forgotten about liminal places of transformation, conceding at once that both the cemetery and the Madam's shack qualified.

The grim work began, and she did it unaided. Even if Elsie were not tending Baby Otto, Adrian wouldn't have enlisted her. She worked with a pie tin, scooping dirt with its rim. It was a clear spring night, still and cool. The moon was so bright that she abandoned the idea of using a flashlight. She labored on, her muscles aching but feeling good. The job would have been easy for Sael, but she had kept Elsie's whereabouts a secret. Often people in town would ask her what had become of Elsie, but with secret delight, she would affect a glazed, half-crazed stare and totter away, muttering incoherently. People soon left her alone.

The pie pan struck the top of the box. She scooped the loose earth from it and threw the pan aside. With her hands, she began to dig the caliche out to free the sides.

Panting, she told Elsie, "Put the baby on the seat in the car. I need help."

Elsie complied and dug eagerly, although her small hands held only a few clods at a time. Eventually when both sides were free, they began to pull, but after they had strained and tugged until they were exhausted, Adrian got another idea.

"This isn't working. Look in the trunk and bring the tire iron. We'll open this box right where it is."

If it ever occurred to her to look upon Elsie as a killer, she might have hesitated to arm her with a tire iron. But she didn't even turn when she heard Elsie's footsteps behind her.

"Give me the iron. I'll use leverage to break the lock."

Elsie was very quiet and when she finally spoke, her voice shook with something like outrage. "Miss Adrian? Shouldn't be no lock."

Adrian grinned in triumph. "I know." She began prying at the lock. "You know, things aren't working out too unjustly. Your daddy mistreated you, but his own greed destroyed the best house he'll ever have a chance to occupy. Ernest got off without paying for embezzling, but he'll have to pay for the death of a corpse he accidentally smuggled out of the country. And he didn't get away with the money, either. Calvin was never charged with rape, but he lost a nose, and he served at least some time as a suspect in Snider's death. Bobby stole my bank note to keep Mobeetie quiet about buying your baby, but he ends up with nothing, and he'll probably serve time for his dad's crime of embezzlement. And bank examiners are sure to take the ranch back from Mobeetie eventually. I get caught up in making money, acquiring things, and Ernest spends all my money living beyond his means. I lose the ranch to Mobeetie or to the bank. But now with your box, you'll have—"

Her own strength surprised her: the lock flew off in two pieces. She pried up the lid and directed, "Make a basket of your nightgown, like your momma carries clothes from the line."

Elsie lifted the skirt of her gown by two tabs and waited while Adrian began to ladle up the box's contents and dump them in the skirt.

"Should have brought a sack. What's the matter with me? I should've had the courage of my own convictions. I knew good and well what *had* to be in this box. Run to the car and dump it in the trunk. Then hurry back for more. We've got to work fast."

They kept it up for an hour, filling Elsie's gown with the green bills her baby had become, and dumping them into the car. When they'd finished, Adrian instructed Elsie to cover them with clothes—for she had spent most of the day casually packing everything of value into the car. Now, as the moon began to wane, she took the pie tin and reburied the box.

"They'll be looking for somebody when they notice this box. And sooner or later, somebody may figure out what was in it."

With dawn the wind began to gather, a favor for which she thanked the gods, because she was certain they had dropped a few bills in the dark, and with luck the wind would disperse them before Cemetery Day. She and Elsie replaced the rocks over the little grave, then got into the car and drove away.

Adrian reached for Elsie's thin hand, patting it with new affection. "Dear, are you sure you put your baby in that salt box?"

Elsie screwed up her face and stared at a spot on the windshield with great concentration. Finally she said, "Times I can't remember about that so good."

"Did you ever give the box to anyone? To Mr. Vogel, say?"

Elsie shook her head vigorously. Then she remembered. "Only to Sael."

"Ah yes, of course. I should have guessed."

Elsie bobbed her head, recalling now. "I wanted to take it home for Momma to cure my baby. Sael put it on his truck when he come to pick me up from Snider's. Only Momma made him take it back on account of it weren't mine."

"Sael must've had it on his truck when Ernest had him crate up the box at the bank. And he must've become confused and put the wrong box into the crate and later placed Ernest's box in the smokehouse." Adrian suppressed a grin out of respect for Elsie's feelings and added, "Your baby is a long way away now, over in Switzerland. Once we're settled, we can get the Red Cross to send her back to be buried properly. You baby will never be cured, dear. But she's been at peace for a long, long time."

She should have guessed that the crate from the bank wouldn't have been large enough to hold the corpse of an adult, just as she should have guessed that Inge Vogel never existed outside of Klaus's arsenal of costumes.

Baby Otto stirred, smacking and looking up at his mother with his Uncle Sael's gotch eyes. They were obviously not just the wandering eyes of a newborn, for the tot was now eight months old. But she and Elsie would fix the eyes. They would dip into the trunk of the Mercedes and pay for the finest surgeons on the West Coast. They would give Otto a chance, at least. And Elsie would teach him things about the world that only she could know.

"We ought to call him something besides Otto," Adrian said suddenly, wondering why she hadn't thought of it before. "He'll have enough battles as it is. He'll need spunk just to keep trying, sometimes—like you've had to do, dear. Yes, the courage of his mother. And cunning, like Snider—"

She shouldn't have mentioned Snider. But now that she had, she went on. "You know, there was always a special something between Snider and me. Used to, I could tell what he was thinking. For a long time now, I've had the funniest feeling that he wasn't murdered at all."

Elsie was lost in the wonder of her suckling child, but Adrian hoped her words would be understood at some level. "He was in terrible health. But he was a hard-headed old coot. I can't believe a small girl could have done more than stun him with that shovel. But he was surprised, and probably so scared of being caught with the dead baby that his heart just stopped."

She glanced at the baby again. "So maybe I'm the cunning one. But we can't name him after me. Let's see . . . he'll need will power. Maybe we'll call him Will." She turned to Elsie. "Would you like that? Will was my father's name. In his sober days, you'd have liked him."

They drove through town just as the sun glinted over the top of the cotton gin. As they turned west by the truck stop onto the highway, Adrian said, "No need to risk running into anybody we know. We'll wait to eat breakfast till we get to Claude."

But hardly anybody inside, including Deputy Pyle, who was having coffee and checking out the new waitress, paid much mind to the passing car. Maybe he didn't recognize the idiot girl and the middle-aged woman, face now weathered by the prairie wind and carved like the grey bark of an ancient mesquite, heading west out the highway.

###